SUMMER OF FIRE

BLACK RIVER CHRONICLES BOOK 1

L. G. SURGESON

Copyright (C) 2016 L.G. Surgeson

Layout design and Copyright (C) 2021 by Next Chapter

Published 2021 by Next Chapter

Cover art by www.thecovercollection.com

This book is a work of fiction. Names, characters, places, and incidents are the product of the author's imagination or are used fictitiously. Any resemblance to actual events, locales, or persons, living or dead, is purely coincidental.

All rights reserved. No part of this book may be reproduced or transmitted in any form or by any means, electronic or mechanical, including photocopying, recording, or by any information storage and retrieval system, without the author's permission.

*For Krieg Clan Dragon and his boundless bravery,
Mori Sil'erbanis and her unswerving faith
& Dakarn Pringle and his hilarious trousers.*

PROLOGUES

The Time Before...

One speaks of the time before the Summer of Fire in the same hushed tones as one speaks of the time before the cataclysm, as though the world was somehow softer then, as though we were more innocent and more lovely. As though no trouble existed. The golden age, not long ago but far away, seen as almost out of reach by those who don't really know of what they speak.

To speak of a time before the Summer of Fire, a time truly before the cacophony of events that chose to confluence in those short months, is to speak of a time more than four hundred years gone by. Very few have a genuine understanding of what led to the time known as the Summer of Fire, of the rising powers that had grown with the patience of mountains, over centuries. Only in looking back could scholars completely understand the full scale of events that preceded it.

It is particularly difficult to distinguish what came 'before', as this is a relative term. Each individual will have a point in time that they consider to be the time 'before', after which their life will have irrevocably changed. General consensus suggests that by 1099 AC it was already too late, but for some it started long before that.

ABERDDU CITY 1093 AC

Severin drained his tankard and slammed it down on the table. He belched languidly and stood up, the brawl outside seemed to be escalating quickly. Flexing his knuckles, he noticed yesterday's grazes were still raw and stinging but he didn't care. He wiped his hands lazily on his threadbare tunic he belched again, then he looked down at his front and shook his head. Three months in Aberddu and this was what he had come to: third-hand clothes, drinking, belching and bar brawls. This was a far cry from Alendria, and this was hardly becoming behaviour for the High Elf Court. Mercifully, this was not the High Elf Court and that was what he loved about it. In Aberddu he was just another elf adventurer, and a grubby drunken one at that. He couldn't remember ever being this happy.

Weighing up his options, he picked up his empty tankard. The bar had more ale and possibly some cheap Albion Brandy but outside the brawl was reaching a crescendo. Metal on metal, shouting and thumping feet told him that the militia was on its way. Celyn was already out there and he wasn't likely to come back inside until the whole thing was done. Drinking alone was dull thought Severin, as he headed towards the door, cudgel in one hand, tankard still in the other.

Celyn slunk back into an alleyway panting as the militia patrol jogged past. It had just started raining and judging by the knotted bulging clouds above him it was set to get heavier. Something big was going on at the city walls judging by the racket. That was the second militia patrol to jog past in as many minutes. He didn't really care what was going on if it kept the militia off his back. The last patrol had been heading for the Eastern Gate with some urgency and their swords already drawn, they had completely ignored the fight. Whatever it was was obviously a higher priority than a bar brawl.

There had been a few lackadaisical rumours of an invasion force coming this way but it was hardly news. As the northernmost trade port of Albion, Aberddu was constantly under threat of invasion even now it had Royal status. If it wasn't the Frisians, it was the Paravelians or even the mighty war barges of Hasselt. Such was life in this cesspool city, among the mongrel nobles and flamboyant ship captains that liked to lord it over the rest of the pestilent rabble. In Aberddu you took your chances. But the ale was good for the price and the adventuring was lucrative, if this hadn't been the case Celyn would have gone back to Frisia where he belonged long ago.

Tonight, however, he was on a personal errand. Somewhere, in the shadows across the thoroughfare that bloody dwarf was lurking, waiting for the rest of his beating. The rain quickened, falling in stinging sheets that soaked him through his leathers. Still, he was wet now and a guilder was a guilder. He would get it out of that tight-fisted stunty bastard if he had to garrotte him, turn him upside down and shake him until his gold fillings fell out. In the distance the sky grumbled, adding foreboding to the sounds of heightened conflict that carried from the Eastern Gates on the evening air.

Celyn exhaled and swung his sword at nothing in particular. His fingers were starting to go numb in the freezing January downpour. The orange light of the tavern spilled into the murk and he saw Severin stagger out. The elf stood stupidly in the doorway looking at the rain, his club hanging limply from his hand. Peering into the darkness, he was clearly wondering where the fight had gone. Celyn was almost tempted to ignore him, let the silly sod wander off alone into the storm. It would be an entertaining few minutes to be sure, but it would probably end in either a temple or a militia cell, neither of which were a good place to go when soaked through to the skin.

The wind picked up, racing up the wide street catching the rain and throwing it into curls. Stepping into the muddy light of the small square, he made himself obvious and waited for Severin to look his way. A third militia patrol passed by, sprinting and red in the face. Like the others they ignored Celyn. Peering into the gloom, he tried to pick out the dwarf. The little bastard had concealed himself well in the shadow of a tall boarding house opposite when the first militia patrol had appeared, however he hadn't moved since. Celyn was prepared to stake his reputation if not his life on that much.

He skirted around the edge of the fountain that blocked the middle of the little plaza. Judging by the rank aroma of the stagnant water in the stone basin, the sluice had been closed for the whole winter and what was sitting there was accumulated rainfall. The raindrops pelted down into the cloudy pool with astonishing force, creating waves that splashed over the edge. The water level had risen in seconds. It would make a nasty dip for his dwarven friend when he eventually found him.

Then, without warning a much bigger wave slopped over the stone basin and a seven-foot figure erupted out of the foul water. It paused for a moment, illuminated by a sudden flash of lightning – the terrifying countenance glowed in the white electrical light. Not only tall but broad and made wider still by hide and furs draped about his shoulders, the warrior was gruesome to behold. His face was painted with fearsome patterns and across his eyes was a deep red stripe. In each hand, he brandished a well-worn bastard sword, ready for combat. His wild starring eyes flickered, and his gaze fell hungrily on Celyn. He stepped out of the fountain in a long sweeping stride, raised both swords to shoulder height and with one brutal, fluid motion cut Celyn down where he stood.

Severin, still in the door way, held his breath; a single movement could be his last. He was beginning to regret not going to the bar. The storm was almost directly overhead now, another thunder-clap deafened him and two more of the massive warriors appeared in the fountain. Their terrifying, greedy eyes glowing in night. They paused momentarily in the fountain, taking in the street. Severin prayed to any god that would listen for the ground to open up and swallow him. In his entire life, he had never seen warriors of this size or ferocity. Their bared teeth and sword blades gleamed as a fork of lightning arched across the city. All around him, chaos was descending. He could hear yelps and shouts of panic as more of these gargantuan soldiers appeared out of nowhere in the neighbouring streets. The Law Temple bells began a frantic, panicked peal, the round notes toppling in disorganised cadences and amplifying the fear he felt. The bells only rang like that when the city was under siege. Ashamed of his sudden cowardice, he slipped slowly into an alleyway and was about to run towards the Docks when he heard a swoosh and felt a cold dull lump contact the back of his head. His head spinning, sweat pouring from his brow, Severin pulled himself to sitting. The Law Temple bells were ringing a complex change in the dawn light. It must be the Feast of the Warden's Keys. He had lost track of time. His heart was pounding and he was fighting to catch his breath as he went over the dream he had just been pulled out of, so vivid it felt like only a few seconds ago. He had no idea why, after nearly four hundred years that memory had suddenly appeared in his dreams but only one word was springing to mind: tartars.

TARTARIA 1093 AC

Clan Stallion Lands

Gathered with the other children in the shade of the mighty *Indaba* tree, Talia eyed the storyteller with suspicion. She had reached the doubting age and found it odd that he seemed to know about everything and have been everywhere, and yet he could only be barely twenty or so years older than her. It seemed like a lot of learning for that short time, particularly as she knew exactly where he had been for the last ten years or so. She had almost reconciled herself with the fact that she would not be able to listen to these stories much longer - more grown up concerns beckoned to her. She was reaching that awkward between point, she had left the age of believing behind her last summer. Too old and too tall to listen to the storyteller in the afternoon before supper; she had more duties and jobs now, brothers and sisters to wrangle, game to stalk, food to prepare - it was rare she got to the tree at all. She was fully grown nearly and it had been many summers in the coming. She wished for the excitement of an older life. But she wasn't yet old enough or tall enough to come back to the tree after dark and a hard day. She was not yet old enough to hear the storyteller's other tales and drink to them. She had not quite reached the understanding age.

She wasn't listening to the storyteller now, she was watching

Syrne. He was a season or two older than her but no more. His dark, piercing eyes were so still they could put you right off thinking. He gazed at the storyteller so intently that he had let his dagger slip out of his hand. Talia wished she could understand why he was still so gripped by this story: *The Legend of Salamander*. She had heard it so often she could pick up where they were without really listening, the storyteller never changed his phrases.

... soldiers stood taller than ordinary tartars, their muscles bound by wicked spirits and the power of the poison totem Salamander. Each one with glistening fangs and eyes like obsidian, a five-foot blade in each hand.

It was difficult to tell whether he was happy or horrified by the Legend of Salamander, his face was rapt but expressionless. Talia wondered what the Chieftain thought of her son spending so long with the bard that he was often late for training. Even now, when he was supposed to be a man, he never missed a tale. Talia thought he must know the stories so well by now that he probably didn't need the teller to speak.

... stepped out of the flames of the camp fires and the waters of the rivers, weapons raised. They cut down all who stood in their way. Lead by a mighty general...

Bored with a story she had heard too often, Talia set out to entertain herself. She shuffled around the circle cautiously, careful not to stir up too much dust. She was going to find out for herself how hard Syrne was concentrating on the story.

... marched south west to the Albion territories. One night a foul storm plagued the port of Aberddu. Thunder echoed across the city and far out to sea. Lightning flashed through the rain that beat down on the buildings and the gates...

She had wriggled to within an arm's reach of Syrne and his gaze had not yet broken. The hilt of his knife was sitting in the dirt, inches from her fingers. She waited for the story to reach its thrilling climax, as Salamander's armies besieged Aberddu and lay waste to the city. Then, whilst his attention was held, she stretched forward until her fingers were wrapped around the hilt.

Her concentration was broken by the sounds of angry feet stamping across the dry earth. Then a voice bellowed

"Syrne," and the teller fell silent. The story spell was broken. Talia looked around with trepidation, as did all the others. Varl the clan war-leader, enraged as he was, in his full fur battle armour with a six-foot broadsword balanced easily on one shoulder, was a terrifying sight even for his own clan. He was standing about ten feet away, his face and neck almost purple with fury, veins bulging and spittle flying as he hollered. Syrne's face still registered no emotion. Even in the face of such anger, he appeared composed and assured. He simply stood up unhurriedly and checked his belt. Noting calmly that his knife was missing, he reached down to pick it up and came face to face with Talia. Talia had her hand wrapped firmly around the hilt of his knife and showed no intention of letting go. Syrne recognised a dominance challenge when he saw one. Unarmed as he was, he was not able to fight her in the traditional sense. Without a pause or even a change of facial expression, he ducked forward, grabbed her ear and twisted. Talia let out a surprised yelp and relinquished the knife. Syrne snatched it up and walked towards the still-seething Varl with a sureness of step that seemed to anger the war-leader even more. Talia snarled at the other children before they could crow, and then turned to watch Syrne's back as he disappeared back into the village.

JAFFRIA 1094 AC

In the heat of the day, Jamar sweated. The white-hot sun glared down on to his head and his back, blistering the raw flesh where Danil's spiked whip had contacted. Splayed on the temple step, heavily armoured acolytes kneeling on his wrists and ankles, he waited for the next lash. Twenty lashes for dishonourable behaviour, five more for cheek and three for squealing like a farmyard beast after the first one. Simultaneously, he heard the whip crack and felt the searing line of pain drawn across his back, adding to the agony. He bit his lip to stop himself screaming and blood trickled into his mouth.

He had lost count, although he was sure there were only a few left to go. He prayed hard for unconsciousness but was unsurprised when it did not come. Amroth could be a vicious master to those that came up short. As Danil prepared for another swing, the echoing harmony of three hundred priests rose up around him as they chanted the next verse of the contrition reel. Their voices resonated around the amphitheatre and another crack rang out. Jamar never felt the hot streak as the peppered leather skimmed his skin. The turmoil that came in the space of that whip-crack superseded all pain.

At first Jamar thought he had managed to faint as the world turned cold and dark, but then he realised that the pandemonium exploding behind him was not part of his unconsciousness. The acolytes on his limbs clambered frantically to their feet and, surprised by his sudden unrestricted movement, it took him a few seconds to follow. When at last he turned to look out over the amphitheatre, he was unable to process what he saw.

A thick, dark grey fog had rolled in, choking the gathered congregation, many of whom were starting to turn blue and purple through lack of air, and some of whom had already keeled forward on their prayer mats. Solidifying out of the sinister smoke were about a dozen dark, winged figures, the size of a tall man - perhaps a foot or so larger. As they began to take shape and detail started to form, Jamar struggled to his feet, adrenaline overriding the pain of his raw back.

The smoke eased and all eyes that were able had fixed on the black angels, that were now hanging two feet from the ground, fully formed and terrible. Their ragged wings spread out, casting chilling shadows over the crowds. The figures were broadly manshaped but made entirely from smoke so thick that they were no longer translucent. Many of their features were ill-defined but their eyes were both bright and hollow. Slowly, with obscene grace, they started to rise up over the cowering crowd, spreading their arms wide in some kind of grotesque benediction. A white freezing mist crept over the ground beneath them, engulfing those who were prone and clinging to the ankles and feet of those who were not. The stunned congregation remained transfixed.

An unholy, guttural hiss filled Jamar's head and he saw several beleaguered clerics clamp their hands over their ears, writhing and contorted with pain. He could feel the surprisingly chilly air circling the amphitheatre in the same way it did on the plains when a whirlwind was rising. Looking around, he could see no exit point that wasn't crowded with people, nearly all of whom were hunched in pain or unconscious. There was nothing he could do for them, he had no power and he could not carry them all to safety. Getting out of here was the only way to survive. Those gargantuan angels floating above him were the opening chorus and he did not want to be here when the main act arrived.

With no feeling of guilt whatsoever, he climbed over the bleeding bodies of the acolytes that had been restraining him only seconds previously and began to run towards the nearest exit tunnel.

The wind snatched his breath and froze his lungs. It was almost crippling to take in the air now, but he persisted. The tunnel couldn't be much more than twenty feet away now. Chased by the wind, angry indigo clouds covered the white-hot sun and day turned to night in an instant. In the darkness Jamar stumbled and lost his bearings. A fork of black lightning arced menacingly across the sky, followed by a clash of thunder that echoed around the amphitheatre, deafening them all. Another lightning arc flashed and Jamar used the bizarre dark-light to reorientate himself in his dash for the exit. This time no thunder followed. Jamar did not stop to look around, he just fled.

On his knees on the altar steps, his face twisted in excruciation, Danil could only gaze up as the figure appeared from the lightning. It was not as big as the angels that had heralded it, but it was far more terrible to behold. It had once been a man - that much was apparent - still dressed in the opulent grey robes of a powerful cleric, although they were now tattered and scorched as though he had run through a fire. What had once been flesh was now charred and scabrous, flaking away in places, exposing the bone,which glowed white in another arc of lightning. More distressing still was the figure's face. Half of the cheek skin had been peeled away and was hanging limply, displaying a livid patch of muscle and sinew around an ugly, skeletal grin. The other half of the face was sallow and clammy, the loose flesh green-grey and rotten. Piercing black eyes looked out at them all, gloating at the agony of the congregation. The thin, cruel half-mouth curled into a smile. Time slowed as Danil watched the figure raise a taloned hand. With a menacing hiss that seemed to resonate around the amphitheatre, the creature conjured tendrils of white fire that fountained from his hand and entwined themselves around each of the dark angels. The angels began to glow and in turn the same white flames poured from their outstretched palms, flooding over the cowering clerics on the ground. Racked with pain, and weeping for swift oblivion, Danil heard the creature hiss again, and within the swarming of the hiss he heard these words: *I am the Defiler, you will fear me and die.*

TARTARIA 1097 AC

Clan Boar Lands

Rurik pulled another chunk of flesh from the slowly charring goat's rump and fell on it ravenously. His horse had been lost to enemy scouts and it had been a long way back to the war-band on foot. He had run further than he had imagined he could to bring the news to the clan chieftain, and he had thought when he had first opened his mouth to speak that he might vomit from the exertion instead. From the look on the chieftain's face he would probably have been less affronted by the puke than by the news that Rurik had been forced to convey.

Within moments of speaking, he had been flung out of the command tent in the general direction of the firepit and the roast and the war-leaders had been called in. Rurik's plan for the rest of the night was to get himself on to the outside of several large chunks of roast goat and oat bread and at least three flagons of the shaman's best. Maybe then he would collapse by the fire and let the storytelling and singing wash over him. Maybe the dancers would dance, although it was unlikely as they hadn't been in battle today and weren't likely to be tomorrow. It didn't really matter because most importantly of all he was not going to move, not even to find a snug tent space.

Far from being a delicate feminine display, Tartarian dancing was martial and adrenaline fuelled, an activity coupled with the heat of fierce battle. As a scout, it was a spectacle that fascinated Rurik. He rarely saw the thick of battle except from a distant concealed spot on a cliff top or at the top of a baobab tree. Different things made his adrenaline rush, his heart pound and his feet run themselves raw - like the news he had heard not twelve hours ago. It was not the kind of rush that made you want to dance all night. In fact, Rurik was hoping that if he ate and drank enough, he would pass out at the fireside quite soon so he didn't have to think about it for too long. He certainly wasn't going to be mentioning it to anyone else. He was chewing his last mouthful and licking the grease from his palms when a deep voice bellowed his name from the darkness.

"Rurik, come here." The voice from the command tent carried out across the chattering night. Everybody at the fire turned and stared at him as he struggled crossly to his bleeding feet and hobbled towards the voice.

"Tell them what you just told me," ordered the chieftain, nodding across at the gathered war-leaders. There was nothing ceremonial about a Tartar war council, the half-dozen war-band commanders were knelt or slouched on hide cushions or sprawled out on a vast patchwork fur rug that covered the majority of the floor of the command tent - only the chieftain sat on a carved wooden chair. The war- leaders were the six quickest-thinking, fiercest fighters in the clan; they felt no need to impress anyone, even the chieftain, with needless formality. It was unlikely that a show of such meaningless pretension would impress the chieftain in any case. The chieftain didn't gesture for Rurik to sit, but given that he could feel the wounds on his feet oozing, he slumped down into a space at the chieftain's feet anyway. All eyes were on him as he began to recount what he had heard.

Maran was the first to react. He was a particularly large tartar, known for speaking softly and slowly but always to the point.

"So," he mused in a soft whisper, as though he was talking to himself, "Ghostbear have fallen, may all the Gods help them and Stonesnake."

"No surprises there," said Iri, a petite but muscular female who had cut down more of the enemy in their tracks than any two of the other war-leaders together. "They've been looking for an excuse to go over to Salamander for years." There were mumbles of agreement from around the room. The chieftain nodded but didn't speak, the voice of the Stonesnake chieftain at the Clans Council still echoed in his head: *Unity can only mean strength, and strength brings the best for Tartaria.* It was a fine sentiment to be sure, when talking about a clan but not about the whole nation. Unity may bring strength, but at what cost? Unity behind such a leader would lead to nowhere in the long run but humiliation, misery and death. "and good riddance I say," she continued, malice in her voice.

"They are a big clan," said Maran mildly, "Almost four thousand lost to him and strong fighters too."

"Strong fighters," scorned Iri, "yeah, sure, but all the same easy to take down, predictable."

"And disloyal," added a dark, burly figure who was leaning back on a bank of pillows and had not spoken since Rurik had come back in. "Strength may be an asset, but not if it is disloyal."

Maran conceded his point with the faintest nod. "As you say, Rhine," he said gently.

At this point, Rhine hauled himself up to his haunches, bringing his sharp, scarred face into the yellow light of the lantern. He was a theatrically striking sight, popular among the clan women - well- poised, almost graceful.

"That doesn't trouble me," he said coldly, "clans are going to fall. This is war after all; chieftains have a difficult choice to face, and they must protect their clan interests and save lives where they can, crossing sides may be their only way to survive."

"Really," interrupted Iri, her thin voice cutting like a knife, "So you think we should cross sides do you? To protect the Boar?" Her voice was cloyingly disdainful and Rurik watched in amazement as a dark cloud of fury passed across Rhine's face. In fact, he was surprised that Rhine did not reach out and strike her.

"That's not what I said," said Rhine through gritted teeth. His ice- cold tone stopped Iri in her tracks, she had sense enough to not provoke him too far. "You need to listen more carefully, *Iriani*,"

Iri's eyes narrowed at the use of a childish nickname that meant, quite literally, in the clan-tongue 'impudent and strong-headed child'. It was an unfortunate deviation of her given name that had plagued her throughout her life. She had just touched her hand to her knife hilt to retaliate when the chieftain spoke.

"Enough," he growled, his usually good-natured eyes steely, he was clearly not in the mood to indulge the war council in petty squabbles. Both Rhine and Iri looked away, bested by a single word. The chieftain continued, reasserting his authority with a firm, fatherly tone. "So, Rhine, if you weren't suggesting we cross over to Salamander what were you saying?"

Rhine, his face betraying an edge of sullenness from the chieftain's scolding, continued to speak.

"The movements of mortals are not as shocking as the defeat of the Phoenix. Men changing sides and armies being defeated are all part of the war. Stonesnake is a loss, but not an unexpected one and we can only pray for Ghostbear. Timberwolf will be the next large clan if I'm any judge and there's nothing that can be done to stop it. All that is nothing more than we expected. The fall of the Phoenix is far more troubling. That Salamander has the power to physically consume and destroy a powerful totem like Phoenix is something we hadn't prepared for. I had heard whispers of this, before you brought the news," he nodded at Rurik, who was still rubbing his aching feet. "I'd heard rumours that Salamander's army had slaughtered every man woman and child, and when the Phoenix appeared to protect them the General himself physically overpowered the totem and somehow imbibed its energy.

Even the idea chilled me to the bone. If he continues in this way, he will become undefeatable. If he can bring down the Phoenix, then tell me which clan remains safe from such an attack?"

"Dragon," murmured Maran, either misunderstanding or plain ignoring Rhine's impassioned rhetoric. "and Leviathan."

Rhine merely glared at him. There was another mumble from the group.

"So, what do we do?" asked a youthful voice who had yet to join the debate. Rurik had not looked much at this youngest member of the war council until now. Perched cross legged on a cushion, knees pulled up to her chin, she was an uninteresting sight. She seemed as out of place here as he felt, she was about his age and therefore very young for this.

He could see now that her plain, weathered face was trembling ever so slightly in the lantern glow. Rurik realised that this was probably Marta's first real war council and if he had to guess he would say that this was probably the most serious war council to be held by Clan Boar for many, many years. No wonder she seemed utterly terrified. The chieftain, wicked and wily in his fatherly way, turned his full attention on the shivering whelp and said

"I don't know Marta, what do you think we should do about it?" Marta was so taken aback that he had addressed her at all that she did not see the glint in his eye. She just turned pale and stuttered, unable to answer the question. Iri smirked cruelly at Marta's obvious discomfort relieved at last not to be the youngest member of the council and Rhine snorted his derision at what he clearly saw as inappropriate levity. Rurik actually felt sorry for Marta, his jealousy of her position greatly outweighed by loyalty to one of his own age. Maran was just about to take pity on her and speak in her place, when, quivering she stood up and said

"We fight, until our very last breath, we fight."

ABERDDU 1097 AC

"Stand back," bellowed Elor, using his staff to shove the more curious and dewy-eyed adventurers unceremoniously backwards. "These ones explode." Just as he spoke, there was a flash of red light and the body detonated spraying blood, viscera and shards of bone over them all.

Elor wiped the mess from his front with a magical flick of the fingers and turned his attention back to the rest of the room, searching for the Guildmistress in the hubbub.

"Erin," he yelled, trying to raise his words above the rumbling of the guild as they tried to regroup. Where the dratted hell was the woman? She never seemed to be about when she was needed. He yelled again, aware that it was horribly undignified. "Erin!" The second call made the elf turn around, gore and sweat smeared across her face, her hand clamped hard against a bleeding wound in her side.

"Just let me get a bandage," she grunted through gritted teeth. Elor nodded, abashed that he had thought her uselessly hiding throughout the attack.

It was true that she was not the most beloved of Guild leaders and Elor was well aware of his tendency to think badly of her in most circumstances. He did have to admit, grudgingly, that this was often unjustified and very unfair of him. At least on this score he had managed to maintain a dignified silence, unlike many of the other older adventurers.

He needed to speak with her because the last attack was troubling him. As a man of scholarship, he had travelled widely, and he was familiar with the clan people that lived on the vast steppes of Tartaria. He might not have found much affinity with the Tartars but he had found a great deal to respect there. In particular their straightforward honesty and their ability to put complex matters into the simplest terms had appealed to him. Born in feudal Paravel and sequestered, as he had been for many years now, in institutions of magical learning, he had spent most of his time with people who were able to turn the simple verities of life into complicated and meandering hypotheses. To see the other end of the scale was very refreshing. However, he had doubts as to the origins of their recent attackers.

It was true that they bore the build and traits of tartars but they were somehow not quite right, like a slightly inaccurate copy. The scarlet eye-stripe on all the warriors was unusual but what worried him more was that these tartars exploded once killed – someone had created a magical detonation device and was using tartars to transport it.

Trying to avoid dragging his coat tails through the pooling effluent on the guild hall floor, he located a clean seat not far from the wounded Guildmistress and sat down to wait patiently. He looked on unmoved, as the other adventurers raced around each other harem-scarem hauling the injured to the side of the room, clearing the floor in case of any further incursion.

Elor mused that even though it appeared to be an utter, chaotic shambles there was a surprisingly ordered approach at work. In this moment of silent contemplation amidst the pandemonium, he wondered wryly what the Law Temple would make of such a thought. Perhaps he would raise it with Ignatius later, if the cleric managed to calm down long enough to listen.

Someone sat down next to him, but Elor didn't look around to see who it was. He was not in the mood for small talk, he had a lot to think about. In spite of this blatantly ungracious gesture, a voice that Elor found somewhat vexing started to talk to him.

"You don't know what they are do you?" it said smugly. Elor turned to look into the self-satisfied face of Severin Starfire, an elf he truly despised. He did not respond, but the barely contained fury in his face said everything.

"I've seen them before," continued Severin with a strange, grim relish. "I've fought them before, and beat them before."

"Good for you," replied Elor, trying not to snarl.

"They're vicious." So far, Severin had said nothing of use and he knew it. He could see the colour rising in Elor's cheeks. He was taking a malicious pleasure in gently provoking this jumped-up little wizard who believed that in his humble forty years he had seen and learnt enough to give him the same authority as a five hundred year old elf. "And?" asked Elor, his voice under exquisite control so that it was cold but not cross.

"Heard of Clan Salamander have you?" said Severin his eyes glowing with mirth. Elor paused for a moment, took in what the elf was saying and said with a chilly tone of morbid curiosity,

"Are you saying that those... *tartars*... belong to General Salamander?" The mirth was gone from Severin's eyes Elor was glad to see, replaced by a steely resolve. It was an insensitive thing to say in jest, but if it were true then it would mean the beginning of events that would touch every corner of the world and would reach out into the future like the dark tendrils of some vile, deadly creeper. The elf did not speak, he simply nodded.

Elor knew the legend. Every mage and scholar who had spent any time in Aberddu for the last four hundred years knew the legend and all its variations. The bare details of Salamander's terrifying rise to power, the iron grip with which he had held Tartaria. The Tartar army that he formed and commanded with his equally terrifying and powerful sister Flamehair. The havoc they wrought across the continent in their quest for power and the thousands that they had killed in the Siege of Aberddu. It seemed hopeless, unstoppable; and then a small, ragtag band of mercenaries stood up - The Aberddu Adventurers Guild, a group of drunken ne'er-do-wells who, according to the stories at any rate, sought little more than their own personal pleasure. The citizenry of Aberddu did not have great confidence in their eccentric protectors. Only a handful of adventurers took the line with the Militia during the siege and when the storm came two days into the stand-off, the city had been over-run. Tales were told of massive tartars appearing from all the waters and every fire. Severin's eyes darkened as he reminded Elor of this, and Elor realised for the first time that Severin was not simply repeating cradle-tales, he was a first-hand account still as vivid in his mind as it had been four hundred years ago. Even after all this time, his face still betrayed the horror of the night when he had seen Salamander's army destroy the city. He had been among the Guild survivors who had fled with everyone else who still had legs to run. The capital of Albion, Auborn was safe and welcoming to the folk from the ruined outpost. For a few months they lay low, until summer came and with it Tartarian troops, marching to meet the glorious Albion Army. Severin had not been on the line that day, but he had heard the tales of the magic that the tartars used against the Albion. Vast columns of water wiped out whole battalions and wild-fire magic wiped out the rest. The flaming creatures that were conjured - drakes and elementals, were unlike anything even the mages could identify. Only a handful of soldiers survived, the tartars did not allow the privilege of retreat, their attacks continued as Albion turned and fled. Disgraced, Albion withdrew from the world stage and when, two months later, Auborn was overrun by the Tartar army there was little resistance.

Aberddu may have been destroyed, but the Adventurers Guild had not. They disappeared and for a while the word was that they had gone to ground across the Sea of Stars, hiding like the cowards they undoubtedly were. As the Tartar armies occupied Auborn and moved their way into Paravel and the Elven Territories, Albion adjusted to life under Tartar rule. Winter approached, and many feared a famine. The occupying forces demanded tithe and food was running low. Preparing for the onset of a slow starvation, the people of Albion waited for the frosts to begin. Then, in the cold white light of the first icy dawn, they awoke to find the Tartars retreating. Salamander and his sister had vanished.

Rumours abounded of terrible warlords, works of dark magic and even the hands of a God. Few seemed to know what had caused Salamander's downfall. The Adventurers Guild of Aberddu, the seemingly useless gang of renegades and reprobates, had executed an act of heroism the like of which bards would sing about down the generations. With little aid, they had travelled deep into the heart of Tartaria and performed a binding ritual on Salamander and his sister Flamehair. They had blocked their powers, removing their command of both fire and water. Powerless, Salamander and Flamehair had fled before the adventurers could kill them. Again, Elor could see from Severin's eyes that this was not hearsay. He lifted his tunic a few inches, exposing his side and Elor saw the faintest trace of a sword wound on his ageing skin. Both men sat in silence, Elor still gazing at the place where Severin's scar had been, as they contemplated the ramifications of the evenings attack.

Erin, now bandaged but still bleeding, hobbled over and said tersely,

"What is it this time Elor?"

ARABI 1098 AC

A fierce wind blew across the gypsum, whipping up clouds of dust. The dirty yellow buildings of Khim Al Salar squatted in clusters around the base of the pyramid. In the height of the day, the streets were deserted giving the dust balls space to tumble and skitter. This was not unusual, few ventured into the white hot sun at this hour. Today though, it was not the heat driving people inside.

Only one building showed any sign of movement. Taller than the surrounding houses, it had a domed roof and a cloistered balcony surrounded by a pierced patterned wall. There was a wide arched doorway on the ground floor of the building and three shallow steps lead down to the road. A stone wall nearly ten foot high ran around the edge of the compound protecting the temple Grounds from the outside world, a large ornately painted wooden gate was set into the wall, providing the only other point of access.

A small obelisk-like tower in front of the main doors housed an iron bell that rang solemnly across the heat-ridden city. The sound of nearly a hundred voices reciting a long, laborious litany of faith spilled out through the walls. It was the only other sound. The volume of the litany reached a crescendo, ending in a resonating declamation of faith. Then there was a moment of genuine silence before nearly one hundred people all got to their feet and streamed towards the wide temple doors.

The Army of Law lined out without a word. Each soldier swathed head to foot in loose green fabric against the heat. Each soldier wore an identical polished breast plate and carried two identical scimitars crossed on their back. The front rank held identical shields bearing the arms of the God-King at exactly the same height. Then, when they were complete in seven ranks of fourteen, they stood at perfect attention and waited.

The massive wooden gate creaked open mechanically and a glorious golden chariot rolled out. The cream horse pulling it was liveried in a flowing green and gold trapper with a polished black leather halter that gleamed in the sunlight. In the back of the chariot, standing nearly seven feet tall was God-King Rabin Ibm Khim Al Salar. His armour, although exactly the same as that of his troops, was more beautiful, more finely wrought and almost glowed in the heat of the day. With terror-inspiring synchronisation, every soldier drew one sword, sank to one knee and raised their blade above their head in salute. In one voice that echoed out across the wastes they cried,

"Khim Al Salar Hail!" and the God-King acknowledged the cheer with a mere nod. Then with more breath-taking precision they rose to standing. Rabin Ibm Khim Al Salar turned to face his troops.

"Faithful," he proclaimed, his voice dry and thin with age, "this is the day, this is the hour. All prayer, all honour has lead our feet along this road to this place. We fight not for glory or land we fight for a thing more precious than worldly concern. Today we stand firm against the forces of Chaos that even now are marching to destroy us. We will fight and we will win or we will go on to the next life knowing we have paid the highest price. For Law" He bellowed the next words and the army echoed them. "To arms." The army turned smartly a quarter turn and in perfect step despite of the uneven ground marched, onward out of the city.

TARTARIA 1098 AC

Clan Boar Land

Marta scowled, her knuckles white on her bridle. Iri's sneering words were still rattling around inside her head but she had not risen to the bait. Not because she wasn't angry but because the imposing sight of Maran and his disapproving glare had quelled her. Even after the last twelve months, Iri's attitude to Marta had not softened and Marta had not quite matured enough to let the deliberately provocative comments pass.

When the chieftain had announced that Marta would be accompanying him to the negotiations, small pink spots of furious envy had appeared on Iri's pale cheeks. It had taken mere seconds for her to turn this on Marta in a low growl. If the chieftain had heard her hiss that it was obvious Marta couldn't be trusted out of sight then he had chosen to ignore it. When you are one of the clan war-leaders, no one stands in front of you. If you choose not defend yourself from attack then it is up to you alone to deal with the consequences. Unfortunately for Marta there was nothing she could do to retaliate that would have any effect on the blatantly jealous Iri. She had turned to make a retort but Maran had been there. His disapproving gaze had silenced her. He knew, even if the younger war-leaders didn't, that there was going to be more trouble on this day than these petty territorial squabbles and power-plays.

Reigning in her vitriolic, humiliated anger, Marta looked down on the camp they were approaching. There must have been two thousand souls living down there on the veldt. In the centre stood the gargantuan command tent of General Salamander, painted with vibrant red and orange knots and patterns, the front opening into featureless darkness. Around it, in the shimmering heat haze, spiralled about a hundred tepees and around the edge a ring of maybe two or three hundred *moktis*: three-poled frames build to support the weight of two soldiers' fur and hide battle armour hung strategically to form a low lying makeshift canopy just big enough for two soldiers overnight. Bare now, as the armour was in use, the *moktis* made a strange frill on the edge of this giant war-like doily.

To Marta, who had never seen two thousand souls in one spot, it was more than intimidating. The year had not been kind to Clan Boar in terms of casualties and there were barely seven hundred of them left all told. It was the first time she had seen the might of Salamander displayed impressively and she could hear her words of twelve months previously.

"We fight, until our very last breath, we fight."

It seemed like childish hubris now, to think that the Boar could stand against this. Surrender and acquiescence, these things were not of the Boar. They did not back down, they were stubborn beyond even what was usual for tartars. This could be seen as spirited or foolhardy given their smaller than usual clan but however it was seen it could not be denied that Boar were as good as their word. Marta couldn't help but wonder if today that might change. The chieftain hadn't said what he intended to do. He had heard them all out but had chosen not to share with them his final verdict.

There had been quite some disagreement amongst the clan council about what the Boar should do next. For once, the voices of the war-leaders had been united against capitulating to Salamander. The shaman had made a case for a more placatory approach, and the elder, whose business was the clan's economic and materialistic welfare, had argued that dead clans held no ground. Marta admitted it was not a decision she would have wished to make. She was grateful, as she picked her way on horseback slowly down the bank to the camp, that she didn't have to.

The pink dots on Iri's sullen cheeks hadn't faded - she was still hot with envy. She didn't bellyache about it, fair wasn't a concept that held any place in the world of the war-leaders. The chieftain had chosen Marta because had wanted to take Marta, he hadn't wanted to take Iri and the reason was largely unimportant. Maran at least had the decency not to scorn her but Rhine on the other hand had simply screwed up his face into a horrid visage of mock sympathy and shaken his head. The conspicuous loss of Kern, another of the war-leaders, not three days earlier and his brother Valdan's overdue return from a scouting mission had left the three of them alone and unnerved. Sitting dejectedly on the steps up to the council table at one end of the great hall they felt and looked oddly diminished. The three of them had very little to say, but that didn't stop them from talking, trying to clarify their thoughts out loud on what might happen in the next twenty four hours. Hunched over with his swords in his lap, Maran did not look at the others as he spoke.

Of the three of them, he seemed the one least certain that the chieftain wasn't about to surrender the clan to Salamander. This was no reflection on Maran's opinion of the chieftain. He had always respected him as a wise and courageous leader, a man with the best interests of the Boar running through his bones. It was because of this that Maran had his doubts. Older than the others by a good five or so summers, he knew that an element of practicality would be involved. Salamander's army numbered more than twenty thousand at the last count and to stand against them would be suicide. If they went over, some of them might survive. Maran really wasn't sure what he would do in the chieftain's position.

In his quiet halting manner, he was trying to find a way to articulate these thoughts to the other two when the warning bell clattering across the village interrupted him. Without a pause all three of them jumped to their feet and sprinted down the hall, their weapons drawn before they had taken three steps. They burst out of the dingy hall into the afternoon sunlight, blinking to focus. The resounding clang of the warning bell filled the air as the clan scrambled into action. Mustering around the bell, every man and woman and every child big enough to wield a dagger was ready to defend. Standing on the bell-plinth, Maran was the only one who could see the full extent of what approached. He swallowed hard, his face white as he addressed the gathered rabble.

His sudden pallor did not go unnoticed, panicked mutters filtered through the crowd as heads turned to see what Maran saw. As they did, they too felt hot lead swell in their stomachs and crash towards their abdomen. Hearts pounded and blood filled ears so that Maran's words were a blur. Outnumbered at least three to one by the fast approaching soldiers of Salamander's army they were starring in horror at their last few minutes.

They knew, without being told that this army were not coming to capture or contain them. This was not the next step in the chain of surrender to General Salamander. This was destruction and they had only one choice: to meet it with their heads held high. As one, a roar swept through them, drowning the last of Maran's useless words.

With giant strides, Rhine took the plinth, elbowing Maran to one side. He was not of such sensible constitution. His eyes glowed with adrenaline, spittle glossed his lips, there was an almost palpable energy exuding from him. As his lifted his sword above his head and bellowed "Boar!" all eyes were on him and the response was staggering. Six hundred desperate voices echoed their name. "BOAR!"

Then, they turned and with few tactics and no restraint at all, sprinted into the open arms of their enemy.

THE ELVEN WOODS 1098 AC

Gul pushed the sweet berries into his mouth and chewed on them haphazardly, spraying juice and pips into his matted beard. The edge of bitterness as he swallowed them made him wonder if he shouldn't have waited a day or two more. But he was hungry now. He grabbed another handful of berries and guzzled them noisily. His slurping startled a sleeping grey finch on the branch above him. The bird let out an indignant caw, fixed him with a look of disgust and took flight. Gul let out a guttural snort of amusement as he gulped down another handful of berries, spitting stray leaves into the air, and forcing escaping juice clumsily into his mouth with his fingers.

Sated at last, he leaned back against the mottled trunk of the towering tree in whose branches he had been swinging for nearly an hour. The warm pale yellow light dappled down through the canopy of leaves above, falling in fussy patterns on his grubby skin. Like a cat he sunned himself, turning his face from side to side to get the best of the soft warmth. A gentle breeze tickled his ears and wafted the scent of ripe summer fruits under his nose. He could smell the elderflower and sugar grass, the strawberries and the cherry blossoms; all singing to him of the glorious sweet taste of summer after the sharp taste of spring and the muddiness of a meat-filled winter diet. Dangling his legs in the air, he felt blessed and free. High in these branches, at one with a mighty tree that had been here before him and would remain long after, he felt safely cocooned in the glory of the Wyld and her munificent bounty.

Gul's bliss was swiftly broken. A strong wind, neither warm nor fragrant, wafted over him. This wind didn't tell tales of the forthcoming delights of summer or of nature's glory. There was blood in the air, rudely spilt and fresh. He sniffed again. Definitely blood. Licking his teeth to rid himself of the smell, he started to scramble to the ground. He jumped the last eight feet and hit the ground running in the direction of his hut, all memory of his blissful stillness vanishing in his stride. With a racing heart, he flung aside the rag curtain and fell straight upon his stones. Snatching up the leather bag and the small clay basin he pelted down to the river and stopped dead on the bank. The portents do not speak to those who harry and force them.

Breathing deeply to force his heart rate to return to normal, he stepped into the river. Ignoring the icy flash as the water touched his feet he waited for a moment and then bent down to dip the basin into the flow. Pulling it out almost instantly, he had caught enough water for his purpose. Moving carefully so as not to spill or ripple the water, he placed the basin on the bank. Then he sat down in front of it, cross-legged and closed his eyes. When, after a few moments, he felt ready, he emptied the contents of his pouch into his left hand and scattered the tiny dozen stones into the water.

The surface quivered and rippled as the pebbles plunged to the bottom. Then, in no time it returned to a still glistening plain and Gul looked down. For an instant his eyes took in the shape of the stones, their positions and proximities and then as though his mind could not compute what he saw, he blinked furiously and rubbed his eyes. It made no difference, the stones had not magically moved – his head swam and his eyes watered. Iolo had been quite clear. He could still feel the old man's breath on his neck as he stood behind him wheezing and rasping as Gul practised reading the stones. He could still taste his unusual scent. It seemed like yesterday when Gul had aligned the stones as they were now and had asked Iolo what it would mean. The silence had filled Gul's head in such a way that he knew he would not forget it even before the old man had finally spoken. In a choked whisper, so much thinner than his usual booming rasp, he had simply said, "pray that you never find out." Gul had had the sense even then not to press the old man, but he had, by the time Iolo died managed to gain enough of the meaning to understand.

Now, as he gazed on them, the world seemed to be spinning. Fighting to remain calm, Gul tried to think. He was not a godly man, his spirit was bound to the Wyld. He was not a worldly man, he knew little of the concerns of nations or faiths. He didn't wield arms, or rally troops, he didn't even have any money. How then was he going to communicate what he had just seen, the portent that was still sitting in the basin, to those with the power to act? He needed to find a priest. Any old one would do, although he did have a specific one in mind. Without a moment's pause to consider anything else, he scooped up his stones, emptied the basin into the river and with as much haste as he could managed began to head towards the road.

And so it began, as troubled times do, not with the dark sense of foreboding that hindsight would suggest but with the gradually building irritation born of knowing that your life will pan out to be less comfortable and easy than those generations before you. The slowly dawning knowledge that the world has laid some unwanted destiny at your door, that the tale of life has somehow scripted you as a hero and not merely a contented extra, is somewhat unpleasant. The poetic vicissitude of such times is lost on those who are unfortunate enough to live through them. Dreams of great deeds of sacrifice and courageousness are not dreamt by those who find themselves having to carry out those deeds when they had been planning a more salubrious and somewhat longer life.

It was not altogether true that those who were to sacrifice themselves in fulfilment of this destiny were planning a quiet life, nor is it true that they found their destiny as wholly unwanted as many. They were, for the most part at least, adventurers. A quiet life to them is like an empty classroom to a schoolmaster, appealing at first glance but soon to become tiresome and pointless.

However, if they were to choose, many would not elect a crusade of such proportion, preferring the relative peace of plunder and pillage. It is not, as has been mooted by some of the more philosophical observers of the adventurers' art, their wish to simply travel the world killing people in new and interesting places. Whilst that is undoubtedly part of their remit, it is not their sole purpose. Simply killing people is a military life, not an adventuring one. To an adventurer, murder is merely a necessary side effect not an end goal – the ultimate plan generally depends on the individual, but it can usually be summarised as the pursuit of three things in some combination: fame, fortune and of course excitement. Some loftier adventurers have claimed they are interested in acquisition of knowledge, protection of innocents and the betterment of civilisation but they nevertheless expect their share of the more material spoils.

In light of these career goals, it seemed somehow strange that at the turn of the twelfth century, it was a group of adventurers that found themselves standing in the eye of a rapidly growing storm.

I

1099AC

THE DARK GATE - NOT YET SPRING

"Papers?" bellowed the towering guard and Daisy flinched. The initial trepidation she had felt about coming to Aberddu in the first place had not died as Mother Tranquillity had promised it would. Instead, it had swollen in her gut until her flesh fluttered and her face prickled. After the dull serenity of the chapterhouse, the tumult and chatter of the Great South road as it approached Aberddu's imposing Dark Gate was almost overwhelming. Carters clattered passed at speed, shouting to the people on foot. People jostled, bantered and quarrelled. It seemed to Daisy, as she drew deeper and deeper inside herself, that all these people knew each other and that she would never know any of them. Surrounded by so many lively bodies she felt totally morose and alone. Unable to face the long walk back and the disappointment in Mother Tranquillity's eyes, she had shuffled into the crush around the gate and tried to pray. She had been uttering the Lady Reel under her breath when the guard had spoken. Nervously, she reached into her pouch and brought out her documents.

The guard opened them mechanically, scanned them, and nodded.

As he handed them back to her, he said,

"Take the left fork of Selliar Street for the Temple District, Sister," without even glancing at Daisy.

"Erm," she stammered unsure even if she was allowed to speak to the gate guard, "I'm not a Sister, and I'm looking for the Adventurers Guild."

"Right fork then," he said gruffly with little actual interest, and before she could speak again, he reached over her dwarven head and bellowed, "Papers?"

It was not Daisy's first time in the City. She had been here on market day before, but only in the company of the Sisters of the Chapter-house and she had always concentrated on protecting the stock in the back of the cart. She could not even have found her way to the market square, which she suspected may have been on the other side of the river. It was irrelevant really, today she was headed somewhere different and in any case she had nothing to sell.

Timorously, Daisy made her way down the wide street towards a large interchange. Wrapped in a green travelling cloak and not conspicuously armed she attracted little attention but she drank in all that she saw. Scowling militia officers dragging a group of scruffy drunks away from a tavern, women with baskets and bundles scurrying in and out of narrow cobbled alleyways, grubby youths throwing a rag ball back and forth, running perilously close to carters who bellowed admonishment and glowered at them but did not slow down. Mounted merchants with disdainful eyes moving quickly lest they be pressed into becoming the unwilling victims of begging, street religion or vagrancy. Tired clerics with streams of children padding behind them waiting for scraps of food or affection to be thrown their way. Daisy pulled her cloak tighter around her and hurried on. At the interchange seven roads met in a chaotic squall of traffic and activity. Selliar street was two of them, running either side of a peculiar wedge shaped building that was flying the flag of one of the smaller Paravelian states and seemed to be either a very cheap hotel or a moderately priced brothel. Daisy averted her gaze just in case and took the left fork, reasonably certain that was what the guard had advised.

Dakarn Pringle chucked the bottle into the alley way and belched. The acrid taste of cheap liquor on an empty stomach filled his mouth and he grimaced. Judging by the fading light, it was approaching evening. He should really get changed and go to the guild. Hopefully a contract would turn up and he could earn himself some guilders before he was forced to sell his boots.

He crossed the street, slipped into a gap between two buildings and headed north. With a bit of luck, Mrs Gamp would be serving dinner as he arrived. He was three weeks behind with his rent, four now he'd finished the bottle, but Mrs Gamp had a soft spot for him. Down on his luck, she reckoned, sounded like a toff even if he didn't dress like one. He'd make good someday, she said, and then he'd remember old Mrs Gamp. Whenever she said it she always sounded so certain, as though she had total faith in him and thought he was more than just a hopeless drunk.

'Stupid old bag,' he thought as he popped out onto Whittling Lane and headed up the cobbled hill. He could feel the contents of his stomach bubbling and somersaulting as though they were actually burning a hole in his gut. Groping clumsily in his pouch, he found the small paper parcel from the apothecary, the one that Mr Arne had actually weighed out and charged him for whilst he was helping himself to the packets of Valerian powders and the poppy seeds from the baskets in front of the counter. Hiccoughing and burping again, he popped a small, foul smelling brown lozenge into his mouth and sucked. It took a moment for the taste of the herbal mixture to fade and be replaced by the familiar flavour of burnt treacle. Noisily, he rolled the little tablet around his mouth as he turned the corner into Dimple End and stopped. It would be a matter of minutes before his tummy was calmed.

Gamp's boarding house for single gentlemen was an imposing, half-timbered building that leaned worryingly into the road like a clumsy drunk about to fall over. It was by far and away the largest building in the small cul de sac, it hung over the smaller houses and drew the eye. Today, it was even more noticeable than usual because where Pringle should have been looking at a brightly painted green front door he was in fact looking at a bright green militia clock. The officer wearing it was engaged in an emphatic debate with Mrs Gamp herself. She had drawn herself up to her full height and in her broad Carthanian twang was explaining with great care that whoever it was they were looking for wasn't in and no they weren't coming in to wait as it was dinner time, and if they were even thinking about searching they could come back with the bailiff and the proper authority. To emphasize the point, she was waving the empty skillet she was holding at the poor man's face. Pringle didn't pause to listen to any more of the officer's protestations nor Mrs Gamp's choice rebukes, he just turned on his heels and with exactly the same gait he had climbed Whittling Lane began to make his way back down. It seemed he would not be getting changed before attending the guild after all. At the bottom of Whittling Lane he dropped into the bustle on Bridge Street, turned left and headed for the Guild District.

Daisy realised her mistake long before she could see the square. She could hear the monotonous litany of a temple's evening devotion, so loud it had drifted through the magnificent clerestory windows and the grimy pauper-slots below. The cadence that bore a striking resemblance to Blessed Be the Lady without the poetry or beauty, rose up into the evening air between the sonorous clangs of the Law Temple bell as it rang out the evening six-hour. As the third peel rang out she paused, looked down at the cobbled street and was suddenly overwhelmed by distance and how far she felt from home. She felt the beginnings of tears wet her eyelashes, but she didn't actually cry them. She could hear Mother Tranquillity, her strong quiet voice scolding the indulgence of Daisy's self-pity.

As the chanting washed over her and the fourth peel sounded, Daisy gathered herself together and made her way into Temple Square. Hemmed in on all sides by the towering, majestic façades of the different temples, it was a strangely large place to find claustrophobic. Daisy gawked up at the gargantuan visage of the Kesoth Temple, like a child in a rather grotesque sweet shop. She had heard of Kesoth only in hushed tones punctuated with dark looks, but here in the city, people saw evil in a different light.

Turning from the arched doorway into this temple of iniquity, Daisy cast about for the Life Temple. She had meant to go to the guild first and establish whether they offered accommodation before she made her way to the temple. She had hoped to avoid having to refuse temple hospitality. The thought of sleeping and living in the Aberddu Life Temple was not appealing, particularly as she had been sent here to escape temple life, but it was certainly better than sleeping on the city streets.

It was not difficult to distinguish the Temple of The Lady's Mercy. The four marble statues showing the faces of Life were said to have been hewn by the hand of the Goddess herself. The beautiful maiden; representing light, hope, birth and renewal, smiled beatifically with soft eyes as she cradled her cornucopia and filled everyone in her gaze with light and energy. Next, the mother cradling a baby, brought comfort and warmth. The warrior, crossed swords on her back and a shield in hand, brought courage and clarity to those at her feet. However, the last one was the most compelling. Wrapped in a cloak, her lined face shaded by a hood, she held empty hands held out in front of her; the Crone. Only the strongest dared to present themselves to her, for she would find the truth in your very depths. Kneel before the Crone and you would have your soul laid bare before you. These faces of the goddess were supposed to be the ultimate in spiritual grace, but Daisy found them simply unnerving.

The temple itself was closed against the night, the gates barred in the last moments of the six-hour. It would remain this way until the following noontide to shield the Sisters of the Chalice from the concerns of the outside world. Other temple devotees could come and go through small doors set into the gate, and outsiders could be admitted if they attracted attention by use of a bell-pull.

Among religious practices it was neither unusual nor extreme. Daisy knew, as a ward of the Chalice, she would be welcomed warmly if she pulled the heavy rope and summoned the Sister-hosteller. She would be taken in, fed and sheltered. She would have no choice but to stay the night and attend the offices of devotion or explain to the Mother Rosetta why not. She would simply have transferred her old life from one temple to another. The seed of yearning for the ease of familiarity tugged at her, but the rest of her fought against it. With a sense of pending regret, Daisy turned on her heels, readjusted her pack on her shoulders and made to walk away from the temple.

"For Gods' sake Elor, will you give us a straight answer?" bellowed Teign, slamming his sheathed sword down on the table making it shake.

"If I could, Teign I would," replied the mage with infuriating control. "I've told you everything I know at this moment. Would you have preferred for me to wait until I knew more details? Like names, dates, weights and eye-colours?" This facetious retort left Teign with no sensible recourse, so the burly Law cleric glowered and turned away.

"It is a bit much to swallow, Elor," said Erin, trying to sound placatory and instead managing to patronise him. "A war amongst the Gods?"

"I appreciate it's not what you'd *want* to hear," continued Elor, ignoring the tone. "I'm not keen on the idea myself. I didn't come down here just to cause a fuss, I'm trying to keep you all informed. You did tell me, if you remember, that it was my duty to keep you all informed." It was Erin's turn to look sour. Elor did not feel the need to apologise, in fact a small rebellious part of him was quite enjoying treating these arrogant warriors in the way they had treated him for so long. Erin huffed.

"I thought Salamander was our greatest enemy. Isn't that what you were saying not three weeks ago?" she said with exasperation. "And the Inquisition. And now, you expect us to drop all that and get involved in some kind of holy war when half of us don't even worship a God."

"I don't expect you to do anything. That's actually not what I was saying. I just said that there was something rising and that it looked as though it was going to be a divine war. I'm afraid I can't help the timing. Unlike a Bards Guild epic, sometimes in life there are two evils, or in this case three and one has to choose one's side carefully."

"Oh very profound," snapped Teign with a look of contempt growing on his handsome face.

"I'm not making it up," continued Elor, needled and defensive as those surrounding him started to mutter.

"Gul has seen it also."

At the mention of Gul's name Teign grunted unkindly, Elor ignored him, "and there have been numerous rumours of unsettling activity from the East. There are reports of a terrible army massing on the Galivara Plains. It is said they are waiting for a holy war."

Teign snorted again, "Why should we care about their heathen armies? Which God do they claim to represent?"

Elor fought to hold back his smirk as he looked Teign directly in the eye and in a perfectly controlled, scholarly tone said,

"They are, I believe, the Armies of Law."

Scowling and burnt, Teign snatched up his sword and stomped away to the other side of the guildhouse, cursing the wizard under his breath. Erin turned to admonish Elor for upsetting Teign but found she was not able to, as Elor had neither done nor said anything that was actually objectionable.

Jason De Vere leaned in uncomfortably close to Elor. He was a tall, sinewy, mean-looking scout who stunk of tanning fluid and sweat. Speaking for the first time in this discussion, his distinctive voice cut through the general hubbub.

"Tell me this Elor, if this is a war among Gods, if this truly is their fight, why should I care? If this is a divine war or whatever you want to call it, why is it any business of ours?" Elor listened politely to the question, then carefully shuffled back in his seat. Looking up at the face glaring down upon him, he lowered his voice to little more than a whisper and said,

"Only a fool would need that explaining to them, and as you are not a fool Jason, I am not going to explain." Jason was just too gob-smacked to respond, he just continued to stare at the wizard, who said calmly,

"If you would all excuse me, I really must go now." Then, with great poise, Elor stood up, picked up his staff and walked sedately towards the door.

Just as he reached out his hand to the door, it slammed open with an impressive crunch and Pringle barged in, barely missing him. The impatient cleric did not stop to apologise to the wizard and Elor, who was already forcefully refusing to lose his temper, chose to ignore the ill-manners and left, closing the door quietly behind him.

Dakarn Pringle strode into the centre of the room and stopped dead. Most people would have paused by the door to consider who was around, instead of making himself conspicuous in the middle of the hall but that was not his style. He looked around the room, interested in who was there. In one corner, a group of shamans were having the kind of self-satisfied, self-righteous conversation that made him want to scream. A group of Paravelian types were having a chat in which he would not be welcome because he was not wearing a frilly shirt or his own body weight in magical jewellery and couldn't remember who his father's father was. To one side, a crowd of older guild members was slowly dispersing, mumbling derisively under their breath. He was seriously considering sitting with the greenskin contingent, who were passing around a flagon and taking bets on some toads they were racing up the middle of a very long table, when his eyes fell on a soft silvery face that was glowering back at him.

"Evening sunshine," he said with an exuberant wink and made a bee-line for the solemn-looking woman. She did not dignify his mocking with a smile or comment, she just nodded in acknowledgement of his greeting which was the least her manners would allow. "How's tricks?" he asked, carrying on in spite of his obviously cool reception.

"Fine, thank you," she said with icy politeness. "Yourself?"

Pringle wallowed in formal exchanges of pleasantry with this sharp woman who he knew only as Mori. She had two appealing qualities to him. First of all, she was stunning - a dark elf of just above average height and beautifully proportioned, with silvery skin had a strange iridescent quality that made her sparkle in moonlight, her eyes and hair were both as dark as the mouth of a cave and just as inviting and on the one occasion he had seen her smile, her whole countenance had transformed. If that wasn't enough, there was the other very important thing: she didn't find him funny in the slightest. In fact, if he had had to guess, he would have said that she found his presence to be somewhere between inexplicably itchy feet and unsneezable sneeze but she never ever let on. Her manners were impeccable. He was smitten, there was nothing he could do.

Half an hour later, when the door creaked open again, Mori looked up hopefully to see who it was. She had been hoping for one of the other Death followers or a priest of any stripe, someone she could excuse herself to talk to. New to the guild, she had made only a handful of acquaintances apart from the odious Trickster cleric who felt the need to entertain her every time he appeared. As it was, she could hardly walk away from him to sit on her own somewhere.

She did not recognise the dwarven woman in the doorway. Wrapped tightly in a woollen cloak that was clearly soaked through, she was shivering and pale. On her back was a pack that appeared almost heavy enough to cause her to over-balance. She had stopped on the doormat and was now gazing around the room with a wide- eyed timorous expression, desperately hoping someone would come over to her before she was forced to attract anyone's attention. Mori was just about to get up and greet the trembling dwarf when one of the greenskins spotted her and bellowed,

"Hey, boss, dere's a wet dwarf in da doorway," attracting the Guildmistress' attention. Deflated, Mori turned her attention back to the prayer book she had been reading in order to try to discourage Pringle from continuing to talk. It wasn't working but it was better than nothing. She was not really interested in the exchange that was now taking place between the newly arrived dwarf and the Guildmistress, so when a moment later Erin called her over, she was quite shocked. "Mori, this is Daisy." said Erin, her jolting formality, putting all three on edge. "She's a new guild member, could you take her out to the pantry and get her some dry clothes and introduce her Madame Du Mare so she can have a room allocated."

Obediently, the dark elf nodded and held out her hand to the quivering dwarf who nervously shook it.

"Nice to meet you," she said, her face still neutral, "Do come this way." Without speaking the dwarf followed her through the hall to a door at the far end.

As they trotted down a dark stone corridor, towards the inviting smell of onions and fresh bread, Daisy became aware how hungry she was. Suddenly they were in a long, narrow and well-lit room. It was clearly utilitarian, not a single item on show that was not entirely functional. A large table with more than a dozen and a half chairs running down each side, taking up most of the space. A sprawling fire place filled the best part of the back wall. Around this table, against each of the other three walls were benches, cupboards and shelves and on which Daisy could see storage containers, cooking pots and piles of woefully mismatched crockery. In the corner closest to the door was a water pump over a stone sluice built into the floor tiles. No doubt the waste water travelled down some short pipe and poured straight out into an unfortunate flower bed in the guild grounds. Beside that were three wooden buckets each with a scraggly mop poking up out of it, two rusty shovels and an almost bald yard broom. An urgent looking note on the wall read, 'hall floor only!!!' and was underlined three times. This was the first thing Daisy had found shocking, as the rest of the room had resembled the chapter-house refectory. She stared at it for a moment before she realised that her guide was looking at her with an expression of polite curiosity.

"Sorry," she said, turning her attention back to the elf.

"This is the pantry," explained Mori, deciding against mentioning the buckets. "Adventurers are allowed in here, and may eat anything that is left unmarked. She pointed to a row of jars, cloches and cloth covered baskets. "There's usually bread, cheese, apples, salt fish, dripping and a few other bits and pieces. Sometimes cooked meat, and stew or gruel," she pointed to a large cast iron pan hanging over a smouldering fire in the enormous hearth. "It depends what they've got left over. Guild members can have four hot meals a week here, but the staff cook most days." Daisy nodded furiously to show that she was paying attention. "The kitchen is through there," Mori pointed at a door in the far wall, "Adventurers aren't allowed in there, Madame Du Mare is very particular about that. If you really must, you may knock on the door."

"Madame Du Mare?" asked Daisy, trying to pretend she was not completely overwhelmed by all of this.

"The housekeeper. She runs the kitchen, allocates the rooms, organises the orderlies and things like that," continued Mori, regurgitating almost to the word the information she had been given when she had first arrived two months previously. "Apparently she gets pretty cross if guild members interfere with 'arrangements'." That sounded familiar to Daisy who having been raised in the chapter-house had fallen foul of Sr. Agnatha, the order's truculent cook, more than once. "Let's sort out your cloak before we bother her."

Soaking wet, Daisy had naturally migrated towards the glowing embers in the fire place and had already swung her pack on to the floor. "So what's the food like?" she asked as she started to unbutton her cloak.

"I don't know," replied Mori, taking a seat at the table, "I usually eat in the shrine."

"Shrine?"

"I'm a priestess of Ankhere," Mori explained,

"A Death Follower?" clarified Daisy as she took of her cloak, her back still to the other woman.

"Yes," confirmed Mori, "of sorts."

"Oh," said Daisy morosely, as she turned around to display the golden chalice on her chest, "That's a shame." Mori looked at her with confusion.

"Why is that a shame?" she asked artlessly, at least given the appearance that she was somehow bemused. "What's wrong with my being a priestess of Ankhere?""Oh," said Daisy somewhat taken aback by this response. "I just assumed that you wouldn't want to speak to a follower of The Goddess of Life."

"Why not?" asked Mori with an almost believable innocence, a twinkle in her dark eyes that the nervous dwarf completely missed.

"Erm, well, er, I just didn't think it was done," she stuttered.

"Well, you're not a devout are you?" continued Mori and

Daisy shook her head. She most definitely was not a 'devout'; a devoted Sister of the Chalice of Mercy to give them their full title. "Because you weren't introduced as Sister and you're wearing a tabard not a habit and scapular, so I don't think I need worry."

"Oh, okay," mumbled the now shamefaced Daisy, who had totally failed to understand the subtle humour of her companion. She just stood, bedraggled and sullen, in front of the fire, softly steaming and wishing she had never spoken.

THE DRAGON LANDS - SPRING

"You have a destiny Krieg," whispered Tian almost pleading, and Krieg looked away from her melancholy eyes. "You have a path to travel, one day you will be our Chieftain." The depth of sadness in her eyes was beyond the tears she was too proud to cry. "You must accept that."

"See?" roared Trell, leaning forward, his crooked nose less than an inch from his brother's. "See?" Krieg dropped back and shot his brother a warning look. He was not afraid of this coming to blows again. He would fight his brother as many times as he had to until he understood. "You are the oldest," said Krieg, for what must have been the tenth time. "You have the Sword. You will be chieftain, not me." A smaller hand grabbed his arm, and Tian tugged him to face her again. "I have seen it," she cried, "Do you think the bones lie?" Krieg cleared his throat and looked her in the eyes.

"Not intentionally," he said quietly, "but perhaps they are mistaken." Tian glowered and looked away. He carried on, his voice steady, determined, "I am not destined. I am not needed here."

"Everyone is needed," growled Trell, "Salamander's army is growing daily. Every warrior is needed to protect the Dragon. If we do not stand together we will fall." Krieg snorted and looked down at the floor. He had heard this before as well, this ridiculous notion that without him the clan would fall to Salamander. He did not look up as he said,

"Trell, I am just one man, the fate of the Dragon does not depend on me. I wield only a knife, it is you who carries the Sword."

Trell let out a sound like thunder rolling across the plains, then white with fury he undid his sword belt and thrust it out towards his brother, just holding back his impulse to throw it at Krieg's feet.

"If the Dragon Sword means so much to you," he hollered, "take it." Krieg simply looked at the sheathed sabre in his brother's hand.

"It doesn't work like that," he said calmly. "You know that as well as I do." He had never wanted the Dragon Sword and he didn't reach out for it now. It had come to his brother and that was close enough, but his brother did not seem to understand that. It was his brother's destiny to lead the mighty Dragon army, not his. He was just a man with itchy feet that longed to follow the road out of Tartaria. He wanted to love Tartaria in the way his brother did, in the way one could love a country when one has at last returned home to it. With his eyes opened by the sight of other places, he would then be able to see his homeland in a different light. He wanted the freedom his brother had had, he needed it and he was prepared to fight for it.

"If you won't listen to me," snarled Trell, strapping his sword belt back around his waist, "You'll listen to the council."

"Fine," conceded Krieg his eyes still fixed on his feet. "Whatever."

The council hall was a large round room at one end of the settlement. It had a low ceiling and narrow horizontal slits for ventilation and light. There was a large fire pit in the centre, which when lit sent its smoke billowing up to an opening in the roof, leaving the space below hot and hazy. Around the fire was a ring of wooden chairs, stools and animal skins on which the council and their guests sat whilst meeting. There was little distinction of rank made in the seating when the gathering was informal and the chieftain fancied, he would sit on the floor, sharing the furs with anyone who would sit with him.

Today, however, he sat on the largest of the carved chairs, his feet raised on a small stool.

Krieg had often wondered if the choice of seating was a power-play by the Chieftain. He selected the floor when he wanted to be seen as approachable, reasonable and kindly, and took the chair when he wanted to appear impressive and dominant, like a king on a throne. For as much as there were no spoken distinctions, the unspoken visual perceptions were unmistakable.

Why he had chosen to enthrone himself like this today Krieg could not fathom. A meeting for such trivial internal business did not need the full realisation of chieftain's power brought to it. Having said that, he was in no way confused by his brother's choice of seat. As the senior war-leader, Trell had taken up the seat on his left hand which would be his customary position during councils of war, important strategic debates and parley with envoys of enemies and potential allies alike. He could have joined Krieg on the floor and been his brother, but he had clearly decided to confer upon himself as much authority as he could manage. As he sat facing Krieg, between the chieftain and Banyan, the surly but fair Clan Elder, he would not meet his brother's gaze. As they waited in uncomfortable silence for the shaman to arrive, Krieg felt small and alone, like a slave cowering at the feet of his masters. He had tried to persuade Tian to come and support him, but she had refused. Burned that her remonstrations had fallen on deaf ears, she was now hardly speaking to him. It was little inducement to stay thought Krieg as he shuffled, trying to get comfortable.

They smelt the Shaman before they saw her. A thick, sickly waft floated through the doorway heralding the tiny woman. Adorned with beads, bones and feathers, anointed with the paste of a hundred herbs and animal parts, her limed hair pulled into four distinct tails, Indya was a mythic sight as she hobbled into the council hall, the rolling gait of age supported by a gnarled staff that was nearly twice her own height. It was strange to think when you laid eyes on this peculiar little figure that she was one of the most respected and revered Shamans in the whole of Tartaria, or she had been before the second rise of Salamander. Now few would recognise her. She bowed her head to the Chieftain in greeting and took a seat on a low stool halfway between Krieg and the others, placing her staff on the floor at her feet.

"Indya, you have read the signs?" asked the Chieftain and the Shaman nodded, looking uncharacteristically grave.

"I have seen times to come," she croaked, her voice still husky from the smoke of the foretelling herbs, "and I have seen dark times for Dragon, as for all Tartaria." This was hardly portentous thought Krieg rebelliously. Salamander was no secret, but he listened with silent respect in any case as she continued. "We will all but fall and then I have seen, like a phoenix, a warrior will stand and lead us from the flames." The Chieftain and Trell nodded sagely. Banyan merely grunted. "A warrior who bears the sword of Dragon. It is clear to me that you have a path, Krieg Clan Dragon, a destiny. That fate will watch your steps and you will be proud and mighty."

Krieg, his bile starting to rise, glared at her with his mouth open. "How is that *my* destiny?" he demanded, almost yelling. "I do not hold the Dragon Sword, that's him." He stabbed an aggressive, pointing finger in the direction of his brother. "He's the warrior, he's the one." His nostrils flared as he said the words, he did not seem to be able to convey that he was not jealous of this. Indya let out a low moan and said, "And you are his brother, and you have a hand in his fate. You will rise alongside him, the Dragon need you. You should not question the signs." Resentment was rising in Krieg's young heart. He could no long keep his tongue civil.

"Oh for pity's sake," he yelled. "What a load of crap. It's his hand on the sword hilt, not mine. I'm just his brother and if I am ever to be anything else, I need to leave." He had said it out loud at last and he felt a certain pressure lift from his shoulders. The four council members in front of him were all silent. Indya's eyes were slit-like and piercing, she was not impressed at his slight on her reading, but it was not the Shaman's wrath that worried Krieg. He felt his brother's eyes burning into the top of his head but he didn't have the will left to force himself to look up and meet his gaze.

The uncomfortable silence wasn't long lived. Banyan was first to speak. When he dared to raise his eyes again, Krieg found himself directly in the eyeline of the Clan Elder who had fixed him with a look of genuine understanding.

"Strong trees don't grow in shade," he said simply. "I don't know about the signs of destiny, but I do know that the road does not have a gate. If a man truly wants to leave the Dragon our say-so alone will not stop him, and neither should it." He heard the Shaman draw breath to speak and before she had a chance, he continued. "We can only provide guidance." Then, turning to the others on the council he added, "I also know that the road goes two ways. He may not be with the Dragon, but wherever he goes, the Dragon will be with him." The chieftain looked at Banyan and nodded.

"You're right," he said, and then turning to Krieg said, "We will miss you, don't forget us." Then he stood up, patted Krieg on the shoulder and left the hall. Banyan, taking the hint that council was over stood up, straightened his belt and loped after him without any further comment to anyone. Angry that she had been overruled, Indya narrowed her eyes and let out a low, menacing hiss. Then, she picked up her staff and performed a series of hand gestures that Krieg hoped were blessings. Heaving herself to standing, she hobbled away leaving the two brothers alone.

Krieg braced himself for retribution, expecting an angry barrage from Trell, but when he finally looked up he found Trell sitting perfectly still, his dark eyes fixed on him.

"If you leave now," he said faintly, "you won't make the border lands before sundown. Better stay till the morning, leave at sun-up, you'll gain enough ground to have you safely in Alendria and away. You might be able to pick up a caravan or something heading west. They leave about now for the Fayre of the Forest, unless you were planning to hop a cutter in Hasselt and go across that way. I wouldn't recommend that with a horse though."

"A horse?" croaked Krieg, thrown off by this uncharacteristic display of brotherly concern. "You're going to let me take a horse?" From the moment the Chieftain had spoken, Krieg had known his brother would have to let him go without too much aggravation, but he hadn't for one moment expected him to offer help, never mind about this.

"You'll need a good horse, you can't go by foot. If Salamander's forces find you, you'll be toast unless you're on horseback. Take Anouk."

"Anouk?" Krieg spluttered, unable to countenance that Trell had offered him one of his favourite horses.

"She's the best over distance," he said, without changing his tone, "She'll see you okay. Don't sell her unless you have to."

"Anouk?" Krieg repeated stupidly.

"Yes, and we'll sort out a couple of spare swords, rations and what have you. Come on, we've got a fair bit to do."

As the new sun started to push back the dark blue of the Tartarian night Krieg saddled Anouk, a glorious eighteen hand Tartarian Bay, and heaved the panniers into place. Taking the thick hemp rope, he strapped his leather pack to the hooks on the back of the travelling saddle and knotted them haphazardly. Looking around, he could see the village was starting to come to life. He wanted to get away before too many of them had roused, not keen on explanations or goodbyes. If he was going to get away without a fuss, he had about five minutes to leave. With a last hopeful look at the doorway of Tian's family home, Krieg flung himself onto his mount and gently eased Anouk into a trot. He could see Trell in the distance, already on his beautiful black stallion Jackal, waiting on the edge of the village to ride with him to the Eagle-eye Pass. "Come on," yelled Trell, his voice echoing in the silence of the early morning, "Time's a-wasting."

The two brothers cantered side by side on the wide, dusty track that lead from the main Dragon settlement to the Eagle-eye Pass at the foot of Nganda Rock.

As they rode the sun climbed, filling the planes with pure white light and warming the air. The wild grassland stretched out before them, so that they could see the majestic orange-brown rocks nearly fifty miles away. They did not stop. For more than two hours they gave themselves over to the pure joy of the ride.

Concentrating only on being at one with his horse, Krieg felt as though he was making his peace with his brother.

As they approached the pass they slowed to a trot and began to pay more attention to their surroundings. Nganda Rock was the edge of Dragon lands, and therefore there was an increased likelihood of hostilities. Nervous, Krieg drew a sword from his back, his eyes darting across the crags and crevices.

Just inside the pass they stopped. Trell reached out a hand and Krieg took it.

"This road goes two ways," said Trell in a shaky imitation of Banyan. "Don't you forget it." Krieg grinned and said nothing. Trell let go of his hand and Krieg was just about to say his final goodbye when his brother let out a squawk and snatched a small brown object from his pocket. "Hang on," he said, pushing it into Krieg's hand. "Tian said to give you this and to tell you to stay safe and to come back a hero or else and that she would have told you herself but she's still not speaking to you." Both brothers chuckled, that was so typical of Tian. Krieg put the object into his pocket without looking and grabbed his brother's arm up to the elbow.

"Thanks," he said, "I'll see you."

"Yeah," said Trell, "I'll see you." Then Trell turned his horse, gave it a sharp jab with his heals and galloped away. As he watched his brother shrinking into the horizon, he pulled the gift from Tian out of his pocket. Opening his hand, he saw it was a small wood carving and on closer examination he decided it was probably a dragon. Turning it around in his hand, he found a small notch that was probably supposed to be for a leather thong so that he could hang it from somewhere, if he figured out where. For now it would have to live in his pocket. Sliding it back, he nudged Anouk into a trot and started to pick his way along the pass.

ABERDDU CITY TEMPLE DISTRICT - SPRING

"No, it's okay," said Mori, "I don't usually go to the temple here. I prefer the shrine." Daisy nodded.

"Fair enough, I just didn't want to keep you from anything important," she said. She had to admit she was still quite unsure of herself around her new friend. Mori's tendency towards still, taciturn expressions left her with the continual feeling that she had spoken out of turn. She was slowly learning that this generally wasn't the case and that more than anything else her new friend was just extremely reserved. They had spent quite a lot of time together after their initial meeting in the guildhouse and on some days, like today, communication between them seemed to run in one long infuriating spiral of nervousness.

"Did you want to go to devotions?" asked Mori hurriedly, sounding a touch embarrassed. "I'm not keeping *you* from anything important am I?"

"No, no," reassured Daisy, "I'm not a devout, as you very astutely pointed out when we first met." They both smiled politely at this reference and shuffled their feet uncomfortably as they dug about for things to say or do.

The Temple District around them was brimming with activity. Gongs and bells were sounding out, the intricate peals clashing in the air into a scrambled cacophony. People hurried towards nearly every temple on the square for evening prayers, rituals and sacrifices. In the short time she had been in Aberddu, Daisy had learnt that evening devotions were by far the most popular amongst a hard working population who could spare no other time. As the bells called them, they flooded from every direction.

Sitting on the edge of the fountain in the centre of the square, Daisy and Mori were away from it all. From their perch they could see the Temple of Our Lady's Mercy and The Gracious House of the Goddess, better known as the Life and Death Temples respectively, resting peacefully side by side as they were. So many had flocked to the Life Temple that the feet of the famous statues were hidden, the Death Temple however was somewhat quieter.

"Why do you think so many people are trying to get into the Life Temple?" pondered Daisy, hoping that Mori would not consider this an accusatory remark.

"They don't," she said stoically against all evidence. "They just want to get into a temple of any kind. You should come down here after a disaster or something. When that ship sank last year, there were so many people trying to get into the Death Temple that the High Priest had to conduct the Dusk Blessing on the temple steps." Daisy nodded and Mori continued. "Life and Death are all they understand. Life for the good times, Death for the bad. What do they care for Law or Amroth or Knowledge. Those are churches for the believers, Life and Death, they are temples for everybody."

They sat in pensive silence digesting this observation for a few more minutes and once the activity in the square had ebbed to a background bustle, they began to gather themselves together to leave.

"Where would we end up if we took that road?" asked Daisy pointing at a broad thoroughfare heading west between the Knowledge Temple and the towering facade of the Law Temple.

"The Docks," said Mori shortly.

"What? Like ships and things?" said Daisy excitedly, having never seen the sea. "That sounds fascinating."

"It is," replied Mori bluntly, "if you like being mugged."

"Oh okay, what about that way?" asked Daisy trying to remain enthused, pointing at a somewhat rougher looking road between the Chaos and Amroth Temples, heading north east.

"The Poor Quarter, the Turn Gate and Tartar Town," said Mori without even looking. To Daisy, who had been cosseted nearly all of her life in a nunnery, that sounded even more intriguing than the Docklands. To the ever-practical Mori it did not.

"We'll only go that way if you really like being mugged," was her terse reply and Daisy was forced to concede this as a defeat, although she had to admit that to visit Tartar Town she might have risked it.

"Back to the Guild then," she said quietly and started to trudge the familiar route home.

They were about a hundred yards clear of the Temple Square when a deep voice came from shadows.

"You ladies look as though you could use a body guard," it said in a tone that was just too confident for a genuine sales pitch.

"Oh do we?" replied Mori, retracting her right hand inside her dark cloak. "And why is that of interest to you?"

"Because if you didn't then I wouldn't be able to do this," replied the man pulling a sword from his cloak and raising it. Daisy squealed, flinched and closed her eyes. No blow struck her and when she opened her eyes she found a very peculiar sight before her. The would-be robber had stepped into the evening sunlight, his weather-beaten face brown with grime, his breath shallow and his bulging eyes flicking between the point of Mori's knife held to his throat and the bony vice- like hand that was clamped around his sword wielding wrist. Daisy could see that Mori was glaring at something above her head and she guessed it was probably the owner of the vice-like hand.

"I was about to say that you two ladies clearly do need a body-guard," said the stranger behind Daisy, "but I can see now that you at least do not."

"Well, quite," replied Mori, "Now if you would mind letting go of this thug I think he may have changed his opinion about the contents of my scrip."

"Of course," said the voice in an accent that Daisy couldn't quite place, and the hand disappeared. "Is your friend all right?"

"I don't know," snapped Mori, now obviously irritated as she lowered her dagger. "Why don't you ask her?"

Daisy, who was essentially hemmed in on three sides by Mori, the mugger and the stranger was starting to feel a little claustrophobic.

"Excuse me," she mumbled, "Can I come out please."

"I beg your pardon Sister," said the stranger, as a firm hand found her elbow and guided her backwards. Then Mori lowered her dagger and dispatched the luckless mugger with a swift kick. The stranger watched as he jogged off, darting down a side alley and then turned back to Daisy. "Are you okay?" he asked solemnly as Daisy laid eyes on him and Mori said flatly,

"She's not a Sister."

To a dwarf from a small, peace-loving temple, the sight of a fully grown tartar warrior was quite a spectacle to behold. More than six foot, rippling with sinew and dressed in piecemeal fur armour he seemed to Daisy like a figure from a Bards Guild Mystery Play, like the embodiment of a heathen god of old. To the somewhat more cosmopolitan Mori, he just seemed to be a nuisance.

"I do beg your pardon again, I saw the cloak and assumed" said the man, clearly concentrating on his city manners. Then he offered his hand and said,

"Krieg, Clan Dragon."

"Mori Sil'erbanis," offered Mori reticently looking at his out stretched hand.

"Daisy," said Daisy heartily, taking the hand and shaking it. "and thank you."

"No problem," said Krieg with a half smile. "Can I escort you ladies anywhere?"

"No," said Mori at the same time as Daisy said, "Yes please." She was desperate for her first encounter with a tartar to last longer than a few apologetic pleasantries.

"Fine," grunted Mori, setting off at pace, leaving Daisy to walk with the tartar.

ABERDDU CITY GUILD DISTRICT - A MONTH OR SO LATER

"Don't kill it, don't kill it," yelled Elor, trying make his point above the bedlam. Jason De Vere, his armour splattered with blood, splinters flying from his shield, ignored the wizard's cry and seeing his moment, sunk the blade of his sword deep into the tartar's side. The tartar dropped to his knees, blood dripping down his chin, still wildly flailing his weapons. Then as though the air had been suddenly let out of him, he crumpled to the floor, his wide yellow eyes glazed and staring.

"Get back, get back," shrieked Elor trying to chivvy fighters away from the body with his staff, "they explode." The majority of the crowd dispersed to tackle other invaders. Jason De Vere, elated from the kill, continued to ignore the wizard and stayed within a foot or so of the body, gurning as he wiped blood from his face. Elor couldn't be bothered to argue, he just left the man to his momentary fate. He was barely clear of the blast himself when, a few seconds later, his diligence was rewarded. The felled tartar detonated, fragmenting into a blast of blood and bone shrapnel. Jason caught the full effect in the face and dropped like a stone into a pool of viscera. Elor looked at the unpleasant display for a moment, before deciding with slight smug satisfaction, that he was probably needed elsewhere.

Racing to the other end of the room, Elor located the Guildmistress shooing a bunch of neophyte adventurers back from another freshly slaughtered body. "Erin," he called above the hubbub, "Erin. We need one alive okay?" The elven Guildmistress looked at Elor for a moment her face brimming with questions she did not have time to ask and nodded reluctantly. Whatever he might be, she could not argue that Elor tended to know what was going on. If he wanted a live one, then there would be a very good reason, a long and almost certainly unintelligible reason but a good one none the less. She turned to the new adventurer who's name she could not yet recall and barked,

"Take the next one alive."

Krieg acknowledged the order with a curt nod and cast about for another to fight. Within moments one had appeared in front of him as though he had heeded Krieg's silent search. Having moved with Krieg into an empty space, Mori and Daisy were also confronted with the berserking figure. Daisy let out a shrill squeal of shock and ducked behind Krieg.

"Get under there," Krieg bellowed pointing to a nearby table with his hatchet, before turning back to the melee. Daisy did as she was told, burrowing behind the table cloth like a giant green mole. Mori glanced over, saw her feet disappearing and tutted. After three months, the dwarf was still a flaming coward. Stoically, she swung her sword and caught the attacking tartar on the upper arm. He didn't seem to notice, he just continued to slash and chop at Krieg's shield, taking chunks out of the wood. A few adventurers sprinted over and joined the conflict as he continued to hack at Krieg.

A bulky fighter in heavy armour and a maroon surcoat shoved Mori aside, and left her looking sour-faced but silent at his back. The armour-clad warrior dived at the tartar, taking his attention from Krieg, pounding him with his hammer. Nothing he did appeared to make any difference, the tartar seemed invulnerable, landing blow after blow on the massive adventurer. Mori stood and watched the pummelling, her arms folded, her lips thin. With one mighty blow, the tartar brought the pommel of his axe down on the adventurer's helmet with a sickening metallic crunch and a streak of blood flew out of the gap in the helmet's visor. The large man crumpled into an undignified heap and the tartar kicked the heap once or twice before turning his attention back to Krieg. With a massive swing, the tartar found a gap in Krieg's defences and sank the axe into his side. Krieg let out a low moan and staggered sideways. Gasping for breath he tried to lift his hatchet again but could not raise his arm. Grunting with rage and determination, Krieg managed to lash out with a poorly aimed blow that glanced from the tartar's fur armour and caused the tartar to hit him again, this time in the solar plexus. Krieg folded, spluttering 'don't kill him' as he fell. One of the other adventurers who had been attending to the bulky armoured lump now scuttled to Krieg and set about trying find bandages for his wounds.

Finally, a clear path to the tartar opened up and Mori stepped into the breach without hesitation. With a half-smile she pointed a hand at the tartar and muttered a cruel sounding incantation under her breath. Instantly, the tartar let out a shriek of surprised agony as blood fountained out of his chest and he folded forward clutching at the apparently massive wound. Then, nimbly and with complete control, Mori slapped him across the eyes with the flat of her sword and before he could regain orientation from this discombobulation she brought the pommel of her sword down hard on to the crown of his bowed head. The tartar tumbled forward unconscious and Mori stepped back, her smile a little fuller. Then, turning to Krieg and his erstwhile healer who was still rummaging for dressings, she leaned over touched Krieg's chest and whispered another invocation. Choking slightly on the blood in his mouth, Krieg opened his eyes and spat. Mori, stood over him with twinkle in her dark eyes and a satisfied smirk on her face, said calmly,

"Have you got any rope? We've got a live one."

Elor licked his lips nervously and looked again. The gem under his hand wasn't quite what he had expected. His efforts to read the magical signature of the stone had left him nauseated and dizzy, with little reward. The small blood red stone set into the top of the tartar's sternum was almost blisteringly hot to the touch and pulsed, Elor assumed, in time with the tartar's heart. The residual magical charge that Elor had attempted to decipher was so strong and obscure that it could have been Divine power.

The only overtone that had come through was the faint tingling buzz of elemental fire magic. He pondered on this for a moment, rubbing his fingers together like a farmer testing the soil quality.

A sickening realisation was opening up to him, the half-formed thought needling him in the stomach over and over again as it grew. A brief jolt of realisation sent a shot of adrenaline racing around his body and he turned to the Guildmistress who was growing impatient behind him, and said as calmly as he could,

"How were they getting in?"

"They kept appearing by the large fire place."

"By it?" asked Elor, his voice a little rude with urgency.

"Yeah, I guess that's where the portal or whatever was," replied Erin ignoring both the mage's rudeness and his questioning inflection.

"By it or in it?" repeated Elor. "It's important." Erin was shocked to hear a wisp of panic creeping in to the wizard's normally assured voice.

"Er," she said, unable to answer under the pressure she felt from Elor's urgent glance. "I'm not sure."

"We need to find out," replied Elor almost yelling as he scuttled out of the back room and into the main guild hall leaving Erin and a handful of others staring at the unconscious tartar bound to the wall.

Elor strode across the guild room, the skirt of his robes flowing in his wake.

"Put the fire out," he barked, hurrying like an old woman shooing pigs. "Put it out," The crowd of adventurers sitting around it just looked at him incredulously. None of them moved. "Don't just sit there. Get a bucket of water from the kitchen," he shouted at a startled neophyte, "In fact get two, quickly!" Then, he leapt into the hearth and started kicking logs apart. To a casual observer, it must have looked as though he was participating in some kind of hybrid between a Tartarian war dance and a polka. "Help me, you fools," he cried as two of the larger warriors tried to lift him from the fireplace amid a muddle of objecting cries.

"He's finally gone doolally, round the twist," said a soft

spoken shaman pityingly. "It's all that indoor work."

"No, no," shrieked, Elor as he tried to struggle free of his restrainers, "The fire, it's how they're getting in, the tartars." At this point the shaman was ferreting through her bag looking for a calming draught. "Let me go," shouted Elor, his face flushing with anger.

At this point, the confused neophyte returned with two slopping buckets of water. Yanking his arm free of the grasp, he snatched a bucket and flung the water in the direction of the glowing embers. The hearth filled with steam and one of the warriors let out a yelp as he was scalded. A volley of abuse hit Elor as he held out his hand for the second bucket, waded into the steam and emptied directly over the heart of the fire. Then, disregarding both the steam and the swearing, said calmly,

"That's better."

"Elor," called an authoritative voice across the hall, "Would you mind explaining exactly what's going on?"

"Ah, Guildmistress," said Elor, trying to maintain his dignity in spite of the fact that his robes were sodden and his long, golden brown hair was plastered to his face. "Yes, of course."

"Well?" said Erin a little impatiently, herself ignoring the complaints of the adventurers now trying to reset the fire.

"It's possible," said Elor, determined to keep it brief but shocking, "that Salamander has regained the power of Fire." This statement had the desired effect. Erin fixed Elor with an 'oh really, well where's your proof,' glare and the previously cussing adventurers around the fireside fell immediately silent.

"They've been travelling through the flames of the fire, that's why they were all appearing beside the fire place,"

"If that's the case," retorted Erin without adding *smarty pants* out loud, "then why have none of them appeared in the brazier in the warming room or the fire place in the pantry?"

"The fire in the pantry isn't lit," offered the bucket-fetcher and as if Elor had cued it himself, there was a scream from the direction of the warming room, the door flew open and a massive blood splattered tartar stepped over the prone corpse of an unfortunate adventurer.

TARTARIA - CLAN STALLION LANDS - SUMMER

Syrne stirred. He could have sworn he heard something on the wind. A dream perhaps? He rolled over and pulled the blanket over his shoulder. The summer night was unusually cold and he shuddered as the breeze crossed his back again.

'Go back to sleep,' he ordered himself, 'long day tomorrow.' Tomorrow he was due to ride out with war band for the first time on a quick sortie to reconnoitre. Salamander's army was on its way and the Stallion would not be caught napping. He covered his eyes with his arm to block out the soft grey of the moonlight. He heard the noise again, like a muffled axe blow on wood and then the faintest sound of a footfall. With incredible control, Syrne rolled himself off his pallet, silently lifted his sword belt and crept out of the hut into the village square. Keeping tight to the building, he took a few anxious steps until he had a clear view across the main thoroughfare of the village, including three the many stables. Syrne's inner clock told him that this was the very trough of the night and that dawn was a while off. It was not the time for saddling up, so any movement in the stables opposite was somewhat suspicious. He saw a glint and recognised moonlight on a blade. Narrowing his eyes, he tried to get a better idea of what he was looking at. Not long ago, he would have assumed these were Stonesnake reivers stealing the renowned Stallion bloodstock to boost their own inferior nags - but those days whilst near memory were well out of reach. Stonesnake were now Salamander and some said gladly. Stonesnake were therefore kill on sight.

Syrne moved slightly, holding his breath in case he disturbed the air. He could clearly see a tall tartar in amongst the beasts in the stable. He didn't recognise the silhouette cast by the plentiful moonlight; the man was almost certainly an interloper. His heart pounded in his chest so loud he was worried it might be heard, he tried to fathom what he could do. There was almost no chance of this intruder being alone. If he raced to the council hall to raise the alarm by ringing the bell he would most likely never make it. He could sneak back to his hut and wake his parents and let them decide, or he could try to wake Talia and see if she had any better suggestions. He was, by now, closer to Talia's hut than his own. His moment of hesitation made the decision for him, as with another muffled thwack and a muted thud, the main tether in the stable fell to the ground, setting loose the ten or so horses it held.

The horses, who until now had been at best restive, became quite agitated at the presence of an unwelcome guest. The air filled with the sounds of bucking and braying objections, disturbing the sleeping village. It was the familiar sound of a rustle and several of the horse-breeders were shod, armed and out into the streets within seconds of the noise. Syrne paused, he couldn't help thinking that this familiar sound was a very clever gambit.

In an instant his suspicions were confirmed, as a shower of arrows fell down on to the first few in the streets, toppling several of them. Then, as though someone had opened a floodgate, chaos broke loose. Tartars streamed out of huts, terrified horses from all over the village bolted into an anarchic stampede. Clan Stallion were dodging amongst their panicking horses, drawing arms and trying to calm their beasts as they searched frantically for the intruders. Figures started to emerge from the shadows. They were tartars, but they seemed somehow larger than the Stallion. Their eyes and teeth glowed ferociously in the moonlight as they sought out their targets. The air was filled with screaming, orders were barked and the clash of metal on metal took over.

Syrne ducked into Talia's hut. She was alone, strapping her back scabbard across her shoulder with barely concealed fury. Her brothers and parents had already rushed out, having insisted she assist them with their armour and weaponry. They always did that to her and it angered her beyond belief, particularly as they would happily own that she was easily the equal of any of them in combat. It was simply because she was the youngest.

"Stonesnake?" she spat, as she adjusted her waist belt, making her sabres clang together.

"No," said Syrne quietly.

"Timberwolf then?" she hissed, picking up her tomahawks.

"No," said Syrne even more quietly, "Salamander." Talia didn't speak she just stared at him.

They had discussed this moment at length, they had even planned what they would do when it arrived. However, they had not expected it to come like this - so swift and so soon. When they had talked, it was a pitched battle, on an open plain far away, where they had chosen to stand. Faced with a midnight invasion those plans seemed pointless and childish; the future was inglorious and uncertain. They should really sprint out into the hubbub, rally on the war-leaders and await instruction, but they were both rooted to the spot just inside the doorway.

It was not cowardice that held their feet. They did not fear what might become of them, but they did fear for the fate of the clan. When they had talked of Salamander, they had each voiced their concerns that the clan council did not take the threat seriously enough. They seemed to think that they could stand against Salamander's slowly burgeoning army and hold them back. Neither Syrne nor Talia were fooled. They knew too well the stories of old. General Salamander would stop at nothing to consume them all.

For a few seconds, they were both frozen in thought, then Talia broke the spell.

"Round up the children," she yelled suddenly making Syrne jump. "We have to get them out of here. They'll be taken as bait - they've done it before." Syrne didn't reply except with a look, he knew she was right. He turned and led the way out into the night.

ABERDDU CITY MAGES GUILD
LIBRARY - LATE SUMMER

Elor cleared his throat before he spoke. He hated addressing the open forum of the Mages Guild, but he also had to admit that he had run out of ideas. He had tried to discuss it with the more academic adventurers before the Guild had all but disbanded for the summer, but he had found himself becoming increasingly frustrated by their argumentative feigned ignorance. Then, once the Guild summer sabbatical had begun, he had had no one to discuss the matter with at all, apart from his bemused apprentices, who had a tendency to agree with him even when he was contradicting himself. It had all become too much and he had put the poor lambs on study leave. For more than a month now he had been neglecting his students and his own research in favour of this, predominantly because he couldn't concentrate on anything else. He steeped himself in Tartarian history. Of course, he knew the legends of Salamander, but he didn't, until recently know the particulars of the ritual that had bound the General's powers. He had been amazed to learn who had been responsible for the act that had saved the world from Salamander and how simply it had been conducted. He was also quite overcome by the implications of what he had seen and heard in recent months. He wondered, although he dare not articulate the wondering, whether this fear had been what paralysed his thinking.

After laying out the evidence he had collected, the spells he had seen, the attacks and all his research, Elor sat down and waited. There was a momentary silence, as the best minds in the Mages Guild absorbed the details and processed them. He had to admit that he had never heard them stay quiet for so long, which in itself was both amusing and troubling. He tried to control his growing nervousness by squeezing his hands together, until he realised he had actually drawn blood with his nails. He was just licking the crimson beads from the back of his hand when a short, rotund man with an abundant black beard who was draped in a voluminous emerald green robe, stood up and let out a gruff groan that was presumably a prequel to speech. Elor knew him as Augustus Cuthbert Theopolitan Bobang, the self-styled 'Adjunct Professor of Portalmancy and Extra-Planar Transport' or as a great big windbag, depending on how tolerant he was feeling at the time. He could almost guarantee that whatever Professor Bobang was about to say was going to be a complicated rewording of what Elor had just said. Then he would say it all again from another angle and possibly again for a third time. After that, he might finally make an original point, but there was a significant chance that, by that time, no one would be listening.

One of Elor's students had once told him that she had taken a course by Professor Bobang that comprised three times as many lectures as normal and that she had been disappointed to discover that it contained only the same amount of learning as an ordinary series. Elor had tried to appear unamused by this fact, but had not quite succeeded.

When he finally tuned back in to what the pompous little man was saying, he found himself to be surprised.

"... would seem that somehow, although by what exact mechanism I do not know, the ritual is slowly unbinding itself and if this continues unchecked, Salamander will regain all his powers."

At this point, a tight-lipped scrawny woman in scarlet velvet with her hair scraped back in a bun, stood up and cut across him. She was a senior wizard in the circle of elemental magic. She glanced down her nose, over the steel rim of her pince-nez and in a voice like a rasp on a gate post, she said,

"Whilst I concur with what our learned colleague says about

the unbinding, I think perhaps his extrapolation that the binding will continue to unravel a little unfounded."

"Madam, I beg to differ," interrupted Bobang, before the last words were out of her mouth. "The binding magic used in the eighth century was highly volatile in nature and based almost entirely on the earlier forms of caeliomancy and pattern manipulation and therefore... "

Elor tuned out, the rest was just so much hot air. He was unusual among the scholars in the Mages Guild, because as far as he was concerned, academic and important were not necessarily the same thing. He had in his possession a cold, hard and fairly chilling fact. These antediluvian know-it-alls could pontificate and hypothesise until they were blue in the face, but it would not change that one solid fact.

At this precise moment, instead of contemplating the exact nature of the magical binding that had been used four centuries ago, Elor was kicking himself for not working it out on his own. When Bobang had said it, a loud clanking sound inside his head had heralded a feeling of extreme foolishness. Now he'd made a pillock of himself in front of the whole Open Questions Quorum. He was almost certain that once the academics had debated his and any other questions brought to the floor, they would adjourn to the refectory and debate how he had ever achieved status of Magus Scholar in the first place. He felt like going up to the reference section of the library, getting down the illustrated leatherbound volume of 'Universal Identification of the Pattern' by R.M. Danderford, which was nearly two feet high and nine inches thick, opening it to page four hundred and seventeen, the first page of the chapter entitled 'The Nature of Magical Interactions' and shutting his head in it. He was still scolding himself when an impatient voice cut through his trance.

"Mister Nybass, Mister Nybass." The way the voice said *Mister* somehow conferred a polite derision on this title that was not of scholarly significance. "Elor, are you with us?" This was then followed by a dry, affected little laugh and Elor looked up from his thoughts into the red shiny face of the Master of Questions, who was giving him a look of irked incredulity, his quill poised to mark the question answered. "Yes," said Elor firmly, determined not to appear as though he had been daydreaming. "Yes, that answer will do nicely, I think. Now, if you would excuse me." Then, watched by the entire quorum he stood up and gathered himself neatly together. Turning to the Master, he said in his best Paravelian manner, "I must now depart for the reference section." With impeccable dignity and poise, he crossed the debating well and headed for the stairs to the gallery. He had every intention of finding page four hundred and seventeen in Universal Identification of Pattern, reading it thoroughly twice, taking extensive notes as he had done when a student and then carefully shutting his head in it.

ABERDDU CITY TEMPLE DISTRICT - EARLY AUTUMN

Daisy shivered. She probably shouldn't have sat on the steps, they were clearly damp and her cloak wasn't as thick as she thought it was. The grey morning was chilly, the first real sign that winter was ambling its way towards the city with a kind of gentle inevitability. Daisy, born and raised in remote parts of the Dwarven Realms, had never experienced a city winter and part of her was quite excited about the prospect. Right now, however, she was too cold to be excited.

She had left the Guild before the cook was up and last night's dinner was now a long time ago. She was annoyed with herself because she had missed the Gate last night, scurrying across the Temple Square only minutes after the bar had been lowered. The mass exodus of Guild members on the summer furlough had left her almost completely alone and to fill in the time she had taken up a commitment with the lay-sisters that worked in the Life Temple orphanage.

She had been living in the temple on and off to avoid returning to the strangely abandoned guildhouse but now most of the adventurers had returned she had been spending more time there. That had been how she had made herself late for duty, and how she had been forced to return to the Guild for the night to sleep in an admittedly much more comfortable bed.

She hadn't slept well. Lying awake, fractious and flushed with guilt she had decided that she should return early to the temple, long before the Gate was due to open, as penance for her lateness. She should have been on the early morning duty which started at sun up, probably about an hour ago and if the Supervising Sister so chose she could open the step-door in the side gate and go out to collect milk as it arrived at the city gates.

Leonora, today's Supervising Sister, was a kindly woman but she did expect complete dedication. Daisy winced now as she thought of the doleful disappointment in Leonora's eyes as she opened the door to make the milk run and found her sitting, hunched under her cloak, on the damp steps. The Sister would probably not punish Daisy any further for neglecting the Goddess' work, well aware that the guilt she was experiencing was a far more effective spiritual punishment than any unpleasant task she might find. Daisy hated displeasing Sr. Leonora, the guilt would go on for days but she had to admit that this was at least better than Sr. Imelti. Sr. Imelti was a humourless old woman with a bitter smile who seemed to enjoy meting out sanctions to unsatisfactory novices and lay-sisters. Had she been supervising today, Daisy would most likely have been birched or even worse relegated her to the orphanage wash house to do the nappies.

The dawn penance had seemed like a heroic gesture when she had decided to do it last night, but it had been nearly an hour and it was starting to feel like pointless discomfort. Only those with true faith could offer up that much irritation up to the Goddess. Daisy did not have that kind of facility, instead she tried to distract herself from the growing damp, itchy patch on her rear by watching the activity in Temple Square.

She was curious to see how different religions greeted the day. A glorious dawn praise rang out from the Temple of the Aesthetics saluting the beauty of the rising sun even though it was concealed by the sickly grey clouds of the city. At the Death Temple, a clutch of subdued and pale supplicants from a night vigil stepped blinking into the light and scattered to the four corners. They scuttled off without a back glance, each to the individual business of their day, threadbare black robes trailing in the mud. The Temple of the Celestial Flame received a delivery of coals which was offloaded by a gang of unwashed faithful, dishevelled in scorched sacking and caked in cinders.

One of the Morning Brethren from her own temple had once told Daisy that these were dedicants of the Flame that had wronged and sought to make amends. He had told her that some people spent years in this penance because it was better than the alternative. When Daisy had asked, naively, what the alternative was he had leaned in close so that she could smell the liquor on his breath and whispered dramatically *'purification'*. She had not asked any further questions.

She scanned the scene, taking in the Knowledge Temple with its high walls and portcullis. Everyone said there was very little inside the compound apart from a library and a small monastery that housed the original chapter of the Brothers of Erudition. If you looked long enough, sometimes you would see a Brother hastily raise the dwarven-made grill and duck underneath. She liked to watch the Brothers of Erudition when they ventured out into the world. Every one of them was extremely bony and thin-haired, they wore brown woollen robes with hoods and peered out at the world over wire-rimmed glasses. They were usually carrying a tome or two that appeared so heavy that it was a miracle their scrawny arms didn't snap. They scuttled about, approaching the world in a way that made Daisy think of overgrown mice on the constant look out for a cat. Daisy had stopped one of them once, and after he had recovered from his initial shock at being spoken to, she had asked him what the portcullis guarded. His eyebrows flew so far up they disappeared into his thinning hair line and in a voice like a squeaky door that was clearly rarely used he had simply said *'Knowledge'*. After that she had taken to admiring the temple from afar.

This morning however, wasn't a usual daybreak. In addition to the normal to and fro of life in the Temple Square, there was something highly fascinating going on at the Law Temple. The heavy oak doors were wide open so that Daisy could see directly into the atrium. She'd never seen it before, the doors were normally shut against the world. Now though, she could see the dark interior with its majestic marble columns and low benches. It was difficult to see too much more detail than that because there were literally hundreds of people swarming around inside. There was the hectic metallic sound of people armouring up. It was activity the like of which Daisy had never seen before. In amongst the scrabbling rabble she could see a number of particularly impressive looking figures bedecked in glorious, gleaming armour and elaborate shoulder mounted cloaks emblazoned with temple insignia. Although Daisy knew it was physically impossible, they seemed to be more than head and shoulders taller than any other people present, their intricate metal helms clearly visible amongst the sea of bodies. Daisy had learnt enough since arriving in the city to know that these were Paladins; holy warriors who held positions of almost untouchable esteem within the temple. The Life Temple had them too, although she had to admit the most of the Paladins of the Lady were far less visually impressive in their armour that those of Law.

One of these Paladins turned and looked out of the temple door, directly at her. Too far away to actually be the focus of his attention, she looked into the foreground for what had actually drawn his gaze. There, striding across Temple Square with a commanding gait was a face she recognised well. It was Teign, although Daisy had never seen him dressed in this way before - armoured in a similar manner to the Paladins, his black and green cloak billowing out behind him in the morning breeze. Under one arm was wedged a sparkling helmet, the other rested casually on the hilt of the sword that hung from his belt. His normally stern face was alight with excitement as he neared the other man, who had come out to meet him. The unknown man offered Teign an unarmoured hand to shake, Teign took it and pulled his companion into a tight bear hug, their armour clanging as it collided. They parted laughing and made their way towards the temple. Daisy was now utterly fascinated. Obviously, Teign would know what was happening. Spurred on by impulsive curiosity, Daisy scurried across to the Law Temple.

"Hey, Teign," she called at the top of voice, "Teign." Teign stopped mid-stride and turned to look at her. She saw a look of mild irritation cross his face before he arranged his features into a look of polite tolerance. Obviously, he thought it important to appear beneficent and gracious in front of his companion. In the Guild, if he had been irritated by her presence, he would more likely have used some colourful and worldly phraseology that Daisy now understood meant '*go away*'. Taking advantage of this, Daisy smiled and said,

"So, who's your friend?" Teign scowled, turning his head so that only Daisy could see but the other man, who had taken his helmet off and tucked it under his arm. More tolerant than Teign, he grinned back and offered her a hand to shake,

"Josef de Clariar, Brother of the Knights of Justice and Duty. I'm one of Teign's compatriots."

"Daisy," she said, her cheeks prickling with embarrassed excitement at meeting a real life Knight. "I'm an adventurer."

"And a Life follower I see," observed Josef cordially.

"Yes, I'm just a lay-sister at the orphanage," she said slightly shamed by her meagre devotion.

"How fascinating," said Josef, sounding genuinely interested. Teign cleared his throat.

"Excuse me Josef," he said with an edge of annoyance in his tone, "Could you spare me a moment? I expect this is important guild business. Could you ascertain from the master of arms how long he thinks they will be until we are ready to leave and ask Judge Hornebold to come down with the prepared blessings? We can't wait too long or we'll miss the tide at the causeway and be held up a full twelve hours." Josef nodded curtly as one would to a commander and strode off towards the temple, his helmet still under his arm. His audience departed, Teign returned to his more familiar dismissive rudeness.

"What do you want?" he demanded of Daisy, with a poorly concealed derisive sneer. "Where are you going?" she asked timidly, regretting her impulse now.

"Away," he said tersely, "For a long time."

"A crusade?" she asked, her voice trembling slightly as she spoke. "If you want to call it that," he said, his voice no longer concealing how irksome he found this conversation.

"But why?" she said, realising too late to stop herself that she sounded like a whining child.

"I don't really think that's any of your business," snapped Teign.

"I'm sorry," spluttered Daisy, panic rising in her. "I just meant, why are you leaving when the Guild, why are you abandoning the Guild when it needs you?"

"The Guild?" he said, snorting in such a way that Daisy realised he had actually been concealing some derision. "The Guild? The Guild doesn't *need* me"

"But what about Salamander?" blurted Daisy.

"Salamander?" he spat, "A Tartarian General? Why should I bother about a Tartarian General. If he's got the gumption to unite his people, then good on him I say. It's not any of our business, we are not tartars." "But," stammered Daisy, desperately fighting for words now, and fretting that she would say the wrong thing. "But, he's got his fire powers back, like before. He's going to try and take over everything, he's going to get more power and then he's going to invade the City and destroy us." Instead of the contemplative silence she had hoped for, her words were met with cruel contemptuous laughter.

"Don't be so ridiculous, girl," said Teign when he had stopped emitting the vile mirthless laugh that Daisy would hear in her dreams for months to come, "You've been talking to that fool Elor haven't you?"

"He's not a fool," she snapped, instantly regretting the petulance of her tone, she might as well have just stamped her foot. "It's happened before," she added quietly trying to claw back some credibility. Teign just looked at her, his eyes almost but not quite pitying.

"Do yourself a favour," he said softly, after a moment, "stop listening to that pompous little wizard and look around you. Whilst he's peddling a four hundred year old tale of horror and overwhelming power that may or may not be replayed in a country a thousand miles away, the world is changing."

"Changing?" repeated Daisy stupidly, "How?"

"The Gods are rising, there's going to be a war and I will not stand blithely by. Take up arms, sayeth the Law," Daisy took a step back as he began to quote, his passion palpable as he declaimed, lost in the words. "Fight against the dark and chaotic, fight against those who would corrupt and defile you, those who would stand in your path. Fight for the innocent and the helpless, for those who can not wield a sword, fight for Justice and Duty. Fight in my name, and you shall be redeemed." Daisy looked up at the glowing eyes of the man in front of her and she barely recognised him as the sullen warrior she knew in the Guild. She couldn't pretend she was not a little frightened by his fervour. After a few seconds, he seemed to regain his composure, and made eye contact with her. He looked slightly deflated at what he saw.

"Do you understand?" he said, gentle for the first time, "That to those of us with faith, there are more important things that warmongering Tartarian Generals and four hundred year old cradle-tales." He looked at her again hopefully, but Daisy didn't understand.

"I'm not going and I have faith," she said feebly.

"Yes, but how much?" shot Teign, his anger rising again. Daisy stared at him blankly.

"You have enough faith to wear the chalice, you do your duty in the orphanage, fine. You have enough faith to offer a simple prayer I'm sure but how much faith is that? Is it enough faith to bless this sword or these people, to ward off evil or feed the starving? Do you have enough to sacrifice an hour a day to your devotions? How about three hours or four? To break your sleep with supplication? How about giving every waking moment in joyful servitude? No? So you have faith but only a little. A little faith is fine, it's respectable and commendable but it is not enough. Until your soul burns and your eyes shine and your every thought, your every step, your every breath is devoted to the glory of your Goddess, do not talk to me about what I should do."

Teign's dark, blazing eyes were burning into Daisy's shamed, blushing cheeks. Her gentle eyes filled with tears and she turned away unable to speak. The cleric's ferocious words had struck her deep in the heart and they carried more truth than she was comfortable with. She may have lived in the chapter house of our Lady's mercy since before she could remember and prayed with the Sisters and done holy works but she had never really been moved. She had a small amount of power granted by the Lady, but she had never questioned why it did not grow because she knew the answer. Teign looked away.

"If that's all," he said tersely, "I've got a crusade to lead." Then, he turned and strode off towards the Law Temple doors leaving Daisy standing alone in the middle of Temple Square. It took a minute or so for Daisy to collect herself together. Then, with what was left of her dignity, she turned back to the Life Temple just in time to see the step-door close behind the tall thin figure of Sr. Imelti. Completely deflated, Daisy turned away from the temple and began to head back towards the Adventurers Guild. With a bit of luck, she might be able to lay her hands on a bit of cold porridge.

An hour or so later, the Army of Justice and Duty were mustered in seven tight ranks in Temple Square. On the temple steps Teign, Josef and one of the other Paladins looked out over the troops. His eyes still sparkling with zeal, Teign cleared his throat and began to speak. He repeated the same holy words that he had declaimed to Daisy and this was followed by a complex peel from the temple bells that all but obliterated the sounds of the morning worship from the neighbouring temples.

From the main door of Kesoth Temple, where worship was not often a collective or demonstrative effort, Jamar looked at the gathering and huffed. He was loathed to admit that it was an awe-inspiring sight and he was racked with jealousy. Whatever else he had found in his new life in the Kesoth Temple, he had to admit that when it came to the carnival elements of faith, they were somehow lacking. These grandiose displays of righteous fury were almost entirely the preserve of the lighter religions, for many reasons. There were so very few things that were common to all Kesoth followers, that the thought of them crusading under a common banner was almost laughable. A rich, rounded voice came from behind him,

"You're jealous of them aren't you Jamar?" said the man

Jamar knew as Callow, although he doubted that was really his name. Jamar liked Callow, he was less creepy than a lot of the other more senior followers at the temple. Dressed in the familiar black coat , which he wore regardless of the weather and a grubby grey bandanna. He came and went without much word on his activities outside the temple, and this time he had been gone for over a fortnight. Jamar, who had seldom left the temple in the three years since he had arrived in this wet, chilly city enjoyed Callow's visits as a way of connecting with the outside world and would grudgingly have admitted to missing him these last two weeks. Callow did, however, have a disconcerting habit of being able to read Jamar's thoughts that Jamar had never enjoyed.

"Yes," he said, aware that it was useless to deny things with Callow.

"Crusading is," he paused casting about for the exact word, "exhilarating, innervating. It's life-affirming."

"It's bloody stupid," interrupted Callow flatly. Jamar just gaped at him. "It is a bloody stupid pantomime and its inefficient.

"You've never crusaded," said Jamar by way of a gentle rebuke.

"True," conceded Callow, "But then, I'm quite attached to my life. Think about it Jamar. When you fight, what works better – striding up to your enemy, shouting about what you're doing, waving your sword about and making ridiculous noises or walking up behind your target and, without a sound, sticking a knife in his kidneys?"

Callow looked at Jamar quizzically for a moment, but didn't give him time to think or answer, "Crusading is the upscaled equivalent of waving your sword around making stupid noises. That's not how we do things in this temple. I hear that they are seeking a divine relic, some kind of magical gauntlet or something that they believe will be key to the rising war. Well they may be right, but the way they are going, it would serve them right someone else takes it before they arrive. They've alerted every temple in this square to the war and these," he paused to lick his thin purplish, lips and then said, "artefacts."

"Artefacts?" asked Jamar, wondering how a yearning for the

wild freedom of the crusade had led to this. "What kind of artefacts?"

"Relics. Actual ones, not chicken bones and old wooden cups. Made by the Gods themselves, so they say. Powerful items. The kind of things that stay hidden in the world until they are needed. Last year, they found a shield they believe had once belonged to Heimdala herself. The Iceni at Meridian have it." he added this last bit as though he was giving provenance for fish in the marketplace. "Since then, all sorts of objects have come up, genuine and fake alike and now temples are racing to get possession of them." Jamar was now listening intently.

"So," he said when it was clear that Callow had finished, his eyes glowing. "There will be a crusade. To find our artefact?" Callow let out a soft chortle, and patted him on the back.

"Jamar, don't you listen?" he said, his voice still dancing with mirth, "Why in the world would we bother with a crusade? All that noise and expense for half the temple to die. Better to just go and get it don't you think?" Jamar stood bolt upright, suddenly half a foot taller.

"Really? You're going to get our artefact aren't you?" he whispered excitedly. "Can I come with you? Please?" Callow chortled once more, his face splitting with a wide grin.

"Oh Jamar," he said, in a old-brotherly tone, "I'm afraid you're far too late." Then, with his back firmly to the Temple Square, he opened the flap of his coat and Jamar saw it. A shining, thin bladed knife was strapped to Callow's chest under his arm. Even without a proper view of it, Jamar could see that the dagger was potent and very very old. He recoiled from it with an involuntary twitch, which did not escape Callow. "Probably just as well you missed it," he said patting Jamar on the shoulder and walking passed him towards the temple door. "If you really want some excitement, Jamar, join the Adventurers guild. They're always recruiting from what I hear."

PARAVEL - A SMALL BACKWATER - WINTER APPROACHES

"Oh that poor little mite," cooed the tailor's wife. "She must be frozen solid in that thin little dress in this weather."

"She's almost as thin as that dress," fussed the baker's wife, "I wonder when she's last had a decent feed."

"Oh Gods love her," whispered the preacher's wife, "it's no life."

The three women were clutched together in a huddle in the village square waiting for the carter with lists and baskets of goods to trade. The small girl in the pink shift with the moth-eaten woollen shawl was across the muddy grass, kicking the heels of her holey boots against the wall of the Inn. She looked so forlorn beneath her bush of untidy hair with her pale, bony limbs. She seemed tall for her age they thought and quite unfortunate in the face but that didn't stop them being compassionate. There was a sharp gust of wind pushing an unpleasant splatter of rain out of the menacing grey clouds. The girl sneezed and clutched her head, the three women let out low sighs of pity and scurried for the shelter of the large sycamore.

Ten minutes later, when the squall had passed and the women had emerged from the protection of the tree shaking water from their cloaks, they hurried over to the poor little mite who was now shivering, her sodden dress clinging to her gaunt frame. The cleric's wife took off her own cloak and wrapped the child in it. The baker's wife pressed a plaited bread roll from the trade basket into her ice cold hand. It was still warm from the bake oven, and the Baker's wife hoped it would warm her before she ate it. The girl smiled wistfully in thanks, her soulful eyes speaking volumes to the kind hearts of the three women.

They were still fussing over her when her bearded monstrosity of a father swanned out of the Inn five minutes later, dry as a bone in a heavy canvas coat. With pointed looks, they nodded their greetings to him and departed muttering under their breath, the cleric's wife taking her cloak as she went. Grabbing the girl savagely by the hand, the bearded man dragged her away around the side of the Inn and out of the women's sight. They were left, lips pursed, shaking their heads. "What the hell do you think you were doing?" growled the man, through the rough fur of his beard.

"Nothing," replied the girl sulkily, through a mouthful of bread. "They felt sorry for me, that's all. I didn't do nothing."

"Bloody marvellous," grumbled the man, "give us some of that." He held out a calloused hand expectantly.

"Sod off," hissed the girl, her voice taking on a strangely masculine tone, "I'm frozen and you promised you were going to delouse this wig and patch this dress and you lied."

"Oh poor baby," snarled the man, scratching his chin vigorously. "At least you haven't got half a badger's backside glued to your chin."

"Come on, let's get back to the wagon," muttered Sylas, taking another bite out of the bread roll and chewing thoroughly. He probably didn't have enough spit left to swallow it quickly. "You have no idea how cold this wind is when there's nothing between you and the air." Parked up on the patch of scrubby grass beside the brook stood a covered wagon. A lick of bright green paint did it's best to conceal the years of poor treatment and even poorer repair jobs. On the fabric of the cover in large shaky letters, was the legend *'Doctor Tolliver: Travelling Wonder Worker, Medicine Man and Rain-maker'*. The man with the badger-bottom beard, the eponymous Doctor Tolliver, scrambled into the wagon and went straight for a cloth covered box at the far end. As he pathologically inspected the money-chest, Sylas his companion hoisted himself onto the back of the cart and struggled to standing.

Being a very diminutive man, Sylas was able to stand up in the back of the wagon much to Tollie's annoyance. Ignoring Tollie, he pulled the damp blond wig from his head, flung it on to his hammock and started to struggle with the dress. Sodden cotton was harder to remove than he would have expected due to its tendency to stick to clammy skin, and having already ripped the dress two or three times this summer, he couldn't really afford any more tears.

"Is it all still there?" he remarked snidely as Tollie finished his compulsive round of checks.

"Mock if you like Sylas," he retorted, "But if it had gone you'd be far less amused." Sylas had to agree that Tollie did have a point, so kept his mouth shut as he pulled on a dry tunic and hose.

"Where to next?" he asked, when he was at last fully clothed and slightly warmer. Tollie was now sitting on a cushion on the floor of the wagon examining a map by the glow of a tiny candle lantern.

"We need to get off the Lilleheim Turnpike," he said without looking up, "head South away from the city. If we're clever we can get across the river at Durodamme and get on to the Old Curien Road. There's a network of valleys up there that basically have only four family names and too many toes per capita. It's lucrative wheat and pottery country but the caravans will have gone by now heading to the Cities for winter. They'll be desperate for some entertainment, and they'll have just been paid."

"Genius," murmured Sylas dropping down next to Tollie. "What routine we going to give them? It's too late in the year for rain-making."

"Doc Tolliver's World Famous Cure-All."

"It's good for what ails you," Sylas supplied smiling.

"Yep, and we've got nearly two hundred bottles left under my bunk and it's starting to reek."

"What's in it anyway?" asked Sylas removing the cork from

the demonstration bottle and wishing he hadn't. "It looks revolting."

"That's because it's a famous greenskin recipe: rat's piss and river water" Sylas who had just dipped a finger into the bottle neck withdrew it hastily, wiped it on his tunic and re-corked the bottle. There were a few seconds pause and then his face fell into anger.

"You rub that on me? During the show, you rub that on me?" he yelled hotly, waving the bottle at Tollie.

"Will you relax," said Tollie with infuriating nonchalance, taking the bottle from his hands. "This one's just river water. The rat's piss just adds a certain *je ne sais quoi* to the smell that makes it that little bit more believable." Sylas scowled at him.

"But still," he continued progressing from a shout to a whine, "You've been rubbing river water into my open sores.

"Yes," said Tollie, ignoring Sylas' tone, he'd groan used to his whining, "I admit it. I've been rubbing river water into your magically created open sores, before cleverly dispelling them five minutes later. I do apologise. I hope you don't get any illusionary parasites from it." Sylas stuck his tongue out, it was the only thing he could do. "Get the horse," ordered Tollie, and without any grace at all, Sylas got up and clambered out of the wagon.

... A week and a half later, in a village on the Old Curien Road

"Roll up, roll up ladies and gentleman for Doctor Tolliver's World Famous Cure-all. It's good for what ails you! Just one drop cures just about anything. That's right madam, step right up, come and see for yourself, Doc Tolliver's instant cure, it's just like magic!"

A reasonable crowd had gathered around the wagon in the village square. The coffers were fuller than expected already from yesterday's show in the village along and Tollie had high hopes for this place. For one thing it was bigger than the two-sheep backwater they had just left, and for another thing a company of soldiers were in town, barracked in a higgledy-piggledy canvas city that had been set up in the long fields. The buxom wench in the Tavern had said they had been there since Sunday and weren't planning on leaving till Tuesday or was it Tuesday week? Either way, they were welcome but only as long as their coin lasted. They hadn't made too much of a nuisance of themselves, even though they seemed to have a large number of priests with them. Tollie had smiled knowingly and nodded as she topped up his pint. He had been charm personified and his sweet little daughter in the pink shift and woolly shawl was a joy, but best not get too close. The wench had bustled out for the show and was standing in the front row making eyes at the Doc. It was funny how people felt inclined to believe a lonely widower, never wondering why if he really had made a miracle cure-all his wife had still managed to die and his daughter was still wandering about covered in weeping sores.

Sylas hopped down from the back of the wagon, pulled his skirt down and trudged around to the front of the van. The oozing, flaking cankers all over his face and arms might have been a clever illusion but every time he looked at them he really felt them itch. It didn't help that Tollie still hadn't deloused the wig. Luckily for Sylas, his expression of sullen resignation was perfect for the performance. He glowered at Tollie as he climbed onto the temporary dais in front of the wagon. Tollie was looking unusually smug and Sylas suspected that was because they had drawn quite a crowd. All eyes were suddenly on him.

Tollie took Sylas gently by the hand and pulled him centre stage, the chattering crowd fell silent.

"Ladies, Gentleman, boys and girls, let me introduce you to my dearest daughter Marielle. Please note her horrifying but completely non-contagious skin complaint. Don't be distressed ladies, she'll be fixed in a jiffy." With a tug on his wrist, Marielle-Sylas was paraded up and down the stage for the horrified village wives to examine and gasp over. "Doc Tolliver's World Famous Cure-all will soon sort her out." Tollie reached into the chest beside him and pulled out two bottles of yellowy-brown liquid with hand written labels, lettered in the same unsteady hand that had painted the legend on the side of wagon cover. Dramatically, Tollie uncorked the first bottle and handed it to the buxom barmaid. She took a sniff from the top of the bottle and reeled back in revulsion. Then, faithful to the genial widower who had poured his heart out to her, nodded approvingly. "Quite potent wouldn't you say madam?" asked Tollie rhetorically, "Pass it around, pass it around." He opened the second bottle and sent that going in the opposite direction through the crowd. Then, with even more theatricality he dipped into the trunk to retrieve the demonstration bottle.

When he looked back at the crowd he was gratified to note that several of the soldiers from the travelling army had joined the back of the mob including a tall dark man who, judging by the quality of his armour, was one of the commanders. He had hold of the bottle and was giving it a very thorough examination. Doctor Tolliver was not worried about this level of inspection of his product and blithely continued his patter as he poured some on to Marielle's oozing ulcerations. Behind the kindly, jovial eyes and coarse badger beard however, Tollie was panicking. As he dabbed a cloth over Marielle's illusionary sores he watched nervously as the commander type re-stoppered the bottle, wrinkled his nose and whispered something in the ear of his sergeant. The sergeant nodded curtly in response and marched away with great purpose. Tollie's attention was focused on this exchange when Doc Tolliver should have been coming to the pinnacle of his performance.

As Marielle's sores began to fade and the usual incredulous mumble of amazement began to ripple through the crowd, Doc Tolliver's eyes met the cold, humourless eyes of the commander. When he should have been extolling the virtues of the lotion and parading the now completely healed Marielle amongst the women directly in front of him, he was in fact trying to work out how fast he could recouple his horse. He did not hear the gasps and adulation of the crowd as Marielle displayed her own arms and tried to carry on as normal. He did not hear them because he was busy coming to an unspoken understanding with the commander.

It went something like this. Sweating profusely, Tolliver had tried to placate him with a feeble smile and raised eyebrows. Clearly unimpressed, the commander had uncorked the bottle and poured the whole content out on to the floor. Tolliver had half shrugged and tried to look as he wasn't really responsible for it and in any case it was all an innocent joke. This also did not cut any ice with the commander whose gaze had turned even more stony. Then, he made a very clear and distinct signal that Tollie could not misinterpret: he drew his finger fast across his throat in a gesture that often indicated the intention to execute. Tollie gulped and noticed for the first time that his badger bottom beard was clumped with sweat and starting to detach.

Speaking faster than he had ever needed to in his long career as a con artist, Doc Tolliver said,

"Thank you Ladies and Gentleman for you kind interest in Doctor Tolliver's World Famous Cure-All, I'm afraid that it seems this batch is not yet ready for public consumption, so I'll have to ask you to wait before you press your hard earned cash on me as I'd hate to sell you anything that might cause you harm or hair loss. Good day to you all." With that, he jumped directly from the front of the dais, and hurried through the crowd towards the commander, leaving Marielle in the clutches of the women folk who were still inspecting her arms.

"*Doctor* Tolliver," said the Commander, his inflection giving Tollie reason to believe that he suspected that his medical credentials might not be legitimate. "A word please."

"Of course commander," oozed Tollie, trying the charm approach. "It's not commander," said the man, "It's Brother. Brother Teign of the Army of Justice and Duty. I am a Paladin of Law. From Aberddu." He did not extend his hand, nor did he smile. Too late Tollie realised that the intricate pattern on the man's gleaming breast plate was an ornamental impression of the Scales of Law. He gulped, suddenly his whole windpipe was as dry as a bone. He was well aware that this man had the power to cut him down where he stood for the crimes he had committed in his life time and he was well aware that this man was also well aware of this fact. The Law man continued to speak in a controlled whisper. "I know rat's piss and river water when I smell it and I can recognise a basic illusion when I see one. Your trickery may fool these simple valley folks but it doesn't fool me.

Now, I'm going to give you one hour to get yourself and your daughter, if indeed *that* is your, or anyone's, daughter, on to your wagon and out of this village and if I see a single bottle of this poisonous muck hanging around, I will come after you and bring you the justice you deserve. Do I make myself clear?"

"Of course, Brother," replied Tolliver, his charm slicked with oil as he tried unsuccessfully to maintain his calm ingratiating exterior. "We'll be going now." He turned, pushed himself back through the bewildered crowd, grabbed the even more puzzled Marielle by the wrist and hauled her from the stage. "Get the horse ready," he hissed through his teeth, "We're going." Sylas-Marielle didn't question he just nodded, his wig slipping slightly as he jogged off to fetch the nag. Tollie then turned back to the stage, fixed his ingratiating smile for the last time, bowed low to the buxom barmaid and heaved the chest of lotion bottles into his arms before she or anyone else could say anything. Within minutes, they were heading up the side of the valley, the wagon rattling over the stony road a little faster than would have been comfortable. Still Tollie had not told Sylas what had occurred. Fighting against the jolting motions of the cart, he struggled out of the dress and back into his tunic and hose. He had learnt when to question Tollie in these past few months, and the best time was generally when a swift exit had been soundly executed and they were well on their way to a new destination.

Slipping himself deftly on to the driver's bench next to his friend he sat in expectant silence for a minute or so. Tollie was concentrating on the road, sweat still beading on his brow and in his badger-bottom beard. When, after another minute or so he said nothing, Sylas cleared his throat theatrically and said,

"So, Doc, what was that all about?" Tollie fixed him with a look for his sarcastic use of the title 'doc' and Sylas noted with amusement that the moustache of his beard was starting to slip from his lip.

"That gentleman is a Paladin of the Brotherhood of Justice and Duty in Aberddu." he said, and when Sylas met him with a blank stare added, "He's a Law cleric. A high ranking one."

"Oh," mouthed Sylas, suddenly very aware of the situation and that they were lucky to have escaped with their hides.

"Yep," said Tollie, tugging on the reins to corner the wagon, "It's almost enough to make me believe in a god. There's clearly something religious and big going down. Did you see the size of that army? They don't field a force like that for nothing you know. I bet the Law Temple in Aberddu is practically empty. Some thing's afoot and I intend to find out what."

"Okay," said Sylas, realising slowly that Tollie's vacant stare wasn't the gape of a man who had just escaped with his life but the slowly dawning mania of a man with a plan. "So, in that case where are we going?" Tollie turned to him, his whole face now glowing with sweat and said with wild eyes,

"Aberddu. Where else?"

ABERDDU CITY TURN GATE - WINTER

The sergeant belched so loudly that the corporal visibly jumped and he let out a laugh that could peel paint.

"Any of you not pilgrims?" he bellowed. "Anyone not a pilgrim?" A grimy woman pushing a barrow of cabbages raised her hands and ambled over. He'd had just about as much as he could stomach of this miracle nonsense. It had been going on nearly a month now and the pilgrims were really starting to get on his wick. Traipsing here from the Middle Kingdoms and Paravel just to get a look at the bloody thing, fetching up around his gate and hanging about, sometimes for days. The embargo wasn't helping. Only twenty pilgrims an hour through the Turn Gate during day time hours and none during the night. How was that helpful? Where did the bastards-that-be think the smelly sods went when they were waiting to get through the gate?

Working on the Turn Gate, he thought he'd seen it all. His dad had said that if you stood still for long enough the whole world would walk past, and nowhere was this truer that the Aberddu Turn Gate. He'd worked this gate for nearly twenty years, and in that time he'd seen an awful lot but he was now realising that he hadn't in fact seen everything.

These pilgrims were a breed apart. Of course there were the usual cripples and waifs who hobbled from shrine to shrine trying to get themselves cured and their attendant relatives, each of whom had their own particular aroma. Then there was the swarm of vulture- like merchants with the carts full of chicken-bone relics and fake holy water. They mostly kept themselves to themselves and at least they had washed some time since the midsummer fayres. Added to that were gangs of priests and adulants from every conceivable corner of the world, many of which were clearly used to warmer temperatures that the Aberddu winter. They set up altars on the verges around the road, some of them had even made temporary camp on the scrub, against the outside edge of the city walls. They performed their rituals for all to see, regardless of weather or time of day. In fact, during his last night-duty, he had been quite alarmed to see a group of elves troupe out of a shack and form a ring. They had then started taking their clothes off and being that at least some of them were ladies, he had eventually looked away for fear of what his wife would have said. Needless to say, they had been the first twenty through when the Gate had opened to them the following morning.

He sent the widow with the cabbage cart through on the nod, along with a drover with a small herd of unruly pigs and three lads with a blanket full of firewood. It was almost time to let the next batch of pilgrims in he fancied. At least no more had arrived since last night he thought. He would be grateful when this was all over. Perhaps that would induce him to go into the temple, because all this miracle palaver certainly wouldn't.

"Anyone else not a pilgrim?" he bellowed again, making his way through the crowd. The locals looked as narked off as he felt, lumbering through the milling crowds with their daily burdens. He exchanged a bout of meaningless banter about long days and welcome pints with a gang of wood cutters returning on their carts. Then, looking down the road he let out a heavy sigh. A covered wagon in the distance, rolling through the slush on the road spraying icy water in its wake. There was probably a dozen or so of these Gods-botherers tucked away in the back of that. Where did they all come from? And more importantly, when were they planning on going back there?

With minimal effort to his lower body, he sidled towards the wagon, which slowed to a halt. He found himself looking at a grinning man with the most peculiar tufts of facial hair dotted in tiny clumps all over his chin, cheeks and upper lip. He smelt faintly odd and seemed to be twitching slightly.

"Good evening sir," began the sergeant in his best 'I'm being reasonable, even though I don't have to because I have a big stick, about twenty blokes with swords and the law on my side' voice, "This is the Aberddu Turn Gate... "

"Excellent," said the man, cutting him off mid-sentence. "Excellent." The sergeant was now escalating towards 'look here mister', his face had hardened and he had tensed all the muscles in his back so he was nearly half a foot taller.

"This is the Aberddu Turn Gate and pilgrims in search of the Father's Tear will wait for authorised admittance."

"The father's what?" cried the man, and the sergeant had to admit that if it was an act it was a good one. "I'm not here to see the father's anything." He circled the wagon, making sure to stick his head inside. There was a small child asleep in a hammock in the back but other than that nothing. The sergeant however was in no mood to let anyone get away with anything right now. His feet were numb in his boots and he was only half way through what was turning into a very tedious shift. He returned to the driver and with a joyless smile continued the exchange.

"The Father's Tear sir. I'm surprised you haven't heard of it. Big news in these parts," he indicated with a gesture of his head to the massing ranks waiting hopefully by the road side. "Can I please ask what business you have in the city?" Tollie knew this question well, he was also familiar with the answer. He pushed his mouth into a self- satisfied smirk and said quietly,

"I have an appointment with Brother Teign of the Knights of Justice and Duty, in the Law Temple." The sergeant, whose name was Greery, had already opened his mouth to start 'well really sir,' before he was brought to an abrupt halt. There was a possibility that this gentleman was legitimate and if he genuinely did have an appointment with Brother Teign then it was not worth his while to hold him up at the gate. That was the kind of grief that made a long week feel more like a fortnight.

"Right you are sir," he said with the measured control of the severely disappointed and then turning to the gate hollered, "Open up for this wagon Corporal."

As the wagon rolled slowly passed, the sergeant observed the grey panel on the side that was clearly an attempt at painting something out and wondered for a fleeting moment what had been written there before and then it drifted from his mind as he moved on to three life priestesses with large cloth bundles on their backs. As he waved them through the gate he sighed again and stamped his feet. 'Never mind,' he thought to himself as he returned to the booth for a cup of tea and five minutes in front of the brazier. At least they were better off than poor bleeders on the Trade Gate, they'd been so inundated they were now working shift and a half. It wasn't until he'd got his feet up in front of the crackling embers and his boots were steaming gently that he remembered that the whole Brotherhood were away on crusade. 'Oh well' he thought to himself as he gulped his tea, 'He'll have a long bloody wait.'

"Who's Brother Teign of the Justice Brotherhood or whatever it was?" asked Sylas groggily, pulling himself to sitting in his hammock. "You remember that large bloke that basically ordered us to leave Paravel?" said Tollie.

"Yeah," replied Sylas, yawning. "Him."

"Oh, okay," said Sylas with an edge of trepidation. That seemed like quite a large lie to tell.

"Relax, will you?" drawled Tollie, sensing Sylas' tension and overdoing the nonchalance. "It's not like he's actually in town is it?" Sylas had to concede that point but he was still puzzled by where they were supposed to be going.

"So, we're not going to the Law Temple then?" he asked as they rattled over the uneven cobbles of the South Wall Slums.

"Definitely not," said Tollie, straining against the reins to stop the horse going any faster than his spine could handle. "There's something big going down, didn't I tell you? Something big and by the look of those priests by the gate it's all happening in the Temple of the Sea God. And like the old saying goes, 'where there's hope there's gold'." Sylas made no response to this, he didn't really understand it, he just hoped it wouldn't involve him putting that dratted dress and wig back on.

The cobbled thoroughfare broadened and grew flatter as they reached an enormous interchange, the confluence of eight or nine different roads. It was crowded and noisy as carters, drovers and pedestrians shouted at one another above the din, bartering their right of way and abusing those who blocked their path. Tollie smiled. He loved cities, especially old ones that had become labyrinthine as they spilled every further outwards and upwards. It was easier to disappear. Looking carefully at the wayfarers' marking painted on the side of the building on the corner of the turning, it indicated that he needed to take one of the two left hand roads for the Docklands. With subtly and skill, he coaxed the nag forward and wielded it around so that they followed a cart laden high with spirit casks, destined either for the trade ships or their crews.

"Hang on," shouted Sylas, above the racket of the street. "If we're going to the temple why are we heading down to the Docklands." "Where do you think the Sea God Temple is you twit?" yelled back

Tollie, his manic smile returning as he steered.

The Temple District – the same evening

Mori dropped down onto the side steps of the Life Temple. She thought she was probably a little early but she wasn't completely sure. It had taken her longer than she had planned to get through the Dark Gate. She had had to fight her way past nearly a hundred pilgrims and one very stupid gate guard. She hadn't heard the Amroth Temple's call to evening prayer in any case, so she definitely wasn't late.

Looking out at Temple Square, she thought to herself that it was much better now there were quite a lot of people missing. Apart from the Law Temple, which was running on a skeleton crew and had started to resemble a City Militia common room, a lot of the smaller temples - Knowledge and Aesthetics for example - had lost their swarms of peasantry. This was because most of them had decanted to the Sea God Temple down on the Docklands, thanks to the excitement and promise of the Father's Tear. Milling amongst the odorous pilgrims gave them a far greater buzz than sweeping the floors of the Knowledge Library, or whatever other devotions they had been undertaking in return for the half-hearted joys of attending temple because it's warmer than their hovel in the winter.

The Temple Square had returned to being a place for those of faith, and if the city could get itself together, then perhaps it would not also need to be a place for those who were sick, hungry, cold or lonely. If the city had a hospital and perhaps some soup kitchens she thought to herself, then perhaps the temples would return to houses of prayer and adulation.

With a melancholic sigh, Mori shook her head. Who was she to suggest these things? Her thoughts were disturbed by the sound of a door opening. Heavy steps approached her from behind her at a laboured pace.

"Hey," said Daisy wearily, slumping down next to her, "my feet are killing me." She slipped her shoe off and started to rub her foot through her thick woollen stockings. "Mother Angelina's had us all over distributing food to these pilgrims. Bread, cheese, apples and ale. It's bloody heavy. Ungrateful buggers they are too. *Haven't you got any meat?*" She imitated unkindly, "*This ale's been watered.*" Anyone would think we were charging for the blooming food. And it weighs a blasted tonne. Then Sr. Imelti decided we should be healing them as well. Well, you can imagine how well that goes down with cripples who have come all this way to touch the Tear. But what can you do? So I tried to heal this old man with a gash on his leg, looked like a festering axe wound if you ask me, and he wallops me across the face. Have I got a bruise?" For the first time, Mori looked around at her friend. The dwarf was pointing at a livid mark on her cheek that was already starting to turn purple. Mori nodded and Daisy carried on prattling away. Mori wasn't actually listening, she was thinking about Daisy. She had been a lay-sister in the Life Temple all her life, she worked hard for them but she seemed to get no joy from her devotion. Mori would never dream of mentioning to her friend that she doubted how much faith she really had. At last Daisy drew breath and said,

"So how're you?"

"Oh, you know, still here," said Mori. She did not feel the same need to ramble on about every single detail of her day. "I had a bit of trouble getting through the Dark Gate but other than that, you know, it is what it is."

"Really? What was the problem with the gate?" asked Daisy. Mori had noticed early in their friendship that Daisy always listened to what was being said to her, whether it was interesting or not. She couldn't make up her mind whether this was admirable or polite to the point of foolishness. She had to admit that it was probably an enviable trait amongst lay-sisters in places like the Life Temple.

"Some jumped up twerp with a badge tried to stop me getting in," she explained shortly and waited for Daisy to ask for more details. She did.

"Oh?" said Daisy, "Why?"

"He thought I was a pilgrim," she supplied with an irritable snort. "And of course that gate's embargoed. He tried to tell me I'd have to go around to the Turn Gate. I told him where to get off. He wasn't best pleased about that. In fact, if I hadn't been armed or I hadn't been alone, I'd have probably been arrested." Mori said this with a deadpan countenance but Daisy was not fooled, she could see the merest of twinkles in her friend's eye. "In the end I had to show him this," she put her hand down the neck of her black tunic and drew out a silver pendant. It was the Ankh, the round topped cross that was the symbol of Mori's Goddess Ankhere. "And I asked him how many Sea God clerics he had seen wearing the Ankh. Whilst he was trying to work it out, I slipped passed him and through the kiss-gate. I hope he's off duty by the time I leave tomorrow." Daisy giggled and Mori allowed herself a half-smile as she heaved herself to standing. The dwarf had replaced her shoes and was now standing up. They needed to make a move.

"Come on then," said Daisy her face a picture of exhaustion. "Let's go if we're going, before the Amroth Temple ring the

Round. I don't want to be swamped by the sanctimonious gits on their way to evening prayers."

They trudged down the Life Temple steps and started out across the Temple Square but they had not gone more than ten paces when a familiar voice behind them said,

"Good Evening Ladies." They didn't stop to greet him but as he kept pace, Daisy said,

"Hello Pringle," and at exactly the same time, Mori said,

"Why don't you change those awful trousers, you smell like a pack of dogs." Pringle let out strangulated chuckle as he scurried around to face them. Bowing low to Mori and saying,

"Charmed as always Mistress Sil'erbanis," as she swept passed him with a snort of irritation. Undeterred he capered onwards, and then addressing Daisy, said,

"I assumed you fine women are heading towards the Adventurers Guild this evening." Too polite to dismiss him out of hand, Daisy slowed and smiled.

"Of course," she said. Mori did not slow down nor did she look back. She just snorted again. Daisy knew that in spite of her better judgement Mori would not get too far ahead.

"Excellent," said Pringle theatrically, now walking abreast with Daisy as they quickened their pace to catch up to Mori. "Then, may I accompany you there?"

"Accompany us?" spat Mori, taking exception to the assertion that they might need assistance. "You want to accompany us?"

"Yes," said Pringle with a fiendish grin, "I'm afraid I might get robbed, and I was hoping that if any felons did happen upon us, that you might subdue and eat them." Pringle couldn't resist a snigger at this image although Daisy fought valiantly to keep a straight face. Mori stopped dead in her tracks and turned to face him. Her eyes were narrowed but her mouth was fighting hard against the urge to curl into a smirk. She let out a single amused snort and said,

"Well in that case fine, as long as you don't speak at all." Pringle inclined his head graciously and bowed low again.

"Of course that goes without saying, pardon the pun." Then

seeing Mori's raised eyebrows finished with, "Of course, my lips are sealed. Do lead on."

Thirty minutes later, the three clerics entered the cloakroom of the Adventurers Guild stamping their feet against the cold. Daisy and Mori paused to removed damp cloaks, gloves and hats. Pringle, having no outer garments to divest, hurried straight through to the warmth of the main hall. Nearly two-dozen adventurers were already gathered around the enormous inglenook in one corner of the hall. Pringle, being very slight in build slid carefully through a gap and folded himself against the wall rubbing his blue-orange tinged hands. Opposite, Elor was sitting in a straight backed chair all alone. His protests regarding the possibilities of Tartarian interlopers had been shouted down by twenty odd people who were too cold to care, many of whom thought a good fight might be the best way of warming up.

"Hi Elor," said Daisy smiling, and he returned the gestured with a polite but solemn nod. Looking around, there weren't many people who she considered friends about. Mostly there were warriors and scouts who didn't want to talk to lay-sisters of the Life Temple who didn't understand their lewd jokes. Also, in recent weeks there had been something going on to which she was not privy. There were little looks and whispers, secrets being shared but not with her. She was comfortable with that, most of the secret keepers were people she did not really respect or like, but even so it got very dull. She preferred to avoid them unless she was required to heal them or worse go on a contract with them.

After the last time, when she had trailed around Albion in the wake of a narcissistic dark elf who didn't deign to speak to her unless he needed healing, a godless scout with a searing sarcasm who thought it was funny to propose marriage and worse to her every few paces and a giant rat that violated every corpse they found or created, she was forced to speak to the Guildmistress. As if her ordeal hadn't been bad enough, she was horrified to discover that the Guildmistress considered this normal behaviour and told her to toughen up and get a sense of humour. Daisy hadn't said anything, she had just fixed Erin with such a look that the woman had relented and said that she could probably keep her off missions with the dark elf and the rat-kin, who hadn't liked her much either, but she was going to find that they weren't that much different from the other adventurers. Daisy then said she was happy to go on fewer missions if she could please be sent with others of a religious persuasion. Erin had grudgingly agreed and then sent her on a contract to the Middle Kingdoms with Pringle and a peculiar man covered in tiny scars who apparently followed Kyrak Lord of Blood, one of the many aspects of Kesoth god of pain and dishonour. It had at least been more enjoyable that the previous jaunt. In fact, although she would never have admitted this to Mori, she was growing to quite like Pringle. This didn't help her right now, as she looked for someone to talk to.

Mori had already padded off towards the pantry in search of food, leaving Daisy standing in the middle of the room gazing around blankly. She did not have to wait long, wondering if she dared interrupt Elor's solitary fury. A rough friendly voice behind her said,

"All right gorgeous?" and with a waft of damp dog and strong liquor she knew Krieg had just arrived, probably direct from a Dockland's tavern. She wished he wouldn't call her gorgeous even though she quite liked it, because it made her blush which made him chuckle.

"I'm okay thanks, clapped out but okay," she said turning and smiling. Krieg hadn't really taken in what she said, he was just nodding enthusiastically and grinning. He looked cleaner than usual although judging by his liquid stare he was clearly at least two, if not all three, sheets to the wind. The end of his weather-beaten nose had turned scarlet. She was impressed at how steady he seemed to be on his feet having been lead to believe that only dwarves could genuinely handle their drink. "How are you?" she said intrigued.

"I'm excellent," replied Krieg, only slightly slurred. "I've just finished a few days' work for some toff, who needed a couple of heavies for some deal. He paid really well too. Not that I've got too much left." He hiccoughed comically and then smiled again. "'scuse me. So what's going down here?"

"Nothing much," supplied Daisy looking a little glum. The exhaustion from the day's rounds was really catching up with her and so far the Guild had failed to provide much inducement not to go straight up to bed.

"Fair enough," said Krieg, looking a little disappointed himself, "I was hoping for a little action actually. It's not natural being this liquored up with nothing to fight. I wonder if there's anything to eat." With that, he wondered off towards the kitchen with what Daisy would have described as nothing more than a slight meander. She gave up, went over to Elor and sat down beside him pointedly.

There was an uncomfortable pause that lasted several minutes. Daisy was too nervous to start a conversation and Elor was still twitching and staring at the fire. She didn't mind, at least she wasn't standing alone. The pause seemed to extend into a serviceable silence and just as Daisy was getting used to it, it was broken by a commotion from the middle of the room.

Expecting tartars from the fireplace, Elor sprung to his feet brandishing his stick and found himself starring down at the convulsing body of one of the older adventurers, a cloud elf that Daisy knew as Til-Dar. He was pale and foaming at the mouth, his eyes rolling back in his head. His companions were gawking down at him in shock, not a single one tried to help him. Acting on instinct, Daisy almost fell upon him. It looked to her as though he had been given quite a serious poison which must have come from one of the four men he had been talking to - but blame was for later. As she checked his pulse, tongue and eyes for what kind of antidote she would need, she felt the muscles in his arms and neck constrict under her hands as his body became instantly rigid and freezing. Then, suddenly, as she turned to her bag to rummage for the most potent antidote she could find, mumbling a prayer under her breath that he would survive long enough for it to take effect, he sat bolt upright. Moving like a giant marionette, he stood up and began to speak. Daisy, who had spun back around to find herself cowering at his feet, crawled backwards as fast as she could. Transfixed with terror by this possessed effigy, she barely registered Elor's protective grasp on her shoulders as she listened to the hollow, reverberating voice that filled the room.

"*I am the creator, the All-Father*" said the voice coming from Til-Dar filling every available space with sound. "*I am Krynok the Hunter and I have returned to you now in this time of upheaval, sacrifice and danger as a teacher, a leader, a protector, a father.*" At this point, Jason De Vere, who had been one of the four men with Til-Dar let out a howling of laughter and started clapping his hands together slowly, he opened his mouth and managed to say,

"Very fun... " before a single look from Til-Dar silenced him. Daisy dared not look, but later Pringle would tell her that for a moment Til-Dar's eyes flashed black, so black in fact that they appeared to be as endless as the night sky. The voice continued.

"*I am the creator, I am the maker of all of you, the All-Father. I created you all as my children but before you I created a daughter, Ankhere and her sisters Kali and Hecate; then, to balance them I created Life the Goddess and so came them all. Law, Chaos, Knowledge, Enigmas, Aesthetics, Celestines, Balance.*" When it said Balance, the voice took on such a deep melancholy that Daisy was moved to tears form the very pit of her solar plexus. "*These are my children also and now, like all spoilt, ungrateful offspring, they are fighting. Squabbling over land and people, seeking to destroy one another for their own gain. They do not care what they do or what they cause. I am sorry. I offer the children of the mortal world my protection and guidance. I ask only their devotion and deepest love in return.*"

There was a pause as silence seemed to echo around the hall. Daisy could feel her heart pounding in her chest, she could almost feel the air in her lungs transferring to her blood stream. She was more awake than she had ever been, buzzing with life she barely recognised the sensation of Elor's hands on her shoulders. She realised later that it was this moment that had taught her the meaning of Teign's words about faith. Years later when she looked back on this moment she would attribute it as the moment her own faith was truly born. She had just managed to marshal her breathing, when the voice spoke again.

"I speak now to you Jason De Vere," Til-Dar's eyes were now revolving wildly in his face, Jason's face drained as for the first time he genuinely believed this was not trickery. "I speak to you of your infidelity, of your fickleness, your anger and selfishness. You have stopped worshipping me for childish reasons, because I did not grant you magic and riches. You have shown me the superficial transience of your so called faith. You are not worthy of blessing. From this moment forward you have been exiled. You are no longer of my children, you will be marked out as prey and you will be hunted." The word hunted rang from the rafters of the Guild hall with an alien metallic tone. Jason's jaw hung open as his voice failed to scream and his face twisted into a grotesque and terrifying visage. Both men collapsed, hitting the Guild Hall floor in muted syncopation and breaking the trance-like silence of the other guild members. The stunned chatter rose to an astonishing volume as adventurers responded to what they had just witnessed. Trembling with adrenaline, Daisy sagged back against Elor's legs and heard the wizard sigh.

TARTARIA - TIMBERWOLF LANDS - THE FIRST SNOWS

Fresh flakes of snow tumbled out of the dark sky, landing on the frozen ground and sprinkling a clean white covering over the scene of bloody destruction. Wide, dead eyes turned towards the sky, unblinking as snow stuck to their lashes.

The silence seemed almost magical as Gregor sat on the frost-hardened earth, letting the cold calm his racing blood. It was a stark contrast to the hours of battle, when the sound of the icy wind had obliterated everything else. Blasts of hail had lashed out as they skirmished, every single heartbeat dedicated to survival. They poured everything into repelling the onslaught but Salamander's army was vast and powerful, even the rain could not quell the power of the flame. The village had burned and the screams echoed in Gregor's ears as people scattered, panicking, into the awaiting army. Blood stained the snow.

Gregor gazed out at the silhouettes of the defeated as they lay motionless in the grass. Beyond them, and in spite of the snow, the *Indaba* tree continued to burn. The sickly orange flames and thick black smoke cast an eerie sheen over the field and the shadows danced, as thought they were the spirits of the departed. He didn't yet know who had been lost. He could not bare to look, but he knew he no choice. As he looked out over the field he could see Timberwolf, shivering and sodden, picking through the detritus for their fallen. He heaved himself to his feet and dragged himself off in search of his brother.

Not two hundred yards away, he found Gilfdan standing over the Chieftain's haggard body in stunned silence. The man's hideous death mask, eyes bulging in terror, gaped back at them. His tongue lolled, his head was bent at an unnatural angle and a horrific scabrous scorch mark around his neck. Seared skin told a tale of flaming hands that had grabbed his throat and twisted, squeezing his last breath from his lungs. Gilfdan reached out a hand and rested it reassuringly on Gregor's shoulder.

"Life is change, we can only travel forwards," he said murmured, the closest thing he knew to a prayer and the words of their departed mother - Clan Shaman in her day. Gregor met Gilfdan's hand with his own, touched it absently and then pushed it gently away. He crouched to close the chieftain's empty eyes, and kissed him softly on his bloodied forehead.

"We need to find the rest of the council," he said, more to himself than his brother.

"What for?" Gilfdan's voice was confrontational, causing Gregor to look up. He really hadn't expected an argument from his older brother at a time like this. Confused, Gregor persisted.

"We have decisions to make," he said quietly, "grief needs to wait until we have determined the future of the Timberwolf," he said in patient clarification.

"What decisions, what future?" spat Gilfdan. "It's over Gregor. It's too late, we've lost. Salamander's won." Gregor couldn't believe what his brother was saying. The savagery of the rhetoric sounded strange coming from his mouth. Not five days ago, he had stood in front of the clan council and given a rousing speech about loyalty and clanship. He had the chieftain, who now lay dead at his feet, and said 'Whilst a Timberwolf heart still beats we have a clan,' and now he was saying this.

Gregor's bile rose.

"What about your speech?" he shouted, hot spit hitting his brother's battle-marred face, "Whilst a Timberwolf heart still beats, you said" he screamed, stabbing a finger violently at his brother. "My heart's still beating. We still have a clan."

"Oh grow up Gregor," shrieked Gilfdan, his voice higher and wilder, the veins on his neck pulsing. "Look around you! We don't have a clan. We can't stand in the way of Salamander, he will kill us, kick dry leaves over our bodies and walk away. You can't be a hero if there's no one left to tell your story. You can join him or you can die, it's quite simple."

"Well I'd sooner die," bellowed Gregor, rounding on his brother, swords drawn.

"You might," screamed Gilfdan, "but I'd sooner live!"

"Well why don't you join him?" screeched Gregor, his voice becoming shrill and petulant, aware that they were gathering a crowd.

"I already have," shrieked Gilfdan, ripping open the neck of his tunic to reveal a fresh wound in his chest which glinted in the moonlight.

Gregor saw the implanted gem, linking his brother to Salamander and felt his heart stop for a moment before it started pounding again as rage filled him.

"Traitor," he bellowed, his voice cutting the night, "You've betrayed me, you've betrayed us all." He let out a guttural cry and charged full pelt at his brother.

"Really?" taunted Gilfdan, feinting and dodging Gregor's angry blows. "You think I'm the only one do you? Open your eyes Gregor, you're pathetic. You're alone. This isn't one of the storyteller's tales, this is real and if you die you won't be a hero - you will just be dead!"

"But at least I'll have died on the right side," hissed Gregor, lunging at Gilfdan again. Now brandishing his axe, his voice cold and harsh, Gilfdan looked at his little brother and said flatly,

"If you're that eager to die, I can arrange it now."

SOUTH WEST ALBION - PORT SELLIAR - A COLD DARK MORNING

The four dozen navy-robed figures paraded from the temple out to the cliff in two rows. Every other pair carried shining orb-lanterns that spilled magical light against the angry grey clouds that covered the dawn. The others held the heavy cast-iron hand-bells and every fourth pace they rang a solemn, simultaneous chime. Under their breath they chanted an archaic litany in a language that onlookers, had there been any, wouldn't have understood. The full moon, low on the horizon, lit the sea below more effectively than any of the lanterns. It cast an eerie aura on the wreck in the cove.

The pair of priests at the front wore white surpluses over their robes. They stopped dead a few feet from the edge of the cliff in the mouth of the cove with a loud exclamation and the other pairs peeled off into a long line. The white clad priest on the left, a reedy cloud elf, pulled a book from inside his surplus and by the light of the lanterns began to read out the prayers of blessing.

"Protect O Lord those you have taken to glory on this night. May their souls reside in the cool repose of your realm in the full understanding of the blessings they have received at your hand. You are the All, you are the mighty, all is yours and to you it shall return. Cleansed are our souls, washed by the waters of your benevolence. We seek only to please you. All Praise to the Sea

God!" He spoke this last line in particular with great conviction, and it was then echoed by the other forty seven,

"All Praise to the Sea God." The words rang out into the dawn, amplified by the silence that followed. Then the priest on the right, a squat pure-blood woman with dirty blonde curls, opened her mouth and let out a note of astonishing purity and beauty. After a few moments, other voices joined the note in harmony until a four part chord was drifting out over the turbulent waves and the wreck. Then slowly, with soul-moving grace, the sound modulated and wove itself into a perfect, complex melody. Even though it had no words, it was so stirring and melancholic that it engendered the very essences of grief and parting. After a few minutes it ebbed away into the whispering of the waves breaking on the rocks below.

The night's storm had passed, the harsh icy wind had started to pull the clouds apart. The moon's glow became brighter, showing more details of the wreck below. Praying in silence, some of the priests looked more closely at the mess of timber shards, ropes and sodden canvas. The two ships had spun together and it was pretty impossible to tell one from the other as they gazed down at what remained of the Albion Naval Galleon HMS Gallant and the Paravelian merchant clipper Pride of Ibngrad. Most of the debris had been battered towards the shore line and was collecting in amongst the treacherous rocks in the cove. It was a common wreck site and within days most of the salvageable material would have been scavenged and squirrelled away by the wreck-reivers of Selliar Old Town. The temple would then be called on to dispose of any bloated green-tinged bodies that had not been taken by the sea the first time.

The silent contemplation was ended by the first priest with another acclamation. This one in the archaic tongue, with pauses for bell ringing. It lasted for nearly a minute and was just reaching a crescendo when one of the other priests let out an ear-piercing yell. The others wheeled around to look at the blasphemous attention seeker. It was a young acolyte with a flop of mousy brown hair, shaking like a leaf in the breeze, one arm flung out, pointing down at the wreck. It was a few moments before he could swallow the terror and articulate what he had seen, his ashen face glowing in the moonlight.

By the time he managed to splutter the word "Kraken," some of the others had seen it too and were whimpering and yelping, their faces drained. The head priest fell to his knees as he gazed down at the wreck below. A cloud shifted and moonlight flooded the scene of devastation below. A vast, dark grey tentacle was lolling over a fragmented quarterdeck, the suckers on almost the size of the helm. It could only be a Kraken, one of the gigantic octopoid creatures that lived below the waves, working the will of the Sea God. It was said that if your ship was brought down by the Kraken, or you were lucky enough to be taken personally by the arms of a Kraken, you would come to rest immediately in the realms of the Sea God. The Kraken were fabled amongst Sea God clerics, sailors and land-loving heathens alike. Most Sea God clerics secretly hoped that they would live their whole life without the blessings of an encounter with the Kraken, whatever they may publicly purport.

A giant milky eye stared sightlessly up at them out of the waves, freezing the blood in their veins. They had witnessed the 'Death of a Kraken'. As they gazed down at the beast, the forty eight priests knew that this moment would become part of the litany of the Sea God in times to come, and that those words would have to be written by somebody else. They would be part of the teachings in perpetuity.

The bell ringers began an impromptu peal. Then the song started, swooping through deep blue of the dawn. Then, without any spoken agreement, they all stepped forward in line to the very edge of the cliff and with the heartfelt acclamation "All Praise to the Sea God" they stepped off.

ABERDDU ADVENTURERS GUILD - FEAST OF MIDWINTER

Neither Mori nor Daisy had ever been to a feast of such proportion. They were not a regular feature of life in the more austere temples. The closest thing Daisy could liken it to was the Harvest Thanksgiving. Thanksgiving meals were largely bread, cheese, fruit, vegetables and the occasional chicken, pig, or if things were really flush, a goat. Daisy had to admit that there was considerably more drunkenness, swearing and nakedness at a feast. Also fewer prayers, more food that she had never heard of and jokes she didn't understand. She also had to admit that she thought the temples were missing out.

Apparently, it had been a very lucrative adventuring year. Erin and the council felt the adventurers deserved to celebrate in style. They had arranged for spread the like of which Daisy could not have dreamed of. There were silver salvers piled with all manner of cuisine from across the whole continent. Spiced meat balls from Jaffria that made the tongue tingle, scented rice, edible flowers from Alendria, griddled fish, strange bitter tasting orange coloured jelly that was supposed to be *the* thing from Arabi this year and of course a whole boar with a large roasted apple wedged into its wryly grinning maw. She had been sitting at the table for nearly an hour and a half now and no one showed any sign of giving up.

Beside Daisy, Pringle was shovelling food into his mouth so

fast that his plate barely had time to get dirty. He hadn't stopped for the entire time they were at the table and Daisy was now wondering how such a skinny man had managed to find room for it all. On her other side, Mori kept tutting at his blatant lack of suitable restraint and table manners. She was sampling the food one dish at a time, and seemed pleased but not excited by the enormous array of choice.

Across the table, Elor was picking his way carefully through a rich shellfish stew. He loved a good meal, well aware that they were a privilege of his station. It was difficult to imagine, when looking at the impressive wizard he had become, that Elor Nybass had been born in a simple surf village in Paravel and that his parents were still living there saving their cash for the great day when they would buy their own freedom and, like so many others, make the journey to Aberddu: city of the free. Elor, who had had to apply to the Baron to be allowed to take up his apprenticeship, had offered to pay their bonds several times but his father had eventually explained that when they finally bought themselves it was going to be through their own toil and then they would be beholden to no one, not even their son. Still, every time Elor found himself in an important meeting or sleeping in a feather bed or eating at a banqueting table he thought of the old man's kind eyes. He took a healthy spoonful of crab meat and blew on it gently.

Gazing up and down the length of the table, Elor could see that quite a few people were extremely merry. Several warriors including the new tartar Krieg Clan Dragon may as well have climbed into a barrel of ale. With absolutely no decorum, they ripped the limbs from the dozen or so chickens in front of them, devoured the meat and flung the bones over their shoulders laughing. Elor was trying to conceal his disgust as he scanned the other side of the table searching for a face he realised he hadn't seen for the better part of three years, since that night in the guild when the blood in his veins had turned to rushing ice water and Salamander's tartars had returned. He needed a vent for the bubbling mess in his head, someone who might be able to understand what he was saying without any yelling. He felt like he was drowning in all of it, being sucked under by the rip currents of a rushing torrent that no one else seemed to be able to see. Most of the people he had tried to explain it to had shouted him down out of fear or incomprehension. He had spent so long being yelled at by the terrified that he was starting to doubt himself. With a tired arm, he picked out a large, juicy looking scallop and chewed it appreciatively, trying to concentrate on the favour of it and push the troubles of the world to the back of his mind. It didn't work he just found himself chewing on the rubbery flesh unable to swallow. He washed it down with a large gulp of cider and put his spoon down. Then leaning back, he rubbed his belly with satisfaction and let the chatter of the others wash over him. This was nothing like the spread the Mages Guild could lay on but there were no foreign dignitaries or aristocrats to impress at the Adventurers table, which probably explained the presence of quite so many pickled dishes. You wouldn't get that at the Mages Guild, they didn't approve of anything that caused flatulence. Elor stifled a belch with his hand and smiled. You wouldn't get that at the Mages Guild table either.

Further down the table, others were bemoaning the pilgrims at the Sea God Temple. Mauna Evanga, a breathy Death cleric dressed in plentiful black robes and expensive silver icons, was lamenting the 'Sea God nonsense' and carrying on about the lack of dignity that all those 'dirty, malingering cripples' brought to a temple with a clear hint of jealousy in her thin voice. As she continued her lament, she gazed at the rigidly upright man beside her, her heavily Kohl-lined eyes wide with adoration. The man, whose name was Whitefire, made polite noises of acknowledgement without actually adding anything of substance to the exchange. Not that Mauna noticed, she just kept on prattling with a wistful gaze. Whitefire was eating a slice of pigeon and ham cutting pie with yellow pickles and drinking mead from a modest goblet.

Elor had to confess that he was a little surprised to see Whitefire at this feast. Whitefire was an Iceni, one of the chosen of Amroth, Goddess of Honour, bound by a divine code to do her duty without thought for his own safety. The Iceni were a race apart, appearing as pure-blood but able to change into animal form at will and imbued with powers and a mandate from their Goddess beyond even that of the high priests. As such they were treated by Amrothians as some kind of sacred walking weapon and their words were treated as gospel. Not being of the Amrothian faith, Elor found most of the Iceni nigh on impossible to converse with. Whitefire, an adventurer of several years standing, seemed more in tune with the common man but even he could be dry and humourless, pious to the point of haughtiness. It made Elor wonder if humour and joy were against the Iceni code, but if they had been then this feast would certainly have been out of the question as it was fast turning from a nice meal into an act of unbridled debauchery. Mind you, Elor thought to himself as he looked at Whitefire, he doesn't seem to be enjoying himself, perhaps that makes it okay.

Elor knew that the Iceni code was nothing to do with the cool look Whitefire was now giving Mauna as she rested her hand gently on his arm. That was entirely to do with the fact that the Iceni found the fawning Death priestess more than a little annoying. Shaking her hand off his sleeve he looked down on her, his face in a supercilious attitude and said with a stiff cold tone,

"The faithful are always worthy, whatever form they take." Staring down his chiselled nose at her with a look of reproachful disdain he continued loftily, "they are an example to us all." Mauna's cheeks flushed red as though she had been slapped in the face, her mouth hung open as she struggled for words. "They have left everything, they have downed tools, left livestock and walked hundreds of miles to experience this miracle. The sacred stone, this gift from above that will touch so many and cure the purest." Mauna had just rearranged her face into a sycophantic simper and was about to agree with him when Elor, who had been listening to Whitefire's puritanical little homily, snorted with amusement. Whitefire turned his sharp gaze on Elor instead.

"What's so funny about that?" he snapped his voice quiet but dangerous.

"Nothing," smirked Elor, poorly concealing his derision. Although he had not intended to join the conversation he did have something to say. "Nothing at all." His flippancy seemed to anger the Iceni. Leaning forward so that his chair scraped loudly against the floor, Whitefire turned his ferocious gaze onto the wizard.

"You find faith funny do you?" he growled as he slammed his spade-like hands on the table, rattling the salvers in front of him. The already unstable table quivered worryingly for a moment under the weight of food and anger but it held out. Shocked by the force of the Iceni's response, Elor flung himself backwards. Whitefire kept going, "You think you're so clever wizard, with your godless magic and your book learning, looking down your hoity-toity fancy nose at the good honest peasant folk who rely on their faith for comfort. You can't even bring yourself to admit something as wonderful as the Father's Tear has a place in this world, because you and your friends at the Mages Guild" he spat the words 'Mages Guild', "can't measure it or explain it. Frankly it's pathetic. You think you're so smart, you think you don't need a god, with your powers a god would be superfluous at best, unnecessary. What arrogance."

His nostrils flared as he shot the words at Elor, who was having trouble concealing an unpleasant smirk. It was hard to think of a statement that would be more incorrect. By now, the Iceni's disproportionate rage had drawn the attention of nearly all the diners at the table, obviously keen for a bit of meal time entertainment. Although he had stopped speaking, he was still glowering at Elor.

"It's funny what assumptions people make," said Elor, his voice barely above a whisper, shaking his head with amusement. This made Whitefire even crosser, he was just about to fling himself to standing when Elor continued. "Sit down and stop flexing your muscles," he said, the scorn rising in his voice, "if you want arrogance then look at yourself." Narrowing his eyes, Whitefire didn't move, Elor was fairly sure that this had more to do with his honour code than Elor's sharp words. "I am a man of faith, just because I don't shout about it you have assumed that I am not. I was born in a surf village, my parents still live there. I may be a man of learning, and of godless magic but unlike you temple types," Elor's voice began quietly acidic over the words 'temple types', "I know how many beans make five." All ears at the table were now on Elor, straining to hear him in his tightly controlled tones. "You know nothing about the Father's Tear."

"And I suppose you do," snarled Whitefire, the strain of maintaining what little was left of his composure was visible in the glistening veins on his forehead.

"Yes, I do," said Elor seeming to delight in the Iceni's infuriation. "I know a fake when I see one." Elor's explanation was lost in a wave of consternation as the earwigging adventures started to add their pennyworth to the debate. He stopped talking and waited for a lull in the hubbub. It didn't come. Smaller arguments had broken out up and down the full length of the table. The Guildmistress, who herself was involved in a heated exchange with the clerics next to her did nothing to stop it. Shaking his head with scornful amusement, Elor helped himself to some grapes and sat back in his chair to let them all quarrel.

ABERDDU CITY STATE - THE PASS FORT - THE TURN OF THE YEAR

In his panic, the first stone Jacob threw missed its mark but the second one contacted smashing the glass and sending both the candle and the oil chamber tumbling into the bone-dry tinder. Within seconds the beacon flared. The orange light flashed over Gideon and he jumped the last four steps and sprinted to his horse. The militiaman paused a moment to watch his comrade gallop away into the night, towards the murky glow of the Trade Gate, then he ran to the ancient brass bell, picked up the hammer and with all his might began to thump the metal. The atonal cry of the warning toll rang out over the dark gulf between the Fort and the City. Although not as well-lit as the city beyond, the shanty sprawl known as Tartar Town was not completely dark. Candle flickers danced in the night like will-o'-the-wisps on a marshland, flashing brighter for a moment as doors were banged open and people responded to the bell.

The Pass Fort blocked the end of a wide mountain pass that crossed the northern border in Frisia. It's stark grey brick filled the gap neatly, stopping would be travellers in their tracks on both sides of the Fort. Built and rebuilt over centuries, the exact age of the structure was forgotten but its pride and glory was a legendary subterranean labyrinth said to be enchanted with pre-cataclysm magic so that the pathway through was never the same twice. Until the last century it had been guarded by a full garrison of Albion soldiers conscious of the potential invasion of their hostile neighbours. However times changed and over the years the threat had waned, Militia replaced Army, and slowly the numbers decreased. No longer Albion, the renegade city state Aberddu, who had snatched its independence from Royal Albion only four years earlier was low on funds and man power. The watch on Pass Fort was held by two low ranking militia officers and a rusting warning bell.

It had been a tartar militiaman who had suggested the bell, nearly a hundred years ago when the garrison at the Fort had first been withdrawn. Although it was not loud enough to summon the town's folk, it would rouse the hundreds of tartars that lived outside the city walls in the ramshackle settlements left to them as second class citizens of the city. When questioned about what the tartars would actually do if the bell rang, the tartar militiaman fixed the questioner with a stony glare and explained very slowly and loudly in words of one syllable exactly what the tartars would do to anyone who tried to breach the Fort. He then explained that it wasn't out of any loyalty to a city who had not even allowed them to live within its walls, but because it was better than the alternative: watching idly as they bore the brunt of an invasion.

As he stood on the parapet of the lookout tower gazing back towards the city, Jacob had no idea what the original tartar officer had said that day but he was certainly glad to see the ripples in the darkness and the glints of the feeble moonlight on blades as the tartars rallied in the dark streets below. He was staring out towards the city, fruitlessly trying to pick out the figure of Gideon on horseback because it was better than turning round. Crossing the valley behind him, approaching the scrub land that marked the very edge of the Frisian borderlands were the flaming torches of the massing army. The flame light didn't allow him to see what kind of army it was or how large it might be, all he knew was that the pattern of torchlight suggested the forces were spread out across nearly a full square mile.

In barely half an hour, he was surrounded by nearly one hundred heavily armed tartar warriors, who had scrambled from their beds and arrived fully equipped in less time than it had probably taken Gideon to get to the Trade Gate or Mages Guild wizard to find the right book in the library. As they had come up the steps to the parapet two at a time he had panicked what commands he ought to give. Now, as he watched the tartars organise themselves along the gantries he realised he needn't have worried. If there was one thing tartars knew about it was battle. War was one of their most infamous exports along with tall tales, prize beef, lethal spirits and the finest horses on the continent. The tartars found and activated every dilapidated siege weapon on the wall, they forced open the rusted hatches of the murder holes in case the portcullis was breeched. They had gathered ammunition for the mangonels and were oiling the mechanisms with some kind of pungent grease that Jacob dare not enquire about. Everywhere was overtaken by frenetic activity, the sound of hard boots on stone and voices giving sharp commands. Every minute more bodies, fur clad and ready for action, seemed to appear.

Jacob was no fool. He could count, even if not particularly reliably. If he was in any way correct about what was standing out there in the dark this tartar band were out numbered five, six or maybe even seven to one by those soldiers that had arrived on foot - never mind about those that would appear when this fodder had been spent. What they were doing on the border was a worry that his superiors could have when they finally got here. For now, he was hoping that the tartars who were slowly psyching themselves up around him would be able to fight them off long enough for his superiors to turn up and start asking questions before he became a smear on the stones.

As the night turned to the chilly blue of early morning, and the outlined shapes grew in definition, Jacob paid them more attention. To the south, he could now just about pick out the Trade Gate which was still closed. Then he turned his attention to the enemy forces in hope of being able to pick out any useful details. As it turned out he had only managed to scare himself again by looking straight into the maw of a gargantuan war-engine, which on further reflection seemed remarkably crude to be Inquisition-built. Clearly the tartars thought so too as there were growing murmurs amongst the ranks and those that Jacob had come to think of as the boss tartars, because he was too scared to remember their hastily exchanged names, were now moving hastily amongst the crowds. As the pale winter sun pushed above the horizon the muttering quietened as Jacob and the tartars learned the awful truth. It was not the Red Army that waited for them in the Frisian scrub but five hundred of Salamander's tartars. Jacob turned to the tartar beside him to comment that he couldn't work out what they were waiting for but did not speak. The look of determination that had been on her face before had morphed into a bitter mask of poorly contained fury.

As darkness fell, Jacob slumped against the slimy wall of a musty passageway. His heart was thumping against his ribs so hard he doubted it would ever cease. The stripe of blue war paint across his eyes had blended with his sweat and started to seep down into his already stinging eyes. None of the tartars seemed to be having the same problem and as he was the only non-tartar to have received the honour of a war-stripe he had no one else to compare himself with. He sunk down to the damp ground and let his brain review the last few hours. As he replayed the horrors in his mind, he tried to tuck the images of his last sight of Gideon away into the depth of his soul where he could brood on it later, should there be a later.

The first assault had come just before dawn, and judging by the looks on the faces of the Aberddu tartars, they knew they were being toyed with in the same way as a farm cat toys with the mice in the grain store. It had comprised little other than a few half-hearted skirmishers with a siege ladder and a shower of boulders from the war-engine. It had taken less than ten minutes for one of the more ingenious Aberddu tartars to set the ladder on fire, ending the bulk of the assault. It seemed peculiar to them. They were not fooled by the leniency, it just left them waiting for the other shoe to drop. It came. As the watery sun pushed its way above the horizon casting a cool bright light over the army, the morning world was plunged into chaos and the Tartar forces on the battlements of the Fort learned very swiftly what had caused the delay. An ear-bursting explosion shattered the calm, the ground under Jacob's feet jolted violently and he was thrown to his knees. Crazes of pain shot up his thighs into his abdomen as he landed hard on the stones. He knew as he heard it that he would never forget the overwhelming sound of the North West watchtower collapsing. The blast had ripped through the tower's foundations, destabilising the walls and causing an avalanche of stone and bodies.

The cacophony of screams and tumbling masonry followed by the dull splashes as everything plunged into the murky water of the moat washed over Jacob, suffocating him. He struggled to standing and gaped at the hole that had been ripped in the stone turret. Gazing out across the moat in the fresh light, he could clearly see the tunnel entrance with plumes of sickly grey smoke billowing up in the breeze. The distinctive smell of the pig-fat incendiaries coiled towards him clinging to his pallet. Too late he turned to shout another warning as another tumultuous blast ripped open the North East turret shooting more acrid smoke into the air. Jacob was thrown to the floor, tumbling as stones beneath his feet fissured and fell. For a brief instant mortality gripped him as he slipped and dropped into a crack, but he managed to wedge his boots tight so that he lay precariously on a slab of crumbling masonry only able to look on, as the less fortunate lost purchase and tumbled, shrieking, past him.

As the billows of greasy smoke dissipated, the war-engines began hurling fallen masonry and flaming rag-bundles at the parapets. Jacob clambered out of the shifting and settling rubble. Beneath him he was relieved to see that the blue tartars, as he had come to think of the tartars on his side, had regrouped and were furiously rewinding the mangonels for a second volley. Below, the ranks of Salamander's tartars, red-striped eyes wide, bayed and hollered but did not charge.

Jacob had no notion how long this exchange of fire lasted, as the siege-engines continued to pepper the ramparts. Slowly the gantries and parapets were littered with small fires from the cata-pulted rag- bundles that flopped harmlessly onto stone but continued to burn. He remembered vividly the feeling of inex-orable but valiant defeat as the war-machines continued to tear into the fortifications and his own side laboured furiously to repay the attack. As he sprinted down the concourse, descended the slippery stone stairs and raced across the down the sloping courtyard to the group waiting to defend the southern gateway, nothing struck him as odd. He flung himself into a small group in front of the portcullis, who had readied themselves in case the attackers tried to breach the gate. His heart thumping in his chest, he prayed to whichever Gods that would listen that the militia hurried up.

The outcome of it all seemed grim but certain, as he stood in the freezing morning air. It wouldn't be long before the gate and walls were breached and their valiant two hundred would be no match for Salamander's forces. The gargantuan warriors waiting for them beyond the fortress wall were bigger and far more vicious than normal tartars. With cold finality, Jacob began to put his thoughts in order.

Then, suddenly, as the grey clouds of what Jacob had assumed would be his last hour started to drift across the watery white sun, a flock of starlings swept down. In the moments that followed, suddenly everything changed. Thirty birds alighted on the grass beside the assembled tartars at the gate, and in one swift movement transformed neatly into thirty wizards from the Aberddu Guild of Mages. There were a few moments of confusion as tartars, taken by surprise, lunged and jabbed and were put gently down. Without pause, the mages split neatly into four groups and sprinted off in separate directions.

One lot headed straight for the portcullis, throwing glistening forcefields of protection over the gateway as they ran. Another sprinted up on to the ramparts, uttering incantations under their breath as they went. Jacob could see balls of green lightning forming in one mage's hands as he ascended the steps. The third group turned and went straight to the dark archway that led down into the bowels of the fort and to the legendary labyrinth itself. He realised that it must have been decades since anyone had been down there. The few travellers that dared enter Aberddu by the Frisian road crossed the central wall of the fort in the same way the militia did; via a perilous arrangement of wooden ladders, ropes and walkways. Presumably the mages were checking the incantations still held.

The final group made for another part of the compound, towards a massive armour-plated door in the western half of the central barrier wall. This had been the entrance that had once allowed the garrison to cross from one side of the fort to the other without having to pass through the labyrinthine passages below ground. The gate had been opened by a series of cogs and mechanisms, powered by an ancient capstan, that crouched like a fat spider in a web of corroded chains and cables, covered in rust and vegetation. It had been unused since the militia patrols on the northern watch towers had fallen below a dozen-and-a-half because it needed nearly that many bodies to turn the capstan.

Jacob watched with fascination as the mages began to cast before they had stopped running. They blasted away the years of dereliction, and with very little apparent effort, forced the creaking, juddering capstan to turn. He was about to sprint over and offer assistance when suddenly the world was overtaken by bedlam. Looking up to the watch tower and the gantries, he was horrified to see a dozen of Salamander's tartars step out of the flames of the rag- bundle fires, battle-tempered swords raised to strike. The blue tartars on the wall let out bellows of alarm, and threw up a hasty defence; the air was filled with spray of hot blood and the sounds of slaughter. In amongst the rampage, wizards flung magic into the melee, blasting the larger tartars with lightening and flames.

A tall mage in a black and magenta robe fountained thin columns of water out of his hands, dousing a number of the fires and creating a plume of boiling steam. Blistering in the cloud, several of the tartars roared displeasure and a tumbling, squalling knot of fur-clad bodies plunged into the courtyard as they lost footing. Frozen in horror below, Jacob just watched as more and more Red tartars appeared from the flames, and suddenly the ragbundle fires made sense. The tartars beside him however decided that this influx was a far more imminent risk than any attack on the gate and sprinted to the steps, leaving Jacob standing alone in the confusion.

As he lay against the freezing wall of that dank alley way, he could still feel the echo of his heart pounding as it had in the brief moment of isolated stillness that seemed simultaneously a lifetime away and a matter of mere moments ago. He remembered vividly the instant where he span around to look at the mages that had been struggling with the gateway to find that by some miracle of magic they had made the capstan turn and the massive gate was swinging open.

He could still feel the hot clamouring of blood rushing to his head as his eyes fell on the massed troops behind the gate. Every militia officer that could be mustered, both serving and retired, had come. Behind them more mages, in robes and tunics, looking dazed and haggard, unused to the early hour. Then, ranks of warriors from the city guild, their fearsome, scarred features set into a strange merry hysteria; and with them the scruffy, rag-tag adventurers with their tricks and traps and their indefinable aura of world-weary arrogance.

Relief flooded over Jacob as he saw his saviours, but there was one face in particular he was still searching for. Gideon, sweat beading on his freckled brow, was in the front rank of the militia line beside a captain that Jacob didn't recognise. It seemed surmountable then, in that moment; he would have a partner in the fight, to watch his back. Now, as he wiped the congealing tartar blood from the blade of the knife in his hand, he let slip a cold, sluggish tear. Gideon had been watching his back, up until...

It was not a sentence Jacob was able to finish yet. A gigantic tartar had come at them. Lunging wildly, in a frantic moment, Jacob had lashed out with his off-hand knife instead of his sword and found himself in the path of the tartar's swing. Gideon plunged forward and pushed Jacob to the ground, blocking the down swing and felling the attacker with a single blow of his bastard sword. But as he turned to help Jacob up from the floor, a laugh of triumph on his lips, there was a dreadful wooden thud. He jolted forward and his face grimaced and went white. Tumbling forward, gurgling and snatching at breath, he fell into Jacob's outstretched arms - Jacob could see that, with his dying breaths, the felled tartar had flung his tomahawk. It had cleaved into Gideon's back perfectly between his shoulder blades, a dark stain seeping slowly across his tunic. Jacob staggered backwards as Gideon's body became torpid and let slip it's last breath.

Jacob could still feel that breath on his neck in the dark of this alley, even though he was completely alone. He gripped the handle of Gideon's knife tightly and desperately wished that he had not been so grateful to see his old friend step through that gate.

The gathered forces that had arrived were not in any way a match for the numbers of Salamander's army; but Aberddu, the tiny city state not long torn from the northern edge of Royal Albion, had always found its strength not in size but in diversity.

As a world famous seaport, Aberddu had become a melting-pot of races, religions and peoples long before it had sought independence from Albion. As the last outpost between Albion and it's great enemy Frisia , it had been a garrison town, a place of strength and courage - and somehow that spirit had spilled out into the soil. Even in this, the first decade of its independence, Aberddu was ready for a fight - not with the proud strutting presence of the glorious Albion army, or the rigid authoritarian propriety of the Inquisition or even the sheer overwhelming force of the tartar horde but with the crazed brutality of a street gang with everything to fight for and nothing to lose.

As fractious day slipped into turbulent night, the air filled with the blue glow of magic as the wizards sought a source of light other than fire. When he tried to recall it later, Jacob couldn't remember much more after that brief moment of reflection in the stinking alleyway. It came in bursts and flashes like scenes from a fever dream. The impressive lightning from one of the mages, the resounding crash as the portcullis fell, the cry of the Warriors Guild as they met the red tartars head on.

These were obvious enough moments to recall, but there were other snippets too. A female mage had tripped over her own feet , tumbled down the stairs and hit the ground with a painful-sounding thud, winding herself. She didn't lie still, even for a moment, she just leapt to her feet and raced back to the fight. A cleric of some indeterminate God quivering in prayer over a fallen militiaman who Jacob didn't know, tears streaming silently down his face. A diminutive wizard in breeches and a frock coat, who Jacob later learnt was with the Adventurers Guild and not the mages, yelling something at an elven woman who was angrily screaming back. The only words he could make out were from the wizard: 'you should have listened,' he had bellowed.

After that, the blur of the night passed into the harsh white light of morning. At some stage there must have been a breakthrough by the Aberddu forces - perhaps it was the forcefield that blocked the enemy magic for a few moments around about midnight or the massive magical shock wave that swept across their lines at some point just before dawn. All he knew for sure, in amongst the chaos and blood, was that by some miracle they had retreated. He picked his way through the bodies on the ruined battlements, placing his feet carefully between the lifeless hands that reached out for dropped swords and the splayed limbs and pools of blood. He knew that the stench that clung to his pallet and seeped into his pores would be with him for a lifetime. He didn't know what he was looking for or even why he'd come up here except to possibly check for himself that the army had gone.

That was when he realised that his feet were taking him back to the north west watch tower to see if Gideon had the stove going for a brew. In that moment, his world collapsed around him like the fortress walls falling again and he remembered - neither the watch tower nor Gideon had lasted the night. He slumped down on a pile of rubble at the top of some steps and put his head in his hands.

He had no idea how long he sat there , completely numb, but when he returned to his senses the cold and damp had seeped into his bones.

Someone was going to have to recover these bodies and rebuild these defences - but it would not be him. Standing up, every muscle in his body crying out in agony, he heaved himself down the steps and started the long lonely walk back to the city.

And so, as the weary Eleventh Century meandered forward into the early days of the Twelfth, life changed from a sweet, simple ebb and flow to a series of sharp, staccato choices that separated kith, kin and Clan. Standing on the precipice, looking into the bitter maelstrom of the future, history had marked its destiny. For better or worse, the world had chosen its heroes. Not the heroes of legend or tale, it had to be said, not then. They were not Emperors or Kings or even Arch-mages. Not gallant knights of a realm nor virtuous priests nor a well-trained army. They were simply those who had stood between, those who had not immediately allied themselves to a side other than that of wanting to survive. A few had listened to the words of one controversial wizard, a man that others considered to be crazy or even worse stupid. Others had merely been standing still when History changed their direction and then they began to walk.

When this time is spoken of, some will say that they were foolish, naive. They will say that they risked everything on a whim, on a surmise. But others, those who have faith or family, those who see hope in the future, will say that their innocence was their saving virtue. They will say that their child-like optimism and the belief that they could face up to those with far greater power than their own, that they could be instrumental in the affairs of the Gods and hope to walk away, was what, in the end, saved the world from the Summer of Fire.

ly
1100AC

BA'AL - THE XAROB WASTES

The beginning of a holy war

Timier glanced back over his shoulder at the massed ranks behind him. It was a stomach-turning sight. In his hitherto uneventful twenty years, he had never seen this many people gathered in one place. He wasn't entirely sure what came after hundreds but he assumed there must be something because as far as he could tell there were more than hundreds of people here. He had made it to the front ranks of the Knights of Justice and somehow he had found himself between Brother Teign and Brother Josef. He wasn't sure if he was honoured or frightened.

The Knights of Justice, an international order, formed a large part of one block of the troops massing on this barren wasteland, but they were by no means the largest force.

There was, beside them, quite a sizeable army dressed in the extravagant lightweight fabrics of gentlemen of the East. Swathed in yards of dark green cotton as they were, Timier thought they were probably more comfortable than he was in his sweat-soaked gambeson and creaking armour, the leather strap of his ill-fitting helmet cut into his slippery neck. He was a little unsure whether he liked being that close to them. There was undeniably an air of heavily-armed and efficient violence about and he was unsure of the wisdom of being in such proximity to an army lead by a commander that was definitely not of mortal flesh. He wasn't sure what exactly the commander was, except that he wasn't any type of undead that Timier was familiar with. His face was wrapped in worn greying bandages and his hands were skeletal and scabrous. From beneath the edge of his dark hood, his empty eyes looked out over his men.

Timier heard the familiar clank of the ranks dropping down to one knee and felt a tight grip on his elbow pulling him down. He had been so wrapped up in his contemplation of the army beside them that he had not noticed that the celebrant had taken up the position in front of the troops for the blessing. The faint words carried out on the wind over the silent ranks of Knights.

"We tread the path of righteousness, of justice, reverence and order," Timier heard, "We seek redemption for all souls misguided from the true way and manipulated by the forces of darkness and disorder." Timier tuned out, this was a standard sermon, he had heard it many times before and could probably have recited it from heart had he so wished. However, he was more fascinated by the easterners and continued to glance fitfully over his shoulder at them.

After a couple of minutes, Timier leant over to Teign who also appeared to be inattentive to the celebrant's speaking and whispered,

"Hey Teign, I don't like the look of them," and gestured with a subtle incline of his head towards the ranks beside them. Teign followed the line of Timier's gaze and smiled, not that Timier could see his expression. Teign was remembering the first time he had heard about Rabin Ibm Khim Al Salar and his mighty army, he had reacted in roughly the same way as the boy.

"That's the mighty army of Khim Al Salar," he whispered, with a deliberate awe in his tone. "and that," Teign pointed surreptitiously at the figure at the head of the ranks, "is His remorseless, illustrious and enigmatic beatitude God-King Rabin Ibm Khim Al Salar - undead and in the flesh, as it were." Teign smirked and Timier shuddered.

"That's a God-King?" he whispered back to Teign frantically, "But isn't he 'an undead abhorrent abomination in the eyes of

Law'?" He quoted the last line of dogma carefully, his eyes rolled up as he fought to remember the exact wording. Teign simply chuckled.

"He doesn't seem to thinks so."

"Okay," muttered Timier, still unconvinced.

"Look at it this way," mumbled Teign understanding the younger man's trepidation, "Where would you prefer him? On the inside pissing out or on the outside pissing in?" With a timorous gulp, Timier nodded slowly.

"I suppose, on the inside," he agreed.

At this point Brother Josef lost his tolerance, reached over and cuffed Timier on the back of the head with his boiled leather gauntlet. "Shut up," he hissed, "And listen to the sermon. Some of us are trying to pray for our souls." Timier mumbled an apology and turned his attention to his navel. Teign had the sense to look away before he smirked at his old friend's sanctimoniousness. Then he bowed his own head and studied the hot grey dirt below his knees.

Two hours later, Timier found himself praying to Law, or really any Gods that would listen, that the army of Khim Al Salar would remain on their side - because if they didn't then he would not see another dawn in this life. The creatures had appeared just moments after he and Teign had joked about the God-King's army. They had come out of nowhere, literally. Slavering dark maws and silvery teeth, an unearthly sound blocking out all other senses. They were unlike any animal Timier could describe, he could find no frame of reference to relate to, he simply dropped down in front of them and waited for the inevitable. Beside him, he heard Josef's shield clatter to the ground and his sword fall on top of it as he too was rendered helpless by these repellent creatures. Had it not been for Teign's presence of mind in snatching them back, they would have been consumed whole as the celebrant had been. Only Khim Al Salar's army seemed unaffected by them, they just drew arms as one mighty machine and charged forward.

Timier and Josef had recovered their senses quickly and flung themselves forward into the melee beside Teign, embarrassed by their cowardice. They battled against these appalling apparitions until the behemoths had arrived. Towering over the forces of Law, they flattened all those in their path, the western armies could only turn and run as Khim Al Salar and his army marched on cleaving into them.

As he sprinted, sweat streaming down the inside of his helmet and into his eyes, Timier felt like a fool. He had believed all the things he had been told. That Law was mighty and Chaos was weak and disjointed, a mishmash of clowns and dissenters that ran around flinging cats at people, enchanting frogs to sing and covering you in honey. They had told him stories of the Chaos Pantheon that had made them seem pathetic, weak and directionless. It seemed that they had left quite a lot of detail out.

No one had told him of Mithras, the Chaos God of War and Fury, whose dark ruthlessness sent forth the colossal beasts that crushed everything in their wake. No one had not spoken of The Faceless One with his cruel, ever changing minions that were called hounds even though they only appeared as giant dogs momentarily. Or Zharalota, the Ice Queen who had actually appeared herself in her chariot, with her deadly whip and her horde of terrible cackling nymphs that ran wild over all in their path leaving raw steaming scorch marks and exposed bone. Her chariot wheels had passed within a matter of feet of Timier's nose as he lay cowering behind a boulder pretending he was part of the landscape.

Even after that, he still could not find her as terrifying as the Hand Maidens of Lilja, The Flower Goddess. He had heard of Lilja, one of the Temple teachers had told him a scornful tale of this Goddess who existed only to scatter flowers at the feet of dancing maidens and dance to merry tunes. Like a simpleton Timier had never questioned this teaching, until a few hours ago. He had seen a woman walking through the melee, looking among the fallen with curiosity. A look, he only realised later, that had been completely lacking in pity, compassion or even revulsion. Wounded and woozy, Timier had mistaken her for one of the Daughters of Salvation – battle nuns of Law who accompanied the armies and acted as medics and armourers. In hindsight, he should have wondered why she was glowing slightly, but through the haze of pain in his mind he assumed it was simply some kind of magical spell he did not recognise. Throwing himself on her mercy, he had ripped open his tunic before he had reached her and had closed his eyes braced for the laying on of hands. Unable to believe her luck the Hand Maiden had clamped her bony hands around his neck with an icy cold touch and let out a delighted shriek.

"My pretty, pretty one," she hissed, "The mistress will love you." He had punched her in the gut and fled. Later, he found out that Lilja's handmaidens picked through the fallen of the battlefields, looking for the beautiful. Lilja would then take them into her court where they would be forced to worship her and pay tribute to her beauty for eternity. After being told this, Timier had struggled to sleep, dreading the return of the handmaiden who had left a collar of black hand prints in the skin around his neck. When he got back to Aberddu, he had written her words on a scrap of parchment, set fire to them and scattered the ashes to the prevailing west wind in a hope that he might forget them. It didn't work.

After that run in with the handmaiden, Timier had spent a lot of time hiding and he was not proud of himself. He was bone-shatteringly terrified by these creatures and he could not, even with all the faith in the world, have pretended otherwise. In the brief moments of safety he reflected on the words of Josef de Clariar as they had marched towards the battle field. In a moment of what had turned out to be an overly-confident piety, Josef had told him loftily that holy war was the ultimate and final test of one's faith. If he survived, Timier would have no further questions. He would either be a truly devout follower of Law or he would have been plunged into the chaotic darkness and left there to find his own way. Timier had to admit it was touch and go which side he would come out on, but given that last time he had seen Josef the good Brother had been lying in an empty ditch clutching his shield to his chest and weeping, he was probably doing okay.

The Celestial Empire of Kchon

The Ambassador's Palace - in the moments before a winter dawn

"Just take it," hissed Samual.

"Why should I?" scowled Iona, looking at the leather pouch the greasy little man was thrusting at her.

"Because if you don't I'll tell the Ambassador about that man I saw hanging around last night, he won't be too pleased to find that you've been playing around on him, will he?" Samual snivelled, with an unpleasant leer.

"What man?" yelled Iona, colour rising into her cheeks, tears of frustration prickling on her eye lashes.

"Oh very convincing," sneered Samual, "I almost bought that. Just a word of advice princess, the crocodile tears are just that smidgen too far. It doesn't matter if there was a man or not my lovely, because his excellency will believe me his trusted secretary and adviser, over some grubby little harlot with delusions of grandeur," Iona's hand twitched, she desperately wanted to slap the man but she didn't dare. "And don't go trying to hit me either girlie, it'll end badly for you." Samual lunged forward suddenly and Iona felt a cold blade pressed against her abdomen. Taking two steps forward, he used his body weight to shove her up against the wall and then leaned forwards until she could smell his foetid breath and feel his saliva spraying over her neck. She strained away from him, closing her eyes. She couldn't fight back against his bodyweight even though she was nearly as tall as him and certainly more muscular, he had her at a disadvantage. "Take it," he snarled and forced the leather pouch into her tunic pocket. "Now go." Samual didn't even pause to see what she would do, he just released her and stalked out of the stable block leaving Iona choking back tears of anger and humiliation. Resignedly, she stuffed the pouch into her satchel and began to saddle up the nearest horse. She led the fractious nag out onto the darkened courtyard. Looking up at the palace, she could see the night-light flickering in the arched window of Lady Rubina's chamber and she felt a momentary pang of regret. Rubina was the only one who would miss Iona, the poor girl was barely of age and unbelievably lonely. She had been given to the Ambassador by her father as though she were a sacrificial goat to appease an angry river god. The Ambassador, an odious pig of a man only a year younger than her father, had tried quite forcefully to press his affections on his young bride on their wedding night only, distressing her to the point of hysteria with his advances. After that, he had never bothered again and largely ignored her. She was forced to follow him around like a toy dog, fumbling her way through the etiquette of one embassy after another trying to make conversation with the haughty, pampered wives of the other diplomats who treated her with scarcely more civility than they treated the staff. Even her lady's maid didn't speak to her. Iona had taken pity on her. When the Ambassador had taken a fancy to her and promoted her from stable hand to 'special ambassadorial aide' she had continued to visit the poor girl every evening. As her horse trotted out of the palace grounds she wondered how long it would be before someone remembered to speak to Rubina again.

Iona picked up speed a little as she made her way on to the cobbles of the main thoroughfare that spiralled down through the Celestial City towards the Oriental Gates. There were no souls on the streets and the city, its white stone glowing in the full moon, was as a dream. The terraces that coiled down the side of the mountain, three, four or five stories high in places were shuttered against the night and silent.

The open frontages on the street level were deserted save for the odd body of a way-sleeper or a sayer deep in meditation. The hoof-beats of Iona's horse echoed from the buildings but brought no attention.

As she rode, she gazed out over the indigo ocean. The dark tranquil expanse reflected the starlight and in the distance she could just make out the edge of The Jewelled Isle of Nippon. A warm breeze carried the scent of the waves over Iona and she felt a tug on her heart. As she carried on down through the city, and the sight of the sea became obscured by the city walls, she came to grips with the knowledge that she would almost certainly never see the Kchonese dawn again.

At the Oriental gates, she nodded silently to the gate-keeper who swung the footbridge across and raised the grille so she could leave by one of the smaller archways. As she left the cobbled streets of the city behind her and moved on to the soft, yielding dirt of the coast road, the glorious red sun began to rise out of the ocean. With the soft wind rushing over her, filling her nostrils and her soul with the familiar, exotic scents of the East, she broke into a gallop and headed out along the cliff tops.

As she rode, her mind raced. Muddled by the complex emotions of this unexpected departure from an adopted country she had learned to love as her own, she fought to formulate a plan. There was no point in heading North into the mountains and Tartaria, and South was not much better. Jaffria and Arabi were not a welcoming prospect for an elven woman travelling alone. That left her with one option, west. A smile broke over her lips as a realisation dawned with the newborn sun. There was only one place she could go. It was months of journey but when she arrived it would be worth it. Plotting out the route in her head, she found herself already planning what she would do when she finally set foot on the golden streets of Aberddu.

ABERDDU ADVENTURERS GUILD

Halfway through the observation of Lynne's Turn

"What about Remy?"

"He's going to Aragon in about three hours."

"Okay, what about Zemuel?"

"He's also going to Aragon in about three hours, hence why he's packing those potion bottles into that bottle-belt."

"There's no need to get sarcastic about it. What about Jason De Vere?"

"I thought you thought he was an idiot?"

"I do, but beggars can't be choosers and all that."

"Well, he's actually on a militia bind-over and can't leave the city for three months."

"What the bloody hell for? No, actually, I don't care." Elor was slowly learning that criminality was an inevitable side product of a number of the more specialised adventuring skills. Jason's crimes were likely to have been violent but ill-organised, hence the bind-over rather than any more severe or final punishments. Usually, the guild managed to wangle some form of reprieve for its members, although hangings were not entirely unprecedented for more serious offences, such as crimes involving accidental demonology or somewhat less than accidental poisoning. This was all irrelevant right now anyway, as Elor was in desperate need of assistance as soon as possible

"Well, what about you then?" he asked Erin, with the air of someone clutching at straws.

"Thank you so much for the personal request for my expertise," she retorted acerbically,"but I'm afraid I'm leading the Aragon trip in about three hours and I could do with getting ready, so can we make this quick?" Elor had ignored the part of the sentence that had come after 'I'm afraid' and was now frantically scouring the guild room. It was remarkably thin on the ground; nearly everybody still in the room was packing travelling sacks. There had been a woeful lack of anyone since midwinter. A fair few adventurers had departed the city for home and not returned, others such as Teign and Whitefire, had taken leaves of protracted absence in the name of one bout of religious hysteria or another. His eyes turned onto a wan woman slumped dramatically on a straight backed seat in one corner, a black wimple and veil partly covering her head and face.

"What about Mauna?" he asked hopefully.

"Mauna?" exclaimed Erin, with a 'surely you're joking' tone. "Yeah, sure. You can take Mauna if you like but we're currently on the eighth day of Lynne's Turn and she's hoping she'll be dead before the end of the week."

"Oh," said Elor quietly. The practices of the Death Acolytes were one of the few things about which Elor was not learned; that he had to admit he would probably never understand. Regrouping swiftly, he then said to Erin in a slightly derisive tone, "So, just where the blazes is everyone then?" Erin, who had decided that she spent enough time trying to placate the crazed wizard, had started rolling her bed-roll but stopped when he said it, looked him straight in the eye and said, with the flat tone of a woman nearly at the end of her limited patience,

"Well, there's half a dozen in Paravel for the Mages Guild, seven on a boat to Ctuma, five who are now three, no four, days overdue from some hell-and-gone hole in the Middle Kingdom, and I've no idea if they're still alive, and of course," she paused at the of course for dramatic emphasis, "I sent half a dozen of our best adventurers to Tartaria on a scouting mission on your say so, because it couldn't possibly have waited until we had fewer contracts, and they'll be gone the best part of two months. So, we're what is colloquially referred to as 'buggered for staff' at the moment."

"Ah, I see," said Elor quietly. He had forgotten about that, he had been so absorbed in the discovery he had made in the Temple of Enigmas that he hadn't really thought about anything else. "Well, this is just as important." Erin took a deep breath before responding.

"Elor," she said with the kind of restrained calm that people reserve for the very small children and the terminally hard of thinking. "It's always really important with you. It's a matter of life and death, or saving the world or whatever, but what you've never really grasped is that this is an establishment of mercenary adventurers not a temple. We are not honour bound to right wrongs and free the innocent from tyranny or whatever, we're here to make some cash and that means when someone who is prepared to pay turns up they gets priority."

"Okay," said Elor through gritted teeth, "But I'm not talking about freeing the oppressed, I'm talking about averting the next cataclysm and if money's the issue I can pay."

"Oh," said Erin, her demeanour changing rapidly - Elor knew it was the mention of the money and not the threat about the cataclysm that had changed her tune. "Well why didn't you say so? I'll fetch the ledger." Moments later, she returned from the back office with a large leather book that contained a record of current guild members and their activities.

"Well," said Erin, opening the ledger with her obviously false business manner. "Let me see who is available. Oh dear, we are hard pressed at the moment." Looking down the rows of the chart, Elor could see that most of the adventurers were listed as being either on jobs or on leave. A number of lines had been stricken, indicating the member had either resigned Guild membership or had been missing without notification for a period in excess of eight weeks. Apart from Elor himself, and Mauna Evanga the wilting Death Acolyte, there were only four other available guild members not already committed to contracts. Even the shaman Gul, who was often passed over in favour of guild members who washed and didn't eat raw fish, had been dragged off on some mission that had been in want of a healer.

"Daisy, that dwarven Life Cleric, is due back from Penitential retreat either today or yesterday. She's a bit limp, but she should do for a healer, provided you don't expect too much combat. Krieg Clan Dragon is available, if we repeal the last three days of his fine period." Erin tapped the book pensively with her finger as she pulled a thoughtful face.

"Fine period?" asked Elor with a frown.

"He was fined one florin and fourteen days for not turning up for a job. It transpired he was being held by the militia on charges of being drunk and incapable to stand, wrestling with a militia officer and urinating on militia property, when he was due to be leaving on the Paravel expedition." Elor could see a black spot in Krieg's row under the current date. It was by no means the only one.

"Er, okay," he said, dubious but not in a position to quibble, "who else?"

"Well, there's Mori Sil'erbanis the Death cleric, provided she's not observing Lynne's Turn as well. And obviously there's Pringle."

As though in response to Erin's words, a pile of rags in the hearth grunted and wriggled. It was only then that Elor realised that the rag pile was wearing boots. "He should come round in an hour or so," said Erin, trying to sound reassuring. "He's quite useful when he's sober."

"When's that?" asked Elor, beginning to regret even coming to the guild. He could have kept it amongst the Mages Guild. They were more than capable of these things, if they thought they were significant or important enough to bother with. There in lay the snag he remembered, it was far more difficult than necessary to convince the mages that something someone else had thought of was important.

Erin had skilfully avoided answering the question. She just

carried on with her business, producing a formal hiring agreement and a quill.

"Shall we say three guilders five florins a head, which as you will know, is a significant discount as you are a valued member of our organisation." She began filling in the parts of the agreement that didn't require much detail.

"Hang on a moment," said Elor tentatively, "I'd like to talk this over with the four of them first, before I sign anything."

"Pardon?" retorted Mori, a little more aggressively than Daisy thought was necessary.

"I just wanted to check that you weren't observing Lynne's Turn," said Elor slightly louder than he had before, failing to grasp Mori's affront at the question.

"Do I really seem like the kind of person that would starve themselves for a fortnight in the vain hope that I would be lucky enough to drop dead and therefore be declared sacred." She fixed Elor with sharp glare and a barely visible smirk on her dark lips. The wizard looked slightly taken aback, then considered for a moment and said abashed,

"No, I suppose not."

"Good," replied the dark elf bluntly, "Because for one thing I'm not *that* crazy and for another thing, that's Hecate worship and I'm a priestess of Ankhere."

"Oh," said Elor, whose knowledge of the Death Temple was purely academic and whose interest in Mori's answer had stopped when she said no. "Fair enough. Then presumably you're available for this mission then."

"Yes," said Mori, still looking Elor in the eye with the same unflinching gaze that was now starting to make him uncomfortable. Daisy suspected that this was the point. Mori had an indefinably air of self- assurance, edging on aggression, that Daisy envied. It seemed to be calculated perfectly to throw people slightly off balance without offending them. It was a glorious sight to behold, particularly when she turned it on the latest guild veteran who was trying to tell her things as though she were a child - or Pringle.

It had taken Elor the best part of the day to track down the four guild members Erin had dredged up for him, and whilst he recognised all the faces, he could not claim to be particularly well acquainted with any of them or their previous work. Much to his confusion, he had located both the Life and Death cleric together in the poor quarter, miles from both temples. He had found Krieg carousing on the Docks - or rather the boys he had sent out looking for him had - and Pringle had at least been in the guildhouse, although as Erin had predicted, it did take him a fair while to come around.

He had been advised by Erin to hold this meeting in a pub, and sitting in a quiet corner of the Quizzical Cat, a crooked four-storey Inn in the Government District, he was beginning to regret not waiting till some of the more experienced and sober members of the guild were back. The priestesses had both arrived promptly stepping into the Tavern with the faint peel of the Law Temple hour bell. Neither of them looked particularly comfortable in the tavern. Mori smiled quickly at him before divesting herself of her plain black wrap. Then she sat down next to Elor, her back poker straight, without even looking towards the bar. The dwarven cleric, Sr. Daisy or whatever her name was, hovered nervously by Elor's shoulder, her damp woollen cloak steaming gently in the cloying warmth of the inn.

"Do sit down," said Elor, the formality of his tone amusing and shocking him as he indicated the wooden bench on the other side of the table, and the shy little thing slid onto the bench without removing her cloak. He did not have much confidence in the assembled party so far.

Next to arrive was Krieg, who swaggered in with a liquid smile, clearly already well lubricated. He made it barely feet through the door before a barman appeared and ordered him to leave his large felling axe in the rack by the door. Unused to this level of civilisation, Krieg argued fiercely with the barman, who was somewhat shorter than him but no less insistent. At last, with great reluctance, Krieg hefted the axe from its resting place on his shoulder and stood it in the rack, glaring around at the patrons seated by the door with a fierce look that suggested he wouldn't need the axe to decapitate anyone who allowed it to be stolen. He stomped up to the bar, thumped a handful of groats down and barked something at the publican, who took the coins in exchange for a large, slopping flagon. Elor was bracing himself for an uncomfortable silence when Krieg arrived at the table, unable to imagine these proper priestesses had any acquaintance with a surly tartar drunk. He couldn't have been more wrong.

As the massive man plonked himself down beside Daisy, everything suddenly changed.

"All right Daisy," he said beaming and nodding convivially to the ladies, "Mori. Good to see you again, interesting mid-winter?"

"Fair," said Mori with a tight, wry, smile, "Less time in clink than you obviously, but still lively enough I'd say." Krieg snorted with amusement into his flagon, his open face curled into a smirk before he took a deep gulp of ale. Once he'd swallowed nearly a quart of ale he turned to Daisy, bared his large ivory teeth, and said,

"How about you, Dee?" Elor was taken aback, first by the use of a nickname and then by the big smile on Daisy's face as she started telling him about what had happened in the Life Temple orphanage over the turn of the year. Elor's amazement only deepened when the last member of the party had arrived.

Elor thought of Dakarn Pringle as a waste of space. He had never seen the man clean, sober and making himself useful all at the same time. Someone had once told Elor that Pringle claimed he was the youngest and possibly only surviving son of some unimportant Albion Duke, but that due to a bout of presumably alcohol-induced amnesia he no longer knew for sure where his father's estate was. Elor thought it was entirely plausible that this was the case, but it hadn't endeared Pringle to him any. When the man walked through the Tavern door all these things passed through Elor's mind as he found himself gazing, stunned, at the apparition that appeared.

Dakarn Pringle cut quite a dash in his adventuring clothes Elor thought. He had changed from the foetid black tunic and hoses into a shirt, long breeches and leather jerkin, and he had obviously found a basin of hot water and a razor somewhere between here and the guildhouse. Had Elor not known better, he might even have assumed that Pringle was sober because his face was fresh and alert and his eyes were clear.

"Good evening all," he said pleasantly, hefting an adventuring pack on to the floor and nudging it under the table with his foot, before sitting down on the other side of Daisy and winking theatrically at Mori, who scowled back but with no real venom. "Together again," he said with a broad smile, "It's been far too long. How's life treating you my old mate?" The conversation began to flow around Elor as though he were a rotting log in a runnel. He looked from one to the other, to the other, to the other with a slightly open mouth as they continued to banter and bicker, chuckling amongst themselves. When Daisy pushed her coin purse over to Pringle and said,

"Get one for yourself while you're there," he shook himself free from his frozen amazement and cleared his throat. It was as though the others had only suddenly been made aware of his presence. The three remaining faces at the table all turned to him simultaneously, smiling politely and Krieg said,

"So, Elor, this job you've got for us then?"

It was only when he started speaking that Elor realised he wasn't sure where to start. He tried to explain about the legends of the Birth of the Younger Gods. These went down like a lead balloon. Mori and Daisy were more than familiar with vastly differing versions of the same stories, each portraying their own Goddess as far more significant than the other. The only point that they agreed upon was that Ankhere and her sisters Kali and Hecate, the three aspects of the Goddess of Death had been the daughters of Krynok The Hunter and that Ankhere had been the first born. After a tense exchange during which Elor suggested they agreed to disagree, Krieg cleared his throat and said,

"I'm sorry, perhaps I've missed something, but I thought we were going to get some helmet or something?" He then drained his flagon and got up, "I need another drink if we're going to have to argue with some Goddess wench." As Elor watched the tartar shoving his way towards the bar he shook his head and sighed. He was making quite a pig's ear of his explanation. Perhaps he ought to try a different tack. Less context was probably the way forward.

"Legend has it," he started, when Krieg arrived back with another sloshing tankard of foul smelling liquid, "that there are twelve items created nearly a thousand years ago, not long after the last Cataclysm, when the lands had come to rest and the seas had fallen back. Twelve new Gods sought to protect themselves from the Elder powers. They created these articles to furnish a mortal hero, a champion, who would fight on their side against any who would seek to threaten their divinity. These items remain hidden throughout the world, never needed until now. Things like these, things of great value and magic, have a way of rising to the surface when their time comes."

"And that's now?" said Pringle, his face suddenly serious as he leant forward onto the scrubbed wooden table.

"Yes," said Elor significantly but not expanding.

"Okay," said Pringle with a curt nod that made Mori, Daisy and Krieg look at him with a range of questioning looks that would have done justice to the cat on the pub sign. None of them said anything, but mentally filed away the queries for another time.

"Look at this," said Elor and with a theatrical flourish he produced an ancient looking scroll. Mori cleared space on the table and Elor unrolled it. The surface of the cracked parchment was covered almost edge to edge with a tightly-packed florid script that had no visible punctuation. "It's all in here," said the wizard gleefully. "I copied this from an archaic text in the vaults of the Knowledge Library. I'm afraid it's a bit of a hack job when it comes to the translation as I didn't have my tomes with me, I may have accidentally mis-rotated the participles and I've slipped into slang here." He tapped a section about three lines from the start of the writing and chuckled, then he looked up to find the adventurers looking incredulously back at him. Krieg looked as though Elor had just suggested he go into battle in a lady mage's silk pyjamas, wearing a bonnet with a huge pink ostrich feather and a bunch of wax cherries on it. Pringle spoke first.

"Elor," he said calmly, "I hope you're not suggesting I try to read that. I may have had a wash and a shave but I'm still as drunk as a skunk and if I try to focus on that tiny writing I will most likely vomit. If you wouldn't mind doing the honours." Elor nodded and cleared his throat. "Peace can not last forever, and disarray will fall on the house of the younger Gods. Quarrels and power play will turn to bitter rivalries and war will descend. The Elder One," he paused, cleared his throat uncomfortably and said, "I assume this is an allusion to the All-Father," before continuing in a more scholarly and slow tone, "will return to the world to confront his offspring and they will rise up and fight. A mortal champion will stand against the Father, again I assume this to mean the All-Father, and will be armed by the Younger Gods." He paused significantly, and slowly the four adventurers nodded in recognition, Krieg and Daisy unconvincingly. "There have been subsequent scrolls and texts that talk about divine items gifted from above, that invoke some kind of deific protection beyond the realms of even the most powerful priests. Some of them are obviously different legends about the same artefact, adding further credence to their existence. The temples are in uproar, well some of them at least. You may have noticed," he looked over at Mori and Daisy and was surprised when Pringle said a very definite 'yes'. "Anyway, to this end, I have located this."

Elor showed them another scroll, with a picture of the helm, and dutifully read to them the legend explaining it's supposed location. He told them of the eastern Kingdom of Al'Raeth, where knowledge was power. A beautiful nation built amongst snow-capped mountains, the Al'Raethan people were protective of their wisdom and wary of strangers. Outlanders were permitted access to only a fraction of this knowledge, and were allowed to leave only with what they could commit to memory. It had taken Elor quite some time to track down enough pieces of the jigsaw to locate the Helm of Enigmas. The secretive Al'Raethan had buried it deep within in a cave system fearing its power might bring an uprising to disturb the millennium of peace they had experienced since the last cataclysm. The adventurers would need to be cautious and subtle, as he said this he looked at Krieg who returned an amused 'what are you trying to say' face.

Elor was surprised to see Mori scribbling down the information fastidiously in a leather-bound notebook. When Elor commented on this, she fixed him with another cutting glare and said, "I understand it is illegal to make notes in Al'Raeth, but this being Aberddu I thought I'd take my chances," and Pringle snorted with laughter. Elor was slowly having to conceded that perhaps he had misjudged these younger adventurers. With that, he handed his cheap copy of the world map and the routes to Krieg who gave them straight to Daisy to put in her bag. Then he put a small pouch of money down on the table and said,

"Right, leave as soon as you're ready, this should get you supplies and passage. Try the market, they may have some horses." Krieg lifted the pouch and snorted.

"Not for that they won't, but I know a man who will," then with a toothy grin he turned to Daisy and said, "Do dwarves ride horses?"

OUTSIDE THE SEA GOD TEMPLE

The day after the end of Lynne's Turn

"Roll up, roll up, Ladies and Gentlemen, finest artefacts for your perusal. Bones of Lucida Anya, from the very hand that touched the Kraken. Bottles of Sea Water from the sacred pools at Gerehazi. Shells and timber from the wreck of La Scarlotta lost in the Santa Rosa Trench five years ago." Tollie was boiling in the heavy woollen robes, the scratchy hood had been pulled up to hide the bits of his face that were visible above his coarse black beard. Sweat beaded on his brow and he wiped it away with a rough sleeve. The cart was heavy, mainly because of the sack loads of potatoes that he was smuggling under the blanket on which he had laid out the relics. He looked over at Sylas, who was done up in the restrictive high-necked garb of an Albion Sea priest. The look of slightly affronted piety on his pale, innocent features was genius although it probably had more to do with the fact that his collar and girdle were both too tight than anything else. He was knelt beside the wagon, pince-nez balanced on the end of his nose reciting from the Albion Book of Tenets.

"The Sea God claims dominion over all waters of the world, and all that touch these waters or depend upon them to live are his to claim," he pronounced and rang a glassy toll on his prayer bell.

"Before you cross the waters, seek the Sea God's blessing lest he grow wrathful and smite you down." He rang the bell again and with a poker straight face kept up the proclamation.

The power of faith was remarkable, thought Tollie as he handed over a cloth roll containing either the better part of a squirrel carcass or the hand bones of Lucida Anya, depending on how gullible you were. There must have been five hundred people pressed into the compound of the Temple to his Divine Bounty. The Aberddu Sea God Temple, standing proud on the banks of the Ddu Delta where the foetid waters of the Ddu River met the turbulent brine of the Aragonese Straits, was one of the oldest in the world. It had stood on this site in one form or another for nearly a thousand years, and this present incarnation had been there for nearly six hundred of them. No one remembered the details of the benefactor who had paid for the building of such a majestic structure with its ornamented vaulted roof and its myriad shrines. Tollie was dwelling on this as Sylas rang the bell again and said,

"Suffer not those who are dark of purpose or vile of spirit, who would commit acts of evil against the Sea God or his possessions." Tollie did not know for sure, but he had heard from a number of reliable sources that most of the true worship took place under ground in a vast network of catacombs and caves that spanned far under the city. He could well believe the stories he had heard about the eldritch beings and doings that went on beneath the temple, although he fervently hoped that the fish-people had been invented by the Bard who had told him. As he slipped the shining guilder into his coin purse he bent slightly and fetched another small fabric wrapped bundle, almost identical to the one he had just sold from beneath the cloth. He did not feel guilty as he watched the pilgrims stream into through the North door into the sanctuary so that they could be bathed in the light of the Father's Tear. If he was any judge, fleecing the odd unwary worshipper of a guilder outside this temple as it welcomed these pilgrims with open collection trays, was like worrying about spitting on someone who had just fallen into the river. In fact, ethically, it was a far better scam than Doctor Tolliver's World Famous Cure-all, particularly as he wasn't entirely sure that the combination of rats-piss and river water that formed the bulk of the cure-all wasn't responsible for the spread of a contagious weeping rash that had broken out in several of the villages they had visited. At least the squirrel bones and bottles of sea water wouldn't do any actual harm.

"The Sea God Bless you madam," he said as a well-dressed old matron handed him a guilder and a half in exchange for a stick of drift wood he had collected from the shore the day before and told him tearfully that her brother had gone down on the La Scarlotta.

Sylas finished his proclamation with a resounding and enthusiastic ringing of his prayer bell and stood up. Most Sea God clerics kept a sacred prayer bell that was supposed to ward off wicked spirits and guide the lost through the mists of uncertainty. They were usually small brass or pewter hand bells which would be made specially for clerics before they took the cloth. However, if anyone were to look closely at Sylas' they would find that it was a brass bell that had been stolen from a drunken town-crier and had a town crest very hastily scratched from its surface. It clattered ominously in its bell doily as he stood up. He had not quite mastered the art of moving with it yet. He was just repacking his bag so that his prayer mat cushioned the bell when he noticed that the incessant babble of the crowds had suddenly silenced. Being no fool, he stopped his packing and before he even paused to assess the situation darted around the back of the cart so he was beside Tollie and more importantly within easy reach of the knives he had stashed there. When he then looked, he could see quite clearly what had caused the silence. A towering cloud elf was standing framed by the gates gazing with distaste at the crush of bodies before him. He was not like any other cloud elf Sylas had ever seen. He was more than seven foot tall Sylas guessed and broad in the shoulder, although some of that may have been the thick sheepskin cloak he wore. He was not elegant or delicate, his face bore the distinct scars of battle and Sylas noted with interest how the scar tissue had grown back in shades of white and blue to match the elf's skin but in such a way that it made it look as though his racial markings, which had presumably once been sharp lines, were leaking. His white blonde hair, which Sylas would have expected to be sleek and clean, was a wiry mesh around his head. The pale blue tips of his exceptionally long pointy ears poked through the nest. It was quite clear that there was little if any human blood in his lineage. What shocked Sylas the most was the figure's voice. It was not the resonant eloquent but ultimately soft sound of a self-possessed high-born elf but the angry commanding tones of a soldier.

"Where is the High Priest" he demanded in slightly broken common that carried clearly across the whole width of the compound. "Bring him to me." Sylas could see he was not the only one overawed by this command, several of the pilgrims were visibly trembling and a few of the children had started to cry. There was a heavy pause as none of them dare speak and the elf waited expectantly. Then as though it was the only sound in the world, a small well-concealed door in the north wall of the temple no more than ten feet from the main North entrance, opened with a deafening creak and a comparatively tiny cleric in long blue robes came scurrying out. Not a prime physical specimen in the first place, the diminutive cleric was balding and sported wire spectacles that made him look like a confused owl. The bare feet poking out of the bottom of his utilitarian habit made a damp thwapping sound on the stone of the courtyard as he hurried to greet the irate colossus in the gateway. Sylas could see the nervous sweat beading on the poor man's bald patch in spite of the fact that it was a chilly February morning and he was barefoot.

"Can I help you?" he said in a wavering officious voice, glaring up over the rim of his spectacles at the angry elf.

"Are you the High Priest of this temple?" sneered the elf with incredulous disdain.

"No," said the little man, looking away from the fearsome visage before him. Then drawing himself up to his full but still insignificant height said as haughtily as he could manage, "I'm the Custos."

"Fetch me the High Priest," bellowed the elf, "now." When he retold the story later, Sylas would say the sheer volume of the elf's voice had caused the Custos face to drain of blood. This was because he was unable to see the knife that the elf had pressed against the unfortunate man's guts. The Custos seemed to grasp very quickly which side his bread was buttered on and rather than staying to argue the point with the elf, turned on his heel and scuttled back into the temple.

Sylas didn't really have a clear recollection of the next half an hour or so. The High Priest appeared. He was a mercifully taller man in a more ornate robe with an embroidered scapular and a blue and white skull cap. He approached the figure with a slow steady pace, presumably to show he would not be ordered about like the barkeep in a cheap inn. He spoke in frantic whispers that elicited grunts and snorts and the elf was escorted inside the temple. The crowd outside waited with bated breath for a few minutes before the babble started again, rumours darting through the gathering like flies on a midden.

The elf had declared the Father's Tear a fraud and was proclaiming himself to be the Chosen of the Sea God. He had struck down a number of the priests, inflicting them with boils and sores in front of everyone. The voice carried as far as the courtyard, even if the words didn't. They could hear the righteous fury that was flowing out of him, and they were secretly glad that they were still in the courtyard. No one had left, because this was far more entertaining than anything else that was likely to happen and there was a certain amount of intrigue as to the eventual outcome of this contretemps.

Tollie, not satisfied with this sideline seat, started to edge his way towards the doors. He wanted to see for himself what exactly was happening. After all, he reasoned no one had said anything about people coming and going from the temple. Even so, he walked as though he were crossing a bog, every step a slow testing tread followed by a pause. As he approached he could hear that some of the yelling was not in the common tongue and he guessed it might be High Elven. Interspersed with this, he could hear the less commanding voice of the High Priest denouncing the elf as a heretic and declaring him to wicked in the eyes of the Sea God. He tucked himself around the edge of the north door, just in time to witness the elf climbing the sanctuary steps to the wide stone plinth on which rested the Father's Tear. With one single giant stride he stepped up and kicked the Father's Tear to the ground. The massive gem hit the cold stone and shattered, spraying shards out around it. There was a cadence of gasps and shrieks and then silence again as all eyes fell on to elf who was now standing on the plinth so that he towered over the sanctuary. He spread his sheepskin cloak out behind him, and in a voice that resonated from every single vault in the roof said,

"I am his chosen, I am protected by his divine mercy and by this holy cloak. I am worthy. Glorious Sea God, I seek to cleanse this place that has become vile and dark of purpose. Bring now your wrath and wash away the wicked, those that would steal, lie and cheat in your name. Only those who are truly worthy remain shall remain when the waters recede after the turn of the tide." The last five words echoed around the sanctuary and hung in the air for a moment. Tollie was too busy admiring the showmanship to notice the panicked looks on the faces of the priests and acolytes around him. In fact, he was enjoying the spectacle so much that his attention was only broken when a frantic cleric shoved him aside to make for the door. Water was trickling from the dark doorways behind the plinth on which the elf stood. It was bubbling and rushing like a storm drain, flowing down over the stone steps and in amongst the benches. Looking around he could see it was rising up out of the small arched doorways along the sides of the temple walls. It was coming up from beneath the ground with an unbelievable force. The sanctuary was already ankle deep and filling fast. The hundred or so pilgrims and clerics that had been attending the Tear were now fighting to be first through the narrow door way out to the courtyard. Tollie forced himself to stop for a moment, he needed a moment of clarity because if he didn't he would be wedged in the main porch with a hundred panicking idiots when the waters rose to cover his head. They were already crashing through the corridors, echoing around the walls. The water was covering his knees. Then, suddenly it was there, the noise in his head was muffled by the pounding crashing as a massive wave that came rushing passed the elf, who was still on the plinth his arms outstretched, a maniacal grin on his face. The clamour in the door way escalated as the water rose to waist height and Tollie's pause paid its dividend. A moment of searching found a sodden black curtain not more than ten feet to one side of the main door. Pushing his way through the swirling brown waters, that were deepening every second, he ducked behind it and found himself looking at the plain back of the door that the Custos had used. Fighting against the rising tide as it reached his chin and started to drag him under, he managed to throw back the top bolt and flung his bodyweight against the wood. It moved but didn't open. Taking a deep breath, he dived under the water and ran his hand over the bottom of the door, grasping the bolt with his frozen fingers. He tugged and tugged and then suddenly the bolt gave way and slid back. As he resurfaced his ears were filled with the frenetic screams of those trapped in the door way and the horrific gurgling of those who were being swept under by the water that was now nearly seven foot deep. With one last burst of energy, Tollie threw himself against the door and tumbled out into the courtyard in a gushing tide of water.

Without pausing to apologise to those who had been swept over by the rush, he splashed through the courtyard that was itself now knee deep in water screaming for Sylas. With the same survival instincts as his partner, Sylas had already readied the cart to leave and was making slow progress towards the gate.

"Leave the cart," screeched Tollie, staggering towards him, "just take the cash and the rope." Sylas, momentarily flummoxed by Tollie's sodden countenance, didn't argue with the instruction to leave the cart. He snatched the money pouch and the rope and started to push towards Tollie. There was an echoing crashing sound as the blockage of people in the doorway was forcefully unstoppered by a torrent of water and the courtyard was suddenly filled with fast moving brown rapids and the limp shapes of the drowned. Tollie was knocked to the floor and for a moment Sylas lost sight of him as the empty dead eyes of a departed priestess looked pleadingly up at him as she floated passed. Then, he saw an arm thrust out of the water. Tying the rope around his waist, he made a large loop in the other end and dived under.

Tollie and Sylas met under the water and Tollie grabbed the lasso. He managed to slip it over his head and poke one arm through it before another tide swept them apart. When he eventually fought his way to the surface and started gulping in breath, he saw Sylas no more than ten feet away doing exactly the same thing. As they were washed towards the gate by another surge, he clung on to the rope. If he survived this with Sylas and the money pouch intact, he was going to give the whole contents of the pouch to a temple. Any temple, he didn't care. Any temple, except this one. With that thought, there was another violent wave and they were washed out of the temple compound and into the river.

BA'AL - THE XAROB WASTES

After the battle

Iona snapped the reins and the oxen team shot forward. Finally, she had managed to move the wagon fast enough to create a breeze that took the vaguest edge off the stifling dry heat. The grey gypsum waste in front of her stretched on beyond the horizon with only two or three sun scorched trees to break up the flat featureless plains. She was heading directly towards the setting sun, it was the only way to hope she was travelling in the right direction. It had been four days of this and by her calculations she ought to be seeing the Jungle on the edge of Ctuma in another day and a half. With a bit of luck, she might run across another settlement before her store of fish leather and bread ran out completely. The map she had glanced at had lacked detail regarding the positioning of settlements because the vast majority of Ba'al sparse population were nomads. There were one or two permanent cities up in the north somewhere closer to the Tartarian border where the land was more forgiving, and hundreds of tiny villages peppering the lush river valleys she had crossed a couple of days before. Iona had not been foolish enough to approach the natives, as a lone western earth elf female she would be easy prey for the blood cults whose spectacular temples to the Sun God she had circumvented with great care. She had heard enough tales of Ba'al slavers and human sacrifices to take no chances. She had managed to shoot a strange ground dwelling mammal that looked like a small furry pig but tasted like chicken, and that had broken the monotony of trail rations, albeit briefly.

As she urged the oxen on, she could see a heat haze that indicated she was approaching a patch of damp ground. The oxen were in desperate need of water apart from anything else and she could do with a moment to stop and get down from the hard wooden driver's perch and stretch her legs. With luck, it would just be a patch of slightly less dry sand. As she approached it, she could see a hopeful looking dark patch that was probably a natural well. She could also make out a line of about ten or twelve long, thin objects that were about the width of a tree trunk and no longer than six feet or so. They seemed to have been deliberately put there, because they were arranged in a regularly spaced line, like rungs on a ladder.

With relief, she saw the water glistening back at her and brought the team to a halt. She leapt down and unhitched them and the stolid creatures ambled towards the murky watering hole without a look back. Snatching the scarf from her head, she hobbled towards the pool calculating whether it was worth risking a drink. She plunged her bandanna into the unpleasantly water, soaked the fabric and wrung it out over her head. It wasn't quite a bath in the ambassadorial residence but luxury is situational and comparative and it was just a relief to have some liquid running over her parched skin. She dunked the bandanna again and repeated the process, not caring that the water smelt stagnant and it was leaving brown trickle lines on her skin. She dipped her headscarf one last time and replaced it. Then, deciding against a drink from the pool, she wondered over towards the trunk like objects curious about anything that would break the boredom. The oxen didn't move from the watering hole, or even look up as she walked away.

She was within about five or six feet of the objects before it occurred to her exactly what they were. They had been covered in a thick layer of dust and therefore were almost a uniform colour, but from this distance they were quite clearly bodies. Far from being repulsed as she felt she ought to be, she was intrigued. With the tip of her boot she nudge the first one, dislodging the dust and revealing a partially desiccated corpse. It could not have been there long because the features were relatively intact. The skin had retracted from the mouth and eyes just enough to give it a pop-eyed, toothy leer but the face was still recognisable. There was a scar across one cheek and a patch of freckles across the nose. The man's long dark hair had become coarse and wiry, and it stuck out at alarming angles from his head. Kicking the dust from the rest of his torso, she found herself looking down on the black and silver livery of a Chaos soldier, judging by his clothing probably from a western temple. The man had been trussed in ropes and staked down with large wooden pegs. Judging from the rope burns still visible on the man's skin, he had been tied up like this for some time before he'd died. Iona recoiled slightly from this brutality. When she had first realised these were bodies she had assumed a burial site or similar. It seemed so incongruous in this deserted place that someone should have killed these dozen soldiers in this strange and cruel way on purpose. Not willing to dig any further, she returned to the wagon and harnessed up the oxen. Then, bound in thought, her skin crawling, she set off again.

Thirty minutes later, Iona was regretting having wished for a break in the featureless plains. The smell of blood and rotten flesh clung on her skin and tongue with the dust. She had not stopped to examine any more of the bodies but she had slowed down to an ambling trot wary of the obstacles scattered across ground. She had found herself driving through the ghastly aftermath of a fairly recent battle, judging by the fact that none of the bodies had turned to bone quite yet. Vultures were shrieking and diving, picking over the carrion banquet, their delighted caws cutting sharply through the stagnant air. Strewn amongst the bodies were broken weapons, shields and the wreckage of several destroyed war-engines. It was grim. Iona tried not to look too closely after a while but she saw enough to realise that the dead soldiers were from both sides of the faith divide. A large number of the bodies bore the colours of different Chaos Armies, eight point stars, spirals and large staring eyes emblazoned in silver and gold on black.

The rest were clad in Law colours, quartered tabards, blue robes with the scales of justice embroidered on them and the loose green gauze and polished armour of some kind of Arabian army.

Iona was not often moved by death but as she passed a young man with wide, bright green eyes staring out from rich dark skin with such pleading that she pulled up the oxen, hopped down and knelt by his side. With a soft hand, she closed his eyes with no idea what stirred such a rush of compassion for this stranger. She couldn't bear to leave him staring. Then with stinging eyes too dry to cry she climbed back on to the wagon, snapped the reins and sped away.

HASSELT

A sunlit forest road, early spring

"If we get stopped by the guard do not, whatever you do, mention that we're adventurers," said Pringle with a deadpan face. After a month and a half of travel including a very uncomfortable boat trip, Daisy was starting to see why Mori found Pringle so irritating. Humour was not a prominent feature of daily routine in the Life Temple and as such Daisy was not familiar with jokes. Therefore, she was a remarkably easy target for Pringle's little jests and he had spent the better part of the journey finding ways to wind her up. He had originally started by winding both Daisy and Mori up. However, after one jovial encounter where he attempted to persuade Mori that steamed toad with anchovy in white wine sauce was an Albion delicacy, she had had a 'quiet word' with him. Neither Krieg nor Daisy had heard what she had said but his face had drained to grey and he had not made a single joke at her expense since. Daisy really wished that Mori had let her into the secret because she was beginning to get fed up with it now.

"Okay," she said to this latest, "whatever you say Pringle. I'll be sure to tell that to the Ice Elves from Nortrol shall I?"

"Actually," chimed in Krieg slowing his horse to a walk. "He's right."

"Oh don't you start," snarled Daisy.

"No, honestly," said Krieg his face set in his serious expression. "Adventuring without a license is a grave offence in Hasselt." Daisy was now studying Krieg's face for any sign that he was about to start laughing. Tartars are not well known for their subtlety and he couldn't keep a straight face for more than a minute or so with these things. He didn't crack. "Genuinely," he continued in earnest, the three of them now riding slowly side-by-side across the width of the road. "King Ein used to be an Adventurer. He knows what kind of things we get up to and he doesn't approve. That's why he's made it illegal to adventure in Hasselt without a royal warrant. The standard punishment is a spell in the fighting pits." Daisy was starting to believe him. "It's up to you though. If you fancy a spell in the fighting pits by all means tell the first guard we spot that we're adventurers and see what happens." Wide-eyed Daisy nodded.

"Technically," said Pringle, taking up the point, "we're not breaking the law, because strictly speaking we're not actually adventuring here, we're just passing through to a transport circle. We're in transit, they'd have a job proving we weren't just private citizens or subjects or whatever they have here. But if you go around telling them we're adventurers then we won't have a leg to stand on."

"Okay," snapped Daisy, feeling as though she was being accused of something she hadn't yet done. "I won't say a word to anyone we don't know. Okay?" With that, she eased her horse into a trot and started to catch up with Mori.

The ride to the transport circle was largely silent after this. Daisy, still not completely convinced that she wasn't being wound up, was determined not to speak to anyone until they had their feet firmly on Al'Raethan soil so that she could not be accused of anything or made to look a fool. The travel had been quite speedy as the four of them sensed the imminent end of six long weeks in the saddle. The circle they were making for was the only one that had a connection with Al'Raeth and the path to it had included a ship across the Sea of Stars.

Trotting amongst the Hasseltine trees in this vast forest,

enjoying the cool bright morning light, it seemed almost blissful to think that at the same time the following day they would be nearly at their destination. The soft comfort of the end in sight was broken by the staccato shouts of violence, causing Krieg to pull his horse up short. The other three halted beside him and listened for a moment. There was a substantial amount of shouting and the distinctive sounds of steel clashing on steel. The sharp slapping of an arrow finding its mark was followed by a shrill shriek and the sound of running feet. The adventurers braced but no one appeared. More cries followed, in which it was possible to make out the words 'STOP' and 'GUARD' and then a crackling pulse of magic and silence.

The four paused. Whilst it was obvious that the scuffle was over, there was no indication of whether any of the survivors remained on the scene. There was a minute or so's worth of bickering as all four of them spoke at once. Krieg, unusually, urged caution and suggested circumnavigating the area off-track and Pringle agreed, but Mori and Daisy insisted that there may be people in need. Krieg tried to argue, but Pringle knew better. He just stood in front of them, his bony arms folded across his narrow chest and shook his head. A wry smile curled across his stubbly chin and snorted,

"Life and Death united, against the Trickster, oh the irony." Then, with a look of long-suffering indulgence, he said, "Come on then. If we don't hurry there won't be anyone left for Daisy to save and Mori will get all the fun." Then he strode off without stopping to check that both women were giving him the exasperated frowns he thought they were. The first thing they found was a well-dressed man hung by his feet from a snare. He was swaying pendulously in the gentle breeze, the arrow that had dispatched him protruding from his chest. On the floor lay three scruffier men as well as four bodies in matching green, brown and gold livery that were probably the Hasseltine National Guard. Daisy and Mori scattered amongst the bodies searching for signs of life. For a moment Pringle and Krieg paused and looked on until Daisy shrieked at them to do something and Mori had more coolly pointed out that the longer it took the longer they would be and the greater chance they had of something going awry.

Nearly all of the bodies were still clinging to life. Daisy and Mori worked diligently acting like a single unit, each patient receiving tender attention and prayers from both. Uninterested in the history of the injuries they healed the wounded in order of need. One of the scruffs opened his eyes, spluttered at the sight of the dwarf and the silver-skinned elf looking down on him and with flexibility that belied his blood-covered limbs extracted swiftly himself from their ministrations. Taking to his heels, he began to sprint back the way the adventurers had come. A barely conscious guard with one hand clamped to a newly bandaged gash in his side leapt up and staggered after him. The nimble crook skidded to a halt as the point of Krieg's sword met the very tip of his nose, making a tiny nick in the flesh.

"No you don't" said Krieg who had, until now, been 'guarding' the area because he had little skill as a medic. The guard who had given chase stumbled pathetically to a standstill and wheezed a painful,

"Thanks," to him.

"What makes you think I did it for you?" said Krieg with a dangerous smile. "I just couldn't help but notice that this young man allowed my colleagues to heal him and then tried to scarper without so much as a by-your-leave. Never mind that you've left your two *friends* behind," continued Krieg, gesturing to the other two crooks that Mori and Daisy had propped up against a tree, and who were now being tended by Pringle, who was fumbling over a dressing. The guard looked nearly as affronted as the criminal as Krieg escorted them both to the road side and indicated by lowering his sword slightly that they ought to sit down. "Sit there," he said gruffly but with a glint in his eye, "and stay quiet, both of you. We don't want any part of this, we're just saving lives not catching villains okay?" He gave the guard's torn and blood-stained livery a disdainful once over and stalked away.

The whole thing took nearly an hour. The unfortunate pendulous man had been cut down, laid out and blessed by all three clerics, Pringle not to be outdone by the solemnity of the last rites of both Life and Death. Everyone else had been patched up and left to finish off their business. Krieg watched as the guards and their prisoners limped away, the dead man strapped to a drag-stretcher. He turned back to make some crack and suggest they went on their way too, only to find the two women kneeling hand in hand, praying over an ankh and a chalice. He opened his mouth to cuss them into action but Pringle flung out an arm to silence him with an unusually ruminative look on his face. Krieg knew enough not to argue, he just slunk back to the horses and sourly made ready to leave. As he did so he glowered at Pringle, who was just standing on the road ponderously observing the women's prayers.

Life and Death are two forces that by their very essence are inextricably linked. Without death, life would mean nothing and without life death would not be possible. One fits with the other in an unbroken cycle, or so it seemed to Mori and Daisy. The temples did not agree. Life and Death stood opposed to each other in the way that Law and Chaos did. The sanctimonious Life clerics preached about the joys of living, mercy, energy, compassion. Secure in the love of the four faces of Lady Life, they railed against the wickedness of the Death Temple. They proclaimed that all Life was the Lady's and hers to end as she so wished. The Sisters of the Chalice, with whom Daisy had lived most of her life, practised a simple doctrine – let none suffer. They embraced all Life's children, healing those that could be saved and easing the passing of those who could not.

Across the Temple Square, the pious Death priests proclaimed the majesty of their great goddess in the form of the three sisters: Ankhere, Kali and Hecate. They preached about the glory of the end of life, about passion and mercy. They expounded the all-pervading power of the Lady Death, who could take your life at her will. The priests of the shrine at which Mori worshipped believed it to be their duty to sit with the dying, to ease the passing of those whose time had come and to make comfortable those who still waited to be gathered.

It was in the long hours of journeying that these two self-contained women with so much to push them apart found that their faiths were not so very different. Mori, steadfast in the love of her Lady, helped the more sceptical Daisy to find love for her own Goddess. Mori laid down a foundation for Daisy's faith that had long been missing. Acknowledging Death as a sacred force allowed Daisy to find peace within her troubled soul. Not by converting her to follow the Three Sisters but by making her see each of the Four Faces as precious and glorious and fleetingly beautiful. For the first time, she had understood what the Sisters meant when they spoke of certainty and serenity and the blissfulness of faith. She knew that when she returned to Aberddu a life as a lay-sister would no longer be enough, it was time to make her vows: sacrifice and mercy, and let that feed the growing flame of her faith. Mori never spoke about whether her faith had altered or grown through her friendship with Daisy but in time it would be hard to deny its potency.

ABERDDU TEMPLE DISTRICT

The aftermath of the Turn of the Tide

Jamar knocked his pipe on the steps and stood up. Surveying the empty square with a sour eye he grunted in disgust and turned to go back inside the Kesoth Temple. Not four months ago, this square had been crawling with people. Every temple had something going on, nearly every hour of the day and night brought more and more faithful. It had been the heart of the city, almost as busy as the market place. Jamar had loved it. People meant profit and in the church of Kesoth the Betrayer, that was a good thing. What use was the soup kitchen or the night shelter if there were no grateful waifs to make use of it? What good will were they cultivating if there was no one to cultivate it in? He knew where they all were. It wasn't a secret. They were all down at the Sea God Temple.

Ever since the Turn of the Tide the Sea God temple had been the place to be, even more than during the time of the Father's Tear. The mysterious elf, known only as Elder Dmitri had walked in and everything changed. The rising waters had washed away the old hierarchy leaving the way clear. It was a genius plan and a brilliant trick thought Jamar - he refused to credit it as divine intervention, he knew showmanship when he saw it. Elder Dmitri had been left with a grateful temple at his feet and none dared to argue with the credentials of it because one does not argue with the Will of the Sea God, particularly when it had been so clearly and unequivocally stated. Everything had had been rhetoric and theatre on a scale that would make the Bards Guild jealous.

Elder Dmitri, by virtue of his loud booming voice, impressive scars and stomach-stirring homilies had brought the city to its knees, in the Sea God Temple. It was sickening really, you heard it all over the market place and the poor quarters, mothers admonishing their children or their idle husbands with sentences like "What would Elder Dmitri say if he saw that," or "What did the Elder say about wasting time and resources?" Jamar snorted again. It was interesting to note that very few mentioned what the Sea God might say. The people of this city really would buy anything, particularly if you dressed it up enough.

One thing was for sure, nothing lasted long in Aberddu. Rumour had it that Elder Dmitri was the Champion of the Gods and Jamar wasn't surprised. He also wouldn't have been surprised if the rumour had been started by Elder Dmitri himself.

"Well," thought Jamar as he went back into the cool darkness of the temple, "let him. It's not a fate I would wish on anyone." As he retreated through the side door into the living chambers, Jamar wondered exactly what Elder Dmitri thought the Champion would have to do because one thing was almost certain: The Sea God Temple had been so busy with their new found popularity, they hadn't had the time to do the same research as everyone else. In this respect at least, it was probably unfortunate for them that they were not located with the other temples, in the Temple Square.

The whispers in the religious communities had leaked across faiths, and for once had not been subject to cruel and ruthless misinformation. Only the Krynok Temple, off to one side physically and culturally, had been left out of this particular mix. Given that this Champion was to be the mortals' aid to the Younger Gods in an attempt to displace Krynok it was hardly surprising.

ABERDDU CITY MAGES GUILD

Late spring

Elor rolled over and dragged himself to sitting. It was useless, it didn't matter how many times he recited Loyola's Matter Sequence or tried to recall the whole contents page of Universal Identification of Pattern it was not helping - he couldn't sleep. The full moon was framed exquisitely by the small arched window at the foot of his bed, its soft white light diluting the dark of his bed chamber. On the desk, he could see the stack of reference books and map-scrolls he had abandoned hours earlier, when he had decided he ought to go to bed. He had been trying to work out where the adventurers would be by now. He had received notification by messenger that they had been through the transport circle eight days ago. They must have reached the cave by now, perhaps they might even be on their way home. Maybe they had had to trade their portal scroll for safe passage or food, or something else. He had stopped worrying that Pringle would steal it and sell it for drink when he had received the notification that they had transported. It seemed unlikely that he would bother to go all the way to Hasselt before indulging in larceny and alcohol abuse, but the devil on Elor's shoulder whispered in his ear that you could never really tell.

In truth, Elor had not slept well since the day he had handed the bag of money and his second-best maps over to the adventurers. At first it was a lack of trust, and then it was a pervading sense of guilt that he had somehow undersold or misjudged them. That had given way to a sickening sense that perhaps he had asked of them more than they were capable and a gut-wrenching panic that he hadn't given them enough information or money. In the last few days it had all segued into a low-level impatience that they were taking so long. This had started to manifest itself as irrationality and a total lack of basic courtesy; two days ago he cancelled all his tutorials, asked the steward to have all his meals sent up and confined himself to his room. Apart from the occasional forays to the library, he was going to stay there until they returned with or without the helm or he received news that they were officially M.I.A. This bout of insomnia was obviously the latest in a long stream of symptoms he could have happily lived without. Any more and he would have to send out for a herbalist. He had two options at this point: he could get up, put on his shawl, light the lantern and continue with his studies or he could keep trying to get to sleep. Logically, he knew he should get up and occupy himself as he was merely making things worse but he couldn't face it, he rolled over and pulled the blanket over his head.

... meanwhile, deep in a cave in the Al'Raethan Mountains

"It's there."

"Where?" hissed Pringle, trying to follow the line of Daisy's pointing fingers.

"There," she said impatiently jabbing the air. "I can't see in the dark," he growled.

"Then you'll just have to take our word for it," grumbled Mori easing herself forward. "I'm going to try and turn it, if I scream and collapse someone heal me." Mori grabbed hold of the large metal wheel and gave it a tug. It creaked and turned a couple of inches, and there was a faint but definite draught in the tunnel. Daisy bustled forward, slipped under her taller friend's arms and added her strength to it. The wheel turned silently and a thin sliver of light spilled over the top of the door.

"Are you just going to stand there and let us do it all," panted Mori turning to Pringle, who was still observing proceedings with a displeased squint. Sullenly, Pringle added himself to the effort and with a shudder, the door opened another foot and a half.

Genetically programmed for life below ground, Daisy the dwarf and Mori the Nachwerten had not struggled to see in the cave system, but the others had been almost blind since leaving the surface. All four of them blinked furiously as the grubby green light from the chamber beyond the door spilled into the tunnel. Krieg, who had been guarding their backs, his short sword held out in front of him, turned briefly.

"Cool," he said, taking in the slowly opening doorway before whipping his head back around.

As the other three hefted the door open, a foot and a half at a time, a scene was revealed slowly before them. When, later, she tried to draw a picture of it, Mori found that she just could not get the perspective right. The first thing they saw clearly was that the green light was being provided by strips of glowing crystal that hung motionless about forty feet above ground. It would have been logical to assume that they were suspended from the roof but for the fact that there was only thick darkness above them. The next turn of the crank revealed the tip of the cage structure that housed the helm. The cage was made from finely worked metal. The next turn showed them that it stood on a rocky pillar surrounded by a chain of armed guards. The guards and the pillar were on a small plinth-like island in the centre of a massive cavern.

The three clerics stood in the tunnel mouth and gaped. It was now blatantly obvious why no one had reacted to them opening a door into this supposed highly protected chamber. Pringle had to admit as he gazed down into the seemingly bottomless darkness that he couldn't think of a better way to protect something you didn't want someone to steal. He also thought that unless those guards could fly, there had to be some way to get across to the island.

"You know what," said Pringle quietly, "I don't often admit this, but right now things would be a lot easier if we had a wizard with us." Neither Mori nor Daisy spoke, they just nodded in agreement. "Any suggestions Krieg?" Krieg had given up pointing his sword at the tunnel behind them and was now staring incredulously into the cavern along with the others.

"We've got two choices," whispered Mori, obviously more concerned than the others about attracting attention to themselves. "We either turn around, go back the way we came and take the portal back to Aberddu or we sit and wait for those guards to change shift." She stared at the others, daring them to make a better suggestion. Daisy simply shrugged and sat down on the tunnel floor. Krieg paused, made a face that suggested his brain was weighing up options, nodded and joined her, his long legs stretched out touching the wall opposite. Pringle looked a little more impatient. His thin face was twisted with argument, desperate to make a clever suggestion that sounded blatantly obvious. Mori just fixed him with her cold, undeterred gaze and said nothing. Eventually, after a couple of minutes of gurning and shuffling, Pringle had to admit silently that she had a point. Until they found out exactly how the guards got to the island on the pillar, it was pointless them creeping off and investigating. There best bet was just to sit down and wait, and pray to their own individual gods that no-one else wanted to use this tunnel.

It was impossible to judge the passing of time in the uncomfortable murky tunnel. Torpor overtook them, and they lolled with chins on chests wondering whether a solution would present itself before they were discovered. Then, suddenly there was a high-pitched whining sound, and Krieg snapped his head up just in time to see a crackle of green light as the guards on the plinth vanished and were replaced by what Krieg supposed was an entirely new set of guards. Krieg had been expecting some kind of bridge contraption to appear and he had been wondering exactly how far they would be able to get across it before they were all slaughtered. Of course, in a country run by obsessive knowledge-seeking wizards, magic was the solution. A broad smile crept across Krieg's battle-scarred face, this was so much better.

"Oi, stunty," he growled elbowing Daisy in the arm, "Wake up pointy and chuckles, I've got a plan."

Back in the Mages Guild…

Elor winced as his bare feet contacted with the cold stone floor. The fresh morning light poured through the window, the City looked far less picturesque than it had done by moonlight. In the grubby streets of the Guild District below, traders were starting to wend their way towards the marketplaces and a group of muscular types jogged around the corner from the Warriors Guild heading for the river path and their dawn run.

As he made his way to the kitchens, he did not ponder that the corridors were all but deserted. It was rare that more than a handful of mages appeared for early breakfast. Not because they were lazy, but because the majority of wizards were by nature night-owls. They tended to stay up later than was good for them tinkering with instruments and pawing over library books. The few naturally early birds found it quite a boon, as they tended to get the refectory, the library and the reading rooms to themselves.

Elor, not a traditional wizard by any means, split his time between the Mages Guild and the Adventurers Guild, where the bed, board and etiquette was a whole lot more rough and ready. As he examined the kippers on offer and helped one on to his plate, he had to admit it was better than the chunk of rock-hard bread and lump of brawn that would probably have been breakfast at the Adventurers. The thoughts of the Adventurers Guild shook him from his morning daze, reminding him why he was awake at this hour in spite of his turbulent night's rest. As he slumped down at one of the long tables and pushed his kipper around his pewter plate, he hoped with all his heavy heart that they were still alive.

Krieg gave the nod and Pringle brought his cudgel down hard on the back of the unsuspecting guard's neck. Then, with a swift hand he stuffed the cloth gag into the guard's open mouth and lowering him to the floor. Without wasting a moment, Mori and Daisy fell on the prone man, stripping his uniform and binding his hands and feet. Krieg snatched up the long tunic and hood and struggled in to it. Then, they dragged the body over to the side of the tunnel and leant it against the other one. Krieg turned to Pringle, who was already suitably attired and said,

"Right, let's go." Then he turned to Mori and Daisy and said, "You know what to do?"

"We'll give it a go," said Mori sardonically, clearly trying to imply that he needn't worry about their end of the task in hand. "Anything else you need?" Her words were dripping with disdainful sarcasm, but that was lost on Krieg.

"Hang on," he said and reached under his tunic. He adjusted something and there was a weighty thud as his weapons belt hit the floor. "Hold this for me will you?" he said, holding out the sheathed blade to Mori, who opened her mouth to point out she wasn't his squire when he said, "I'd give it to Dee, but it's nearly as big as she is." Mori let out an amused snort, shut her mouth and took the sword. Then, Krieg stuck his hand under his tunic again, fiddled in a pouch and turned to Daisy. "You better take this, just in case," he said thrusting a scruffy parchment sheet into Daisy's hand. She opened it, silently read the word 'by this scroll, portal', folded it carefully into quarters and tucked into her prayer book.

Pringle and Krieg added themselves discretely to the end of the line of guards heading towards the transport chamber. Krieg had been spot on in his assertion that the dwarf and silver-skinned dark elf would have been out of place in the mix, because mix was entirely the wrong word for the group of guards they had joined. They were all tall, muscular, male and judging by their visible features all pure-blood humans or thereabouts. Luckily Pringle and Krieg passed easily in this demographic, at first glance at least. First glance was all that turned out to be necessary. No sooner had they marched smartly into place by the age-old method of following the bloke in front than they were subject to a popping sound and a magical transportation effect occurred.

Krieg felt oddly sick as his body was compressed and pushed passed something, then he stumbled on the spot as he appeared about two feet from the edge of the central plinth and almost staggered into the thin air. The guard next to him muttered something in a sharp, snappish dialect that was probably the Al'Raethan translation of 'easy fella' and then smirked under his breath and whispered something to the man next to him, that judging by his expression was probably an unkind remark about new recruits. Krieg just smiled genially at him, nodded and shuffled back into his position. He had just realised the first flaw in their plan. Krieg and Pringle had spread themselves between the guards so that they were not stood beside each other. However, this meant that in their current positions in the outward facing ring around the central pillar they were no longer in each other's line of sight. This left them with a dilemma; both men wondering if they were going to be forced to make the first move.

Time passed. Standing guard gazing out at the darkened edge of a cave with few features to recommend it was one of the most breathtakingly boring experiences of Krieg's life. It was only since coming to the City that Krieg had encountered buildings bigger than the clan council hall. Indoor spaces this large were alien to him and he was beginning to pine for the sky when he heard something behind him. It was the sound of someone dropping a dagger. Krieg hoped that was the signal and it wasn't just someone being clumsy. He turned in time to see the flash of fire as Pringle shot a magical scourging at the unfortunate guard next to him, who staggered blindly forward over the edge of the pillar and let out a yell as he fell. The light and noise seemed to cartwheel the rest of the guards into action, three or four of them converged on Pringle. The others, conscious of the restricted space, hung back. At this point, Krieg sidled up to the smirking guard beside him with a mock look of confusion on his face. The guard was about to give Krieg some good rookie advice when he found himself on the receiving end of a cast iron knuckle duster that Krieg had been given as a birthday present by his brother three or four years ago. The guard's jaw broke, blood and drool sprayed out across Krieg's smiling face. Behind the broken-jawed smirker, the next guard drew his short sword – none of the guards had weapons longer than their arm, presumably because of space considerations – and lunged for Krieg. Krieg brought his boot up, and sent the man skidding back to within inches of the edge. Then, reaching into the top of his grieves produced a pair of hunting knives and headed straight across the plinth, bounding up the steps at the bottom of the central column and down the other side so that he was beside Pringle. Without a word, he boxed the ears of a man who was trying to wrestle Pringle to the floor. The pommels of his knives connected with the man's ears, there was a faint popping sound and his eyes rolled up into his head. Pringle extracted himself just in time as the guard fell forwards, the faintest trace of blood trickling from his ears.

"You get it," screamed Krieg to Pringle over the noise of the melee.

Pringle didn't need telling twice. It had been the plan in any case. Krieg would cover Pringle as he shinned up the pillar and snatched the helm from its perch. With a wide grin, Krieg turned his attention to the oncoming guards and Pringle sprinted for the column.

In the transport chamber, Mori cursed. They had waited for the outgoing guards to exit down a narrow tunnel opposite the one that the incoming shift had used. Then, they had crept into the chamber to look at the transport circle. She was no expert. Her elven was rusty to the point of almost non-existence, but she had managed to pick out one or two things from the symbols on the circle. It would be simple enough to activate when the time came she thought, but the problem was that there seemed to be no way of transporting specific people. It was all or nothing which meant that they would be transporting about a dozen angry guards along with Pringle, Krieg and the helm. Daisy had padded back down the corridor to act as look out and watch the theft through the door, so she could let Mori know when the others were ready.

Crouching in the tunnel, her eyes firmly fixed on the island, Daisy's heart raced. Pringle had managed to scramble nearly halfway up the stone pillar, Krieg was in the centre of a clutch of dancing blades and inexperienced as she was Daisy had no idea if he was winning. Then, she saw something that cast no doubt at all. She didn't see exactly what had led up to it, but suddenly Krieg was rolling across the floor and over the edge of the island. Judging by the lack of screaming, and unable to countenance any other explanation, Daisy assumed he was hanging on to the edge by at least one hand. This seemed to be backed up by the fact that several of the guards were still looking down where he had fallen, although the majority had turned their attention to the swiftly ascending Pringle. There was only one thing to do at that point, and Daisy did it admirably - she panicked.

Sprinting as fast as her little dwarven legs would allow, and shrieking at the top of her lungs, caution thrown quite swiftly to the wind, Daisy headed for the transport chamber. Mori, poised and ready for action set the protocol in motion before Daisy had even appeared in the room, shouting to Daisy to ready a weapon and their own portal scroll as she did so. There were less than twenty seconds between Mori activating the circle and the appearance of the dozen or so angry guards that Mori, but not Daisy, had been expecting. Some of them were mid swing. Unprepared for transport, they stumbled forward and toppled over. Others were more aware. One of them brought their short sword swing down towards Daisy with frightening rapidity. Trembling and white with terror, she managed to fling her axe haft up in front of her with moments to spare, blocking the blow. Mori, who was off to one side, was able to see that neither Krieg nor Pringle were among the guards.

"Where are they?" she yelled at Daisy, who was still wrestling with the determined guard with the short sword.

"Send them back," returned Daisy, panting and unable to provide any other information in brief.

On the island, both Pringle and Krieg had been momentarily shocked by the sudden disappearance of the guards. Then, neither one the type to look a gift horse in the gob, they made use of their sudden advantage. Krieg, several of his fingers smashed by the boots of men trying to get him to lose his grip on the edge of the island, heaved himself back up. Pringle, propelled by what he presumed would be only a momentary advantage, shot up the pillar, snatched the helm and slid down the pole landing in an inelegant heap at the bottom. At this point, there was a squeezing sucking sensation and a faint pop.

The next thing they knew, they were standing in the transport chamber which was empty apart from Mori, who was leaning over a heavily bleeding Daisy.

"Come on," yelled Pringle, clearly having trouble containing his adrenaline. "We need to get out of the portal ward."

"Hang on," hissed Mori, pushing healing magic into Daisy.

"Is she alive?" shouted Krieg urgently.

"Yes," replied Mori through gritted teeth, clearly resenting the interference, "but not conscious, and certainly not able to walk."

"Okay," said Krieg, bending over and hoisting Daisy onto his shoulder. "Let's go."

To the hurrying adventurers, the tunnels were labyrinthine. Pringle, Mori and Krieg carrying Daisy over one shoulder, sprinted for all they were worth doubling back and taking any path they could find. The lack of a palpable alarm response was only heightening their anxiety because they expected to run into a massive drop-net, an armed guard or a massive steel door at any moment. They just needed to find a gap that would lead them to the outside world and out of the portal warding. Panting, Krieg paused and sniffed. Cold air was drifting across his face from the south west.

"This way," he barked at the others, who had hung back when they saw him stop to shout at him to pick up the pace. "Fresh air," he bellowed by way of explanation and they turned on their heels and fled. It was a matter of moments before they saw both the source of the fresh air and the first glimpses of the response to their larceny. A guard patrol of perhaps four or five very slender but intimidating men, were clustered around a fissure in the rock that was perhaps six-foot square. It was clearly some kind of vent, and it was possible to see the white afternoon sky behind them. "Where's the portal scroll?" shouted Pringle as they bounced to a halt, staring face on at the guards.

"Daisy's got it," panted Krieg, his eyes fixed on the situation in front of him.

"Where?" screamed Pringle at Mori this time.

"One of her pouches," returned Mori who, like Krieg, was sizing up the opposition.

"Which one?" cried Pringle, almost hysterical as the guards started to walk slowly towards them.

"I don't know," hissed Mori through her teeth, drawing her knife from her belt with a determined look. Pringle, who couldn't quite understand why Krieg and Mori both seemed so calm began to empty the contents of Daisy's pouches willy-nilly. Empty potion bottles and coins clattered on to the tunnel floor. Krieg ignored him, he was trying to balance the weight of the scantly breathing dwarf so that he could lunge at the guard coming towards him. He didn't fancy his chances. He didn't want to put her down because he wasn't convinced he'd be able to pick her back up again and he didn't trust Pringle to carry her. Mori, who seemed to have anticipated the problem whispered to him, "When I shout run, head for the gap, okay?" Krieg, willing to put his life and Daisy's in Mori's hands nodded slowly with his eyes still fixed on the slowly approaching guards who were now trying to engage them in conversation in a language he didn't even recognise much less understand. Pringle was just about to toss Daisy's pray book aside when Mori hissed, "wait!!" at him and he stayed his hand. Pringle looked down, and saw poking from the edge of the book a scrap of cream coloured parchment. His heart thumping in his ears, he snatched it from the book tearing pages as he did so and flung the epistle carelessly away. With the guards now within sword reach, Mori bellowed

"Run," so loudly that the echo of it filled the whole corridor. Neither Krieg nor Pringle hesitated, they pelted towards the guards, swords drawn to parry blows rather than deal them and pushed past. Mori however ran head long into the group with her dagger. Krieg didn't see what she did, he was only aware of the sound of her racing towards him. When he turned to look he saw two guards on the floor, arterial spray fountaining from their chests as the other guards, stunned by their comrades fate, stood stupidly over them covered in glistening red. Seeing the incredulity on the men's faces, Mori yelled,

"Don't ask, just jump," grabbed both of their arms and bundled all four of them towards the hole, pushing them through the tight gap with scraped skin and bruises. Pringle already holding the scroll open had begun to say the incantation that ended in 'by this scroll portal' before they had even left the tunnel. It was thanks to his presence of mind that they four only plummeted ten feet through the air before landing hard on the cold tiles of the central atrium of the Aberddu Mages Guild.

Elor had been slumped face down in the centre pages of 'Encyclopaedia Arcanum Magicas Edition 7' for maybe three or four hours, dozing on and off and drooling in the margin. He hadn't read anything properly all morning, he had just started off looking at the beautiful script too preoccupied to translate the florid elven dialect as he read. That was when he had put his head down on the velum.

He had sent a terse note to his students requesting a paper about something or other that would almost certainly keep them busy for a week or so. He had only just dispatched this mail and already he had forgotten what it said. Looking out of the window at the Guild Square below, he sighed heavily. He could see mid-afternoon business was taking place as usual. The Warriors Guild were outside their frontage doing a serious of physical training exercises that would have made most wizards vomit at their mere suggestion and the Bard's Guilds afternoon Matinee was in full swing. It was then that Elor realised that he had heard the afternoon three bell from the Law Temple, but that no one had arrived with his lunch. This did not improve his mood. A knock stirred Elor from his torpor. The steward came in and, before Elor could give him the flat end of his tongue for forgetting his lunch, said,

"Mr Nybass, you're wanted in the atrium."

TARTARIA – DRAGON LANDS

Late summer

Marta's horse reared and bucked but a tartar is not easily unseated. She had ridden it to within almost arms reach of the borders of the Dragon lands. It was, or rather it had once been, unusual for a clan to demarcate their boundaries so clearly but in times of conflict things change. The bones of the Dragon Fallen made a striking display as the first line of defence, interspersed at they were with ten foot wooden stakes cut to a point and driven deep into the ground so they would skewer any mounted attackers who approached incautiously. Marta was close enough to see that many of the points had been stained brown with blood. However, this array of spikes and bones was not what troubled her. The stakes would be easily destroyed by fire and the bones would be ground under-foot as the horses charged through the smouldering remains. What did trouble her were the two creatures that she could see beyond this fence. She reached back into her realm of experience and had to admit she was coming up blank. The Boar had had nothing like this. Bones and spikes and symbolism would have been their limit, possibly a little fire-side hokum but nothing more potent. Perhaps that was why they had fallen and the Dragon remained strong. Only Clan Leviathan had matched the Dragon's resistance and even they were starting to crack.

She paused for a moment, her cheek pressed against the rough hide on her horse's neck. She whispered gentle, calming words into the animal's ear and continued to stroke it. She sometimes wondered if her horse knew she was a turncoat; if the animal who had been with her for seven or eight summers, ever since she was large enough to have her own warhorse, realised what she had done. He must have been aware that she was no longer Boar or at least that he was now tethered with different horses. She wondered if he thought she had gone on some kind of scouting mission and was waiting for her to return to the clan. She hoped he didn't know what she had done. He was a fiercely loyal creature and he would probably have died rather than betray her. She tried to convince herself that horses didn't disapprove of things but she just couldn't bear the thought that he might know.

Hooves approached behind her perhaps four, five or maybe half a dozen sets.

"What's the problem?" shouted one of them.

"Those," she yelled back, pointing at the creatures that prowled back and forth beyond the spike wall. They were more than twenty feet high if she was any judge, and reptilian. They stalked up and down on four clawed feet, their dark penetrating eyes fixed on Marta and her companions.

"Dragons," snorted another of the commanders, a sinewy sallow-faced former Stonesnake called Janx that reminded Marta unpleasantly of Iri. "How quaint."

"A cheap shamanistic illusion," snarled the General coming into line with Marta and Janx. "That won't present a problem." He waved an arm and another mounted figure broke away from the main gathering. Glancing over her shoulder, Marta let slip an involuntary shudder as she realised who was approaching. The Flame shamans drove fear and hatred into Marta's soul. Wild eyes, staring out of a mask of woad and lime, unable to hold your gaze as though they were staring into a different world. Their deep intrusive voices that crept in through the ears, and the unworldly aura that seeped from them some how managed to wobble her solar plexus and left her on edge.

The one that Marta thought was called Gilfdan crossed the field with remarkable speed and levelled with them. The General leant across and whispered in his ear. Gilfdan let out a stream of guttural chanting and clapped his hands together.

Seven Fire Drakes appeared in front of them. The drakes, a few feet taller than a large man, were vicious looking two-legged lizard creatures wreathed in flames. As the fire danced across their yellow and orange scales, they opened their jaws to reveal hundreds of needle sharp teeth and streams of fountaining flames. Marta held herself rigid so that she wouldn't be caught cowering back from the beasts, wary of their cruelty and power. With another clap of the hands, they scattered, dancing through the spikes and the setting the wood alight. On sinewy hind legs they moved, spreading the flames quickly until they had ignited the whole seventy-foot expanse, smoke spiralling up along its length.

Marta observed the whole scene uneasily, not willing to dismiss the Dragon's power as swiftly as the others had. It was little more than four seasons since she had been Boar and Boar had been allied to Dragon. She knew better what they faced because she suspected she was the only one who had seen first hand what the Dragon were hiding. She placed a reassuring palm on her horse's flank as it began to stir.

Through the flickering flames, the mounted commanders could see the massive Dragon totem effigies turning slowly until they were lined up directly facing them. Looking with disdain on the much smaller drakes, as though they were children that needed to be kept in place, one by one they opened their gigantic mouths and effortlessly expelled a stream of crackling blue flames. The streams met and entwine, like threads in a rope – killing the impudent drakes almost instantly. Then, the largest of them shot another jet of fire at the gathered commanders, who scattered outwards leaving a patch of yellow grass to catch and blaze. Marta did not need to see any of the other commanders' faces to imagine the looks of shocked surprise that would be trickling into affronted anger right now. Through the coiling smoke from the swiftly spreading grass fire, Marta could see the others regrouping. She cantered towards them, and just as she did so one of the shamans reached out a hand and a stream of water fountained up, dowsing the flame. The plumes of steam that shot up from the ground disorientated her as she rode. It took her a few minutes to find her way to the edge of the stinging cloud, and when she reached the others , It was blatantly obvious from their expressions that they had seriously underestimated the power of the Dragon apparitions – and none of them would ever, ever admit it. Marta was glad she was junior enough to be ignored right now, because she hadn't. In spite of what the General might have said, it had never seemed to be merely shamanistic trickery to her.

ABERDDU CITY - GALLOWS HILL

A wet autumn evening

Tollie had to admit the Militia had, for once, put on quite a spectacle. The baying crowd on Gallows Hill could have been at a Bards Guild late-nighter or even the fighting pits. The steady stream of condemned had been going on for nearly half an hour. They had erected two extra scaffolds so that they could conduct five hangings at once. The bone-wagons rattled up and down One Way Walk with alarming frequency. They had all three of the rickety carts on duty for the occasion, ferrying the convicts across the Singers Bridge from Blackwall to the infamous Gallows Hill and returning the cooling corpses to the municipal pit. The clunk of the lever silenced the crowd momentarily again as with bated breath they watched five more drop. Then, they let out a roar so powerful it was almost palpable, making Tollie's ears ring as the five danced their final jolting, shuddering waltz and slowly asphyxiated.

Tollie couldn't watch any more. He had known all five faces in the last batch. All of them were men, and boys, he had worked with at one time or other. None of them were exactly what he would call friends and certainly none of them had known his real name which was probably the only reason he was in the crowd and not the bone-cart, but still. As he watched the guards cut the five motionless corpses free from their ropes he felt sick. Running a clammy hand around his neck, he pushed his way back through the crowd as they whooped and hollered at the next batch of condemned that were rattling their way up the street. It really was grotesque and Tollie couldn't help feeling that it was only a matter of time before he was looking out of the bone-cart at the jeering masses with their rotten produce.

On another level he was finding it difficult for a totally different reason. It pained him to see so many people gathered together in one place in a situation like this, where there was so much opportunity to be exploited and so little leeway for exploitation. With the Militia clearly out in force on a day like this, it was ill-advised to try and circumnavigate them. Running a book, flogging flasks or something was beyond foolish and would probably lead to an impromptu addition to the days 'festivities'. Added to that, Tollie had now recognised so many of the faces in the death parade that it was probably just as well in any case, as making money from the fate of one's former colleagues seemed somehow distasteful. Tollie wasn't sure why he felt like that, because he could have almost guaranteed that if the boot was on the other foot, or to be more exact the noose was around the other neck, then most of them wouldn't have thought twice.

As he pushed passed a bunch of cackling fishwives with armfuls of screaming brats, he could see a clutch of militiamen in green tabards standing in the entrance to Cup-n-Ball Lane. That was inconvenient. Whilst he had done nothing that could be considered an arrestable offence recently, he would rather not have to face them, given that the face he possessed was quite familiar to at least two or three of them already. Looking around, he realised he had little choice. The only other way out of the square on this side was the narrow passageway known as Conical Trot, and the entrance to that was on the far side of a massive swath of screeching dockers and at least two other militiamen. He needed to get out of here and find Sylas as quickly as possible. He would just have to brazen it out.

Tollie's swagger came straight from the hip although today it didn't come from the heart. He had forced himself to look nonchalantly straight ahead as he approached the cluster of militiamen. Any sign of nervousness or weakness would be pounced on in a heartbeat, and he wasn't convinced he was up to talking his way out of a possible arrest today. He was guilty of plenty of things and it probably wouldn't take much to make him confess to any of them right now. He kept his eyes fixed on a battered wooden door hanging precariously on its hinges on a house about three doors from the end of lane. It was nothing special or even noteworthy, but it did hold the gaze. He considered whistling under his breath but he thought that would probably be over-egging the pudding and besides he couldn't think of any tunes other than The Lady's Grace – a Death Temple burial standard.

The militiamen were gossiping under their breath like kitchen maids in the scullery. They weren't really paying any heed to Tollie as he strode towards Cup-n-Ball Lane and he thought he was home dry as he drew level and overheard the tail end of a throaty, smoke-ridden chuckle and snigger. Clearly, they were just taking in the view like everyone else in Gallows Square. Then, just as he was about to step off the cobbles on to the dirt road, the same throaty voice said,

"Well, well Mr Marchant, fancy seeing you here," and Tollie froze. It was pointless to run, even if he could out-distance them all, they had his face and only a guilty man flees the militia.

"Good afternoon," he said turning slowly to examine the man who had addressed him although he already knew who it was. "How are you keeping Private Standing? Long time no see."

The man leered and gestured to his shoulder stripe. "Ah," said Tollie with mock courtesy, "I do beg your pardon Corporal, it has been a very long time."

"Yes, Marchant, it has," smiled Standing with a crocodile grin. "But as you can tell, we've been very busy." Tollie pulled an uneasy grimace that would probably pass for a smile if it had made it anywhere near his eyes. As it was, it barely made it to the edge of his mouth.

"Yes, of course," he said hoarsely.

"To be honest with you," continued Standing, clearing his

throat noisily, "I was a little surprised that we didn't meet up sooner than this. I have to say, I was expecting our paths to cross."

"Oh were you now?" muttered Tollie through gritted teeth, his grimace flattening to a scowl. "Well, apparently you were mistaken."

"So it would seem," conceded Standing, dropping his greasy pretence at civility, "so it would seem." Tollie turned on his heels and started to walk away. The corporal, unable to leave it at that, shouted after him, "I will see you soon Mr Marchant, oh yes I will! And we'll meet again in this square." This was met with whoops of approval from Standing's comrades but Tollie didn't stop to dignify it with a response. He was too scared that it might be the truth.

The collapse of the Aberddu Guild of Assassins and Thieves had not be as impressive to behold as one might have expected. There had been no public proclamation or 'witch-hunt'. That would have been kinder and almost completely pointless. The Militia had been very clever on that score, a little too clever a cynical mind might think. It had started very simply with three or four low-profile arrests, which seemed innocuous enough. Being arrested was an occupational hazard and those who were lucky enough to be overlooked learned to look the other way when their gang-mates were being led away in cuffs – eye contact being a fatally expensive luxury in these circumstances. However, this time it hadn't been the usual shake-down. Those three or four arrests had each lead to three or four more arrests, which had then each lead to more arrests. It seemed that something was making them talk and so the wave spiralled outwards whipping up everyone in its path – nearly eleven dozen all told by the time the trail ran dry. Blackwall had been heaving at the seams. Then, it came: the proclamation from the High Council. To relieve the over-crowding in the gaol, all those who had been convicted of murder, serial thefts, more than three counts of intention to endanger the public welfare, impersonating military or militia personnel and a host of other more obscure offences were to be put to death for the 'public good'. It wasn't difficult to pin three counts of intention to endanger the public welfare on any member of the Thieves and Assassins Guild even if you couldn't get them for one of the other things. Sylas hadn't hung around long enough to wait for the proclamation, he had seen which way the wind was blowing the day they had started hauling the street kids. He had mumbled something about the Middle Kingdoms being pleasant at this time of year before he had fled but had given no more specific details than that. The only thing Tollie knew for sure about Sylas' location was that the last place he would be was the Middle Kingdoms. He did however have a suspicion that Sylas hadn't gone nearly that far.

ABERDDU CITY - OUTSIDE THE TURN GATE

Three days before midwinter

"Would you take that ridiculous wig off?" snapped Tollie.

"It's no worse than your badger's bum beard," grumbled Sylas, stubbornly refusing to remove it.

"It's going bald, and it's got lice," spat Tollie, leaning over to snatch it from his head.

"It's realistic," retorted Sylas ducking skilfully out of his grip.

"It's revolting," groaned Tollie making another grab for it.

"Would you two just shut up," snapped Jason De Vere irritably. He was leaning against a nearby tree just off the path trying to pretend that he wasn't with them. Next to his feet, Pringle was sitting cross-legged on the floor, his hammer across his knees, playing with the grass. It had been a very long walk from Neckard not because it was far away but because Tollie and Sylas hadn't shut up the whole way. After a particularly joyless contract it was the last thing Jason had needed, and now here they were sitting outside the Turn Gate behind a stinking Arabian trade caravan. The gate guard seemed to be registering every single wagon and trader, and as many of the traders didn't speak common there was a lot of shouting and wild gesturing going on. The patient creatures that pulled the carts stood languidly chewing the cud and crapping on the road. Jason smirked to himself.

When the caravan eventually moved an enterprising soul could make a small mint from the manure that would remain. Jason thanked his lucky stars that since joining the Adventurers Guild, that enterprising soul was no longer him. He looked down at Pringle about to pass the comment, saw the top of the priest's greasy head and changed his mind. The quicker they got back into the city and he could speak to someone who didn't annoy him so much it made him want to gouge his eyes out, the better. At least it wasn't raining right now he thought.

"It's bad enough that you hid in the orphanage," Tollie was saying when Jason turned his attention back to them. Sylas made a garbled retort that was largely curse words.

"As one of the orphans!" continued Tollie, his volume rising as he got into his berating stride. Sylas swore again but said nothing useful and this only served to feed Tollie's fire. "One of the *girl* orphans," he exclaimed at the top of his voice. "You hid in the girls orphanage in the Life Temple to avoid being arrested!"

This was too loud thought Jason, and very unfair of Tollie. Sylas didn't say anything in response he just punched Tollie in the nose, causing it to crunch loudly and bleed. Tollie, far from being thrown off by the violence of this response, used it as an excuse to yank Sylas's wig off. He tossed it into the drainage ditch, where it sank beneath the stagnating gunk almost immediately. Sylas sprang from standing and clamped himself on to Tollie's front, his teeth going for Tollie's neck and ear, his feet kicking. Jason just watched the performance, he couldn't be bothered to intervene. Pringle didn't even look up.

The muscles in Iona's legs were agony and she could feel the spreading blisters on her damp feet. Her oilskin cloak needed patching again, hopefully before the next deluge leaked through the tears in the back of it and into her clothes so it could join the rest of the rain. She could feel the rough cotton of her breaches chaffing and was hoping that her skin didn't rub raw before she got to a warm bath. At least, today the end was in sight. She had seen, from the prow of the last hill she had just trudged down, the famed City Walls of Aberddu Free State or whatever it was called. She had also seen, although not in much detail, the mammoth queue at the gate. From her years in the orient, she recognised the camels in the caravan and guessed that its country of origin was more likely Arabi than Jaffria given the shape of the wagons. She stopped for a moment and closed her eyes. She could smell the rich spices on the damp air, twining up out of the sweet-sour mix of leaf mould and camel dung. She wondered if they had confectionery with them, this far from Kchon a little eastern promise would be very welcome. Even though she had been raised in the Elven Forests, Iona's heart was in Kchon and Eastern delicacies were one of the things she had fallen in love with. Even soaking and frozen to the core as she was, she could imagine the sharp acidic explosion of the highly flavoured sugar crystals which made her think of pure sunshine.

As she travelled the last hundred yards or so to join the back of the massing queue outside the gate she slowed down, the blood was pounding through her feet and each step was hobbling, stinging torture. When she saw the man on the main path in front of her, his coarse black, shoulder length hair poking out in all directions, his smile wide, she immediately dropped her hand onto her knife hilt. She was just far enough away from the gathered people to be out of ear shot and she didn't really want to be beholden to the protection of strangers in any case. The ragged man just continued to stand in the road and Iona tried not to make eye contact. Keep on walking, she thought to herself, just keep on walking. She was just about to get within arm's reach of the man, who showed no sign of stepping aside to let her pass freely when he opened his mouth, showing off the black rotted stumps of what had presumably once been teeth and said genially,

"How be lovely?" Iona stopped dead in her tracks, and realised that this had been a mistake moments later when she heard the sound of a pair of feet landing in the mud behind her as either a small child or a very short woman dropped from the branches of the tree above her. Why hadn't she looked up? This was a gambit as old as time itself, and as an elf from a Forest land, she had seen it done in many guises. With lightning speed she drew her knife and stabbed it backwards. Judging by the grunt she contacted with her unseen assailant, but not to much effect as there was no warm spray of blood on her hand. Having fumbled this blow Iona realised that she had lost already. She could feel the grasping hands from behind on her shoulders and the jagged point of a cold blade in her own gut from the front. She could smell the liquor on the man's breath as he leaned in, and feel it sticking to her neck as he wheezed,

"Very clever, precious, very clever. But not clever enough, what's in the bag?"

Sylas and Tollie were now sitting side by side like bookends, studiously ignoring each other as they tended their various injuries. The brawl had been extremely short lived. Once Sylas had broken Tollie's nose and Tollie had snatched Sylas' wig, there had been a lot of pointless tussling and a black eye apiece –before they stopped out of sheer boredom. Neither Jason nor Pringle had stirred themselves in any way regarding the fight, Pringle had just continued picking the grass and Jason was still lolling against the tree gazing into the distance down the road. Then suddenly Jason started and stood up properly. It was almost as though his ears had pricked up. Then without a word, he jogged off up the road. Not wanting to be left with the squabbling pair and in need of some entertainment, Pringle leapt up hefted his hammer over his shoulder and strode after him. Pringle had to admit he had no idea how Jason had seen what he had seen, because it only became apparent to Pringle what he'd seen when he'd run about thirty yards.

A short elven woman was being held at knife-point by a wretched-looking man with wiry black hair, as a scrappy-looking woman with grubby pigtails went carelessly through the contents of a travelling pack on the side of the road. Jason cleared his throat and said loudly,

"Good afternoon,"

"Piss off," hissed the man without turning around to see who had spoken to him, "If you know what's good for you."

"No," said Jason quietly, "I don't think I will." This was followed by the very impressive chinking sound as he ostentatiously drew his sword. The woman, who could see Jason over the man's shoulder leapt to her feet dropping a large sparkling amulet as she did so.

"Agnita," cried the man, "what are you doing?" but the woman didn't answer she just continued to back away as Jason slowly raised his sword and Pringle swaggered up grinning with his enormous hammer over one shoulder. Jason tensed his arm muscles as the sword reached the top of its arc and Agnita, eyes wide, turned on her heels and fled.

"Agnita," bellowed the man, "Agnita," but she didn't stop. "A wise move," said Pringle softly.

"I told you to piss off," growled the man.

"I think you should turn around," advised Pringle ignoring this, "very slowly."

"Why should I?" hissed the man.

"I would if I were you," said Iona, a smirk dancing over her lips. "It might be less painful in the long run." The man just leered at her and then there was the sound of a sword colliding with an old woollen coat and a damp thud as he hit the floor.

"You just can't help some people," said Pringle stepping over the body and offering his hand to Iona. "Are you okay?"

"Yeah," said Iona patting herself down, "Yeah, I think so. Thanks." She didn't offer her name, but determined Pringle said,

"I'm Dakarn Pringle, and you are?"

"On my way to Aberddu," replied Iona guardedly, stepping back. "Thank you gentlemen for your help."

"It's no trouble," grunted Jason sardonically still wiping his blade on a scraggy cloth. "It's a pleasure I'm sure." Pringle, who was looking less than impressed by his cool reception from Iona, was not satisfied with this limited exchange. As far as he was concerned, if one went to the effort of saving a lady from a scurrilous robbery then the least one should get in return was a dinner invite, never mind about a name.

"Where are you headed madam?" he asked, utilising his best manners.

"Into town," evaded Iona, now crouching on the road side, squirrelling her personal items back into her pack.

"That much I had surmised," replied Pringle greasily, "I was just wondering if I could be of some assistance, knowing the city as well as I do." Iona stood up, having refilled her bag and gave him a cold appraising look. Jason had already ambled back to where Tollie and Sylas were sitting, leaving Pringle to ingratiate himself. Iona, aware that she was about to enter a large city in search of someone, knew she was going to have to ask for directions sooner or later. It was probably safer to ask the - she hesitated to use the word - gentleman who had just saved her from a mugging than it was to take her chances with someone else.

"There is one thing," she said coolly, trying not to sound as though she was encouraging Pringle's clumsy advances. "I could do with directions to this tavern, if you would be so kind." With that she thrust a scrap of grubby paper into Pringle's hand. He unrolled it casually and glanced down at the spidery scrawl. He recognised the name all too well, and he really hadn't been expecting that. He looked from the paper to Iona and back again. Clearly there was more to this woman than he had originally surmised. However, he had a feeling she was about to be sorely disappointed.

In a year that saw the fall of the Thieves and Assassins Guild and the rise of the Sea God Temple, the dynamics of the city slowly shifted. Somehow, faith became more important than guild allegiance or even family. Talk turned to Gods more often than not. Opinion was divided - many had turned to the All-Father seeking solace from the divisive younger gods.

The news of the war on the Galivara Plains had spread through Aberddu. The Crusades and The Champion had captured the imagination. The bare bones of the legend were common knowledge: A mortal to fight Krynok in the name of the Younger Gods. The details, however, had been lost in time. Who this champion would be, which God he would follow and how exactly he would take on the All-Father were all still grey and hazy but it didn't matter. As the citizens of Aberddu, along with the church-followers around the world, turned their attention to this and submerged themselves in the fervour and legend, all eyes turned away from Tartaria. What was a mortal threat when compared to a divine war?

III

1101 A

TARTARIA - THE BORDER OF STALLION AND TIMBERWOLF LANDS

Sunrise, early in the year

Talia dropped from the tree and started running the moment her feet touched the ground. The grass fire was spreading up across the plain with frightening rapidity, heading for this small clutch of woodland. She simply couldn't credit what she had just seen. As she sprinted across the grassland toward the others she prayed to whoever was listening that none of the monsters spotted her. They were barely recognisable as tartars, as massively big with wild, terrifying eyes. They did not seem in possession of themselves as they stalked about the tiny settlement setting fire to every dwelling. They had been ruthless and thorough about their destruction even though this outpost had been deserted for months after that dreadful night eighteen months ago when the Stallion had fallen.

Talia had remembered this village and it had been a distant paradise to them all as they moved across the veldt. It had taken them two months of walking around in increasing circles to find it. They had been hiding on the Dragon land, almost certain they would be safe if found by the clan. Syrne was adamant that this was the place to turn. Their hopes of salvation had been dashed when they attempted to find a settlement. It seemed that before they had declared their resistance to Salamander, the Dragon had taken every available opportunity to protect themselves. Every area of population was surrounded by grotesque effigies, enchantments, creatures and traps. They had lost three of the little ones before they had realised they needed to approach with the utmost caution. They gave up in the end, and conceded they would need a new plan.

It had been an awful winter, the hunger had been fatal and the cold had been worse. Syrne and Talia had done their best to provide and some of the others had definitely stepped up. In fact, the spirit with which the kids had embraced their fate was indisputable and the tartar tendency to train even the youngest children in survival was certainly paying off, but even so. Talia had been lying sleepless one night, with Zua and Eva, two of the smallest, clutched to her for warmth when she had remembered the village. If they could find it then they could have a home, and maybe for a while pretend that everything was going to be okay. As she sprinted back to the others, hot angry tears prickled her eyes.

Syrne could see from Talia's face that things had not worked out, before she was even within earshot. He exhaled sharply and frowned. Nicci, who was only a year or so younger than Talia and Syrne, saw this gesture and nodded acknowledgement. Obviously they were going to need a new plan. She sighed and looked down at the children sitting around her feet. There were half a dozen or so very little ones, and another five or six who were not yet ten. They had the world-weary eyes of those much older, and some of them were remarkably tough but underneath they were still just children she thought. They had all seen too much and lost too much. She, and Talia and Syrne, had built this village up in their minds as something to hope for, fight for, dream of. If it was not to be, then there needed to be something else better to grasp at. She crouched down and said quietly,

"First person to bring me back a pot-ready rabbit gets to wear my hat,"

"How long for?" squealed Jacobi excitedly springing to his feet.

All day tomorrow," she said with a grin and as one, all dozen or so children stood up and sprinted off towards a patch of scrub behind them at which Nicci had been pointing. Syrne turned, watched them go and said,

"What was that about?"

"They're getting dinner," said Nicci calmly, "while we work out a plan and something to tell them."

Just as she said that Talia reached them slowing to a jog, her hand on her axe handle.

With the little ones gone there were maybe a dozen of them left, possibly fifteen. They gathered around in a circle and sat cross-legged on the ground like a proper clan council. They all looked to Syrne, who wore the mantle of acting chieftain uneasily but firmly and he, like many a chieftain before deferred to Talia, his would-be shaman with strong silence and uttered,

"What happened?"

Talia told them in a hushed but urgent tone what she had seen. They all listened without a sound aware that they had only a matter of minutes to hear this and make a decision before one of the children raced back to Nicci waving an inexpertly skinned and gutted rabbit over their head. When she had finished the silence hung on. No one knew what to say. It had been their only idea. In fact, some of them had started to silently cry, tears glistening on their cheeks in the watery morning sun. Syrne stood up and shook his head. All eyes were on him, it seemed like a defeatist gesture. What was he thinking? What was he about to say? Hearts pounded, and mouths opened but did not speak. Then, at length he cleared his throat and said so softly it was barely audible,

"Aberddu."

ABERDDU CITY DARK GATE

A glorious early spring morning

On a golden morning such as this, Aberddu was almost beautiful. The sunlight danced amongst the scum and algae on the surface of the water in the horse trough by the gate. The cobbles glistened with dew, a group of half-hearted sparrows croaked out a chorus from a tumble down roof top. The wide street that lead into the city from the Dark Gate was normally a bustle of activity but today it was overwhelming. Arriving home in triumph was something that happened a lot in Aberddu, particularly amongst the Temple types and crowds could be arranged to look almost spontaneous with judicious application of enough free fruit, cake or ale. The Law Temple had sent runners ahead with enough florins to purchase two dozen barrels of pears and the streets were packed. As the trumpeters sounded, the heavy iron counterweights let out a creak and the vast wooden gate swung gracefully open. Softened by their complimentary fruit, the crowd let out a rousing cheer and waved anything within arm's reach that would flap appropriately.

Five shining mounted knights in highly polished, discretely pock-marked armour rode in a spearhead formation on five proud chargers. The rider at the point of the spear seemed enormous, his silvery chest plate reflecting the morning sun, his long blue cloak stretched elegantly out over his horse's rump. He was widely recognisable as Brother Teign of the Law Temple and Adventurers Guild, well known locally. On his hands, he was wearing massive, gleaming gauntlets. Each one reached nearly to his elbow and was covered with fine silver and aquamarine metal scales, making it look almost like fish-skin in the sunlight. Although it wasn't actually palpable, the gauntlets had a strange aura about them that drew the gaze immediately. It was clear that these were items of significant magical importance.

These knights were followed by a rank of mounted cavalry, in expertly patched livery depicting the scales and book of Law. Behind them, were row on row of similarly mounted men and women, becoming shabbier as they went on. Then following this, about forty or so troops in shirt sleeves. The foot soldiers were followed by a wagon train that was looking surprisingly dilapidated but by the time the last cart had rolled through the gate nearly everyone on the route had gone in any case, most of them following alongside the shining knights and cavalry men.

"Oh dear, oh dear, oh dear" sighed Tollie, leaning against the wall of a wash-house and biting into a pear. "That's an interesting development indeed." He examined the fruit flesh carefully, picked a bruise away with his nail and flicked the offending pulp into the air.

"What?" grunted Sylas as he climbed into the nearby barrel to help himself to the crushed contents at the bottom. Then, having stuffed nearly half a pear in his mouth, straightened up and spluttered, "Wha' interes'ing?"

"Well, two things really," said Tollie, taking another bite and swallowing it before continuing. He was now trying to avoid watching Sylas' frantically masticating maw, the slurping sounds alone were bad enough. "Well, the first thing that struck me was how few of them seem to have returned. I'm fairly sure there were more than one hundred and fifty when they left last year, and the ones that have returned look rather worse for wear. I wonder if we'll ever find out what actually happened."

Sylas snorted swallowing the pear with a discussing sucking noise, grunted in acknowledgement of this fact and said, "I doubt it. What was the second thing?" Tollie paused for dramatic effect, took the last bite out of his pear and threw the core into the gutter idly.

"I don't think Elder Dmitri is going to like it."

A few days later, in the Temple Square

Tollie's supposition that Elder Dmitri was going to be unhappy was only the tip of a very large iceberg of unrest that sailed into the Temple District of Aberddu on the tide of the returning Law Crusade. Whilst never exactly friendly with the Chaos Temple, the Law Temple had at least existed in a state of tacit stalemate. There had been a certain understanding that a balance was necessary, that they could not condemn each other out of hand. There had been the usual rhetoric and finger pointing but it had been many years since it had been any more than that.

The soldiers that returned from the crusades were changed. Many of them had retreated behind glassy gazes, lost in the horrors they had witnessed on the Galivara Plains. No one spoke of what had happened, except in hushed whispers to others that had been there. It was forbidden to speak to or aid in anyway a member of the Chaos brethren, even a child. The punishment for infringement was anything from twenty lashes to isolated detention. The atmosphere in the temple became tensely purposeful, many of the returned who had not previously done so made vows.

For their part, the Chaos Temple took this new development with somewhere between laissez-faire lethargy and poorly-stifled amusement. A declaration to mirror the Law Temple's, regarding contact with follows of Law, was not the Chaos Temple's style and would not have been enforced in any case. However, it did become noticeable that there were more and more people openly wearing the eye of Chaos, the spiral or the eight point star than before. Then, three days after the return of the crusade a group of priests released one hundred and fifty possessed frogs into the Law Temple sanctuary, declaring it a blessing from Selatina, the lesser known Dark Goddess of Amphibians and Needlecraft. As is often the case with finely balanced diplomatic situations, it takes one tiny nudge to break the floodgates and the frogs did it.

There followed an all-out riot in the Temple Square. Law followers, many of whom felt they had little left to lose, charged the Chaos Temple and were met head on by the Soldiers of Mithras – Chaos God of War and Fury in battle, who it seemed had been lying in wait for them just inside the Chaos Temple grounds, almost as though the frogs had been part of the plan. The fighting spilled out into the public square, drawing the Life and Death Temples into the sordid mix. Sisters of the Chalice remonstrated with anyone who would listen to cease the violence, but to no avail. A clutch of black-robed Hecate worshippers waded into the fight then, screaming that conflict was natural and that the priests should be allowed to fight. When one of them raised a hand to an elderly Sister, breaking her cheek bone and blooding her nose, the Paladins of Life joined the melee.

The whole incident was only brought to a stop when the militia intervened. As Daisy lead a wounded and weeping Sister back to the temple she glanced over to the Death Temple steps. She glimpsed a familiar figure wrapped in a large black cloak, a look of horrified disgust on her face. Daisy's eyes met Mori's for the briefest moment, but there was no smile of recognition between them only a deep sadness in the elf's gaze met Daisy, before she turned and went back into the temple. Choking back a sudden rush of tears, Daisy patted her charge on the back and steered her carefully towards the temple sanatorium.

ABERDDU GUILD DISTRICT

A chilly evening, late spring

The sight of a slightly crazed wizard running pall-mall across the Guild Square, hair and robes flying in the breeze was not unusual enough to make the passers-by stop and stare. This one was shouting, also not that out of the ordinary. As far as the usual inhabitants of the Guild District were concerned, wizards throwing all dignity to the wind in this manner were about as much theatre as watching a small boy poking a dead bird with a stick. What did make things a little different was the direction in which the man was headed. Usually screaming Mages headed for either the Merchants Guild, Temple District or Adventurers Guild. This one seemed to be headed to the Mages Guild itself and away from the Adventurers Guild. As he reached the centre of the Guild Square he seemed to have shouted himself out and had progressed to muttering under his breath. Scurrying some way behind him was a rotund dwarf dressed conspicuously in the robes of a Sister of the Chalice, who seemed to be concentrating all her energy on catching up with him.

As he crossed the central square and she gained on him she yelled in a hoarse panting voice,

"Elor, Elor, wait up, what did you say?" The wizard paused in his stride for a moment, let out a muffled and highly disgruntled exclamation and then carried on at an even faster pace. At this point, Daisy was forced to start running in order to keep up. Even after all this drama, the carter who was delivering a consignment of bolts of Arabian Silk to the Weavers and Dyers Guild still found the colour of his ear wax more entertaining.

It was not unusual for rows in the Adventurers Guild to escalate out into the courtyard or even the Guild Square, however they didn't usually make it quite as far as the main reference library of the Mages Guild. Usually, they were the kind of arguments best resolved by a bout of good, old-fashioned fisticuffs and rarely the sort that required reference material. This time was an exception. When one accuses a wizard of 'talking out of his rear end' one can normally expect one of three responses: finding oneself magically transformed into a mouse, frog, snail or similar, a scathing or witty retort, possibly in an ancient language that one doesn't speak or, as in this case a loud exclamation of 'oh am I really?' as the aforementioned wizard stalks off to the nearest source that can provide writ of for his claim. This is why the Mages Guild open questions forum would make such an excellent entertainment spectacle, if only the Bards Guild could persuade them to license it as such. And also why the Mages Guild reference library was open twenty four hours a day.

The exchange that had led to Elor storming across the Guild District in search of empirical proof had gone on for a significant length of time before it had descended into childish name-calling. It had started with Elor, Severin and Erin and had, like ripples on a pond, spread to encompass nearly every member of the Guild that had come into the hall at any point during its duration. It was the kind of argument that had been made infuriatingly longer by people arriving, taking an interest and jumping in with both feet before establishing what had already been discussed.

Elor, in a fit of hysteria, had rushed into the guild clutching an old vellum scroll and talking faster than most people could listen. He had ignored all greetings and marched straight up to Erin. Without pausing to find out if it was a convenient moment, he launched into a complicated explanation of the facts and thrust the scroll at her. Erin had been discussing the concerning situation in Tartaria. Severin, an ancient elf who had been with the guild the first time Salamander had tried to take over Tartaria several centuries before, was giving her, a much younger elf, the benefit of his age and wisdom. When Severin objected to Elor's interruption, Elor told him in no uncertain terms exactly where he could go and what he could do when he got there. This rapidly escalated into a full scale stand-off with both men explaining calmly through gritted teeth exactly why they were clearly right.

"Was it not you who brought the Tartarian threat to the guild's attention in the first place?" snarled Severin, blinking furiously over his fixed smile.

"Yes," conceded Elor with equally dangerous civility. "I did. Which would put me in the better position to understand what I mean when I say that I am talking of a more pressing concern."

"A more pressing concern than a tyrant warlord trying to take over Tartaria and subsequently everywhere else?" shrieked Erin in disbelief, to which Elor had replied without irony or levity,

"Yes." It was at this point that it had become a bit of a free for all. Half the gathered crowd wanted to hear Elor out, even if they didn't believe him they thought it was probably worth listening for a few minutes. The other half of the crowd however were intent on belittling and heckling him. Jason De Vere dismissed him out of hand after only a few sentences, exclaiming that 'God problems' were the jurisdiction of the Temple District not the Guilds. This had then provoked quite a bit of not entirely good natured religious to and fro between devotees of different Gods which Elor had ended by stating loudly and categorically that none of the temples could solve the problem, because it would need them all to work together. This was the point at which Jason De Vere lost all interest and Severin told him unequivocally that he was talking out of his rear end. At that point, Elor went very quiet and stalked out of the Guild room. To their credit, none of the adventurers laughed until they had heard him slam the heavy oak doors. Daisy had looked to Krieg with a concerned questioning gaze and Krieg's eyes had mirrored her own. They, at least trusted Elor's opinion ever since he had sent them to retrieve the Helm. No one thought twice as the dwarf leapt up and scuttled after him. They were too busy loudly agreeing what an idiot Elor was being. Krieg said nothing, he just sat to the side with his swords on his lap, waiting for Daisy to return.

Several hours after Elor's tantrum, in a dark riverside bar by the name of the Coxon's Oars Daisy had managed to convince the rest of the gathered crowd to sit down on the grimy benches and attempt the cider. In the end, she had had to put her cloak down before Elor would sit. Krieg and Pringle, who had both seen their fair share of seedy taverns were eyeing the tankards suspiciously but not passing comment, Mori was resolutely not drinking having discovered they had no wine of any kind. Mollified with a cup of very cheap and warm spirits that had been sold as Brandy, Elor had calmed down enough to explain to the others what was going on. Krieg, as a native of Tartaria, had a vested interest in the rise of Salamander and had initially reserved his judgement on what Elor had to say. The other three, all clerics, were spellbound by the legend that he presented. As he rolled out the stained and cracked vellum scroll that he had gone back to the Mages Guild to retrieve, they sat like children around the story teller.

More than a thousand years ago, at the time of the first cataclysm, the Younger Gods had expelled Krynok from the world, banishing him to a realm beyond the stars. In fact it had been the force of this conflict that had caused the cataclysm in the first place. A handful of mortals that had survived the rising waters and the great cratering tears in the ground made a thorough and substantial record of the days before and after the darkness. Some of the content, if not the actual physical forms, of these records remained in temple vaults, the private libraries of rich elves, and according to popular myth The Al'Raethan Court. These records, however factual they were at the time, became peppered with more apocryphal yarns and soon it became difficult to separate truth from fiction. In later years, Mages had dedicated whole lifetimes to trying to decipher the truth and there was now in the chain of Mages Guilds that stretched across the continent a cache of accepted wisdom. Beyond that, there was much conjecture and little actual concrete proof. As a younger man, Elor had toyed with the idea of becoming a cataclyst, as they were called, and had read a number of the more obscure scrolls, including the one he clutched now.

The scroll was in a florid hand and the writing was very obviously in High Elven. Elor didn't even pause he just began to translate, skipping over the more intricate language and paraphrasing the important points. When Krynok had been banished and the world had righted itself, the younger Gods had devised a scheme in case he should return. They created items of strength and power that could be united into a suit of armour for a champion, a mortal champion. This champion would be able to fight Krynok should he return and if he won, banish Krynok once more. The fighting amongst the younger Gods, which had been becoming more and more evident recently, had made them weak and had drawn Krynok's notice from his exile and brought his interest back to the mortal world. Now as well as fighting amongst themselves, the Younger Gods faced the threat of the All-Father returning to take back his lands.

As he finished the story, he rolled up the scroll and sank the last of his liquor with a twisted grimace. None of the others moved, they were all still gaping at him open mouthed. Krieg was the first to speak. "Are you actually saying that unless someone finds all those items and unites them to create a champion, then there's going to be another cataclysm?" It takes a tartar to put something of such proportion so succinctly and Elor smiled wanly as he said,

"Basically, yes." Krieg nodded slowly, took a deep gulp of his ale, belched fruitfully and said slowly,

"And to do that we have to convince the gods to stop arguing and get on, so that their champion can kick Krynok in the arse and save us all?" Krieg continued in his simple way, the three clerics silenced by the enormity of what was being mooted. Elor closed his eyes, exhaled and with a wider curling of a smile said,

"Close enough."

Krieg picked up his tankard, drained the contents in one long swallow, his Adam's apple bouncing up and down furiously, put it down and said almost imperceptibly,

"Oh."

ABERDDU CITY TEMPLE DISTRICT

As the blossom fell

Pringle stood on the steps of the Trickster Temple and gazed out over the Temple Square. He'd popped out for some air the overwhelming smell of aniseed was becoming somewhat nauseating. It was a beautiful evening, the soft warm sunlight seemed to hide the harsher edges of the city as the sun sank slowly into the sea. Evening devotions could be heard floating in the air from most of the temples on the square. He picked out the faint edge of a melody from the Life Choir, the glory of it was stirring, even to a Trickster like him. He took in a deep breath, the hint of the orange and cherry blossoms from the Life garden penetrated the aniseed coating his nostrils. Closing his eyes, he took another breath.

As had been the case since the early spring, the Law Temple was crowded. He could see the late comers standing in the doorway. Hopefully they could hear more of the garbled homily that was issuing from the sanctum than he could, although he doubted they would care if they couldn't. Since the return of the crusade, the Law Temple had taken on the mantle of the 'place to be' seriously diminishing the numbers at the Sea God Temple. It was said that Elder Dmitri had become less merciful and more vitriolic in his condemnation of those who had chosen to seek solace elsewhere. Pringle didn't really care. When it came down to it and all the theatricality was over, the only temple that would care about the poor, the downtrodden and the hopeless was his own. They would still be waiting to pick up the fallen after all this had ended. Perhaps, he thought to himself sadly, the champion should be a Trickster. After all, they were the only ones whose God could really understand the mortal condition, having once been mortal himself. He had cheated his divinity out of the Goddess of Balance and had spent every day since trying to win back his mortality. It was this dichotomy, the melancholy of getting what you wish for only to wish you hadn't, that appealed to Pringle. Far from being the God of jovial practical japes and merriment, the Trickster was the God that dealt with the frailty and transience of mortality, the twisted dark humour that was the only antidote to the moribundity of living. That was why the aniseed, the custard pies, the whoopee cushions and the rest of it annoyed him.

Pringle was just about to go back inside when his attention was drawn down a side street to the Krynok Temple. The front door was opening slowly, and people were spilling out. As he watched, Pringle realised that whilst he was aware that people must go in and out of the Krynok Temple - their congregation was more than healthy enough within the city - he had never seen anyone use this door. His eyes were drawn and held by the figures as they formed into a crowd. The whole square seemed to fill with a sweet, unworldly sound that tumbled into music in Pringle's head, completely engulfing the melody coming from the Life Temple. As the crowd moved towards the main square, Pringle was drawn to walk towards them and he could see he was not alone. People were appearing on the steps of other temples, some having walked out in the middle of evening devotions. They were all heading down into the square to greet the crowd as they moved into the plaza. Pringle was about to start down the steps himself when he was jostled from behind by a group of White Face acolytes who were racing towards the crowd themselves when he caught hold of himself. White Face followers take pleasure in the cruel pain and suffering of others, they are the sort of people who think it's funny to put ground glass in the porridge pan, they don't run excitedly into the square to see any sort of spectacle other than possibly a particularly gratuitous public hanging. There was clearly some kind of magic at work here. Fighting against his urge to be part of the crowd, Pringle let himself descend the steps but moved no further.

As the crowd approached, he was in a better position than most to take in the whole view and in his state of relative clarity was disturbed by what he saw. There was no question that the crowd was largely mortal and mostly human, although there was a fair smattering of dwarves and elves, and even one or two greenskins. However, they were all shimmering with a faint golden haze. Their wide open eyes were bright and shimmering, their faces smiling and serene. They were all singing, their arms outstretched in welcome. The people, who were now pouring into the plaza by the dozen from nearly every temple except Kesoth, were running joyfully into the crowd embracing the singers, laughing and smiling. Pringle hardened his heart as he felt another pull toward them. The homily in the Law Temple had come to an abrupt end as those standing in the sanctum had flooded out, and the Paladins had appeared in short order on the top of the Law Temple steps, arms readied. They were now staring in confusion down into the square, unable to act. Some of them were even edging their way down the steps towards the embracing mass now.

Pringle found that the longer he resisted, the more clearly he was able to see what was happening. He could see the golden shimmering tendrils that were snaking up to the temples and in through the doors. He saw the ones that had swept past him and in through the doors of the Trickster Temple, curling around whoever they touched. He could see amongst the mortals of the original crowd were other creatures. They were trying very hard to look like mortals but they were just too beautiful. If you just glanced over them you would never have known, but if you looked at one long enough you could see its countenance slip for an instant. The Fae thought Pringle with a shudder. The fairyfolk, the immortals, the chosen, whatever you wanted to call them, the children of Krynok were creepy. They had largely been the stuff of myth since the cataclysm, but with Krynok's rise they had been more and more apparent. It had started as shimmering in the night, the occasional wispy presence on the wind, almost intangible, until one day they had started to appear in physical form. They were beautiful, there was no denying it, even the vicious ones with thousands of needle teeth were in some way resplendent. They could even seem charming and kind for a while, until you realised that they had no grasp of the realities of a mortal existence. Pringle had distanced himself from them as a champion of the Trickster, the most mortal of all Gods. The same could not be said for some of the other adventurers, who had been drawn by the offers of power and bewitched by the glamour of the Fae. He could see, among the crowd, a face he realised he had not looked upon for nearly twelve months. Til-Dar, through whom Krynok had spoken to the Adventurers Guild nearly eighteen months ago, was there. His skin was translucent, his eyes silvery and his hair shimmering. His mouth was open in a wide smile as he embraced all those who came near him. Then, he began to speak, his words echoed around the temples with unnatural resonance, although it was indisputably his own voice, just amplified.

"The All-Father calls you home, Krynok the creator of all welcomes you his children and calls you to his side. Come with us and seek sanctuary in our temple." As the joyful, embracing masses made their way clumsily back towards the open doors of the Krynok Temple, watched open mouthed by among others the Law Paladins, three of whom were being forcibly restrained from following, Pringle hung his head. Taking a deep breath and hoping the aniseed had in some way dispersed, he climbed wearily up the steps and back into the Trickster Temple.

ABERDDU CITY STATE

The road heading North through the woods ,- almost lunch time

Daisy sneezed again, and with an exaggerated look of forbearance Mori handed her a pristine white handkerchief from somewhere within the folds of her tunic.

"What did she say?" she asked as Daisy wiped her nose.

"She told me that it was not our concern, and that I should remember the vows I was hoping to take and that mercy and sacrifice didn't cover glory-seeking, and that I should think about the repercussions of my actions as an adventurer on my work for the poor, sick and dispossessed." With that, Daisy sneezed again, and let out a small groan. "I think I'm allergic to that long grass stuff," she mumbled thickly, pointing at a clump on the road side.

"Keep the hanky," said Mori stoically.

"What did the head of your temple say?" asked Daisy, wiping her nose again.

"I couldn't even get in to see him," growled Mori bitterly, "The Master Pardoner told me I was wasting his time and suggested I leave unless I wanted to offer a blood sacrifice."

"A blood sacrifice?" shrieked Daisy, slightly louder than she had intended.

"He's a Hecate priest," muttered Mori with a dark look,

"They're into that sort of thing. Why do you think I don't go in there very often? The Ankhere faithful are becoming less and less welcome." Daisy nodded, she was familiar with the politics of the Aberddu Death Temple.

The three sisters that made up the pantheon did not cohabit so peaceably as the four faces of Life. Hecate, the sister whose followers worshipped the process of bloody and cruel death, the ending of life in all possible ways and Kali, whose devoted sought out the glorification of death were at odds with the quiet caring sister who sought only mercy and cool repose. The temple in Aberddu had once been controlled by Ankhere worshippers but in recent years the Hecate cult had grown and now they had the lion's share of the followers including the High Priest and his Pardoner. The Ankhere worshippers had been sidelined and pushed out, and were now being treated like an embarrassing hangover from the Life Temple. Mori didn't really care, she had never really attended the main temple, but in the current circumstances it was going to prove problematic.

They reached the fork in the road and turned off down the narrow path that headed around the bottom of the nearby hill. The two women walked in silence for a while before Mori said quietly,

"Have you seen Pringle at all?" They had obviously both been thinking the same thought – had Pringle had any more success with his temple? Even though he was no more powerful than either of them magically, he was in much better standing within his temple and at least he would probably have had a fair hearing from his High Priest. Daisy knew the answer to this already and had not really wanted to share the news with Mori just yet.

"I saw him yesterday," said Daisy slowly, "and he had been granted an audience, that's what they call it in the Trickster Temple apparently." Mori nodded. They had stopped beside a small brook where a dip in the bank lead to three rather slimy stepping stones.

"And?" she demanded when Daisy failed to continue swiftly. "Well," started the dwarf, "The High Priest was very interested in what Pringle had to say, but he then pointed out one very pertinent fact." Mori raised her eyebrows questioningly. "The Trickster wasn't a God during the last cataclysm. If the legend of the champion is true, then the likelihood that the Trickster had been involved in creating the items was next to nothing." Mori exhaled loudly and closed her eyes. Daisy could see the fine silver skin of her eye lids was trembling. "Right," she said quietly after a moment. "Okay." Daisy had always appreciated Mori's cast iron hold on her temper and emotions. Daisy who had been raised amongst priestesses of Life was used to highly- strung sensitive women who wore their heart on their sleeve and flew into a soggy fluster at every set back. Mori's admirable control fascinated her. "Let's go before we run out of time." With that, Mori stepped deftly off the bank and on to the first of the stepping stones.

The rest of the walk to the shrine was silent with Daisy trailing about three feet behind Mori. They were both lost in thought as they rounded the corner and saw the small glade. Their gait changed, from the preoccupied urgency of women with their minds full of otherworldly concerns to the dignified strides of priestesses approaching worship. It had been three days since they had both been free to come to their shrine and in that time little had changed. Daisy noted with satisfaction that someone had been past and left a bunch of wild flowers at the feet of the statues. Judging by their wilted appearance, they had probably been there for a day or so. As she knelt down in front of the two statues, one of Ankhere and one of the Crone she thought how similar they looked. She knew the similarity of appearance was almost certainly because the artisan who had made the statues had only been able to carve one face and that they both probably looked just like his sister, but even so it still touched her. She took her cup and wine flask from her scrip and bent down to kiss the statues' feet. Beside her, Mori was silently doing the same thing.

KCHON - A QUIET PATCH OF WOODLAND

A summer night, just after dark

"Unless you've got a better idea, of course," said Jason smiling. Tollie and Sylas looked from one to the other and grinned.

"Nope," said Tollie after a moment, "sounds great to me."

"Yeah," agreed Sylas, "I like it."

"You're joking?" shrieked Jason with a snort. "Are you seriously telling me that you don't have some convoluted scheme involving I don't know, a goat, a parasol and a fake badger hair beard?"

"No," said Tollie calmly, "sometimes simple is better, and that plan is the essence of simplicity."

Jason nodded appreciatively and said,

"Now all we have to do is get the other two to agree." "Yep," said Tollie and Sylas in resigned unison.

It had not been an easy trip. The trouble with adventuring was that one often had to do it with other adventurers, and whilst it was possible to develop comradeship beyond even the bonds of brotherhood it was also possible to develop a depth of hatred it was difficult to conceive elsewhere. It was incredible how deep the feelings could drive themselves when one was forced to go questing with someone with whom one did not see eye to eye. This was one of the primary reasons that murdering other members of the Adventurers Guild was expressly forbidden by guild law. In fact that and the clause about not being a demon or demonologist were often the only guild laws anybody ever bothered explaining to newcomers. It seemed simple enough - don't kill anyone in the room, don't take up with a demon. Then, you spent more than six months in the Adventurers Guild and found out why these two rules were so completely crucial to everyone's continued survival. It was the only reason that neither Jason nor Tollie had clubbed Mauna Evanga over the back of the head as she slept. Sylas didn't have so much of a problem with her, largely because she tended to side with him in arguments. She made no secret of the fact that she thought Tollie was a pig and Jason was a bounder. She was right, but she didn't seem to understand that just because Sylas was whelp- like it didn't mean he was incapable of standing up for himself, nor did it mean that he couldn't deliver the sharpest jab in the ribs Tollie had ever encountered. She had made a nuisance of herself all the way across the continent by arguing continuously, sometimes seemingly just for the sake of it. Sylas had discovered however that if he put on a particularly querulous tone and tried to look hungry he could get her to agree to just about anything. He did this just as soon as he tired of watching Tollie and Jason getting an ear-bending. Unfortunately for Tollie and Jason it amused Sylas far too much for him to ever end it quickly.

Mauna Evanga however was nowhere near as irritating as Gul. Gul was a shaman, and if you caught him when he'd just been shaved and washed you'd be able to tell that he was wood elf. However, he considered washing and shaving to be against the spirit of the Wyld and hence only let himself be subjected to such worldly humiliations once every few months. If you could stand the stench and the fact that he shared his beard with ten or eleven different species of insect, then he was perfectly affable, provided you could understand what he was saying. He had spent many many years alone in the Elven woods, living on berries and raw fish and studying the portents. He tended to talk in strange cryptic phrases and whenever he was being spoken to seemed to stare over the left shoulder of whoever was trying to address him.

It was often difficult to tell from his response whether he had understood what you had said to him or not. All four of them were silently sick of him by the time they had boarded the mule train in the Middle Kingdoms and that had been nearly three weeks ago. Unfortunately for them, or fortunately for Gul, he was an almost uncannily good healer and none of them could match his skill in this regard, nor could any of them sense magical signatures so well. Both these skills were vital to the mission. This was the only reason that Tollie and Sylas had agreed to take him when Erin had suggested it in the first place. They had taken Mauna because before this adventure Tollie and Sylas had never spoken to her, and judging entirely on appearances – she was clad head to foot in a fitted black robe and adorned with silver jewellery – she looked as though she would at least be entertaining. They had found out before they had left the city state that she used the robes and jewellery to camouflage the fact that she was actually breathtakingly dull on an almost spiritual level. The only entertaining thing she had done on the whole trip was to repeatedly fall off her mule and the fuss that followed that had started to get old pretty quickly.

Jason, Tollie and Sylas had been working together for a while now and had probably been out on half a dozen or so missions. They had developed a mutual respect and friendship that kept them coming back. Jason liked the way Tollie and Sylas worked and Tollie and Sylas liked the fact that Jason didn't think they were immoral or at least any more immoral than he was. He was also fairly game when it came to acts of confidence trickery and almost too enthusiastic regarding dressing up in various disguises. This was the first time that he had dared express a plan in front of them and he was still a little confused that neither of them seemed to think his idea was too pedestrian to succeed. He looked over to where Mauna was lying by the fire wrapped in a blanket, her chest rising and falling slowly. Even if she wasn't asleep, she was doing a good enough job of pretending that he wasn't about to wake her up to be shrieked at. It could wait till morning.

Disturbing Gul when he was in a trance was a bad idea anyway. Jason stood up and stretched out his aching legs. Weeks on a mule train and three days trekking up the mountain sides of Kchon and he was walking as though he'd just sat on a red hot poker.

"I'm just going to visit the little adventurer's room," he said with mock coyness and ambled slowly off into the dark trees leaving Tollie and Sylas chuckling into their rations.

Three minutes passed during which the only activity of note was Gul letting out a resonant and substantial belch that didn't seem in any way to break his catatonic state but caused Mauna to whimper and pull her trail blanket over her head. Then the air was rent by a piercing scream that was cut off abruptly, Gul's eyes sprang open. He leapt to his feet and sprinted into the darkness before the other three had had time to react. Mauna shot to standing, screamed

"Don't leave me," and flung herself at Sylas as he and Tollie made to follow Gul into the darkness.

Dragging the priestess behind them with no thought for the safety of their camp, Sylas and Tollie made after Gul.

They didn't have far to go. Barely fifty yards from the edge of the clearing Gul was standing covered in the glistening blood of a fearsome looking creature whose head he was holding in one hand. Lying on the floor at his feet was a heap of glistening viscera wearing Jason De Vere's boots. For once in his life Gul was perfectly clear.

"Red cap," he said by way of explanation, holding out the creature's head. "Body's gone. So have the others." The wide open eyes of the head seemed strangely alive as they gazed back at Tollie, Sylas and Mauna. It's mouth hung slack, showing hundreds of bloodied needle- like teeth in its maw. It's tufts of hair were stiff with blood, its white nostrils were flared even in death. The bloodied neck stump was dripping onto the dark ground. Gul must have grabbed it by the hair, and by sheer brute strength ripped it from its body. It was a sight that Sylas knew he would see in his nightmares for years to come.

Tollie had dropped to his knees beside Jason but it was too late. There was nothing, apart from the boots, discernibly left of

Jason De Vere Tollie wasn't even sure if all the flesh in the heap was his.

"Gul," he said softly, desperation causing a lump to rise in his throat, "Gul, can you do anything?"

Gul grunted and dropped to his knees, thrusting the decapitated head into Mauna's hands before she could coil back in revulsion. Her hand had been on the head barely a second before her eyes rolled back in her head and she dropped into a dead faint, letting the head go as she fell. Sylas let out an irritable sigh as he sloped after the head thinking to himself that a Death cleric, particularly one who professed to practise in the ways of Hecate, really ought to be able to stand a little more gore than this.

ABERDDU CITY EAST GATE

A wet summer morning

"Tartar Town, that way," bellowed Greery before Syrne had even opened his mouth, waving a muscular arm north along the city wall. "Just keep walking, you'll see it." Talia looked at Syrne, who was a poorly contained ball of rage these days, and stepped between him and the guard before Syrne had time to raise a fist.

"Why do you assume we want Tartar Town?" she said coldly, kicking Syrne swiftly in the knee to stop him gesturing in a way that might be considered an arrestable offence.

"You're tartars?" replied the guard glibly, already looking passed them to the merchant's wagon behind. "That's where tartars go, unless you've got specific business with someone of note, I don't have to let you in." Talia did not, as the guard had expected her to, step back as he leaned towards her.

"How do you know we don't have specific business with someone of note?" she retorted, her own rage boiling up now. The sudden burst of summer rain had chilled her to the bone, at first a welcome break from the heat but now a discomfort as her furs were still damp.

"Oh, I do beg your pardon," Greery retorted with mock courtesy, "and whom did you wish to see?

"Krieg Clan Dragon." hissed Talia, the guard's taunting tone the last straw for her temper. At this point, Syrne pushed her aside to take over. "Is that so?" sneered Greery. A combination of boredom and irritation with these arrogant youths was starting to bring out the pig-headedness that had enabled him to rise to the rank of Gate Sergeant so very swiftly. He wasn't sure exactly what he was going to do, but he was sure of one thing: if these kids were coming through this gate while he was on duty they would need a hand written, gold embossed invitation from the Albion Ambassador himself and quite possibly a diplomatic escort.

"Yes," snarled Syrne, even closer to the guard than Talia had been, his hair plastered to his red face and his hot sour breath mixing with the stale tobacco and cider of the guard's.

"And do you have that in writing?" asked Greery, upping the ante ever so slightly by leaning forward a little more and smiling.

"Writing?" snapped Syrne, "why would we have that in *writing*."

The guard, himself barely literate, was always cruelly amused by the way that tartars made the words *reading* and *writing* sound like acts of extreme obscenity. It was his favourite trick, on a slow day, to demand to see a tartar's papers and make them fill in the pass ledger with the details of their reason for visiting the city and expected date of departure. Strictly speaking, the ledger was only used during certain lock-downs, times of martial law and religious crises but any gate guard was within his rights to ask anybody passing through the gate to fill in the ledger if they believed them to be of, now how did the rule book phrase it, 'suspicious intent'. It was perfectly reasonable to claim that you felt any tartar to be of suspicious intent just because they were a tartar.

"If you had read the ordinance of gate passage dated 1068 AC you would know that in order for me to permit entry to a group of tartars I need written instruction from a noted person as to their destination, purpose of visit and expected length of stay. That noted person must then agree to be responsible for any moral or financial repercussions of their visit to the city, " spouted Greery. What he didn't add was that this rule had not been used on a regular basis since 1072 AC, even after the rise of Salamander, because a gate ordinance was not likely to keep an army out.

He also didn't add that all ordinances were applied, during peace time, at the discretion of the Gate Sergeant and that he was simply just being an arsehole.

"Oh really?" bellowed Syrne, raising his fist above his head and stopping dead. Talia's bony fingers formed a solid cuff around his wrist.

"Yes really," said the guard smugly, "like I said missy," speaking directly to Talia over Syrne's shoulder, "Tartar Town is that way."

As he watched the back of the young tartars stomping off in the direction of Tartar Town, Greery reached into his oilskin and pulled out a grimy clay pipe and a small pouch. He let the Merchant's wagon through on the nod as he packed his pipe bowl and received a florin for his trouble. Seeing the traffic had cleared, he was just contemplating getting one of the privates to put on the pan for a brew when he saw something in the distance that caused him to shove his pipe angrily back inside his cape and let out an infuriated grunt. It was yet another party of pilgrims. God bothering types were always easy to spot, they tended to walk as though they were doing the world a favour and usually arrived dressed in some bizarrely uniform manner. This lot were wearing deep red robes with rope belts and brown cloaks. Every single one of them was carrying a glowing storm lantern regardless of the fact that it was mid-morning and bright in spite of the rain. It was getting beyond a joke now, between the bloody tartars and these religious types, this gate was registering more daily traffic than both the Dark Gate and the North Gate and was starting to equal the Turn Gate. Greery scowled, it really wasn't on. He had worked blooming hard to be made Gate Sergeant of the East Gate, having calculated long ago that it was the city gate that got the least traffic. Most of what it did get were westbound trade caravans who'd come along way and were fully prepared to grease wheels for a swift pass through the gate as soon as they could smell the salt air. The East Gate had become remarkably efficient under Sergeant Greery. In fact for the last few months, he'd been fighting hard against being promoted to Gate Captain elsewhere. Now, he was beginning to wonder if he ought to think about it.

He didn't mind putting up with these peculiar foreign types if they were willing to throw a silver or two his way, but the tartars were argumentative and the clerics were supercilious and they were all flat broke.

Greery had no notion exactly why his cushy little world had been invaded by displaced tartars and streams of god-botherers. He hadn't been to the Temple District since his old mum had died ten years ago and the only news he took an interest in was the results from the Fighting Pits. In all probability, if someone had paused to explain it to him, he was have considered it to be flaming stupid reason for all this inconvenience and would probably have stopped listening after less than a minute anyway.

As the clerics waddled closer he wandered into the middle of the road and said in his most commanding tone,

"You have reached the East Gate of Aberddu City, stand and state your business."

ABERDDU GUILD DISTRICT

As summer turns to autumn

"Why do you come here Elor?" screeched Erin, "Do you know what we do here? This is a Guild of merchant adventurers, not a temple." She was flailing widely, waving a sheaf of notes at the wizard, who was standing with his arms folded and his head tilted on one side, calmly watching her with pursed lips. "Why, in the name of all the Gods do you think we'd be interested in this?"

"Well, funny you should mention all the Gods," said Elor quietly in a tone that suggested he didn't think it was funny at all, "But it's actually in the name of all the Gods, the younger ones anyway, and the rest of us that we're doing this."

"What are you drivelling on about now?" demanded Severin butting in. Elor had noticed that he had assumed more and more authority in the Guild of late, and no one had challenged him. Elor had avoided the guild for several months after the last row and this time he was determined to keep his head. He had heard from Daisy, Mori and Pringle that there had been little interest displayed in anything other than the ongoing situation in Tartaria. Even the unfortunate and sudden death of Jason De Vere at the hands of a pack of redcaps had not stirred any real curiosity. The common consensus being that he probably had it coming.

Elor had originally despaired and then, having decided that despair was counterproductive, he put together a collection of incontrovertible evidence and research. It was this that Erin was currently waving at him. Severin snatched the sheaf of papers from the Guildmistress and began to leaf through the pages with a disdainful sneer on his face. It was quite clear he wasn't even reading the words, he was just trying to disparage them. Elor reached over and snatched them back.

"I realise that this isn't the most popular idea in the whole world," he said through gritted teeth, a very firm grasp on his temper, "particularly as none of us remember the last cataclysm and therefore can't swan about acting important and offering sage advice," he directed a pointed look at Severin who narrowed his eyes in return, "but if we don't stop this, there will be another cataclysm and it won't matter one iota what Salamander does because there's a significant chance none of us will know anything about it." To the Guild's credit, they had at least done Elor the courtesy of listening to this last announcement without interruption and when he finished there was a moment of absolute silence, the like of which had rarely ever occurred in the guild. Then, before everyone could start talking at once Severin opened his mouth and said spitefully,

"Oh please Elor, the Bards Guild's across the square." After that, the guild descended into babbling, squabbling chaos. Elor turned white and began to quiver with poorly-contained fury. He was just about to explode in a flurry of screaming and arm-waving when he felt a hand firmly on his shoulder. A soft voice in his ear said,

"Come on mate, let's go get a brandy."

Krieg steered the fuming wizard towards the door of the guild hall and into the courtyard. Elor, who was still quivering gently, was about to open his mouth to protest at this high-handed treatment when Krieg said firmly,

"Just hear me out Elor before you explode and then by all means shout as much as you like, and if then you're not too rude I'll buy you a brandy." Elor went swiftly from white to puce but held his tongue. "Do you know what an *indaba* is?" Elor, completely wrong-footed for a second by this seemingly irrelevant question, stammered for a moment as he searched his head for an answer and then said, "Er, isn't it the Tartarian word for an argument in a horse market?"

"Close," said Krieg smiling, he loved it when outlanders tried to explain Tartarian clan-speak, because the explanation nearly always involved something to do with a horse market. "It actually has two meanings. When the Clan Elders need to tell the clan something they invite all those of age to the *Indaba* tree to make a decision. They tell us things and we take the information and make of it what we will. Then, somehow, a decision is reached. It's chaotic for sure, but it's a living process. Beautiful in its way. It may not be how they do things in Albion or the Mages Guild, but it's served us well in Tartaria so far. They all listened to you, they're all talking about what you said, whether they like it or not – they are talking about it. That's what *indaba* means. You've planted the seeds, now let them grow." Krieg smiled broadly at Elor and gave his shoulder a reassuring squeeze. Elor's brain fought to process the words and deflated slightly. Weakly, he said the only thing he could think of, which was

"actually I'm from Paravel, and you've obviously never been into the Mages Guild." Looking up at the broad-shouldered man beside him, Elor wondered when exactly Krieg had gone from being the scrawny drunken youth to the chiselled colossus in front of him, with the bearing of a chieftain and the self-assurance of the ages. Krieg smiled at the mage but didn't say anything, he just let out an amused snort. He wasn't going to tell Elor the other meaning of *indaba* – a loud and disproportionate disagreement between drunks, that escalates far beyond its trivial starting point – usually over the disputes at the horse market. *He clapped* Elor on the back so hard that the slender wizard staggered slightly and said,

"Right, I promised you a brandy."

Left inside the Guild Hall, Daisy was contemplating hiding in the kitchen. The guild had exploded into a complex web of bickering and shrieking as everyone seemed to be disagreeing with everyone else. It was the kind of argument where people started arguing against people who they had previously been agreeing with and it showed no sign of abating. The Guild-mistress had initially tried to take control of the discussion but to no avail. The noise and temperature in the room were becoming unbearable and Daisy was starting to feel quite uncomfortable. Mori and Pringle had both dived head long into the argument in full-throated defence of Elor. Pringle was re-explaining the finer points of the champions armour to a group of sceptical clerics who couldn't understand why they hadn't heard about this from their temples. Mori was trapped in the corner with a snooty looking Paravelian by the name of Lord Ferrin de Andro who was explaining to her that people would take her more seriously if she didn't pay so much attention to 'that idiotic wizard', by whom Daisy assumed he meant Elor. Judging by the tight-lipped grimace on Mori's face she was trying to work out the best place to stick a knife. Daisy wondered where Krieg had gone with Elor, guessing it would probably involve a bar. She wished he had taken her too.

Iona climbed the guild steps with more than a little trepidation. She could hear the sounds of a heated exchange before she had even opened the towering wooden doors. Nearly a dozen voices seemed to be raised in cross-purposes, some of them angry, some of them merely overexcited. It was not a welcoming sound, particularly for Iona who had been putting off this night for several weeks.

It was sheer desperation that had dragged Iona to Adventurers Guild, nothing else. Having discovered to her horror that the Thieves and Assassins Guild had been recently, publicly and very fatally disbanded, she was left with very few options. Not without commercial skills, she had tried to market herself as a freelance hunter but not being local to the area she was little use as a scout or pathfinder and in any case she found work of that variety difficult to come by in the city. Eventually a kindly man at a vegetable cart had explained to her that business of that nature was conducted by the Guilds and very few people who were worth dealing with would hire outside of the Guild system. Iona had resisted. She had heard tales of the Adventurers Guild, she had been in enough alehouses. In fact, the tales of the Aberddu Adventurers Guild had stretched far and wide, becoming hearth yarns in the Middle Kingdoms and bardic epics as far afield as Tartaria. If the bards were to be believed, they were doers of great deeds, righters of great wrongs and drinkers of much ale. They had an uncanny knack for being the last people standing in the middle of a catastrophic and unholy mess, and most of them had been barred from every tavern in Baylis, Nedlund, Carthane and The Vale of Hahnn. It did not seem like the kind of life Iona had imagined when she had galloped out of the Oriental gates of the Celestial City. Even as she had rode the wagon train across the Galivara Plains she had hoped for something more stable; petty theft and a comfortable bed. It was apparently not to be and city life is expensive compared to rural existence. She had sold everything, even the gem she had been given, but she still did not have enough money to live. Cutting her loses, she moved out of the city into the woods to the east. Living rough was not beyond her and during the summer months could even be considered quite pleasant, but winter was fast approaching and she didn't fancy her chances alone against the Aberddu snows. The first morning she woke up shivering in the heavy dew she realised she had no choice, she would have to find work. In a city with such a vast free peasant populace there were very few available jobs. Freedom had a price and money meant work even if it was spending twelve hours a day on the docks up to your elbows in barrels of fish guts or walking the streets leading the pony that pulled the bone cart or the slurry truck. At last she had to concede that she had only two options and it was an unenviable choice: adventuring or prostitution. Adventuring had not been her first choice, but she couldn't even afford a skirt and the Dockland street-walkers scared her more than the idea of possibly having to save the world. With that in mind, she forced herself up to the top step and with her heart pounding in her ears pulled down on the heavy bell rope.

Nothing happened and Iona was forced to conclude that the

sound of the bell had gone unnoticed because of the noise. She was tempted to turn around and go back to the Docks when her stomach rumbled. Letting out a resigned snort she pulled the rope again, this time harder, and was gratified to hear a clanging sound somewhere behind the door. There was the definite sound of movement, the noise became louder and then quietened again as though someone had opened and closed an internal door and then at last, after what had felt like a lifetime the heavy door groaned and started to swing open. Iona hadn't planned what she would say when confronted with an actual person and had given no thought to what kind of reception she was expecting. It was probably just as well she hadn't wasted her time, because if she had she would never have thought of what actually happened. She was studying her feet out of embarrassment when the door finally opened and so didn't see who was standing there, she just heard a faintly familiar voice say,

"Oh it's you, I was wondering when you would show up."

Looking up, she found herself gazing into the smiling face of the man who had rescued her from the muggers outside the City gates. He had told her his name but that had been months ago and she couldn't even remember what letter it had started with. Totally taken aback by this greeting she stammered,

"Hello again," and looked back at her shoes.

"It's Pringle," said the jovial voice, clearly amused by her awkwardness. "As I doubt you remember and you never told me your name."

"Iona," mumbled Iona into her chest.

"Well Iona," said Pringle with poorly contained glee now, "I'm guessing you've either come to tell us to keep the noise down or you'd like to join the Guild." When Iona didn't respond, Pringle eased back on his exuberant tone and said more quietly, "in all seriousness, you've picked a bloody awful moment to join. There's quite a ding dong going on and the Guildmistress is apoplectic."

"Oh" muttered Iona, turning to leave. Whatever she had hoped would happen, being sent away like a child that had disturbed its father in the library was not it.

"Hang on," said Pringle, his tone changing again, this time it was gentler. "I was about to leave myself. Let me get my cloak and I'll fill you in on ... well, everything." With that, he ducked back inside the door and reappeared momentarily wearing a luxuriant looking brown velvet cloak trimmed with golden beads. Not in a position to object, Iona accepted the proffered elbow.

TARTARIA DRAGON LANDS

Around the autumnal equinox

Tian dismounted and raced to the motionless heap lying prone in the grass. Tears streaming down her face, she fell upon the bulky form and with all that was left of her strength she rolled it over praying silently that she would look down into an unfamiliar face. It was a false hope she knew, Jackal was an unmistakable horse and he wouldn't have stood over anyone else. Blinking furiously, so that her gaze was not smudged by tears she pressed her ear to Trell's chest, begging the fates and the Gods that something would let her know he was still alive. She lay with her head on the sticky fur of his armour far longer than the necessary few seconds that it took to ascertain that there was no breath and no heart beating. He was still warm, he was not long gone. With no thought for anything else she flung her arms around him, buried her face in his furs and began to sob.

The Chieftain rode out. Nursing the axe wound on his arm, he walked his horse carefully amongst the fallen. He hated these sickening moments of calm after the frenzy of battle, when you could not avoid counting the cost. He had seen Talvic's distinctive helm in the distance, presumably he at least had survived this most brutal onslaught. Kira and Leni had already brought in Banyan's body, and it had been laid out as peacefully as possible.

The chieftain had reflected sadly that the tired, kindly eyes of the Elder seemed to smile in death even more than they had in life. The Chieftain sighed, too many of these bodies were Dragon, and not nearly enough were the enemy. He had given up looking into the faces, he knew them all even if he could not remember names. It was with a certain degree of shame that he admitted to himself that he was in fact searching for only one face. It was not the face he saw first, it was the sleek black stallion.

Jackal remained perfectly still as Tian and the chieftain heaved Trell's body on to his back, every muscle and sinew taut. Then, with majestic pride in this final duty, the horse trotted carefully back to the command tent, Tian and the Chieftain riding either side of him. As they approached, the crowds around the base fell silent. They knew it had been a hard fight, no one had needed to tell them that. They were lucky to be alive, unlike so many. The chieftain and Indya had survived, there was still Clan, still hope. As they looked on Trell's lifeless back, the deep grief in the dark eyes of his beautiful horse was reflected in theirs. The Dragon Sword hung uselessly from his belt, no more use than a toothpick now. If Trell had gone perhaps it was the dead and not the living who were the lucky ones.

The body was taken into the back of the command tent behind the plain cloth screen, and laid beside Banyan. The shamans came to clean and tend it, as in stoic silence the warriors carried on collecting themselves together. They had been given until sunrise to surrender, retreat or face another attack. Retreat was the only option, surrender was unconscionable and they would not survive another attack. The chieftain slipped behind the screen for a moment of quiet with his trusted friends on the council. Without Banyan, he would not be able to navigate the subtle politics of keeping the can together, and without Trell, how would he convince the warriors to fight? He knew the self-doubt was fleeting and would pass with the night but it was here now.

He didn't register Indya's approach, in fact he didn't even notice the screen move. He knew nothing of her presence until she put a hand on his back. It was unusual for Indya to arrive anywhere so quietly or to remain so once she had but she had not risen to her revered position without a certain degree of empathy. She did not let the silence linger too long, she bent forward placed a hand on Trell's clammy forehead and muttered the ancient ancestral blessing. Then she straightened up, fixed the chieftain with eyes as hard as whetstone and said in a low but definite tone,

"Find Krieg."

ALENDRIA - TEMPLE OF AESTHETICS

The Sleep of the Sun

The sleep of the sun; an important time of introspection and self-regulation on the Aesthetics calendar. The start of this period is marked by an opulent ritual telling the story of the fall of the blossom and the dying days of summer – days of outward beauty and indulgence in the gifts of creation. The ritual is performed by thirteen priestesses, all young, lithe and exquisitely beautiful and watched by all the faithful who wished to welcome this time of deep, spiritual reflection. Twelve of the priestesses this year were slender, raven-haired fire elves. Their wild hair cascading over their shoulders and down to their waists, held back from their faces by only their delicately pointed ears. The thirteenth, the high priestess, was a white blond, grey-eyed cloud elf nearly a head taller than the others with almost translucent white skin. Fine blue veins coiled up her arms, on to her shoulders and around her long, elegant neck. Her hair was trusted in two bunches and braided with the tiniest blue flowers. Dressed only in folds of floor length white silk, belted at the waist to make simple, sleeveless robes, they were quite a breathtaking sight.

The sanctum was silent as the high priestess performed the ritual, then she climbed on to the dais. All eyes were on her. She opened her mouth and let out a note of almost heart-stopping purity. Then, holding them all spell-bound, she swooped up into the familiar melody of the blessing. She sung the old words, that they had heard year on year down the generations. Some of the congregation closed their eyes and let the beautiful music flow over them, others openly wept. Then, at the crescendo point, the twelve waiting priestess joined the song and began to dance, each one raising their arms above their heads. Then, from nowhere thousands of soft pink petals raining down on them all, showering them all with myriad gentle blossoms.

At this point the song changed to a minor key, as the sun began to set behind the ritualists, visible between the temple pillars. The congregation fell to their knees, heads bowed, each silently offering their inadequacies to their Goddess, promising that by the waking of the sun they would be a better, more balanced person. The priestesses danced out of the circle and started to weave between the congregation touching their heads and scattering more blossom over them.

The wind rose, imperceptibly at first, then a loud gust rushing through the sanctum rustling the carpet of petals. No one reacted, the ritual carried on. Then another, louder gust, that left an unusually icy chill hanging in the air. One or two of the congregation paused in their reverie to look out at the weather. Their attention was caught by the gathering storm clouds visible beyond the pillars. Their lingering attention drew others to look. The ritual paused; several people ran to the edge of the temple to look out at the blackening sky and the evil whorls forming on the horizon, moving fast towards them and laced with crackling bolts of lightning. The air rushing through the temple moved with a fractious urgency as though it were being chased. It was unlike any storm front anyone remembered in Alendria and living memory in an Elven kingdom such as this stretches back nearly a millennium.

Then as the storm arrived over the temple, hail pelting down, there was a deafening roll of thunder followed by an arching fork of blue- white lightening and an ear-piercing scream. The congregation spun around to find the high priestess lying prone on the dais stone, blood trickling from her ears and eyes. Standing over her were two translucent figures. One was a stunningly beautiful young woman, her perfect heart shaped face twisted in a shrieking grimace, her long honey blond hair whipping around her. The other was a dark angel nearly twice her height. It's face was shrouded in shadow, it's ragged wings spread wide and it's outstretched claws snatching for the woman. She screamed again, darted backwards and lashed out. A ribbon of white light flew out of her hand and the terrifying effigy recoiled momentarily. Then, from an unseen mouth, it let out a hideous rasping sound and dived forward. The woman ran into the middle of the congregation crying for help, drawing the creature with her. The worshippers scattered, unarmed and unsure who this woman was they were unwilling to intervene. Two of the priestesses took the opportunity to rush forward to their leader whose lifeless pleading eyes gazed back at them.

The dark angel lunged and snatched at the woman again, whose panic was pathetic to behold. She lashed out three or four more times with ribbons of white light, although they had less and less effect on the creature, who just seemed to be toying with her. The worshippers looked on in horror as with one final lazy swipe, it grabbed her with both claws and held her fast. At that moment, there was another fork of lightning and a thunderous roar and a man appeared. Human in appearance, he was dressed in a finely tailored black frock coat, breaches and knee boots, his collar and cuffs were crisp white cotton and his black hair was slicked straight back. His sneering face was strangely handsome in a way that either drew you to stare or forced you to look away. He fixed the struggling captive with a penetrating steely glare and curled his mouth into a cruel smile. When he spoke, his voice was a rich whisper that carried across the whole of the temple.

"Don't struggle," he said with disdain, "you cannot win against me."

Threateningly he leaned in, so that he was barely inches from her terrified face. "Do you know who I am?" All colour had drained from her cheeks, her lips were trembling, she did not answer. He shot out a leather-gloved hand, and grabbed her throat so that she could not speak even if she wanted to, "Do you know who I am?" he asked again, lowering his voice menacingly. At this point he turned his gaze on to the frozen, fearful crowd and smiled cruelly again. Without looking back at the woman, he squeezed her throat and she let out a gargling choking noise. "Well?" he demanded. "Do any of you know, as I crush the life out of your Goddess, who I am?"

The word Goddess jolted the gathered crowd into life, a number of them flung themselves towards the man trying to pull him away from the woman and were met with nothing but a derision and languid flicks of the man's hand. A shimmering screen of light appeared momentarily between him and the lunging faithful, causing them to cry out in pain and recoil from him. He laughed as he squeezed harder, his hand starting to burn into the woman's flesh. The faithful were now pressed helplessly against the forcefield, some were crying, some shouting. The woman's face drained to grey and her eyes rolled up in her head, she let out another rasping, gurgling noise as she gasped her last breaths. Her flesh started to fade, becoming transparent and crumbling. Kesoth let out a whooping laugh of exhilaration, as in a stream of flickering lights he drained the last elements of power from the Goddess and she let out a final strangled screech as she disappeared. Rounding on the worshippers, his eyes wild, his breath escalated, he said in a high pitched, sinister voice,

"I am the Betrayer, and you will ever more know who I am," before vanishing as swiftly as he had appeared.

News of what had happened in Alendria swept across the continent within hours and by the morning the once uneasy truce between faiths was strained beyond breaking point. All-out war was only a breath away. Lines were being drawn. On midwinter's night, an allegiance was formed and in the cold light of day a proclamation was posted in temples across the world, announcing the formation of the Dark Alliance. The Temples of Death, Chaos and Kesoth would stand together. They would work together against the other, softer, less powerful gods and against Krynok. They had seen an opportunity, the present instabilities provided a perfect route to power. That night, no one slept well.

ABERDDU CITY EAST GATE

A cold, dark morning

Greery stamped his feet and shoved his hands into his armpits. The brazier was guttering, so he shouted to the new private whose name he couldn't remember because he usually thought of him as 'the kid', to fetch some more logs and fill the water pan. If he was any judge, and after all his years on the gate he wasn't bad, it was more than an hour before dawn and if this rain got any heavier he probably wouldn't completely dry out again until the new year. The only thing to do was get the kid to brew up and huddle in the sentry box. It wasn't market day, so traffic would be light unless any more sodding god-botherers turned up. He must have let in nearly a hundred all told over the last week, and as yet none of them had passed back the other way. He only hoped they were leaving the city by the other gates, or else the Temple District would be fit to burst soon. The other lads had all been saying the same, knee deep in religious types, some of them heavily armoured and all of them looking grim. News of the God War had finally made it to Greery's ears but he hadn't paid it much attention, the only impact it had on him was all these bloody foreign clerics that wanted letting in. The kid arrived with an armful of wood and slopped water out of the pan in his other hand as he lumped the sticks into the brazier. Greery contemplated his pipe and decided that he would wait for the rain to ease a little bit. Then once the pan was safely on the fire, he sent the kid back into the store to find the tin with the lardy bread in it. If nothing else did, that would warm them up. Another fifteen minutes or so, and he'd slope off into the office to fill in the report for the last couple of hours and put his feet up for a while. Best make sure all was clear first though, thought Greery, heaving himself to the gantry to look out up the road.

It was quite a good view along the main road from the top platform, gave you an idea of what was on its way for nearly a mile and a half down, unless it was coming cross-country. Lifting the lantern high, he peered into the grubby blue night and his heart sank. Just under a mile away were two or maybe three figures mounted on horseback. Judging by the size and silhouette of the horses and the physique of the riders, coupled with the direction of their approach, Greery reckoned he had a pretty good idea of who those riders might be or at least where they had come from. He sagged and stood for a moment on the gantry, motionless. Then, the kid's reedy voice broke the silence of the night.

"Lardy Sarge," it yelled up the steps, "and the tea's nearly ready."

"Excellent," muttered Greery in response as he hitched up his oilskin cape and stumped down the ladder. "Just what we need before we get any more bloody tartars."

It was lighter when the mounted figures approached, although visibility was still poor. They had been moving at a slow walking pace and the riders looked weary, as though they had been in the saddle for a long time. Tartarian warhorses were famed for their intelligence and stamina and it was entirely possible that these riders had slept on horseback. Greery drew himself up to his full and not inconsiderable height and inflated his barrel-like chest. The driving rain spat and bounced off his cape and created rivulets down his pock-marked forehead and elephantine nose. He was an imposing sight to most people but tartars are not so easily cowed. This was another reason why Greery didn't like them. His stomach rumbled, the lardy had barely touched the sides. It was hopefully going to be breakfast time soon, just to deal with this lot first.

"This is the Aberddu East Gate," he boomed, "dismount and state your business."

The riders did as instructed and Greery was taken aback to find that whilst two of them were towering fur clad warriors, the third was a tiny, shrivelled woman with nearly a whole chicken's worth of feathers braided into her hair. She sprang down from her horse without a moment's pause.

"We seek Krieg Clan Dragon," announced one of the warriors in an over-loud voice. He too was used to having the physical advantage over people, as he tried to loom over Greery and found him looking him in the eye instead. Greery was not impressed. He had no idea who Krieg Clan Dragon was, but he was getting far too many house calls.

"Oh do you really?" he said in his favourite, dry derisive sneer. "How very nice for you, Tartar Town is that way." He jabbed a sausage-sized finger North. He noted with disgruntled irritation that it was now possible to see the edge of the ever-expanding shanty settlement that clung to the North Eastern walls of the city.

"We seek Krieg Clan Dragon, in the Adventurers Guild," restated the warrior, his over-loud voice edged with distaste at Greery's callous tone. "Not in... *Tartar Town*." He almost spat the words Tartar Town back at the guard. The Adventurers Guild, thought Greery with amused malice, of course; the home of all no-good, interfering, layabout, bounty-hunting, bleeding-heart, useless scum. Worse than the temples for attracting the wrong sort to the city and performing little in the way of useful service. Admittedly Greery didn't know what the Adventurers Guild *did* do, but seeing as they didn't make or sell anything and spent a lot of time apologising to the temples and the Militia, they couldn't be that important. He had been to see a number of the Bard's Guild epics about their so-called exploits but he was well aware how theatrical types tended to embellish things.

"The Adventurers Guild?" he said, adopting the same tone as law-men worldwide who have decided to play things 'by the book', specifically the book that contains the instructions on how to be as unhelpful and unfriendly as possible whilst not actually breaking any rules, laws or guidelines on conduct. "The Aberddu Adventurers Guild? I see. Well, I'm afraid in order for you to be admitted to the city, I need to see, in writing, an invitation from Mr Clan Dragon," Greery knew full-well that the term 'mister' was *never* applied to a tartar, "stating your names and that he is prepared to take full responsibility for you whilst you are guests in our fair city."

The warrior's eyes glazed over and his mouth opened to retort but no words were forthcoming. His companion, who until now had not moved let alone spoken, discretely placed a hand on his sword hilt and shifted his weight so that he was in combat stance. Greery grinned. They really were as dumb as they looked, murder a gate guard in Aberddu and you'd be dancing your last polka before the next sunset. The open-mouthed warrior met Greery's gaze and recognising the predatory leer, closed his mouth. The other didn't budge. They had reached a stand-off

At this point there was a rattling cough like silt unclogging from a downpipe and the tiny woman stepped forward. She barely reached Greery's chest, but she stood with her head craned back so she could see his face. Two sharp black eyes peered out from amid the weathered creases and locked on to his and he felt a cold shiver dance down his spine. The wind had whipped up as the woman had stepped forward and the driving rain seemed to sting more as it pelted his raw skin.

"Listen carefully," said the woman in a quiet but dangerous voice, "because this is important." Greery obeyed, for all his ignorance he was not stupid. The wind was beginning to whistle and whoop now as it spun around them. "I am Indya, Shaman of the Dragon and I seek Krieg, who is in your city's Adventurers Guild. You will let us in." Greery opened his mouth to retort but found no words. Although he didn't argue, he also didn't move. The woman paused, took a step back and waited. When Greery failed to act after a minute, she opened her mouth and in a voice that bounced back off the massive wooden gate behind him and echoed around Greery's head, bellowed the word

"NOW!" Greery found himself with no choice, the power of the word would not let him disobey, he thumped the gate and shouted to the kid to open one side. The three tartars climbed back into their saddles and still spellbound, Greery stood aside and let them trot up to the gate as it creaked open. The two warriors did not even make eye contact as they rode passed but the woman paused. She beckoned to Greery with a claw-like hand and once more he had no choice but to obey. She leaned down close to his ear and in a rasping tone whispered,

"Learn from today. Tartars are not simple tribes-folk to be corralled like cattle, we are proud and we are strong, and you underestimate us at your peril." Greery found himself nodding, still unable to articulate his thoughts into speech, as she eased her horse forward through the gate.

As he watched the three tartars disappear down the road into the city, and the gate swung closed Greery was left shaking his head and wondering what had just happened. The blue of the night was paling into a dismal, chilly morning and his stomach growled. Best he could tell, the temple six bells hadn't chimed yet. It was going to be a tricky day by the look of it, best get the kid to do breakfast quickly while he filled in the ledger with 'three admitted on horseback'.

IV

1102AC

As the residents of Aberddu woke on the first day of the new year, 1102 AC, they felt no different than they had any other morning except possibly a little more delicate thanks to the previous night's revelry. As they hauled themselves from their beds and dragged themselves about their business, they were scarcely aware of the significance of the year ahead. Even the adventurers could not have predicted the enormity of what would come. Like rats in a maze they chased about, feverishly trying to escape from the turmoil they had found themselves in. They tried to fix things, but like someone trying to plug the holes in a rapidly disintegrating dam with their fingers, they were fast running out of hands. Unfortunately, they were so concerned with keeping their feet dry, they hadn't yet noticed that the dam was about to burst.

In the wake of the declaration of the Dark Alliance, the other temples started to band together. Law, Amroth and Life stood tentatively shoulder to shoulder against their opposite numbers. Others, like the Sea God and the Celestial Flame declared themselves neutral. It seemed that instead of uniting against the All-Father and his children the younger Gods, or at least their mortal followers, were preparing to pit their strength against each other in an almighty power grab.

ABERDDU CITY NORTH GATE

An overcast morning

It was easy to see from Daisy's swollen face and blood shot eyes that she had been crying. Mori didn't say anything, she just nodded in greeting and the pair proceeded out of the North Gate as they did every day when they could. When they had first started to go to their shrine in the woods, they had chattered happily on the walk there and walked back in glorious, reflective silence. Since they had taken on the task of trying to unite the champion items, they had had much to discuss and the walk to the shrine had become valuable time for private conversations. However, since the Temple District had factionalised and tensions had risen, it was difficult to pretend that nothing had changed. There had been several sullen, silent walks to the shrine since the end of the previous year, the dismal weather had not helped matters.

Mori was well aware that Daisy had found the upheaval of the recent months tricky to deal with, not least because of the sudden departure of Krieg. The first couple of times the dwarf had dissolved into tears over it all Mori had been sympathetic, if not actually understanding. It wasn't that she didn't miss Krieg, it was more than she couldn't see the point in crying over it. However, he had gone nearly a month ago and Daisy still kept weeping. It was becoming very wearing and Mori had taken to ignoring it. The only problem was, it became impossible to hold a conversation whilst you were pretending that your companion wasn't crying. This had definitely made walking to the shrine less of a joy. Pulling her cloak around herself, Mori shivered. She wouldn't be sorry to see the back of this winter, she couldn't remember the last time she had felt properly warm, the cold and damp seemed to somehow penetrate everything this year.

As they rounded the bend in the track that approached the shrine, it was obvious even from this distance that all was not well. It had been nearly a week since they had been able to get up here, and in that time the shrine had been desecrated. The statue of Ankhere was missing completely, and the Crone had been roughly decapitated so that the fragments of the body were scattered over the ground and her upturned face gazed at the priestesses with wide, sorrowful eyes. Daisy burst into tears and dropped to her knees, lifting the white stone head gently in her cupped hands. Mori stood back for a moment, scanning the area but there were no clear tracks or any other indicators of who had been here.

Nothing. They seemed to be completely alone, but she didn't drop her guard as she could easily be mistaken.

"Who would have done this?" stammered Daisy, collapsing into the damp grass, tears running down her face. Mori let out a low, cynical laugh. She knew exactly who it was. Not names or faces perhaps, but she knew.

"Can't you think of anyone?" she said in a slightly incredulous voice. "Can you really think of no one?" She let out an almost silent snort of poorly concealed disdain. Daisy's naivety was starting to grate on her fraying nerves.

"Well, Mother Angelina did say something about Hecate cultists in the area, rampaging," sniffed the dwarf sitting up and looking Mori full in the face. "It seems like the sort of thing they might do."

"Hecate cultists?" said Mori sourly. Admittedly, she had her own problems with the beliefs and practises of the Hecate cultists, but she was equally irritated by the way Daisy had implied it was clearly the doing of the Dark Alliance. "Hecate cultists?" she repeated dangerously slowly, "so it couldn't possibly have been anyone else could it?" Daisy didn't hear the edge of accusation in Mori's tone.

"Well no," snivelled the dwarf, sitting up in the grass, cradling the statue head to her chest. "it couldn't have been, could it." Mori rounded on her, anger flickering across her dark eyes.

"So the bright and shining paladins of Life have never desecrated a shrine I suppose," she said quietly.

"Well no," said Daisy innocently, so wrapped up in the agony of events that she still had not picked up on the aggression in Mori's voice. Mori went from poorly-concealed sarcasm to searing derision as she lost her grip on her temper.

"Oh really," she hissed. "Really? Is *that* what they've been telling you in that temple of yours? What do you think the Paladins do with those great big shining swords they ponce about with then, trim the hedge?" Daisy was speechless, she was used to gentle mockery and even poorly concealed irritation from Mori, but she had never been spoken to like this before.

"Er, er," stammered Daisy, tears falling thick and fast and a stream of mucus snaking from her little red nose. "They aren't for desecrating shrines, they're for smiting Godless unbelievers, the unholy, the undead and those which must be returned to the demonic Pit." She reeled off this line of dogma without really listening to what she was saying as she had done so many times before.

"Exactly," hissed Mori, "and who do you think those Godless unbelievers are?" Her dark eyes were narrowed and blazing as she leaned in towards Daisy's flushed and grimy face, "Just exactly who do you think they are?"

"Er," wailed Daisy, snottily, "I don't know, Kesothians I guess?" Mori let out a derisive grunt.

"Kesothians?" she sneered, "and the rest of the Dark Alliance, Daisy are you really that foolish? They mean all of us, Kesothians, Chaos-followers and Death followers," These words were like a slap in the face to Daisy who stopped snivelling and gaped at her friend. "They mean Death worshippers. They mean me." Some people would have shouted these words but Mori spoke them in a threatening whisper. Daisy could no longer contain herself, she let out another self- indulgent howl and fell forward. Mori snorted. Usually, she was more tolerant of Daisy's melodramatic traumas, but not today. She turned around, folded her arms and then suddenly found herself striding away. She hadn't meant to walk away from the shrine and Daisy, but as she started moving back to the path she found herself picking up her pace until she was running across the forest floor, desperate to put distance between herself and everything. She kept moving until she could no longer hear Daisy's pathetic yowling and then she stopped by a tree and sank down into a squat, her head in her hands. She couldn't think straight any more, her head was ringing with turmoil. She could imagine exactly what dogmatic propaganda Daisy was being fed in her temple, it was almost certainly the same as the rubbish being spewed by the Hecate cult that ruled the City Death Temple, except the Life Temple tended to pretend that they were doing it for merciful, self- sacrificing and highly moral reasons instead of just because they liked it. Mori had distanced herself from her own temple for that very reason, but she couldn't seem to make Daisy understand that she needed to decide what she wanted – the security blanket of a well-established institution or the uncertainty of this new renegade faith. She didn't even know what Daisy really believed. They had talked about it, the cycle of Life and Death, the similarity of their beliefs and they had prayed together for a long time now. Mori had only felt stronger for it but she couldn't answer for Daisy.

ABERDDU CITY TEMPLE DISTRICT

A snowy afternoon

Tollie knew the thin end of a wedge when he saw one and as he watched the mustering clerics in the Temple Square, he recognised the very thin edge of what was likely to be a gigantic wedge. He paused for a moment to take in the growing numbers of well-armed men and women stamping their feet in the slush, gathered around braziers trying to fight off the chill. Then he sighed and ducked down an alley way. Sylas was waiting for him somewhere around the back of the Aesthetics' Temple, which had become one of the safest places in the city to conduct unorthodox or illegal business since what Tollie thought of as 'the unfortunate incident' about six weeks earlier.

'Unfortunate incident' was a masterful understatement for the death of one deity at the hands of another, but really as far as Tollie was concerned, the biggest misfortune was that in the following hysteria the whole Sisterhood of Lucinda – a cult of charming and vital young priestesses who had a tendency to wear translucent silk robes – had committed very elegant suicide by poison in the inner sanctum. As far as the religion went he could take or leave it, but he had enjoyed the spectacle of the Sisters on their high-day. The whole cult of Aesthetic were, Tollie felt, ever so slightly limp and useless. Seekers of inner peace, tranquillity and beauty were not, in general, inclined to put up much of fight and neither was their Goddess. It was that that had made her such an easy target, Tollie supposed. Far from bristling with vengeance-seeking paladins prepared to fight to death and beyond to get their Goddess back, the temple was all but empty. Only a few lone believers haunted its dark corners, deep in meditation trying to seek out the answers.

As he stepped into the narrow passage that ran along the back of the temple, he could see Sylas slumped against the back wall, picking his nose. A glorious and ironic juxtaposition to the previous life of this grand building thought Tollie as he scuttled forward through the icy muck. As he got nearer, he could see from Sylas' body language and the part of his face that was visible among the shadows, that it was not good news.

"No joy," croaked Sylas, hoarsely as he looked up to check the approaching sound was Tollie and not someone coming to attempt to mug him. "He wasn't interested. He threw me out." Absently, Sylas rubbed his elbow and grimaced. Tollie could see he was soaking wet and shivering. "Miserable bastard, so much for Guild loyalty."

"Guild loyalty?" grunted Tollie, "I think that might be stretching it a bit. Guild loyalty doesn't usually extend past the lifetime of the Guild."

"Yeah, well," grumbled Sylas, clearly still put out by his reception. "Although now you mention it, I'd never thought of the Guild."

"Well, it's a bit late seeing as you've just pointed out the Guildfolded," grumped Sylas turning away from Tollie, his bottom lip stuck out like a spoilt child denied sweets.

"I wasn't thinking of that Guild," smirked Tollie, never able to take Sylas' sulking seriously. "What day is it?"

Whilst it was true that the Adventurers Guild of Aberddu was open for business at any hour of the day or night via that heavy rope bell-pull in the court yard if the main door was locked, you were better off calling on week days between midday and the evening ten-hour. The door tended to be open between these hours, and someone would most likely be around even if it was only the somewhat surly cook who could take a message and then fail to pass it on. However, it was a well-recognised fact that if you actually wanted to talk to a significant number of Guild members all at the same time then you had to go down to the guildhouse on a Thursday evening. Quite often, there would be enough of them there, sober and raring to go, to solve two or three world threatening problems or alternatively half a dozen minor crises. Tollie didn't even need them to deal with a small inconvenience, he just wanted some information and given their propensity for being the biggest gossips in town they were probably the best people to ask.

Tollie and Sylas had taken up with the Adventurers Guild when they had felt the winds of change rustling through the safe haven of the Thieves and Assassins Guild and had had a fairly illustrious career. They hadn't exactly mended their ways, but were now being far more cautious about when, where and how they plied their usual trades. The bottom had all but fallen out of the fake religious accoutrements market mainly because of a militia crackdown. The medicine man routine wasn't going work in the city, there was far too much access to temple healing and Tollie had spotted that snotty Law paladin in the Temple Square a couple of weeks ago in any case. Besides which, Sylas was currently refusing to do anything that involved him wearing a dress. This had left them with the trade in information and given the current climate, the only people who were prepared to pay good money for knowledge were Dark Alliance clerics. Tollie had to admit that Brother Nathaniel gave him the creeps, but dealing with him was a better alternative than starving slowly to death although Tollie mused, Brother Nathaniel in his role as Master Pardoner of the Death Temple might not see it that way. He had given them quite an intriguing poser some days ago and so far they had failed to get any information at all. They had tried nearly everyone they could find who had survived the end of the old Guild and several other sources but now they had been reduced to asking the Adventurers. This was probably going to cost them dearly, and very likely more than just money.

The snow had turned a watery muddy brown under foot but the angry clouds looked like it wouldn't be long before they covered it with a fresh white top-coat. Sylas was still sulking by the time they had tramped across the city to the Guild District. He had tucked his hands firmly into his armpits so that wrapped in his heavy cloak he looked like a woolly cone waddling down the road only his head and feet visible, poking out from either end. His ears and nose were red with cold and his scraggy hair was plastered against his face. He looked thoroughly bedraggled. Beside him, Tollie, with a fur lined hunting cap jammed over his ears and a heavy coat clasped around him looked only marginally less ridiculous as his breath misted out from beneath the peak of the hat.

The Guild Square was a hive of activity just before the evening six bell, and even though it was already dark, people were scurrying to and fro looking business-like and stern. An officious-looking man with a large leather portfolio darted in front of them and disappeared through a narrow wooden gate labelled 'Scribes and Cartographers Guild, Aberddu, for service enquire within' without so much as a nod of greeting. Judging by the noise issuing from the open door of the Bards Guild, someone was juggling a toad, a kitten and a Paravelian battle horn, possibly on purpose. The racket mingled with the staccato barks of the Warriors Guild drill master conducting evening training and the sounds of a raucous auction taking place in the Merchants Guild. The Adventurers Guild was set a little back from the main thoroughfare, beside the vacant plot that had previously contained the now defunct Bakers Guild. It was surrounded by a tumbledown-looking brick wall, the majority of which ran ten feet high around a courtyard and attached itself on to the unprepossessing Guild building at each end. In the middle of this weary-looking wall was a large wooden gate, which looked as though it had been left ajar deliberately to keep the gateway lintel from falling down. There was a hand-painted sign nailed to it that read: Aberddu Adventurers Guild, enquire within, in case of emergency ring bell. There was a crooked arrow that indicated a grubby rope hanging a couple of feet away. The words "ring bell' had been scratched out twice and replaced with sentiments that had been blacked out, then the words had been repainted in different hands over the top of the black paint. Tollie saw the sign and snorted with amusement. Sylas just shoved passed him and through the gap in the gate.

There was no drama taking place in the desolate courtyard outside the Adventurers Guild tonight, although there was a very well-trodden path through the snow from the gate to the front steps, and a slight less well-used one around the side to the stable block and privies It was strangely quiet as they approached the main doors. Usually at this time on a Thursday night there was a spirited argument or a fight, or on one memorable and terrifying occasion a sing-song, going on. Tonight, there was barely the low rumble of conversation.

As he climbed the steps, Tollie conceded it was perhaps a little early for the bulk of the adventurers, many of whom didn't rise until noon and considered the six-hour to be basically lunch time. It was okay, they could probably cadge some food and wait in the warm for a couple of hours. It wasn't as though they had anything better to do tonight anyway.

Several hours later, Tollie was sitting against the chimney wall yawning. Sylas was curled up on the hearth snoring, under one of the coarse blankets that one of the orderlies had brought in half way through the evening. It had probably been liberated from a stable somewhere if the smell was any indication. There weren't yet ten people in the Guild room and that had been the situation all evening. According to the Guildmistress, numbers had been thin on the ground since Mid-winter because most of the religious guild members had not returned from temples after the turn of the year.

The Guildmistress was a woman that Tollie couldn't quite fathom, mainly because she seemed to be neither completely charmed by his sense of humour nor displaying any violent intent towards him, which were the two most common responses he got from women. She just treated him with a chilly but not impolite business-like indifference that Sylas found highly funny. When Tollie had asked her why she thought they hadn't come back, she fixed him with a stare that could have curdled milk and said quietly,

"Oh, I can't imagine." She had then excused herself and stalked out of the main hall in the direction of her office. She hadn't reappeared for more than two minutes at a time since, and Tollie got the distinct impression from her carriage and demeanour on her last reappearance that she had been drinking. Not being regular attendees at Guild meetings, Tollie and Sylas were not over familiar with many of the current Guild members. They only really knew the more outspoken ones and of course those who had had dual membership with the 'other Guild'. The more outspoken Guild members tended to be religious types and to a body they weren't there, not even Pringle – who Tollie and Sylas couldn't really imagine taking sides in anything more complex or important than a bout of arm-wrestling. Lord Ferrin had been in briefly, but had left at pace via one of the side doors when a sour-face young elven woman arrived stalked in with her hair pulled tightly back from her face and her arms knotted firmly across her chest. There were two fresh-faced warriors sitting on a straight-backed settle to one side of the fireplace both of them looking down at their suspiciously new-looking boots. Opposite them in an armchair, sat a young wizard with a slight overbite and an impressive widow's peak for his age. He was reading a heavy leather-bound tome entitled 'The Arts of Elemental Manipulation'. He coughed twice but didn't speak. The only person they had had any kind of entertaining exchange with was Ellidahl Beauchamp, who claimed to be a bard but actually worked a handful of low-lit taverns in the Trade District in a badly fitting blonde wig and a threadbare, low-cut bodice. She at least was pleased to see them, albeit with a professionally glossy smile and was happy to chat. However, chit- chat about the new trade in the market was not what Tollie had come to the guild for. Eventually, she decided she would have a much more lucrative evening down at The Scholar's Vault, particularly as there was a trade caravan in from Jaffria that would have just been paid.

It was a little after the ten-hour when the door creaked open theatrically and Tollie jolted awake. The fire had warmed him into a soporific daze, and he'd let his head loll. Elor was standing in the doorway looking about him with a slightly disgusted expression.

"Geratti," he snapped, addressing the young wizard with the book, "I would appreciate it if you didn't disappear without leaving a note and without asking if you may help yourself to my books." The young wizard snapped the book shut and sprung to his feet, tucking the tome hastily under his arm as he did so.

"Er, sorry Professor," he stuttered, a deep crimson flush rising to his soft cheeks. Then, turning to the room in general, Elor exclaimed,

"Where in the name of all that's holy has everyone got to?" It was at this point that a bitter laugh cut the silence and from behind Elor the Guildmistress said,

"That's a particularly fortuitous choice of words, Elor." Elor spun around. His countenance snapped immediately from teacherly disapproval to carefully calculated civility.

"Good Evening Erin," he said somewhat tight-lipped as he stepped aside to let her sway through the door.

"They are," she continued, ignoring Elor's courtly courtesy, "as you so rightly have said, busy with pursuits in the name of all that is holy. They have abandoned us for their temples." As she said this, she wobbled dangerously and Elor shot out a hand to steady her. Angrily she snatched herself back from his grip and tottered into the wall. "They have decided that their Gods mean more to them than their fellow Guild members. We are nothing now. Look," she gestured wildly at the room, causing herself to stagger sideways. Elor, his kindness having been shunned once, stepped back and allowed her to fall into a chair beside the door. "The Adventurers Guild of Aberddu is nothing," screeched Erin from her ignominious perch.

"Actually, Erin," said Elor firmly, "I disagree."

"Oh, imagine my surprise," slurred Erin in reply, "Imagine my shock, you disagree with me! Wasn't it you that said we should be tackling the warring Gods? Weren't you in here not even a year ago, screaming at me that we should ignore Salamander and go hunting for some champion? Well, now they have and they are and you should be satisfied,"

Elor had listened to this tirade largely open-mouthed, and then before Erin could continue any further bellowed,

"Madam, will you be quiet." Erin was so shocked by this outburst that she shut her mouth and glared at him, purely because she couldn't work out what else to do. "I'd actually come to talk to you about Salamander, but it seems I am going to be disappointed."

"Salamander," shrieked Erin, trying to stand up and failing. "Salamander? You have the front to walk into this Guild and tell me that you think we should do something about Salamander?" She let out a high-pitch derisive cackle. "You're too late, you've already sent them off to solve their little God crisis, and this is what's left!"

"Madam, would you *please* stop shrieking," said Elor as calmly as he could over the sound of Erin continuing to harangue him.

"No I will not," she carried on, "I will not stop shrieking. Look at my Guild? Look at what it's become? Four hundred years of heritage gone. It's only a matter of time before the City disband us. Because of your God War,"

"My God War?" interjected Elor, raising his voice for the first time, "You're blaming me for the God War?"

Erin did even pause to hear him. "I hope you're proud of yourself," she was screaming, as she hauled herself to standing by grabbing hold of the Guild Banner that was hanging from the wall behind her seat, "You've destroyed us."

At this point, Elor looked around and found that the other people in the room were all gaping at them and that the two fresh-faced warriors had got uncertainly to their feet. They were clearly unused to guild histrionics. Elor decided it was probably politic at this point not to say anything but it didn't help. Erin began to howl uncontrollably, letting out a string of obscenities directed mainly but not entirely at Elor. She then with one final painful yell, yanked the Guild Banner from its hooks, flung it at Elor knocking him to the ground and flounced from the room.

The mesmerism that had frozen the others in place broke and they all acted at once. The wizard called Geratti dropped his tome with a resounding thud and dived forward to try to extract Elor. The warriors sheathed their weapons and one of them strode purposefully out of the hall door after Erin. Judging by the sound of the heavy oak front door banging a few moments later he had gone straight out of the building. The other one paused for a moment and looked on as Tollie and Sylas burst into a flooding fit of laughter that they had been poorly containing during the row.

Elor, beneath his heavy canvas shroud lay perfectly still. Geratti, who obviously had no idea about the real world, was dancing around the edge of the banner trying to lift it up and failing. A substantial piece of canvas is quite a weight for anyone, let alone scrawny book- learnt noble. From the wobbling of his flabby face, he was either convinced that Elor was dead or severely maimed, or he was fighting off the world's most enormous sneeze. Either way the young warrior, a local lad a farming family in Welton Henry on Ddu, took pity on him. He walked over with the soft, strong gait of the unflappable working man and set about taking quiet charge of the agitated wizard and the large banner. Tollie and Sylas tried to stand up to help him, but gave up. They merely collapsed on to the floor again, arms folded across their stomachs, silent tears of mirth running down their faces now laughing at each other's hysteria.

After a minute or so of extremely patient direction, the warrior and the wizard managed to peel back the banner to reveal Elor lying flat on his back on the floor, stock-still with an enigmatic half-smile on his otherwise blank face. Geratti rushed forward to help him up, caught his feet in the folds on the edge of the banner and ended up sprawled face first on to the floor beside his motionless mentor. Elor didn't react to his pupil hitting the floor, he just continued to gaze up at the ceiling with the same expression, a little as though he were reading a very gripping piece of slightly racy poetry. At this point, the warrior, whose name was Derek Peterson, held out a firm if somewhat unwashed hand which Elor completely ignored. He simply let out a low-pitched grunt of sudden realisation, scrambled to his feet and hurried out of the room. Geratti, lying in a heap on the banner groaned and accepted Derek's hand.

TARTARIA DRAGON LANDS

A bright chill morning

Looking up at Krieg, where he stood on the rock in front of the *Indaba* tree, Tian felt small. It was strange to think that not two years ago Krieg had been, well that was the thing, she didn't know how she would have described what Krieg had been. A joke? Second-fiddle? Overshadowed? None of it was flattering. She had always loved him but even she had thought of Trell as the better brother and not just because he was the oldest. Trell was strong, dependable, a vast, comforting presence in the clan. His death had left a huge void amongst them. When Indya had sent for Krieg, Tian couldn't help feeling that this would be the wrong thing to do. She had feared that Krieg would return from the city changed, weakened by comfortable living and trivial concerns and the stark comparisons between him and Trell would be even more noticeable.

She had been right about one thing: Krieg had changed. He was barely recognisable except for the deep brown eyes - they were still Krieg's, gazing out of the sharp, weathered face with the same laughing kindness they had always had. The rest however was quite a shock. He seemed nearly a head and a half taller, and two feet wider. Balanced above the mustering clan, there was no doubt he was a presence in his own right. No one even whispered

Trell's name, not even in comparison. Beside him, the chieftain in his impressive martial furs and Indya, her hair dressed with lime and adorned with the wings of a Hawk, seemed tiny. Had it not been for the carved wooden dragon that Tian could see hanging just inside his tunic, Tian would have wondered if it was him at all.

Even the children had been brought to this *Indaba* which was unusual, but Indya and the Chieftain had both agreed with Krieg that this was too important to exclude anybody at all. It brought a lump to Krieg's throat as he became aware of exactly how few Dragon were left. Once, not so long ago, the gathering around the tree had stretched from the rock to the river. Now, they barely spread a hundred yards across. Many would have looked out on that meagre gathering and felt the sinking sorrow of defeat. That was how Salamander had won so many, by the tireless attrition of numbers and spirit. Even Leviathan were falling they said, but not the Dragon. Better they were all dead and the Dragon was no longer than it was subsumed by Salamander. That was worse than death, that was defeat. As he cleared his throat, Krieg was grateful for the wise words of his brother. The road did indeed go both ways.

"Dragon," he said and even though he had spoken the word softly, it had carried out across the gathering and they all turned to look and listen. "There is something to decide upon and it is so important we have invited all of you to hear and, if you so wish, speak your piece."

ABERDDU CITY

A passage in the Trade District - a damp evening

"Why should I?" demanded Iona. It wasn't a childish retort, it was an honest question and she fixed Pringle with an icy glare that actually made him shiver.

"Because I'm asking you to," replied Pringle with a smile that was just on the greasy side of charming.

"And that's supposed to be enough motivation to make me put my life in danger is it?" retorted Iona folding her arms and raising her eyebrows. She wasn't smiling, Pringle caved.

"Look," he said quietly, fixing Iona with the first genuine expression she had probably ever seen on his gaunt face. "It's really important, on a vast scale. A world shattering scale." Even in the murkiness, Iona could see the poorly concealed fear in Pringle's eyes. His grin had become a worried grimace and she could see he was trembling. Looking away, determined not to let him know that his distress had had an effect on her, she swallowed hard and before she could stop herself found herself muttering,

"I'll think about it." She closed her eyes and exhaled. Why had she given even the slightest hint she was prepared to help him or that she cared what happened to him? Glancing back at Pringle for a moment she could see the relief in his posture.

"Thank you," he said softly, and brushed her arm with his hand. Iona looked back down at her feet, determined not to meet his eye and let him know she had tingled under his touch.

"I'm not promising I'll do it," she muttered, aware that her cheeks were flushing. Then, without another word, she turned and strode away.

She knew he hadn't moved, she couldn't hear him splashing down the alley in the opposite direction, but she refused to let herself look back. As she ducked down a narrow passage that led directly to Fisher's Bridge her mind was so full of the exchange that had just taken place that she was paying no attention at all to her surroundings. She was just listening intently to the inside of her head as it buzzed with questions. The primary one was why exactly Pringle thought she was the best person to wander into the Kesoth Temple, a building she had previously not even set foot in, and steal, or at very least attempt to steal, a sacred relic. She would have assumed it was because Pringle considered her a disposable resource up until the point he had touched her arm. She scolded herself. Make someone think you care about them and they'll do anything you like. That was the oldest trick in the book, a book that she was fairly certain Pringle had read cover to cover, memorised and was probably writing a sequel for. Hot prickling spots of embarrassment appeared on her cheeks as she started to chide herself for letting her guard down. She didn't notice the stranger as he stepped into her path. In fact, in her daze, Iona almost walked straight into him.

Iona let out a squeal of surprise and tried to dart back from the man as she almost collided with him, fumbling at her waist for her knife before she'd even looked up. The man didn't move, he just let out a slightly cruel chuckle. She tried to duck backwards to make a rapid retreat but the man shot out an arm with surprising speed, clamped a vice like hand around the top of her arm and yanked her back towards him. Like lightening her other hand shot to another knife, this one concealed in the top of her boot, which she had raised under the man's chin before he had a moment to react. He didn't let her go as she'd hoped, he just let out another sinister laugh and her knife turned to ash in her hand.

Startled and terrified, Iona let slip a strangled whimper and made a grab for yet another knife, this one a small stiletto blade in a tasteful, discrete thigh strap. Anticipating this, he seized hold of her other wrist and raised her arm.

"Oh dear me," he said with an unctuous smirk, "you are a fiery one." Iona spat at him but the glob of saliva froze in mid-air and dropped to the floor where it shattered. The man's expression didn't change. "That was uncalled for," he said emotionless, bringing Iona's second arm upwards so that he held both her wrists above her head, putting her in a considerable amount of pain. "We don't want any unpleasantness." As he said this, Iona felt her muscles lock, momentarily paralysing her. "Now, listen."

Forced into such drastic submission, Iona looked at the stranger for the first time. He was a little taller than Pringle, and broader. He was dressed in a double-breasted black silk frock coat, with expensive golden buttons. The whitest neck cloth Iona had ever seen was visible inside the collar of the coat. Above this was a face that was at once both the most beautiful and terrifying thing Iona had ever laid eyes on. It was almost, but not quite, the image of perfection: smooth, heart-shaped and just strong enough to not be feminine. The eyes that looked down on her were sparkling icy blue and had a slight hint of mischief hiding in them. They seemed oddly familiar but at that moment she just couldn't place them. His hair, a rich reddish-brown, curved around his cheeks and ears, although the majority of it had been pulled back into a ribboned tail. The lips, which drew Iona's gaze almost as powerfully as the eyes, were soft, pink and curled into a dangerous smile. Perhaps the most disturbing element of the whole apparition, because Iona was beginning to doubt that this was a mortal man, was the scent that coiled up from him. Usually the foetid smell of stagnating mud and effluent clung so tightly to the nose that one no longer really smelt much at all, but Iona could smell a sweet, spicy musk that permeated the air. It was heady and alluring and completely unlike anything else Iona had smelt before, even in the East. She stopped fighting against the paralysis in her muscles. He clearly wasn't the usual kind of street scum that went mugging in the Trade District back alleys - if he'd wanted to kill her, she would be dead already. He must have felt her relax because he let go of her wrists and as he did so her muscles unlocked and she staggered backwards as her arms dropped under their own weight. She didn't know what to say or do next, she just stood looking down at her feet not wanting to meet those eyes again. There was a moment of silence then a strong but surprisingly soft hand lifted her chin so that she had no choice. The eyes danced and she saw nothing else as the stranger said in a low whisper.

"I know what you are about to do, and I can help you."

ABERDDU TEMPLE DISTRICT

Early in the spring

"She's gone," murmured Mori, dropping down on to the Life Temple steps sadly, her whole face sagged with defeated despair. Pringle slumped down beside her, there was not even enough spirit left in him to swear.

"Well," he said after a moment, starting a sentence he did not yet know how to finish. Mori just looked at him, and he shut his mouth.

"There's nothing we can do," continued Mori in a tone so low it was barely audible, "If she's made her choice, and she's gone with the crusade then there's nothing we can do." Mori closed her eyes slowly and swallowed. Pringle knew that for most people there would have been tears now, but Mori didn't cry like that.

"So," said Pringle, wondering if he would manage to get to the end of his sentence this time. "So," he hoped the second run up would lead to more words. It didn't.

"So," said Mori, picking up his false start without humour, "so, it's just us now." Pringle nodded heavily. It seemed like an incredible journey, from gods' knew where he had come from to here. Sitting on the steps of an almost empty Life Temple with a dark elf Death priestess who thought he was a moron; charged with the responsibility of preventing a God War that every temple in the city apart from his own seemed hell-bent on having. Sagging forward, Pringle rested his gaunt face on his bony knees and sighed. First Krieg, now Daisy. Perhaps the Adventurers Guild, such that they remained, had been right. This was a temple concern - except that he knew that it wasn't. If it had been left up to them then the champion would never be found and if Elor was correct, which Pringle whole-heartedly believed he was, then the New Gods would fight and none of them would win and Krynok The All-Father would step in to the breach. Pringle had difficulty articulating why he was so bothered by this possibility. He did not trust the All-Father. Everybody seemed to have conveniently forgotten that he had once been called the Hunter and his children were the Fae.

It was true that Krynok's was the only temple that was in anyway thriving, all the others were empty shells, drained as their faithful marched to the Middle Kingdoms. The mortal 'children' of Krynok now numbered in the hundreds and could be found, not just scurrying about the Temple District like a peripatetic rash, but in every nook and cranny of every slum and Poor Quarter in the city. Their distinctive white robes and glassy, joyful smiles made them easy to spot as they ministered to the destitute and despairing that had been abandoned by the other temples, spreading as they did so their poisonous message of Krynok as the benevolent All-Father. It made Pringle angry, because he didn't trust it. As a devoted follower of the Trickster, the most mortal of all the Gods, Pringle wanted to run screaming into their citadel and declaim heresy but he was just one man and he could not fight alone. As he sat with his ear pressed to his knee he thought of life after all of this, if there was to be any, and wondered idly if he could persuade Iona to go to some kind of Ambassadorial Ball with him. He had never seen her out of woodsman's clothes, but he was prepared to believe that if he threw a handful of gold at the right people, she could be scrubbed up to something quite acceptable indeed. With a sour chuckle, he realised that now was hardly the time for planning his courting.

About ten miles outside the city walls...

"Sister, if you can carry this water skin, that'll free up some more space." Sullenly, Daisy reached out and took the heavy leather skin from the priest who was waving it behind him without looking to see if anyone was actually going to take it. "Thank you," he said tersely, his attention already back inside the cart. Another wave of nauseating regret washed over Daisy as she gazed back down the road towards Aberddu. The last few days had passed in a blur, she could barely recall the dawns and sunsets that had separated them. When the crusade had been announced there had been such elation and then there had been flurries of preparation and dedication. Mother Angelina had called the postulant Sisters to her and told them that, if they wanted to, they would be given permission to take orders immediately because of the extreme circumstances. She had said it was entirely their decision and that if they wanted to stay in Aberddu and not come to war then she would support them in that choice as well. She had looked directly at Daisy as she had said this.

When she had returned from Al'Raeth, Daisy's heart had been full of faith. She had wanted to take vows then and there and Mother Angelina had kissed her on the forehead and rejoiced and taken her to pray. Then, time had tumbled away from them in the crush of turbulent conflict that had followed and it had been forgotten. Daisy had started to pray with Mori more and more, and her faith had shifted and solidified. She was no longer sure that she needed to take vows of mercy and sacrifice because she lived them every day, her promises made directly to her Goddess. She had opened her mouth to decline Mother Angelina and found that she could not. Now she was standing on the road to the Middle Kingdoms wearing the full habit and cowl of a priestess of the Chalice, having made her vows only days before. She had not spoken to Mori since the shrine had been desecrated. She did not know how to approach her. She felt stupid and empty. She hoped in vain that Mori would seek her out, not really calculating that a Death priestess could not walk into the Life

Temple in this climate any more than she could expect a warm welcome in the Death Temple wearing the Chalice.

With nothing else to cling to, Daisy had thrown herself into temple life, but it was not right. Her soul did not sing when she went to the sanctuary for devotions, she could not find the beatific smile that the other Sisters wore as they ministered and prayed. She wore her habit with a grim resolve, a heavy heart and a long face. Every sting of her bare feet reminded her not of the service she was giving to the Lady but of the friend she had left behind. She had hoped distance, if not time, might be a healer. When they had left for the wars she had thought that she might leave her guilt behind her on the temple steps but the further she moved from Aberddu the more painful it had become. Now as she hefted the water-skin on to her shoulders, she could no longer hold back the tears.

THE MIDDLE KINGDOMS

The place that would become the Plains of Blood - late spring

Keryn raised her swords and brought them down hard into the back of the weeping knight in front of her. They cleaved deep into his flesh, cutting cleanly through his leather back-plate with little resistance. Hot arterial spray drenched her, filling her eyes and mouth. She spat and wiped her face with the grimy sleeve of her tunic. The metallic taste of her victim's blood danced on her tongue and her heart pounded as she turned to find the next one. here were plenty to choose from, Knights of Law, piety washed away in the visceral horror of it all, Life Paladins with sickened, wretched expressions, even Amrothians with deep-rooted sadness in their eyes. The Light Alliance. Their foolish weakness was showing through, as their righteousness was crushed by the Dark Armies. Grim determination was nothing compared to the might of the Kali Paladins fighting side by side with their Goddess, joy in their hearts and a smile on their blood-splattered lips as they sought out the most glorious of the deaths on these plains of blood. A guttural cry cut through the cacophony and Keryn stepped aside in time to watch a Greater Avatar of Kesoth immolate a Paladin of Amroth, his armour glowing in the flames as he burned. She paused a moment too long and didn't see the deft elven warrior in with the bear claw blazon until his battleaxe had glanced off her breastplate, grazing her arm. Cursing herself, she spun around and sunk both blades into him, plunging them so deep that she had the satisfaction of hearing them exit through the warrior's back-plate. His eyes bulged with silent agony and blood welled up into his mouth as he choked on his last breath. With a cruel leer she stepped forward, planted a boot firmly on the bear claw blazon and yanked her swords free. Letting out a trilling war cry as her body flooded with adrenaline, she sprinted off into the melee.

As Alisandra ducked and scurried amid the chaos, the small part of her brain that was still capable of such thoughts pondered on the fact that her habit seemed to be more effective than armour at keeping her safe. The simple robe and the fact that she was barely five foot tall she seemed to make her almost invisible, even to the psychotic and maleficent paladins of Kali who offered up every euphoric killing blow to their nefarious Goddess. They seemed to regard the Sisterhood of the Chalice as hardly worth the trouble. Alisandra would have thought of it as an act of mercy, had she not known better. She stepped cautiously over a prone figure soaked so thoroughly with blood that she knew there was little hope of anything other than resurrection. As she passed she recognised the unstained scraps of tunic, the sword and shield device identified him as one of the Amrothian Brethren. The Amrothians would no doubt gather up their dead in time. She looked away, heading for the bunker about a quarter of a mile ahead.

She had volunteered to take this run because she was looking for a specific face. Mathias had not been seen since the last charge, and no one seemed to know where he was. He had been holding the line with the other Life Followers until it had been shattered by Chaos servitors. The Life Paladins had scattered into groups and in the panic Mathias had vanished. He wasn't the only one, but he was the only one Alisandra could think about. Until she found him, alive or - she could barely bring herself to think it - dead, she wouldn't be able to concentrate on anyone else. She was looking around her for the familiar shock of blonde curls with growing desperation, afraid that she would see it but more afraid that she wouldn't. She picked up the pace. So far all she had seen were downed Amrothians and two or three groaning Law clerics, who were patching each other up with pitiful slowness. In exact obedience to her vows, she ought to have stopped to aid them but if they were making noise and moving then they were not in dire need of her help. She pressed on, almost certain that the lump she could see on the edge of horizon would be Mathias.

Pulse quickening, sweat beading on her brow, she drew closer and saw that it actually was him. She even recognised the checked under-shirt he was wearing beneath his tunic, which was now in plain sight. She couldn't see any obvious blood stains, which had to be some kind of blessing she thought. As she picked up her speed she began to pray under her breath. Focussed completely on Mathias, she was not aware of the sound of the battle encroaching around her. She had no real concept of how close she was to the current front line. With a bolt of adrenaline, she vaulted over another, much larger body, and landed on her knees beside a mercifully still breathing Mathias. She rummaged in her bag, pulling out salves and clothes and tiny glass phials. His forehead was clammy and his breath was coming in feverish snatches. She guessed he had been stabbed with a poisoned blade. A crimson stain had blossomed from his gut and was slowly growing. It was within her scope to mend this. In her relief she did not hear the shrill cry or see the woman driven forward by fury. All she ever knew of Keryn was the sudden agony of two razor-sharp blades piercing her flesh and then just a gradual gurgling darkness.

Darkness was falling, although it was difficult to tell if it was night time or whether the sky had simply turned black. Daisy's fear had escalated to a cold, clammy numbness that filled her with a certainty that she was witnessing the end of days. In a brief moment of respite, she had flopped down on a mound on the edge of the camp. She was supposed to be eating a chunk of bread but her mouth was too dry to chew, her arm too bone-weary to lift it to her mouth and her stomach tight beyond the point of hunger. She just lay on her back gazing up at the sky, the bread clutched in her hand slowly soaking up the sweat. Listening to the echoing exhaustion of her brain, Daisy gazed up at where the stars should have been. Even if it were night, it would have been impossible to tell. The swirling indigo clouds, edged with the livid orange glow of battlefield pitch fire, would have obscured the moon and stars anyway. It was strange to think that only a few days ago, she had taken the stars and the quiet safety of the temple for granted. The jarring, jolting noises that drifted over her from the still-raging battle had become common place so fast she barely heard them now. It had been a long time since she had felt the pure, beautiful silence in her soul that told her the Goddess was with her. She wondered why, in the middle of what was supposed to be a holy war, she couldn't feel her faith. A harsh shout brought her back to the here and now. It was a call for her patrol to go out again. She scrambled to her feet, flinging the sweaty chunk of bread into a ditch. Dragging energy from nowhere, she made her way to the camp gateway and joined up with the others.

Sometime later, Daisy was scurrying among the carrion, following in the trail of Sr. Alma bandaging whatever the terrifying nun instructed her to with a gruff grunt and a fierce point. She had stopped vomiting at the sight of the wounded now, she had seen enough dismemberment and evisceration to desensitise even an innocent soul like hers. She had learned not to think, she just tried to fit the pieces back together and ply them with any healing she could. When there was nothing to be done, she just laid out what she could find and if possible closed their eyes before offering a few words of blessing and rushing on to the next, who might be saved. She was praying almost constantly now, although she felt less and less when she did.

Kneeling beside another sodden corpse, she began to gingerly pick her way through the destruction. To her horror she realised that she was tearing aside the habit of a Sister of the Chalice. She hadn't paused to look at *who* she was working on, she had just started work. With the thump of a terrified heart ringing in her ears, she tugged at the robes until the much taller woman, slack in death, tumbled on to her back. Daisy let out an involuntary squeal as she met the anguished gaze of Sr. Alisandra, whose eyes were wide open. There was a thin trail of blood running from the corner of her mouth. Her skin was cold to touch and grey from blood loss. Daisy fought the rigor mortis to close the Sister's eyes and because Alisandra had always been kind to her, she wept gently as she prayed the whole of the Repose in the Lady oblivious to the sounds of the still continuing war around her. Only when she had done that did she turn her attention to the body on which Alisandra had been lying. With stomach churning dread she realised that it was still breathing, although barely. Beyond that she didn't pause until she had tended the more obvious wounds, which were several hours old and partially healed, presumably by Alisandra. It was only when this was done that she took in the face, grime spattered as it was, and let out another horrified squeak. Brother Mathias' shock of curls marked him out among the Paladins, many of whom were indistinguishable to Daisy with their sleek brown crops and dour expressions. She had always liked Mathias although she had never spoken to him, because like his sister Alisandra he had always seemed kind and friendly. She finished ministering to him and with some considerable effort rolled him on to his side in a position that would mark him out as still alive to the stretcher-bearers. She was supposed to bring him around at this point, but she couldn't face it. Someone else could explain to him what had happened to his sister when her mutilated body had been taken back to the camp and tended properly. She clambered on to her feet and shouted to an orderly that there was one for a stretcher and one for the bone-cart.

As she walked the battlefield, her hand absent-mindedly tucked into her bandage pack, Daisy was enveloped in the here and now. She hardly thought of life before the war and she couldn't imagine a time when this would all be over and she could go back to Aberddu and the quiet of her faith. Sr. Alma barked out the order to return to base, and gratefully Daisy complied, picking her way through the debris without much thought. She didn't bother to make her way back to the main group, no one worth listening to would have anything to say right now and she found solitude easier. She was not looking down as she stepped over the prone black-clad figure. When a claw-like hand shot up and grabbed her ankle she let out another yelp and staggered. It did not occur to her to scream for help, nor when she actually looked down did it occur to her to panic or be afraid. The pleading eyes looking up at her were so filled with anguish that she was almost moved to tears. The woman who had grabbed her was trembling with the effort of it.

It was impossible to tell whether the blood covering her was her own or someone else's, because she was drenched in it. When she spoke, her voice had faded to a gasping whisper.

"Help me," she croaked, pulling Daisy closer with surprising strength. "Mercy."

Daisy did not hesitate. This woman was obviously a paladin of Kali but Daisy's vows had not had an equivocation for times of war. She had taken the three-fold vow, the first pledge of a Sister of the Chalice, not two months ago and every day the words rang in her head: faith, mercy, sacrifice. She had sacrificed nearly everything already and her faith was waning but she could at least offer this woman mercy. She dropped to her knees beside the woman's head without a thought that it may have been a ruse or trap. With a practised eye, she scanned down the body for the most serious injuries and located a slow-bleeding stomach wound that was seeping across her abdomen. Reaching for her bandages, she was about to set about treating it when the woman's hand shot out again and grabbed her wrist, staying her hand.

"No," rasped the woman, her gaze so intense that Daisy could not mistake its horrific meaning. "No." The last word trembled on the woman's pale lips and she closed her eyes in agony. Daisy knew what the woman wanted her to do. Mercy. The blood rushed into Daisy's ears as she realised what she the reality of the woman's request washed over her.

"I can't," choked Daisy, "I'm unarmed." It sounded so feeble, but it was true. The Sisters of the Chalice didn't often carry weapons. Without breaking her gaze, the woman reached down and with a shaking hand, and pulled a knife from her own belt.

"Please," she breathed, as she handed it hilt first to Daisy. "Please."

With soul-sinking sadness, Daisy took the proffered knife and with an unsteady hand pulled it from its sheath. The blade was surprisingly clean, she thought as she looked at it, unable to take the woman's gaze any longer. The woman let go of her arm and pulled the neck of her armour open. Daisy took a deep breath and attempted to aim the unfamiliar knife at the woman's vulnerable neck, but her hand was shaking too much. Wrapping her other hand around the hilt to steady it she looked away, and, before she could think about what she was doing, stabbed downwards. As the hot blood gushed over her hands she started to cry.

She had tried to pray but found that she could not. The words would not come. She closed the woman's eyes with tenderness and because she could not offer a prayer, bent forward and kissed her forehead. Then, soaked in this strange woman's blood and still carrying her knife, Daisy picked up her bag and hurried back to camp.

ABERDDU TRICKSTER TEMPLE

A relatively light evening

Pringle didn't often go into the temple to listen to the preaching, mainly because the preaching tended to be done by pompous windbags with nothing to say but he had to admit that Ninian Kindle, if that in fact was his real name, certainly had something about him. Pringle had managed to listen to the whole of the first three minutes before he had drifted into his own thoughts. It wasn't difficult to get lost in the thoughts in Pringle's head at that moment, they were a squalling cacophony of ifs, ands and maybes that was enough to make most people dizzy. Pringle was not most people, they just made him grey and grim with determination. He recited the list that he had now learnt by heart: sword, scabbard, shield, knife, cloak, gauntlet, buckle, scroll case, helm, armour, and gemstone. They had the helm and the shield, because say what you like about Amrothians and Pringle had said plenty, they were open to persuasion and reason. They knew the location of the gauntlet and the cloak, and with some luck in a couple of days would also be in possession of the knife. Elor thought he knew how to get hold of the scroll case and they had people currently in hot pursuit of the armour. That wasn't too shabby, thought Pringle. It only left the buckle, the sword and the scabbard and the bloody gemstone.

He shook his head, oblivious that he was now drawing the attention of a gaggle of bored acolytes who were sitting in the pew behind him. He was almost one hundred percent sure that the Temple of Death had the sword, but they had had no luck retrieving it. Mori and Elor had both tried to reason with them but the High Priest and his Pardoner were disinclined to negotiate. Pringle was convinced that they were up to something. Elor was less certain but as clever as he was, he did not know the world like Pringle did. Current conjecture regarding the scabbard of Life placed it on the Plains of Blood. Elor's reading had thrown up several possibilities for the buckle, the current favourite being that any buckle would do as the moment it was united with the other items it would be imbued with divine power by the Chaos Pantheon. If this proved correct, Pringle had every intention of handing over his own belt and watching the ritual with his hands in his pockets to keep his trousers up. That just left the gemstone, which was proving to be somewhat elusive.

It wasn't possible to inquire at the Aesthetics Temple any more, because the building had been all but deserted and those that remained were not really capable of answering questions. Having found a dearth of information in the Knowledge Temple library and unsure where else to turn, Elor had opened it up to the Questions Quorum as the weekly hypothetical a month or so previously, not keen to explain too much of the context of his question. As he had expected, the Quorum had thrown themselves at the question with alacrity. After half an hour of frantic note taking Elor was still none the wiser and had been left with a niggling concern over a suggestion made by the thin-lipped woman with pince-nez that was still rolling around his head when the Master of Questions had grandiloquently thanked him for his 'most engaging hypothesis' at the end of the debate. She had pointed out that as the Aesthetics was technically now a dead or 'fallen' Goddess, then perhaps deific items created by her were now defunct. Seen in one light, that might be good news – one less item for them to acquire. However, Elor doubted it was that fortuitously simple. He had spent three sleepless nights worrying that without the gemstone the whole suit wouldn't work and that it would all be in vain. On the fourth day, he had expressed these concerns very eloquently to Pringle who had hit him across the back of the head with a roll of parchment and handed him a pewter hip flask with instructions not to drink more than a tumbler full and not to remove the stopper before he blew out his candle. It was the foulest smelling liquor Elor had ever encountered but it knocked him out flat for a dreamless twelve hours. It hadn't solved the problem, but at least it gave him a clearer perspective on it. It was likely to be a very impressive gemstone, internationally renowned for its beauty and magical properties, and there was at least one group of people Elor could think of who might know about really valuable jewels.

The Law Temple bell chimed the evening nine-hour and Pringle sprang to his feet causing the gaggle of acolytes to cackle wildly and Ninian Kindle to stop mid-flow and glare at them pointedly. Pringle didn't even bother apologising, he just nodded curtly to Kindle and made his way out of the temple.

The Bird and Bottle was the very definition of a back-alley pub, except that it was on the ironically named Charm Street – a sizeable side arm of the even larger Bridge Street. Pringle entered at pace, aware that he was quite late and pushed his way through the crowd. Sure enough, Tollie and Sylas were waiting as per arrangement, in a dingy corner. Both of them were gazing irritably into their now empty tankards and muttering back and forth under their breath. Pringle elbowed his way to the bar and in voice just loud enough to carry through the hubbub said,

"Alright Sam, the usual please and whatever those two in the corner are drinking." He gestured clumsily over his shoulder but kept his eyes firmly on the three tankards as Sam filled them all from the cider cask and pushed them across the bar. Picking all three up carefully, he turned into the crowd and was gratified to see that his ploy had worked. Both Tollie and Sylas were sitting bolt upright and watching him like a hawk as he barged passed a table of rowdy dockers, narrowly avoiding a flailing arm.

"Sorry I'm late fellas," said Pringle genially as he thumped the three mugs down on the table and flopped down on the settle beside Sylas. Without waiting for any response, he reached over and grabbed one of the tankards and took a long swallow. Then he let out a long contented sigh and slumped back. Tollie and Sylas were both now gingerly pulling slightly overfull tankards towards them, all eyes on Pringle. "So," he said and both of them paused, waiting. "How's tricks then?" Tollie gave him a frozen glare and said shortly,

"What do you want Pringle. You didn't drag us out here for small talk and cider."

"I do beg your pardon," retorted Pringle with a sardonic smirk, "Do excuse my manners. We can get straight down to business if you want." "Please," said Tollie, sinking nearly half of tankard in one gulp. "We've got things to do." Pringle nodded not really offended by this bluntness.

"Sure," he said. "Well it's like this, there's a gemstone I need to lay my hands on and I think you gents might be able to find out how, where and how much." Tollie opened his mouth to object to this statement but before he could get anything that sounded like 'I don't know what you're implying' out of his mouth, Pringle continued. "And don't come that with me. Don't make me embarrass you by telling you how I know you know." Tollie shut his mouth. He had always suspected there was more to Pringle that the colourfully trousered clerical that appeared around the city. "You wanted to get down to business and this is it." Sylas, who was far less suspicious of Pringle said quietly,

"Well we'll need some more information than that but okay."

In a low voice, Pringle explained that he was searching for a significant, probably renowned, gemstone of some considerable age and that he expected it would have something of a reputation. He didn't know the exact details. Had they heard of a stone that fitted this description, and if they had how could he can access to it, not necessarily on a permanent basis? He could see from the subtle changes of their facial expressions that Tollie and Sylas were intrigued and on some level already had an idea as to what he was looking for. He knew better than to mention this though. As he left the pub, having handed over a small but weighty bag of coins, he was hopeful if not necessarily confident of a positive result.

Pringle was lost in thought as he walked back across the city to the guildhouse. Crossing the city after dark was a risky business in a dazed state but he made it across the Brightling Bridge and into the Guild District without mishap. He was now a common enough sight in the city to be afforded some protection from most petty criminals who would not risk angering either the Adventurers or the Trickster temple by jumping him for his pocket change. The crooks were also well aware that it was likely that he was well-armed under his long brown cloak and, however dopey he may appear, adventurers who had survived more than two years tended to have lightning-fast reflexes when it came to survival.

An unholy din issuing from the Bards Guild broke his dazed state. Apparently, even at this hour they were rehearsing for the authentic Jaffrian opera spectacular. The activity in the well-lit Bards Guild was a stark contrast to the Adventurers Guild building which languished in darkness across the square. Dwindled to barely a dozen resident members, the guild was unofficially disbanded. Erin hadn't been seen since she had walked out on the day she had flung the banner at Elor and the majority of guild members with any religious allegiance at all had moved into the Temple District due to the current political climate.

The same political climate was the largest contributing factor in Pringle's continued residence in the almost totally deserted Adventurers Guild; that and the fact that most of the clerics in his dorm either snored or had a tendency to roll in drunk considerably after curfew. Even after the cook had walked out, followed swiftly by the laundry orderlies, stable hand and the chap that swept the floor, the Adventurers Guild was still a more appealing prospect - at least here he had his own room. It was strange seeing the building deserted on a Thursday. There should have been a raucous guild meeting going on even now, but times had changed and there was only so long one could sit in the guild hall waiting for work. He wondered idly if anyone was still about as he ambled across the dim courtyard, there were occasionally a few people hanging about the kitchen fire if nothing else. Pringle quite liked Derek, one of the new members who seemed happy to hang around and wait for things to pick up again. The boy had quite a lot about him for a farm lad. Margog, a shady dwarf, was usually reliable for a jug of mead and a game of dice and there was a troll whose name he couldn't remember who was presumably a guild member as he had taken up residence in one of the rooms at the far end of the corridor.

Maybe, he thought hopefully, Iona would be back. She had vanished after their meeting in the alley way and he was starting to worry. Perhaps she had made an ill-fated attempt at the theft and met an ignominious end. It was unlikely though, because the Kesoth Temple tended to widely publicise the fate of people who crossed them to save time and effort of having to explain on a one at a time basis. Perhaps she had left Aberddu completely, frightened by what he had asked her to do. He hoped not, he was strangely fond of her for all that she seemed to despise him, or perhaps *because* she seemed to despise him. When this was over, he thought to himself, he'd take her to a smart ball if he could get himself invited to one. Being a Duke of Albion, albeit it an alleged one, had to be some kind of social advantage. Maybe he'd even ask her to marry him. Then they could leave the Adventurers Guild, buy a nice simple house in Albion and have a family.

This dizzying romanticism carried him around the side of the guild building to the kitchen door, which was the standard way in these days. He was disappointed to see a lack of lantern light through the pantry window. Everyone must be in bed already. Bother. Mindlessly, he popped the latch and wondered through the scullery into the main kitchen. As expected, it was empty and dimly lit. Someone had left the lid off the cheese board so Pringle helped himself to a slowly drying chunk of nicely pungent Dockside Darlington and replaced the heavy cloche. He poured himself the last of the cider from the pitcher and moved it to the stone sink. He would draw some water in the morning and sort it all out then. He probably ought to check out the state of the pantry as well and possibly organise some provisions if he could get anyone to give them any more credit. It really came to something Pringle thought, when he was having to take on domestic responsibilities. He yawned. There was no point in lighting the lamp and sitting up here, he might as go up to his room and hide under his blankets.

Pringle's feet were burning and stinging, his boots felt like lead as stumped up the main stairs all the way to the second floor. He had achieved his objective for the day, they were on the way to gathering all the items together. He'd sleep better tonight he hoped. As he shouldered his door open, it didn't occur to him that he had left it locked when he ventured out very early that morning. He was too busy kicking off his boots and rummaging for a candle stub to take in the fact that there was an unexpected lump in the shadow of his bed. As he struggled with the flint and tinder, the shape shifted to a sitting position so that when he finally wrestled the candle aflame and turned around he was greeted by Iona sitting on his bed. Pringle let out a high-pitched squeal of surprise and dropped his candle stick. Mercifully, the candle hit the stone floor and went out. After a moment of stamping and swearing, and Iona cackling, Pringle relit it and Iona said,

"Hello Pringle."

He looked at her open-mouthed. Not only was he unaware that she had the skills necessary to break into his bedroom he was also completely taken aback as to why she would want to. He could see in her eyes that she was amused by his reactions. It struck him that she looked a little different sitting there on his bed, not wearing the scruffy brown tunic and hose he had last seen her in but a smart black bodice and well-tailored skirt. As he studied her more closely, he could see a number of subtle differences in her. Paranoid, he briefly checked her for any unwelcome magical signatures but found nothing. Apparently, the woman sitting on his bed was completely and entirely Iona, it was just that someone had given her a bath, a hairbrush, a corset and possibly some charm classes.

"I have something for you," she said softly, in a voice that Pringle only barely recognised as belonging to Iona.

"Oh?" said Pringle stupidly, unsure how to respond.

"Yes," she said with a big smile, "and I've brought you this as well." As she said this, she produced a thin cloth bundle from behind her and held it out to him. Wordlessly, he took the parcel and unrolled it. Sitting amongst the scrappy black cloth was the most malevolent knife Pringle had ever seen. The blade, which was intricately serrated down nearly it's entirely length in such a way that it would do as much damage coming out of a wound as it would being driven in, glinted darkly. The hilt was encrusted in obsidian shards and the pommel had been moulded intricately with a hideous serpentine visage.

"Oh my good God," uttered Pringle as he looked down on the evil- looking artefact clutched in his hands. "Is this the dagger." He said the word dagger with whispered reverence. Iona snorted.

"The High Priest certainly seemed to think so" she said coyly. Pringle knew the difference between a carefully worded statement such as this and a direct yes.

"And what do you think?" he said with a wry smile.

"I think *this* is the dagger of Kesoth," she whispered, reaching into the top of her bodice, carefully extracted a much smaller, far more utilitarian knife from her décolletage. Pringle held out a hand, and Iona handed it to him. Instantaneously, he felt the iniquity of the knife's magical signature jarring through him. Gingerly, he turned it over in his hand. The blade was also black, but it wasn't glinting theatrically in the candle light. It was thin, well-made and straight edged and there were two narrow blood channels along its length that were only really visible once you had found them by feel. It had a plain metal crosspiece and the pommel was just an inch long extension beyond the soft black suede of the hilt. As Pringle closed his hand around the grip he was intrigued by how comfortable it was in his grasp. He had raised his arm ready to strike before he realised what he was doing. Far from looking threatened, he realised Iona was smiling at him.

"How did you find it?" mumbled Pringle hoarsely, struggling to hold the knife by his side.

"With a little help from a friend of mine," replied Iona cryptically, "Let's just say he was better qualified than the High Priest when it came to identifying the knife."

"Oh," said Pringle, not quite understanding. He returned the knife to Iona's outstretched hand, and she placed idly on the cabinet beside Pringle's bed.

"There's something else I came here to give you," said Iona, standing up and holding Pringle's gaze with a confidence he had never seen before. She reached up and pulled a silver comb out of her hair. With a practice shake of her head, she sent her auburn curls tumbling down her back and shoulders. Then, stepping forward so that Pringle could feel her breath on his skin she said softly, "blow the candle out."

Five days later, in a deserted patch of dockland.

"It'll cost you," said Tollie. "A lot."

"How much is a lot?" asked Iona shrewdly,

"Upwards of a thousand guilders," Tollie said it quietly, hoping to break this prohibitive news gently. Iona whistled through her teeth but Pringle simply nodded grimly. He seemed unsurprised by this exorbitant figure.

"Okay," he said at last. "And how difficult will it be to get hold of?" "For a thousand guilders?" asked Tollie, who was frankly amazed that this was still under discussion. "not particularly hard at all. For that money you can purchase by direct sale. Mind you, it'd probably wouldn't cost you a whole lot less to have it stolen, it's not a job I would fancy and since the guild dissolved... " Tollie didn't finish the sentence because he didn't need to, Pringle was already scribbling figures in a notepad.

"Can you arrange the sale?" said Pringle intensely, without looking up from his scribblings.

"I should think so," said Tollie slowly, completely taken aback. He had not expected this. He had expected Pringle to reject the whole thing out of hand, or possibly come up with some crazy, half-cocked plan to steal it. A thousand guilders. The thought kept coming back to Tollie. A thousand guilders.

"Okay," said Pringle, closing his notepad and meeting Tollie's gaze for the first time, "fantastic. It'll probably take us a couple of days to get our hands on the cash."

"A couple of days?" shrieked Tollie before he could stop himself and Iona sniggered.

"Yep," she said smugly, "Let's just say we've got it covered." "Okay," said Tollie still stunned by what he had just been asked to do. "But can I ask a question, and I want an honest and comprehensive answer or I'm walking." Pringle nodded, he was used to this now. Iona had made the same demand in exchange for the dagger.

"Fine," said Pringle, "but just be warned, I can't untell you what I'm about to tell you and it will keep you awake at night."

"He's not kidding," said Iona, speaking for the first time without any hint of amusement in her voice or eyes. "But if you want to know..." Tollie nodded, not completely convinced that the pair weren't having him on, but aware that a thousand guilders was serious money. With a sinking feeling of inevitability, he let his curiosity get the better of him. "Go on then," he said with a resigned sigh, "tell me." Pringle's face split into a broad grin and he said enigmatically, "Tell me Tolliver, do you follow a God?"

Pringle related the whole tale to an open mouthed Tollie, from the reappearance of the All-Father, who had once been called Krynok the Hunter and his challenge to the younger gods through to the legends of the Champion and the armour that would allow a mortal to defend them from Krynok.

"So let me get this right," said Tollie slowly once Pringle had finished, "if the younger gods don't get it together then Krynok will gain power and the Fae will take over and we'll all be forced to serve them?" "Yep," said Pringle more cheerfully than Tollie felt was appropriate given the news he'd just received. "That's about the size of it."

"So," said Tollie still trying to digest, "just out of curiosity, why exactly are you in charge of sorting this out? I'm mean, no disrespect but you're not exactly a High Priest or anything."

"Well," said Pringle, "it gets worse."

"Worse?" said Tollie, his forehead creasing, "how?"

"You may well be aware that the Temple District is pretty much deserted," Tollie nodded, he'd watched a number of the war bands leave town, in some cases it had been more like the Bards Guild carnival. "Well, instead of uniting against the common threat, Krynok, Kesoth decided that the panic caused by the appearance of the All-Father was a perfect opportunity for a power grab. That was why he killed the Aesthetics."

"No?" exclaimed Tollie incredulously, "what a bastard."

"Yep," said Pringle, "exactly." As he said this he fixed Iona with a significant look and she returned a cold narrow glare.

"I think you'll find it depends whose side you're on," she said tightly, before letting her face slip into a slightly cruel half-smirk. Tollie was aware that he had missed something, but wasn't interested enough to pursue it right now.

"So," continued Pringle, turning away from Iona and back to Tollie, "Once one of them had started playing silly buggers, the rest had to follow. The Dark Alliance was the beginning of the end, the lighter gods could hardly sit back and let Kesoth, Death and Chaos raised havoc. So off they've all gone to the Middle Kingdoms and there they are, as we speak, killing each other for nothing because unless they stand together Krynok will come down and swipe them all aside."

"Really?" said Tollie, who was still trying to process this world-shattering information.

"Yep," said Pringle, "You think Kesoth is a bastard? Well frankly Krynok makes Kesoth look like your great Aunt Jessie." Tollie responded with the only thing he could think of,

"My great aunt Jessie's a lovely woman." Pringle chuckled at this bemused response,

"That would be my point," he said. "If we think Kesoth doesn't care about the mortal world, wait until Krynok turns up with his Fae children. They're beautiful sure, and some of them even seem friendly, but they can't die. They don't understand the fragility of a mortal life and they'll play with us like heavy-handed children trying to catch butterflies."

"Wow," said Tollie, leaving his mouth gaping after he had said it.

"I did tell you I couldn't untell you, didn't I?" sniggered Pringle, amused by Tollie's reaction.

"Yeah," said Tollie. "but I didn't think it would be that bad." Pringle snorted again and Tollie carried on. "So, this gemstone is something to do with the champion's armour?"

"Yep, it's the gift of the Aesthetics," chimed in Iona, "and frankly, we need it enough to pay for it at this point."

"Okay, fair enough," said Tollie because it was all he could say, "I'll see what I can do."

"Thank you," said Pringle and Iona simultaneously.

THE MIDDLE KINGDOMS

The Plains of Blood - first battle of the God War

Ferrin replaced his sword in his back scabbard and wiped his brow with his shirt sleeve. The midday sun on the plains beat down on them all, baking the blood dry on the scorched grass. The ground in front of him was like a charnel house, body upon body lined up in unmoving ranks. Some were mutilated beyond all recognition, limbless or headless, flayed or immolated. Others were all too recognisable.

The Dark Alliance army had hit them hard and fast in the middle of the night, an unrelenting assault of mortal troops mixed with servitors and angels and the most foul beasts. The Death Servitors, gargantuan effigies towering above the armies, firing dark lightening into the sky and raining down fire. A Greater Avatar of Kesoth, in all its terrible majesty cut great swathes through the ranks and a fleet of Zharalota's Harpies picked off stragglers like vultures circling carrion. By dawn, the Life and Law armies had fallen back to regroup not willing to face any more and unable to persuade the Amrothians to retreat. Ferrin had petitioned hard for a strategic withdrawal but to no avail. It had been during the prayer session following this near suicidal decision that She had appeared.

Heimdala the defender was the aspect of Amroth concerned

with the protection of the innocent. She appeared in the material world as a tall, flame-haired woman wearing a wolf-skin cloak and armed with a sword and shield. She was an impressive, if not obviously divine, sight. When he saw her, Ferrin had dropped to his knees in deference like the others and when she had beckoned them to, he had stood. His heart was pounding hard with relief that she was here but he couldn't help feeling that Heimdala was not who he had expected to see on these killing fields. He would have expected Gunnar the Hunter with his vengeful wrath or Vathnir the Warlord. It was only later when he had time to reflect, that he realised exactly who the innocents Heimdala had come to protect were.

Although a soldier of some prestige, Ferrin was not important enough to be in the select gathering clustered around the Goddess as She listened to the commanders relating the last twenty four hours to her as though She was unaware. It was strange to think that this woman surrounded by the generals was in fact their Goddess - her divinity was not obvious from her appearance, apart from the fact that she was taller and cleaner than the other soldiers. Apart from that, and the fact that she was wearing a wolf-fur cloak and not sweating in the noonday heat, she seemed like any other. She let the generals talk themselves out and then with supreme grace, blessed each one, turned without saying a word and marched towards the Dark Alliance battle lines. Ferrin watched, his heart in his mouth, as the figure grew smaller on the horizon and then he returned to his men.

Jamar was bleeding, again. His tunic was already rigid with dried blood and some of it his own. The final skirmish in the light of the rising sun had been deadly. His gang had come up against a pocket of mounted Law Paladins, whose strength denied that they had been fighting all night. They had charged into dark soldiers, cutting down dozens of them where they stood, Jamar had not waited around to see what happened next. He fled away from the battle, and down through a gorse-ridden hollow, skirting the rest of the fight without really taking in his surroundings. There was a solitary yew tree on the far edge of this dip, and Jamar had scrambled up it so that he had the perfect vantage point as the final Dark Alliance assault swarmed over the Light Armies like a terrible plague. The attack was brief, like a final cruel taunt. Left with little choice, Life and Law pulled back a significant way and then, when the Amrothians refused to follow, partially unretreated and then retreated again. Messengers on weary horses with stained livery had been darting between the three camps all morning.

Jamar had drifted off, it was not an exciting sight after the first hour or so. A bright flash woke him with a start causing him to topple from the tree, opening an old wound and covering him in fresh gashes. As he limped back to base camp, he could see a column of light shining out of the Amrothian battle line. He didn't stop for a closer look. He couldn't remember the last time he had been clean, or rested or full. Life before the continual agony of war wounds and stinging feet, before the flies and the terrifying magic, before the constant fear and indignity of it all, was just a blur. Even though he knew that the dark creatures of Death and Chaos were supposed to be on his side, it was small comfort. The Greater Avatar of Kesoth was bad enough, and he'd seen that before. The Handmaidens of Lilja and Zharalota's Harpies scared him to witless never mind about the Hecate army revelling in the slaughter and smearing the blood of their enemies into their mouths and hair. Aberddu was calling him home, and if he thought he would survive the journey alone, he would have left then and there. Jamar was almost at the edge of the camp when he felt a wave of sinister magic pulse over him. He managed to stay upright, although he staggered as a stabbing pain rippled through his body. Looking up, he could see a dark, unnatural cloud swirling over the Kesothian camp. Jamar broke into a run, overriding his pain signals - he wasn't prepared to miss out on whatever was causing this.

Beauty is in the eye of the beholder they say, and all those who behold Caros the Beautiful are left with the same deep-routed, cold sense of awestruck terror from the sight of her dreadful beauty. Gazing up at the towering figure that hung ten feet above the battlefield, encircled by a dark pulsing halo, Jamar was overtaken by the bizarre impulse that he would not be able to look away however much he wanted to. His eyes were drawn to her, studying her in minute detail. Looking closely, he could see that the monumental apparition before him was in fact naked. Not that this was immediately obvious, because long tendrils of black hair wound and swirled around her, carried as if on the wind. Every inch of flesh that he could see was covered in sigils and scarification. She raised her arms above her head, opened her mouth wide and let out a shrill echoing cry. As one the Kesothians surged towards her caught in her thrall, swords drawn and ready to follow her anywhere. Everyone else shrank away in fear, even the other Dark Alliance who were supposedly on her side. All cowered back from Caros. She opened her chasmic mouth even wider, showing her thousand tiny razor sharp teeth and let out a full-throated wail so loud that it knocked the air out of Jamar's lungs. She gazed down on the cringing mortals at her feet and closed her mouth and her soft pink lips formed into a strange, benevolent smile. With a sweep of her hands, she gestured for her devoted to stand and as one, with joyful hearts, they obeyed. Caught up in the rapture, Jamar was swept along in the tide of hysteria. The press of bodies moving forward pulled him with them even though he felt nothing but cold terror at the sight of the Goddess. He drew his sword, to protect himself more than anything else and tried to keep his wits about him.

In fact, Jamar was not a Caros follower; truth, pain and beauty being things he valued about as much as integrity, honour and courage. Each to their own, he felt, and as far as he was concerned Caros' main use was in keeping all the nut-cases out of the useful bits of the temple. If they wanted to poke each other with hot needles and whatnot then let them, as long as they didn't make too much mess. He was more interested in other aspects of Kesoth. The Betrayer was more to his taste - victory at any cost, self-preservation and playing to win. Not that there was much chance of the Betrayer deigning to turn up here. Pulling his mind back to the chaotic present, he drew his off-hand dagger and kept his eyes peeled as he was swept along in the charge. Coming towards them with determined stride was a statuesque woman with sword and shield, her long red hair whipping around her.

For a moment, Jamar thought she was a general and he would not have dared to argue with her whoever she said she was. She was approaching at quite a pace, although she didn't seem to be moving faster than walking speed. It was only as they drew nearer to the woman that Jamar had any idea how tall she was and how long her stride must be. As he looked closer, he could see the faintly shimmering aura surrounding her and for the first time it occurred to him that this woman was no more mortal than the soaring creature above him. The warrior's piercing blue eyes were fixed firmly on Caros and even at this distance, Jamar could see they glowed with pure hatred. He heard one of the priestesses beside him utter the word 'Heimdala'. He should have known, he had once been one of her priests - how long ago and far away that life seemed now.

Heimdala broke into a run and with a roar like a lioness defending her cubs, took off and met Caros in mid-air. With a fluid motion, she raised her shield against Caros' talons and brought her glimmering sword hard down on Caros' back. It rent a long wound in the flesh , causing Caros to let out a deafening shriek. Heimdala raised her sword to strike again, but Caros feinted away. Below, the Carosites stood frozen and gaping. Jamar could see that the wound on Caros' back was beginning to knit already. Soaring higher, she flung her arms wide and shot a stream of black fire at Heimdala. With lightning fast reactions, Heimdala brought her shield up and the flames rebounded. Angered by this, Caros flew at her, mouth wide and talons splayed, but again Heimdala was too fast. With nothing more than mild irritation, she batted Caros away with the flat of her blade, like someone swatting flies at a picnic. Even more enraged, Caros dived at Heimdala once more, this time flames spilling from her mouth, a knife suddenly in her hand. Heimdala dropped into a crouch, raising her shield to catch the worse of the fire and unable to stop herself, Caros tumbled over her. For a moment, it looked like Caros would press this sudden advantage as she spun around and sank her claws into the back of Heimdala's neck, but the defender was ready for her. Barely had Caros contacted with the back of her neck when Heimdala turned and drove her sword deep into Caros' chest. If she had been mortal it would have pierced her heart. Caros let out a gurgling screech that sent a shot of pain down Jamar's spine and she fell to the ground.

Jamar hadn't expected that. He gazed in bemusement at the place where She had landed, and then a movement beyond caught his eye. Galloping towards them, in uncharacteristic disarray, were about fifty mounted Amrothian Knights led by a figure Jamar recognised from his days as an Adventurer as Lord Ferrin de Andro. Oddly, he could see that Ferrin had out-ridden all the identifiable generals and none of them had paused to wait for the foot soldiers who were sprinting in their wake. The Carosite army braced for the onslaught and Jamar took the opportunity to cast about for a safe place to hide.

Having seen the dark goddess fall limply to the ground, the Amrothians were spurred forward, many letting out victorious cries as they charged towards the Carosites. Ferrin was barely in control of his faculties as his horse galloped onwards, he had not stopped to look up. If he had, he would have seen what Jamar saw. Heimdala, far from appearing jubilant was gazing down on her approaching faithful in horror.

"NO," she screamed, returning to the ground without breaking stride. "No."

From his position, on the edge of the Carosite army, Jamar could see what she was screaming at. The supposedly lifeless remains of Caros the beautiful, surrounded on all sides by charging Amrothians was no longer lying prostrate and bleeding in the grass. She was upright again and smirking cruelly. She let out a pitiless chuckle that was the first Ferrin knew of her presence. Then, flinging her arms wide she filled the air with anguished screams as all the Amrothians within a hundred yards of Caros were paralysed with pain, tiny cuts appearing all over their bare skin. She watched and laughed, revelling in their agony. Heimdala, fury replacing the hatred in her eyes, abandoned her mortal affections and with a brief flash of white light vanished and reappeared in front of Caros. The rage on Heimdala's face only made Caros laugh harder. She had no weapon now, she just stood, arms folded and watched as Heimdala brought her sword down again. Then with inhuman speed, Caros shot out a hand and caught the blade. There was a moment of deadlock as Caros tried to disarm Heimdala and failed. A nasty grimace curled over Caros' face and she was forced to let go. The paralysing pain stopped and the Amrothians scrambled to their feet.

"This is not their fight," bellowed Heimdala, flying at Caros with her sword raised again.

"Oh really?" hissed Caros. Her voice was serpent-like. "Tell them." She waved a taloned hand at the Carosites behind her, and as one they charged passed her into the waiting Amrothians. Heimdala let out an angry yell, turned and raced towards her followers. She did not see Caros smile. Jamar did.

Wading through the clustering Carosites, cutting them down by the half dozen with her mighty sword, she pushed through to her own. Wrong-footed by the sudden charge, and still covered with tiny, painful cuts the Amrothians were not at their best. They were putting up a valiant fight but against the enraptured pain-worshippers they were at a distinct disadvantage. Heimdala looked about, momentarily bewildered. Some of her faithful lay bleeding and dying, others had lost control completely and were berserking through the enemy with no thought or humanity. It was too late to shield them, and she could not, like Caros had done, attack all the enemy fighters at once.

It was only a moment's pause but it was long enough for Caros. Silently, she flew at Heimdala's back and clamped her talons around her neck. Heimdala struggled and tried to turn but Caros, in her position of natural advantage, was too strong. Caros rose up, dragging Heimdala with her. The Defender tried to turn to face her attacker and struggled constantly to no avail. Then, once they were about thirty feet above ground Caros opened her awful maw and sunk her thousand teeth into Heimdala's jugular. Scarlet blood gushed from the wound, and filled Caros' smiling mouth. Caros let out a shriek of triumph and lifted Heimdala's limp form above her head letting Heimdala's blood rain down on them all. Jamar had no intention of becoming part of a body count that looked like it may include a Goddess. Breaking away from a pack of Carosites who were about to find themselves in the path of a dozen berserking Knights of Vathnir, he jumped and rolled into a gorse-filled dip. Struggling free of the prickles, he crouched out of sight and watched. The ferocity of Vathnir Knights surprised Jamar, he hadn't factored in the force of their fury as they tore through the Carosites. Ferrin's breath was coming in sharp, stinging bursts. He had never in his life fought so hard for anything. The sight of his Goddess above him, helpless and dying in the arms of the dreadful apparition of Caros was more than he could bear. He had been driven beyond the rational, and he found himself fighting with every fibre of his being against the cruelly goading Carosites in front of him. He wanted to kill them, and he didn't care how. It was not a feeling he'd ever experienced before, he was struggling not to lash out, to maintain his honour. All of a sudden, Caros let out another violent, gleeful cry and dropped the pale lifeless remains of Heimdala to the ground as though she was discarding a chicken bone at a banquet. Then, She flew up into the air, trailing flashes of lightening and coils of black hair, and with a clap of her hands let out a thunder crack so powerful it knocked them all to the ground.

Ferrin had no memory of what happened after that. Even when he heard the tales recounted years later, it was still a blank. He had been standing only feet from where Heimdala's body had landed and had been the first to drop to his knees to aid Her. Without thought that it might not work, he began to bandage the Goddess' wounds with the same herbal bandages he would have used on his fallen comrades. All the while praying under his breath, cold saline tears snaking down his cheeks. When Caros had clapped, he had been kneeling there, applying pressure to the gaping neck wound, his hands soaked in Heimdala's blood. He had no reason to doubt the accounts of the events that followed, although he was simultaneously shocked, appalled and awestruck by them. Overcome by the power of Caros' triumph, Ferrin had sprung to his feet, drawn both his swords from his back scabbards and charged ferociously at the nearest Carosites. Without mercy or honour, he hacked through them as they lay on the ground cowering at the sight of the screaming Amrothian. As he did this, berserking for all he was worth, breaking noses with the swift application of a boot, driving his swords into already dead corpses just for the pleasure of watching the blood seep, Heimdala lay unattended. Then, something happened that was later described as a miracle by a clutch of the more hysterical variety of nun.

Unobtrusively, a faint white glow about the size of a small ball appeared, hovering in the air no more than twenty feet from Heimdala. It was like the soft light of morning sun. Slowly, it grew into an elongated oval and formed itself into a person: a young girl with grey eyes, translucent skin and white hair. She was wearing a simple light-green shift dress, her feet were bare. She ran across the battlefield to Heimdala and as she arrived at the scene stopped for a moment. Her innocent face fell into a look of soul-wrenching grief as she took in what lay before her: bloodied corpses, berserking warriors and Heimdala's body, apparently lifeless. She began to cry and as her tears fell on to the scorched grass it turned green and lush and began to spread. As the revitalised grass touched the corpses, some of which had been dead long enough for their spirits to depart, their wounds started to knit and they began to stir. The patch of green radiated rapidly from her feet, forming a circle about one hundred yards across. Most of the berserking warriors calmed and slowed, many of them dropped their weapons and fell to the ground weeping. Indiscriminate of which side they were on, the wounded and dying started to come around.

Only Ferrin continued to berserk, although he was blundering about struggling to find a target. He seemed completely oblivious to the girl or the miracle that was occurring around him. Still crying, tears falling harder as she lay her eyes on Ferrin, the girl walked deliberately towards him. Stretching out a tiny, perfect hand, she rested it on Ferrin's outstretched sword arm. He stopped mid-stride and turned to look at her, his rage dissipated. With deep sorrow in his eyes, he fell to his knees at her feet and wept. Gently, she leaned forward and touched her lips to his forehead. Instantly his face became serene and he slumped sideways into a deep, dreamless sleep. Then, she turned back to Heimdala, knelt down and pulled the much larger woman's head into her lap, stroking her bloodied cheek. In a warm flash of pure white light, they both vanished.

As that happened, Caros let out a shrill screech and dived down from where she had been somersaulting with triumph. She reached the ground just too late to stop them and in her fury she turned the fresh green grass to rotting black sludge with one malevolent wave of her hands then vanished. Jamar climbed out from behind a suddenly decaying gorse bush and, with his mind full of what he had seen, made his way back to the camp.

The defeat of Heimdala was a catalyst that forced events to tumble towards their monstrous and inevitable conclusion with startling rapidity. Overnight Law, Life and the beleaguered Amrothians united under the single banner of the Light Alliance. News travelled fast and by the morning they were being joined by hundreds of soldiers from other faiths who were keen to make a stand before their own Gods fell prey to Kesoth. The Brothers of Erudition from the Temple of Knowledge and the Army of the Celestial Flame were among those who took to the field in these days. The world was now in the grip of what would become known by those who survived as the Summer of Fire. For those caught up in the tumultuous days that followed there was little time to reflect or even catch breath. For all those entangled in it, it was both an aeon and a heartbeat. Those who survived would never again sleep without dreaming of those who did not.

ABERDDU CITY – THE BANKS OF THE RIVER DDU

A week after the Fall of Heimdala

Iona was sitting in the shade on the banks of the River Ddu, Pringle lying with his head in her lap. It was a blisteringly hot day in the City with no breeze to relieve the heat. Even the Docks were steaming, the banks of the river were the coolest place to be found. In the bright sunshine, the grey river looked almost inviting as it meandered towards the delta but Iona wasn't stupid enough to jump into the pestilent stream to find out. The pair were having the same conversation they had had every day for nearly three weeks now, ever since they had got their hands on the Gem of Aesthetics. Raising the thousand guilders, through the ancient triumvirate of borrowing, begging and larceny, had been a doddle compared to the rest of their colossal task. The problem was that even though they knew the location of nearly all the items, they weren't in a position to put their hands on them. At least three of them were with the armies on the Plains of Blood and another was in the hands of, or rather on the back of, a man who would sooner die than let them have it.

"We can't do this alone," said Iona sadly, for the third or fourth time that week. "We need more help."

"Like who?" snapped Pringle. He was getting fed up with Iona saying this.

"Well you could do worse than the Adventurers Guild," said Iona sourly, not keen on being snapped at.

"The Adventurers Guild is finished," sneered Pringle sitting up and fixing Iona with a morose hang dog expression. "Just another casualty of the God War."

"Oh don't be such a drama queen," retorted Iona. "It's not like they're all dead and believe me getting them back together is going to be easier than killing Elder Dmitri to find out if we actually can prise the Cloak of the Sea God out of his cold, dead hands."

Pringle snorted with laughter as she said this. He had to admit that she had a point about that, although he was not as optimistic that reuniting the Guild would do anything other than cause more trouble. At least he supposed it was a direction, and if there was going to be a divine war then the more people on his side the merrier.

"Okay," he said decisively standing up and offering Iona a hand which she ignored. "Where do we start?"

"Well," said Iona, pushing herself up of her own volition, "You go and find Elor and Mori and I'll go and dig out the Guild membership ledger."

Meanwhile, on the Plains of Blood...

Daisy had originally been grateful for her reassignment to the field hospital, but now she was beginning to wonder if it wasn't even more soul-destroying than work on the battlefield itself. Most of the cases that made it as far as the hospital had the kind of wounds that could not be treated easily by magic, many of them were horrifying disfigurements or cursed, seeping sores. The smell was often just as overwhelming as the sight of them. She had learnt quickly to always breathe in before bending down to remove a dressing. As always she was more than grateful that she had, as she found that the spreading necrosis was starting to ooze thick black pus. The delirious soldier whose leg she was treating twitched in her torpor as Daisy redressed the wound and poured more healing magic into the gaping sore. It was a pointless procedure, the poison from this wound was already coiled around the warrior's soul and she could not be healed. She would be departed in less than twenty four hours. Dearly, Daisy wished she could do for her what she had done for the fallen Kali follower she had found on the field, whose face was there every time she closed her eyes. Two chilly tears dotted the clean bandage before Daisy could turn her head and move on to the next bed.

The patient in this bed was a puzzle – his physical wounds had healed easily, he was simply asleep and had not stirred since he had been brought in. The healers had tried everything they could think of to bring him around but so far nothing had worked, he just remained in a deep, restful slumber. Daisy had volunteered to tend to him because she recognised him. When she had been told his name was Lord Ferrin de Andro she had remembered where she had met him. He was a member of the Aberddu Adventurers Guild, and although sporadic he was still a familiar face to Daisy, which she found comforting. Like everyone else, she had heard the tale of how he had come to be asleep. It had been the talk of the Life army that he had been kissed by an apparition of a young girl that was now widely thought to be one of the faces of the Goddess of Life and that the kiss had stopped him berserking and put him into this deep sleep. Why he was still asleep now was anyone's guess, but several of the more hysterical Sisters had sung blessings and lit candles at his bedside.

Daisy had not even uttered a prayer for him. If he had been put to sleep by the Lady then he was lucky, he was probably in a much more pleasant place than she was right now. Looking at him enviously, she sunk onto the canvas stool beside the bed. She had engineered her rounds so that she finished her duties by this bed. It meant that she was free to talk to him. She found it oddly easy to pour out her woes to this man who never responded. She didn't have to pretend to him that she believed in any of what the temple was doing, or that she had any faith that they might win. He didn't judge her or pity her, he just lay there. Over the course of the last couple of weeks she had told him repeatedly what she had learnt from Elor about the champion of the Younger Gods, and how this whole battle might be ended by the uniting of the items. She had wept thousands of tears of regret that she had not stayed in Aberddu to help her friends, and even more tears of grief for all those who had died on the fields. She had spent even longer with her small dwarven fingers clamped around his large clammy hand, her head on his arm, just sitting in silence. This was the only contact she had. She had tried so hard to pray but she could not sense her Goddess and she felt breathtakingly alone.

In the orange glow of the candle lantern, she took his hand and started to cry again. She had nothing left to say, except to repeat over and over again how meaningless and pointless this all was and that was a waste of breath. Unabashedly she wept for several minutes, when the thinnest words escaped her lips.

"I want to go home," she breathed into her sobbing. "I want to go back to Aberddu." As she said this, she felt the hand in hers tense and squeeze and a faint voice in the darkness replied,

"So do I."

Daisy sat bolt upright and let go of the hand. The lantern light was so dim that she had not noticed until now that Ferrin's eyes were open, even if only slightly. He was smiling beatifically.

"I'm so sorry," howled Daisy, standing up and flushing with embarrassment. "I... I... " There was nothing else she could say in this moment of abject humiliation.

"Daisy isn't it?" murmured Ferrin, heaving himself up into a sitting position.

"Yes," choked Daisy hoarsely, her nursing training taking over as she leant forward to adjust his pillows. "Yes it is. How did you... " Her voice tailed off again.

"How did I know?" whispered Ferrin, looking around for a drink. "You're an adventurer aren't you? You hang about with that tartar, Krieg I think his name is? Can I have some water please?" Daisy nodded, stunned, and vanished almost instantly to fetch a cup.

"So let me get this straight," said Ferrin quietly, after he had made Daisy recount everything she had told him about the Champion and the items, "you're saying this whole fight is needless? That this is just a power-grab by Kesoth and that the real danger is Krynok and that to defeat him, the Younger Gods have to *unite*?"

"Yes," said Daisy slowly. "That's pretty much it."

"Okay," said Ferrin, fixing Daisy with the kind of deep determined stare she had last seen in Krieg's eyes. There was an air of something moribund about this man as he lay in the bed, clutching a beaker of water and taking in Daisy's words which he had already heard in his dreams. He seemed somehow sorrowful, regretful of something. Daisy didn't know whether she ought to keep talking, because the silence Ferrin was creating felt so definite. It was as though when he said 'okay' that had drawn a line under the conversation and the next sentence ought to start a new chapter. After a few minutes of uncomfortable silence, Daisy realised that Ferrin hadn't spoken because he was praying. She could see the tears streaming down his face and his lips trembling as they shaped the silent words.

Daisy looked down at her lap, embarrassed again. She didn't like seeing him so vulnerable. She didn't really know where to look or what to say, she just sat quietly not willing to leave him. Even though this was uncomfortable, she had a feeling it was leading somewhere. After about ten minutes her patience paid off. Ferrin reached out a hand and touched her arm. She looked up into his blurry gaze and in a tremulous voice he said,

"Fetch me a quill and parchment, I need to send a message."

Daisy protested vociferously over Ferrin's message to Teign. She was well aware that Teign thought of her as a waste of space and air and would no more want to hear what she had to say about the Champion of the Younger Gods than polish her boots with his tongue. However, Ferrin had insisted and Daisy wasn't really in a position to argue too much with him. At least she had been able to avoid taking the message herself as she wasn't strictly speaking permitted off base. She just handed the small folded note to one of the messengers and went to bed.

THE MIDDLE KINGDOMS

The Plains of Blood , as the God War rages

Jamar scrambled up the tree. He had just about been able to cope with the Kesoth Avatar and the handmaidens, even Caros had not been too bad but now the field crawled with foul divine creatures which made the handmaidens look sweet and friendly. The massive white angels of Life that were in constant evidence were no more reassuring. For creatures that were supposed to be the embodiment of all Life's goodness, they were certainly terrible and terrifying to behold particularly if they were coming for you with cold fury in their eyes.

As he clung on to the branch for dear life he looked out over the battlefield and was forced to consider whose side he was on. This was no longer a mortal war, this was a divine battle which would ultimately crush mortals underfoot and discard them. It wouldn't matter whether you fought for the Dark Alliance, who would honour only those strong enough to survive or for the Light Alliance, who would lie and call your death heroism, you would be no safer. Faced with the prospect of a possibly lethal journey back to Aberddu or an almost certain death on this battlefield, Jamar made his decision. He was fairly sure he could outrun most bandits even with his injured leg but if he was forced to spend another night on this (he laughed bitterly as he realised that the term 'godforsaken' was so far from the truth) field he might actually go and offer himself to the Handmaidens of Lilja before he met the wrath of an Amrothian avatar who he was convinced would recognise him as a turncoat. As he wriggled on the branch to get comfortable, he made his decision: it would be safer to wait until the battle had moved away from the bottom of this tree and he knew exactly whose side he was on - his own.

Whitefire had a way of looking straight through you as though he was examining what was going on in your soul instead of listening to what was coming out of your mouth. It had usually made Ferrin feel slightly inadequate but today it was actually making him feel really on edge.

"I like you Ferrin," said the Iceni after a long silence, "And I respect you, but what makes you so sure you're right?" Ferrin had been waiting for that. It was going to be difficult to convince him, as a chosen of Amroth, to leave a battlefield on which his Goddess had lost an aspect. It had surprised Ferrin that he had been willing to listen in the first place. At this point Teign interrupted,

"Look Whitefire," he said in the voice he reserved for when he was trying to sound measured and learned, "I can't say I'm any more taken with the idea of walking away from this fight than you," he didn't quite add although at least the Law Army aren't trying to claim back a Goddess, "and I have to admit at first I thought the whole thing sounded like enough bilge to drown a battle fleet." As he said this, he gave Daisy another one of the contemptuous glances that she was becoming used to. "But the more I think about it, the more it seems to make sense." As he said this he turned away from her, not wanting to look at the dishevelled dwarf when he conceded she might be right. Then, he escalated to the absolute height of condescension in one mighty stride. "I realise that you are less able to make free choices that those of us who are not chosen but I think this bears serious consideration."

It was difficult to tell, thought Daisy, whether Teign had just clumsily insulted Whitefire or whether it was a very clever play.

Either way it had the desired effect. Whitefire fixed Teign with a haughty stare that looked as though it could bore a hole through his breastplate and turned without a word to Ferrin.

"Ferrin, I need to know, why should I come with you?" said the Iceni earnestly, his back firmly turned towards Teign.

"I can't put my finger on it," said Ferrin, deciding that honesty was probably the only sensible policy at this moment. "This just doesn't feel right." As he said 'this' he gestured to the battle behind them. "We can't win against them. They're too strong and they know it. They're just going to wipe us out because they don't play by any rules. There has to be another solution, and this feels right."

The moment he said 'feels right' Whitefire held up his hand as if to say he had heard enough.

"Okay," he said slowly, "when do we leave?"

"First light," said Ferrin hoarsely, shocked that he had an agreement. "How very traditional," replied Whitefire so dryly that Ferrin didn't dare chuckle, he just nodded and turned away.

The Iceni stood by the camp gate. It was well after midnight, perhaps Mauna wasn't coming. Perhaps he had misjudged their relationship. Had he been the kind of person that was given to panic he would have started now as thoughts of betrayal flooded into his head. He doubted these thoughts but not enough to dismiss them completely. He liked Mauna in spite of her religious persuasion, not least because she tended to accept what he had told her on face value and without questioning it. She had agreed to do what he had asked this time even though it was potentially very dangerous and against her own religion. He wanted to think that she liked him enough to take these chances and that she had not gone straight to the high priests and told them what he had said. She was very late now though. As he always did when he was uncertain, Whitefire prayed. Without dropping to his knees or moving his mouth, he opened his heart up to the Goddess and hope.

After ten or so minutes, he was distracted from his prayers by a small movement on the sky line that drew his eye. Even his eagle-eyes couldn't quite make out if the movement was a person.

He just kept watching. The sound of footsteps above him told him that the gate guards had also spotted the movement and they would have a telescope.

"Soldier," he barked, "what can you see?" Judging by the initial response to this question, Whitefire must have taken the guard by surprise.

"Sir?" came the quavering reply from a weary night-watch guard who had just realised he was being watched by someone he should definitely be calling 'sir' and therefore should probably not have belched, slouched or picked his nose in the last hour or so.

"There's something moving on the skyline soldier," said Whitefire patiently, concealing his amusement at the guard's obvious panic, "What is it?"

"Oh, right, yes, sir. It's a woman sir. A death priestess I think, judging by her clothing sir." Whitefire smiled and nodded and then realised that the guard, who was couldn't have seen this gesture even if it hadn't been dark.

"Okay, soldier," he said "open the foot gate and let her in."

"Yes, sir," replied the guard trying to sound like he didn't want to argue with an Iceni. Whitefire smirked at the tone of the guard's response and moved to meet Mauna.

"I'm coming with you," insisted Mauna through tight lips. "I can't go back now. Not after taking that," she gestured at the long, cloth-wrapped parcel on the bench between her and the two Amrothians. "Haven't I proven myself enough?" She looked pleadingly at Whitefire. "I did exactly what you asked. I brought you the sword, I wasn't followed, I didn't tell anyone. What else do I have to do?" Her voice was whining and it was grating on Ferrin's nerves. It made him want to say no to her begging even more but he could see the look on Whitefire's face and he was smart enough to know he was going to have to relent. Teign was not going to like this, he hated riding out with women at the best of times. The weepy dwarf was bad enough but adding the fawning Death cleric was only going to make matters worse. He would just have to lump it. They needed the sword and he couldn't argue with her logic.

"Fine," conceded Ferrin at last with ill-grace and was met

with a stoic, sulking silence in response. Whitefire filled it by murmuring 'thank you'. "Right," said Ferrin irritably, "If we're going let's go."

ABERDDU CITY TEMPLE DISTRICT

Pringle darted out of the Trickster Temple and immediately ducked down the alley that ran between it and the Celestial Flame Temple. The whole square was crawling with people flocking towards the new Krynok Temple. Strictly speaking the new Krynok Temple was the old Aesthetic Temple. The Krynok followers had expanded their base of operations into the abandoned building on the main plaza with what Pringle and a number of the other Trickster clerics considered to be indecent haste. It could be argued that they needed the space, although Pringle was sceptical as to how they were gaining such large numbers of followers. He looked over to the stark, black frontage of the Kesoth Temple. He was supposed to be collecting Iona before they went up to the Guild District, but quite honestly he wasn't sure he could make it across the square. Perhaps rescuing was a more appropriate word than collecting, the crush of bodies was really quite overwhelming. Gods only knew what was going on, but the overflow of newly converted Krynok Worshippers was filling the square.

Pringle had never asked Iona exactly what it was she did in the Kesoth Temple for hours at a time. It wasn't generally a sensible question, in case some actually told you. She generally came out clean and didn't have any obvious scars so he was prepared to venture she wasn't into the ritual bloodletting that went on in some of the Kesoth Cults. He didn't know if the alternatives to this were better or worse. In times of turmoil such as this, who was he to question anything that provided people with faith and comfort, even if it was the Betrayer? As a Trickster, his heart and soul lay with the mortals and his first thought was always the mortal condition. If Kesoth was what Iona needed to get through all of this, then that was fine. He was, however, less sure of the validity of the new-found Krynok fixation. He was all in favour of religion for the masses if it served their interest, he was however not in favour of religious hysteria. The nonsense and carry on at the Sea God Temple had been bad enough. All the rubbish about the Father's Tear and the Pilgrims, and the dramatic arrival of Elder Dmitri was not in any way to his taste but even so he had to admit it was preferable to what he was witnessing now. Call them fairy-folk if you like, but you would be naive to believe the Fae to be that simplistic. Krynok's children made him nervous, as did anything else that could not really die. He shuddered as the bodies pressed forward, desperate to get into the temple.

As he continued to watch the Kesoth Temple, trying to work out how he was going to get there, he saw one of the side doors open and a figure pop out. Iona was unmistakable these days, in both dress and stance. She began to elbow her way through the crowd, kicking and cursing anyone who ignored her "excuse me" s. She was making a bee-line directly for where Pringle was hiding. Another man would have been embarrassed that he remained cowering as a woman fought towards him, but not Pringle. He just looked on and admired the way the sun danced over her cascading auburn hair. He would quite like the chance to find out how that hair looked against the white linen of his pillow. Desperately, he hoped that after all this was over he'd have some time to spend with her, when they weren't fixated on saving the world.

As Iona reached Pringle's earshot, she shouted across to him,

"Bugger this for a game of soldiers, let's go the quick way." She reached out a hand to him and pulled him towards the nearest sewer hatch. He was about to object when she gave him a complex wink and expertly tipped the hatch open with her boot. After watching Iona skilfully navigate her way through the top layer of the Aberddu sewer network, reading the carved tags and gang marks and navigating them both swiftly, Pringle was the kind of amazed that you can really only be with a person you think you're falling in love with. However, being an adventurer of several years standing he also had enough sense to be equally concerned as to how Iona knew where she was going in a world predominantly controlled by the Other Guild.

Elor was sitting on the fire side settle in the main guild hall, tapping his feet nervously. This was one of those moments when you have an idea that you dearly want to work but in all reality expect to be a complete failure. The Adventurers Guild, although not officially defunct, had been on hiatus since the night Erin had flung the Guild banner at Elor. The main hall had gathered dust in the months since, the few remaining Guild members had stuck to the kitchen and their rooms and the staff were long gone in search of jobs that might actually pay. It had taken long enough to get the word out that the Guild was re- opening. A significant number of adventurers were temple affiliated, hence why many of them were long gone before the closure. Getting them back was even harder - the front-line of the God War didn't have a postal address. The rest of the Guild had scattered far and wide, some of them had gone as far away as Kchon, and were still on their way back. Elor had been gratified by the general response, he had to hand it to Iona and Pringle, they had left very few stones unturned trying to dredge up old adventurers. There were faces there he hadn't seen in a good many years, and he doubted that Pringle and Iona had ever met them. They must have made an eloquent and impassioned case to bring them out of retirement. He just wished that they themselves had turned up on time. An undercurrent of muttering was starting to develop and he could tell they were growing restless. Some of the more reluctant attendees were glancing towards the door every few seconds as if weighing up the merits of pushing off to the pub instead of staying for the meeting. Just as he was contemplating taking the floor himself, the door opened with a theatrical bang and Dakarn

Pringle, Duke of Albion walked into the room. It was a truly impressive entrance, Elor had to admit. He did not sidle in with his normal grubby smirk and a wink, he strode confidently in through the door way, walking tall and proud with his warhammer slung casually over one shoulder - an impressive feat in itself when you took into account the weight of the solid metal head.

Looking at him like this, his long legs clad in the striped trousers of his religion, a brown velvet cloak hanging square from his shoulders, Elor had to concede that he had never realised how tall or dashing Pringle actually was. He could tell from the slightly discombobulated expressions around the room that he was not alone in thinking this. It was clear to see that this man, who everyone had assumed to be the court fool had actually been the King in motley all along. Judging by the glowing pride in Iona's eyes, she was the only person gathered who was not completely stunned. She stood a little back and to his left, hovering in his shadow, her eyes fixed on him as he began to speak. She didn't take in the words, only the passion and conviction of them. She was left buoyed and ready for action. Looking around her she could see she was not alone.

Aberddu City Turn Gate

The noises of the battle field still rang in Daisy's ears as plainly as they had five days earlier when they had left. As they departed the field, the Light Alliance were about to mount a dawn offensive on the Dark Armies using the first rays of the sun against the foul creatures that belonged to their enemy. The prematurely triumphant war cries of the Light Army gave way to the clash of steel and the fearsome clamouring and caterwauling of bloodthirsty beasts. The sound had been in the distance like a cruel whisper, as they rode away from the Plains but it had still be loud enough to have an effect on Daisy. Judging by Mauna Evanga's subdued countenance she was not the only one, although Daisy was not daft enough to broach the subject with the Death priestess. Mauna would sooner chew off her own thumb than admit she had anything in common with a Sister of the Chalice. As they stood waiting at the Turn Gate, Daisy was taken back to the day years earlier when she had first arrived in Aberddu at the height of the Father's Tear Pilgrimage. She barely recognised herself as she was then, timid and almost completely faithless. She had grown in everything but stature since and her faith had blossomed beyond all recognition. Deep in her heart, she was not sure that it was the faith of a Sister of the Chalice. Suddenly she was overcome by a plummeting feeling of grief. She realised now how much she missed Mori and the faith that they had, in essence, shared. Perhaps they still did. Her beliefs had not changed in all the time she had been on the Plains in spite of the best efforts of the other Sisters, she still held that Death was as sacred as Life. In fact, hadn't she shown mercy to that woman? Daisy was wrapped tightly in her own thoughts when the gate guards finally reached them to check papers. Apparently the war on the Plains of Blood had made the Turn Gate, already the city's busiest gate, even worse. The Sergeant, whose dirty blonde hair had been slicked against sallow cheeks by an earlier summer squall, had a face like a particularly disgruntled ferret. His rodent-like features made him look mean, and his voice didn't help. He stalked up to Whitefire and, removing the pick from his teeth, and said in a bored drawl,

"This is the Aberddu Turn Gate. State your business."

Whitefire explained the details to the guard whilst trying to lean tactfully out of the range of his rancid halitosis. Teign, who felt he was the senior, stood beside his horse his arms folded looking on sourly. He tapped his magnificent gauntlet against the side of his rerebrace, producing a sonorous clanking that was clearly irritating the guard, who glowered passed Whitefire as the Iceni was speaking. The guard had even appeared interested in what Whitefire was saying until he said the word 'Adventurers'. This elicited an acerbic grunt and he shouted up to a woman on the gantry.

"Cox, open the gate. It's more bloody adventurers." Then, without another word he wondered on to the next contingent.

The words 'more bloody adventurers' had piqued Daisy's

interest enough to tear her away from her self-pity. Almost immediately as they stepped through the gates her barely formed questions were answered. Plastered on the side of the first building they saw, a tumble-down inn called the Fiddler's Elbow, was a massive painted message. It must have been as tall as Daisy, and twice as wide. Each bold black letter a hand high:

"***Adventurers Needed - Guild reopened.*** **Past members welcome.** *Interesting Times ahead*

See D. Pringle Guildmaster."

It brought the whole group of them to a standstill as they stared up at the words in bemused shock. After a moment of silence, three adventurers spoke at once.

"Since when did the Adventurers need to advertise?" exclaimed Ferrin, as Whitefire whispered,

"Guild reopened? When did it close?" and Mauna shrieked, "Pringle, Guildmaster?" and let slip a cruel laugh. Teign was too dumbstruck to speak and Daisy simply groaned. The words interesting times did nothing to inspire her, instead they just topped up her existing dread to levels beyond those which she had previously thought possible. At least this meant that something was happening and they hadn't walked all this way back from the Middle Kingdoms to find Pringle alone and drunk on the Guild Hall hearth, at least she hoped not. After another pause during which they all tried to digest what they were seeing Whitefire said quietly,

"I guess we should head for the Guild then".

The guild was buzzing when they stepped wearily through the door. Pringle came striding out into the entrance hall and threw his arms wide like the ebullient host at the season's most notable party.

"Teign, Ferrin, Whitefire, Mauna," he exclaimed with a wide smile. His eyes fell greedily on Teign's impressive gauntlet and for a moment his smile became a leer. "Take off your cloaks, go on through, dinner's ready," he said congenially, pulling his face back into its suave welcoming expression.

Daisy, who had been dreading this moment since the Turn

Gate had opened in front of her earlier, looked away. Obviously Pringle wasn't pleased to see her. She let slip a silent tear and turned to go as the others divested themselves uncertainly at the behest of a man whose authority they had previously felt they should be questioning. Now they could see him, they were thinking that perhaps they had been hasty. Though none of them said it, as the four made their way into the bustling hall they each wondered if in fact Pringle's time had come. As Daisy took a step back towards the door she felt a firm but gentle hand on her shoulder, pulling her round.

"Where are you off to?" said Pringle softly, grinning down at her, his lashes damp with tears. "It's good to see you Dee, Mori will be so relieved." Then, he pulled her into rib-cracking embrace. It was too much, the exhaustion and fear just flowed out of her as cold, hysterical sobs and as it did so, she distinctly felt several heavy tear-drops fall into her parting. Then, as though this was as much emotion as he could stand, Pringle pushed her out to arm's length and said with glee in his eyes,

"It's all coming together, come in and let me show you."

Pringle lead the overwhelmed dwarf by the arm into the main guild hall. The transformation was astonishing. Even though physically it was unaltered since Daisy had last been there, it was barely recognisable as the same room. It was alive with activity, every free inch of space had been filled with trestle tables, chairs and bodies hard at work with their noses in books and scrolls. There must have been close on seventy people, Daisy estimated. Looking around, she could pick out maybe two dozen faces she recognised, among them Severin Starfire, the most condescending elf Daisy had ever met, Gul the shaman that Daisy thought of as not so much a shaman as an excuse for a myriad of pervasive and peculiar odours and Tollie and Sylas, who had once told her they were purveyors of genuine religious relics, medicine men and urban pathfinders. She suspected they were lying and therefore were up to something dodgy she didn't want to know about. Even in spite of that she had to admit it felt good to see the familiar faces.

The rest of the people in the room were both a shock and a

mystery to her. Where in the world had Pringle suddenly found all these willing volunteers? They were an unusual array of people. In the back corner an enormous contingent of mixed greenskins was sitting around a large scroll with looks of comical concentration on their mottled faces as a harassed looking scrawny young man with a long mousy brown pony tail and virtually no chin read aloud from it. There were also a surprising number of tartars mingling amongst the groups, all of them very young. They didn't seem to be remotely interested in the paperwork but were largely intent on sharpening and cleaning any weaponry they could lay their hands on. This was no surprise to Daisy, Krieg had explained to her long ago that tartars didn't usually read because they considered written language to be in some way destructive. Write things down and they are set in stone, they are dead and can no longer change and grow. Write things down and you have an excuse to forget. Tartars that learnt to read kept it very much to themselves and Daisy could understand why. They also gave their children weapons as soon as they were big enough to lift them.

The third obvious group of new comers were either mages or clerics judging by their clothing. At each table, and circulating around the room carrying books and scrolls like some kind of peripatetic reference library, were nearly two dozen delicate looking souls in clean- looking ankle length robes. Most of them were pale and willowy, and looked as though they had never seen such uncomfortable looking chairs in their whole lives. Several of them had their noses buried firmly in their reading matter, as though they were trying to pretend they were in a great library and the rest of them had the slightly discomforted expression of someone who had suddenly found themselves surrounded by too much weaponry and far too many people who couldn't read but did know how to kill them.

After taking a few minutes to absorb it all, Daisy turned to Pringle.

Her curiosity was so vast that it would not fit into words, she resorted to a questioning look.

"We reformed the Guild," he said beaming, "It was Iona's

idea." Daisy narrowed her eyes, that wasn't the name she'd expect to hear nor was that a look she had expected to see in Pringle's eyes.

"I can see that," replied Daisy weakly, unwilling to take Pringle to task about Iona just yet. "But where did all these people come from?" "A lot of them are ex-adventurers, some of the temples sent some clerics on loan and the tartars and greenskins responded to the advert, although Gods know who they found to read it to them." He chuckled as he said this and Daisy forced herself to smile. It was clear that Pringle bore her no ill will for leaving. "The rest," Pringle waved and arm indicating the delicate doilies in the robes, "are Elor's students. He told them that they needed practical experience of research and problem-solving and that they couldn't pass his course without it. That's why most of them look so terrified." Pringle chuckled again and this time Daisy's smile was more relaxed. "On the other hand, that guy," Pringle pointed to the chap who was reading patiently to the Green skins and absently guarding a small silver gyroscope from further prying fingers with one hand, "wants to join up. Don't scare him. His name's Geratti." Daisy just looked at Pringle. Don't scare him? She had never effectively scared anyone in her life. Pringle raised his eyebrows at her expression and then, suddenly the tension broke and both of them collapsed into fits of laughter.

At that point, a figure quietly approached them proffering two bowls.

"Soup?" said Mori, smiling at Daisy and pushing one of the bowls into her hands, "It's quite good actually, although I'm not sure what those yellow lumps are." Daisy breathed out. She knew her old friend well enough to know that this was as warm a welcome as she could expect and that any discussion or reproof would wait. Mori gave the other bowl to Pringle and the three of them shuffled across the crowded room to a clutch of empty seats. Daisy couldn't deny she was hungry and set about the soup gratefully. It took her only a few minutes to finish and Mori held out her hand for the empty bowl.

"More?" she said quietly, and Daisy shook her head. Hunger

staved off for a while at least, she had too many questions swimming about in her head.

"What are they all doing?" she burst out before she could organise the thought in a more articulate manner.

"Well," said Mori taking up the reins of explanation to allow Pringle to continue with his soup. "They're working on the ritual for the Champion," she waved to a group of four or five tables at the far side of the hall. "They're trying to locate the scroll case of Knowledge," she indicated a clutch in the middle. Then she pointed to another bunch nearer to them. "They're trying to work out how to get the cloak off Elder Dmitri without actually killing him and the tartars are organising the armoury."

"What about them?" asked Daisy, pointing to the wizard and the green skins. Mori smiled.

"Oh," she said with a smirk, "and Geratti is reading the greenskins Paravelian Cradle Tales to stop them 'helping out'. Apparently they particularly liked the story of the Scathach." Daisy shook her head and smiled.

"Okay," she said, her smile now uncontrollably wide, "What should I do?"

"Come with me," said Mori smiling back at her, "we have a shrine to rebuild."

Aberddu City Docklands (the nice end) - sunset

Pringle looked down at the ring on his right hand. He couldn't remember how he had come by it, mainly because he'd had it for longer than he could remember. This was not much of a feat given that most of his past was a gaping hole and his earliest memory was only five years previously. He had turned up at the city Dark Gate, drunk as a skunk with a nagging feeling he had forgotten something. As it turned out, he had forgotten everything and the only connection he had to his past was this plain little silver ring. He had never really paid it much attention until now, its total lack of embellishment meant that it held no clue to anything whatsoever. The only reason he was thinking about it now was that he had just noticed it was warm and shimmering.

He had just been about to take it off for the first time in five years and put it in his pocket so that he could pull it out at the opportune moment but now he decided that was probably not wise.

Iona would be here any minute. He tried to smooth his hair down again and looked out to sea. The setting sun was cooperating nicely, pushing a soft orange path up the gentle blue-green waves as it sank slowly towards the horizon. It was the best he could do for romance right now. He turned back to the city, and saw Iona appear at the end of Fisherman's Walk. His heart quickened as he tried not to think about how she had navigated that less than reputable alleyway at this time of day alone. He waited breathless as she looked around for him and then as she laid eyes on him and smiled, he felt his stomach flip. With an urgent, scurrying run Iona crossed the main thoroughfare and stopped just short of Pringle.

"What's so important?" she said, her face fixed in a pleased but curious expression. "Have you found a champion?" Pringle just shook his head. Now the moment had come he was lost for words. It hadn't occurred to him that Iona would think this was a business meeting and he now found himself inexplicably nervous. "You've found the scroll case?" she said, smiling excitedly but Pringle shook his head again he really didn't know how to say it. He'd planned all sorts of grandiloquent speeches for this moment but now none of them seemed to fit. "The ritual's been written?" said Iona, now getting frustrated with this guessing game, "because you didn't have to drag me out to the Docks to tell me that." Pringle shook his head again and fixed Iona with a determined look that had the desired effect - she shut up. He reached out and took both her hands, dropped to one knee and immediately grimaced, not daring to look down at what he had just knelt in. Iona didn't laugh - she was too shocked by what seemed to be happening.

"Um," Pringle said, still fighting for words. After another moment or so of Pringle not knowing what to say, Iona said,

"Oh for heavens' sake stand up and stop trying to pretend that we're other people." She hauled him to standing, let go of his hands, gave him a glowing smile and she said, "Now what did you want?" Pringle folded his arms and grinned back at her with a look of enormous relief on his face and realised for the first time that he wasn't fooling himself in thinking he loved her. The words came so easily now.

"I think we should get married," he said in the same emphatic tone he used to talk about the God War. "As soon as possible."

"Okay," said Iona with a grin so wide she could barely contain it on her face, "how about now?" Pringle smirked and said,

"Why not? Your temple or mine?"

Many unfavourable things could be said about the Trickster Temple and many of them often were. However, there was one inarguable fact that was often conveniently glossed over: The Trickster was the God of the Everyman. Having once been a mortal himself, his affinity with them was far greater than any other deities, in fact some even said he missed the mortal life and deeply regretted the hubris that had led to him steal his divinity. The majority of his followers were among the most open and accepting of clerics welcoming all states of the mortal condition, all ideas. Unlike the Kesoth Temple that considered a lot of things beneath them including allowing its followers to marry those of other 'lesser' Gods, the Trickster Temple welcomed Pringle and Iona with open arms. One of the acolytes even lent them a ring to be going on with.

As they walked across the city hand in hand, neither of them spoke.

They wore the blissful half-smiles of people who have just experienced a moment of wonder amongst a plethora of atrocities. As they reached the guild building, they could tell from the noise issuing from the hall that something had happened. It was a part excitable, part argumentative buzz. They looked at each other with resigned smiles. There was no way that they could ignore it.

A charitable mind could describe what they encountered in the guild hall as a passionate exchange of ideas. An all-out row was more accurate assessment of the situation. Elor, Teign, Whitefire and several of the gathered clerics were involved in a heated and voluble debate around Mori and Daisy who were having little success refereeing the discussion whilst the greenskins and tartars waited with bated breath in case there was an outbreak of fisticuffs and they could join in. Pringle, still hand in hand with Iona, strode into the centre of the room and cleared his throat. It was testament to his current standing as Guildmaster that everyone fell quiet and looked at him. Several of the shrewder and more socially aware adventurers then looked at Iona who was standing next to him, taking in their clasped hands. None of them said anything.

"What's going on?" he asked genially, and everyone spoke at once. He simply raised his hand and they all stopped. Then, with a growing air of authority, he turned to Mori and said directly to her,

"What's happened?"

It's not often that a man turns up on the doorstep claiming to be the Champion of the Gods, so it was understandable that a disagreement had broken out. Nearly every temple was in some way represented in the Guild and most of them wanted the honour of providing the Champion. Elor on the other hand had done his reading. Unfortunately, this had not stopped Teign, Whitefire and few others shouting him and each other down as they tried to put forward their own cases. Pringle listened as Mori explained, and just as Teign opened his mouth to add his groat's worth held up his hand again to stop him.

Pringle had listened to Elor and knew exactly what question he needed to ask and to whom. He let go of Iona's hand, walked passed the group of open-mouthed debaters and held his hand out to the serene-looking man sitting on a low bench off to one side watching the whole scene with infinite patience. The man stood up, took Pringle's hand, shook it and said,

"I'm Jarell"

"Dakarn Pringle, Guildmaster, a pleasure to meet you," said Pringle pleasantly. "I understand you believe yourself to be the champion of the Younger Gods?" Jarell nodded but before he could speak, Pringle continued. "Excellent," he said with a broad grin, "In which case I have only one question for you." The gathered adventurers and clerics looked on with bated breath, readying objections to either the question or the answer on the tips of their tongues. "Which God do you follow?" The pause between the question and its answer was a mere few seconds but it felt like a lifetime to those waiting for the response. Jarell looked steadily at Pringle and said in a half-whisper

"All of them." The answer was greeted by stunned silence from everyone except Elor who said, "See," in tone of uppity self-justification before turning to stalk away.

"Excellent," said Pringle grinning even wider, "You'll do." He patted Jarell on his well-armoured shoulder and said flippantly, "Welcome aboard, the dwarf'll find you a room." Then he turned to the adventurers and clerics, who were all poised to start shouting at once including Daisy who was irritated at being called 'the dwarf' and treated like the housekeeper.

"Now, ladies and gentleman," he said with a grand theatrical gesture, "It's my wedding night, so if you don't mind I'll deal with your objections in the morning." With that, he swept Iona heroically into his arms and strode out of the room towards the stairs.

As he lay her gently down on his bed, he could tell from the quiet below that the room was still stunned into silence. As her beautiful auburn hair tumbled over the pillow, Pringle sighed. It looked exactly how he had imagined.

ABERDDU ADVENTURERS GUILD

Sunrise

Mr and Mrs Pringle's honeymoon was extremely short-lived. It ended a few minutes before the morning six-hour the day after their wedding, when the whole guild was woken by the frantic ringing of the warning bell. The peals echoed up the stairwell stirring all the resident adventurers unceremoniously from their rooms. Pringle sat bolt upright and leapt out of bed, diving into his trousers and pulling them up as he went. He snatched a shirt and started to run for the door, leaving Iona looking about in the murky morning light trying to find her tunic. The hallway was pandemonium as the bell had sent all the adventurers racing towards the hall in varying states of dress. As Iona appeared dazed in the doorway of the Guildmaster's chamber, she was greeted by the sight of the entire greenskin contingent piling down the stairs apparently all having emerged from the same room, their weapons belts already on and their boots hanging around their necks on knotted laces.

"Morning," snorted one of the orcs and gave her a knowing wink. Iona just grunted and found her way into the crush on the stairs. By the time she finally pushed her way into the main hall Pringle was slumped, shaking, on a bench with his head in his hands. A quivering messenger with the distinctive insignia of the

Trickster was babbling on, unsure what to do about the fact that he couldn't tell if Pringle was listening. The scrambled adventurers were milling about the hall, some of them had dropped into chairs and were resting their heads on the tables. Elor, still in his nightshirt and cap, was bustling about snatching up books that were at risk of crinkled pages or drool puddles. It didn't take long for the bleary silence to become disgruntled muttering. When, after five minutes or so, Pringle still hadn't told them what was happening Iona realised that something was really wrong.

Crouching down beside her husband, she was horrified to see that he was as white as his bed-sheets and tears were snaking down his cheeks. His eyes were fixed on a patch on the floor about a foot and a half from the end of his boots and his hands were trembling. Unsure what to do, having never seen Pringle in this state before, Iona knelt beside him and softly put a hand on his thigh.

"What's happened?" she asked quietly, so that Pringle could answer her without having to say it publicly.

Pringle just looked at her, the sparkle of excitement had completely vanished from his eyes and had been replaced with cold, dull despair. He opened his mouth to speak but no words came out, he just shook his head sadly. Iona looked imploringly over to the messenger who was also pale and shaking but seemed more able to communicate than Pringle. It seemed cruel to make him repeat the obviously devastating news again but she had no choice.

"What's happened?" she said, louder this time in hope that the messenger might speak up so she didn't have to. She was no longer sure she wanted to repeat this news, whatever it turned out to be, to the gathering. The messenger swallowed hard and in a quavering voice said,

"We were attacked, the temple's burning, we've lost more than a hundred clerics and... "

At this point his voice faded out and he was overcome by sobbing.

"and what?" demanded Iona, hoping the harsh tone would

snap the messenger out of his distress. It worked well enough. In a voice strangled by crying he managed to splutter.

"and the Trickster's dead."

Iona went numb. She suspected that she already knew the answer to the question she was about to ask but she couldn't avoid it.

"Who attacked?" This question seemed to steel the messenger a little and he spat the word back at her.

"Kesoth."

There was nothing she could do or say, she didn't even know if she ought to get up and walk away. Would Pringle want her to go? She didn't know. Would he blame her? She hoped not. She had been aware that something was happening, it was difficult to spend that much time in the temple and not be aware of that. For one thing, they had been concealing quite a sizeable strike force who had been preparing for something in the underground levels. Iona had just assumed the target would be Light Alliance, consolidating the position against Amroth. She had been down there to help with preparations. She felt sick.

She looked up at Pringle with tears in her eyes, scared of what she would see looking back. Like him, she was now lost for words and could only shake her head slowly.

Pringle took hold of the hand she still had placed on his thigh and squeezed it. Then, he looked into her eyes. It would have been impossible for him to conceal the hurt she saw, even if he had been trying. In a murmur, so that only Iona could hear, he said

"I have to go. I don't know how long I'll be, but I will come back." He emphasized the word 'will' with another squeeze of the hand. "I love you."

"I love you," choked Iona, her voice thick with emotion. Then, Pringle stood up and, without pausing for anything, left the room. The messenger, slow on the uptake, scuttled after him leaving Iona sitting on the guild hall floor with her head in her hands.

The messenger's just about audible announcement and Pringle's swift departure opened some kind of flood gate. The other Trickster followers departed in short order, with only marginally more decorum than Pringle and the room suddenly descended into pandemonium, almost everybody started speaking at once. This very quickly degenerated into the half-awake adventurers yelling over each other and hurling abuse at those from other temples.

Iona remained on the floor, unable to move, whilst around her everybody else continued as though this were a shortage of fish in the market-place. Hot, angry tears were streaming down her cheeks. She was furious with herself for falling for Pringle. If she had kept her distance, not let her guard down, then she wouldn't be sitting here crying now. She would very probably be in the Kesoth Temple celebrating. As she thought that she let out an anguished yelp of self-disgust. In all probability, if Pringle hadn't married her, he would have been in the Trickster Temple tonight, and quite probably dead. At this thought she let out another wail and began to sob hysterically.

Most of the guild were too wrapped up in the current business to pay any attention to the weeping woman in a heap on the floor. Elor was now coordinating a frank exchange of opinions and trying to turn it, unsuccessfully, into a plan of action. He was on what Pringle liked to refer to as a 'hiding to nothing' because most of the people who were giving their frank opinions were not interested in a guild plan of action so much as giving voice to their panic about the future of their own gods.

Amongst the clamour and people grumbling that they had been dragged out of bed for nothing, two women maintained a grip on the situation. Mori and Daisy were both still fully-dressed having not been to bed in the first place. They had been at prayer most of the night and had only come back when the glow of the flaming temple had risen above the city walls. They were not shocked by the news, because they had passed through the Temple District on the way to the Guild. They had paused for a minute and looked around at the bedlam that was slowly escalating out of control.

Mori laid eyes on Iona in her isolated grief and made her way silently through the hubbub towards her. She placed a gentle silver hand onto Iona's shuddering shoulder and the woman turned to look at her. The sight of Iona's blood-shot eyes and the absolute fear and anguish of her expression filled Mori with sadness. She took Iona by the unresisting hand, helped her to her feet and lead her out of the room and into the quiet of the reception hall.

Daisy just stood for a moment on the edge of the growing chaos, soul-wearied by the self-righteousness and ignorance of many of the arguments she could hear. She let out a deep sigh. Once again, no one was saying anything important and Elor was failing to control the conversation. She turned to wander into the kitchen when something stopped her. Deep in the pit of her stomach, a sharp fiery passion compelled her to take an action she would not have thought possible. She leapt up on the bench against the wall so that she was at least of comparable height to most of the humans and elves in the room and took in a deep breath.

"Stop," she bellowed, her usually thin voice echoing from the walls and rafters of the hall. "Stop and listen."

The shock of Daisy shouting was powerful enough to silence the whole room. She flushed red as all eyes turned to her, many of them glowering but all of them intrigued. "Don't you get it? This is it. This is the time for action. We need to move quickly. We need to get the ritual started as soon as physically possible and bring all this to an end." Daisy's voice petered out, as astonished as everyone else by this outburst, but the quiet remained for a moment, until Elor said,

"Exactly what I was trying to say," and gave Daisy a look of grudging admiration.

The Fall of the Trickster Temple shook the city. All but a handful of its clerics had been wiped out. The few that remained picked over the rubble in desperate but waning hope. Pringle was nowhere to be found. It was a dispiriting sight. Rumours from the Plains of Blood filtered back into the city in the days that followed, the whole Temple District held its breath to find out which God would be next. Although many reports were garbled and some were certainly fanciful, several of the more unpleasant tales were easily corroborated. It seemed that dissatisfied with the murder of Heimdala by Caros the Beautiful, Kesoth had seen fit to take to the mortal plain again, this time in the form of the Betrayer. Other Gods followed suit. Amroth, not to be defeated again, appeared as Vathnir the warlord - a more suitable opponent for the Betrayer. Their strengths were well- matched and the battle continued for some time.

Law and Life also appeared as did Death and Chaos. So far, the balance was in some way maintained. Then, the smaller, neutral Gods took to the field. The Enigmas, The God of Knowledge and The Celestial Flame appeared, allied to no-one. Easy prey as they were, Kesoth picked off Knowledge and The Enigmas without a second thought, absorbing their power into his own, black and silver lightening crackling around him. The power of the Dark Alliance was growing immeasurably as they continued to fight, fielding more and more dark creatures alongside their mortal armies, now energised by these significant victories.

The Celestial Flame, a Goddess more savvy in the ways of warfare than either Knowledge or the Enigmas, put up at least a cursory defence. She had lasted nearly twenty four-hours until she was surrounded by Kali and Hecate, two of the sister Goddesses of Death. They destroyed her in minutes, releasing a pillar of fire that was visible from Aberddu City. The Temple District was in turmoil. The followers of the Fallen Gods reacted in myriad different ways. Every man, woman and child that could walk in the congregation of the Celestial Flame marched together to the Plains of Blood to join the Light Alliance and seek retribution for the death of their Goddess. The Brothers of Erudition, the principal order of Knowledge followers in Aberddu, barred the temple gates against the world and refused to let anyone in or out. The Enigmas worshippers simply vanished.

It was on this backdrop, with Pringle missing and the guild barely reformed, that Mori and Daisy took over the task of the ritual that would save them all.

ABERDDU CITY STATE

The Day of The Ritual

In the seven days since the Temple of the Trickster had been razed, the Temple District of Aberddu had become a war zone to equal the Plains of Blood. Those that remained behind in the big temples were unable to maintain the uneasy truce that had existed in the months before. The Death Temple had suffered the most, bearing the brunt of retribution from the Light Alliance forces that were still in the city as well as a significant amount of hostility from the followers of the All-Father, who had added an extra dimension to the war in Aberddu. The Children of Krynok were strange and awful and the mortals in their thrall were little better.

Thrall was perhaps too strong a word thought Mori as she darted down a side street and away from a gang of them. They had taken to roaming the streets ostensibly with the intention of providing sanctuary to those troubled by the violence. However, if you refused or in any way objected to them they became aggressive. Mori already bore a livid cut on her cheek from an earlier run in with a different group and she wasn't planning on getting a second. She should have felt triumphant as she rushed back towards the Guild District, she had accomplished exactly what she had set out to do; she had located an Enigmas follower.

Granted, the woman was currently high as a kite and in militia custody but neither of these states were permanent

However, Mori could not see this as a victory, even though this was supposedly the last piece in the puzzle. They had obtained all the items which were now under constant guard by a whole infestation of greenskins, as was Jarell, who was showing no signs of regretting his decision. Elor and his team of wizards had cooked up a ritual and they had, up until an hour ago, managed to recruit a follower of every younger God except the Enigmas. It had taken three days, and a considerable amount of money, as well as every contact nearly every guild member could call on to locate the one they had found. She had been in the nick on the day the Enigmas had met its demise and had therefore not disappeared with all the others.

The Militia were happy to accept a few silvers as bail, mainly because she was driving them up the wall. They couldn't work out what it was she had taken, but it was showing no signs of wearing off and she kept telling them they sounded spotty and smelled of yellow. None of them could work out if this was insulting and therefore, so far they hadn't charge her with disrespectful behaviour directed at an officer of the militia. It was getting to the point where the Sergeant was about to declare the words an insult so that they could at least charge her with something. She had originally been hauled in for being drunk and offensive to the public, which usually resulted in a small fine and a stay at the Militia's first class hotel until you were sober enough to leave without bumping into anything. She had been in there nearly a month and was still did not appear to have come down, they were beginning to think she wasn't high at all and that she was just weird. Unfortunately being weird wasn't actually a bookable offence, which, the sergeant thought, was probably just as well as they didn't have anything like that kind of cell space.

Raising the bail would be no problem, then all they would have to do would be tie her down long enough to get her to enact her part of the ritual and they were home and dry, in theory. Mori knew she should be elated but realistically there were two things troubling her. Firstly, the words 'in theory' which followed every statement that Elor made about the ritual and the second thing was that she had a deep seated suspicion that they had missed something. She scurried across Bryony Bridge and pulling her cloak around her against the chilly dawn air, rushed across the empty Guild Square. The war in the Temple District had emptied the Guild District like a hole poked into a water tank. Only the Adventurers, Bards and Scribes were still in operation, everyone else had suspended trade or had lost so many members to the conflict that they were temporarily shut down.

Oddly, she missed the noise of the warriors Guild doing what she had always thought as their early morning showing off. The square seemed dead without it. The Adventurers Guild was a hive of activity. Mori divested herself of her cloak quickly and ducked into the hall. She wanted to see Elor and Daisy before she was bombarded with questions by people trying to be helpful. She appreciated their help she really did, but she was not naturally in charge and it bugged her that people needed to know everything. Looking around for a moment, she located Elor with his head down over a large piece of parchment that she recognised as the ritual transcript and Daisy at the end of a large table of people who looked like they could probably write. She was instructing them to do something, but Mori didn't listen to what. It was strange enough to see her shy friend giving orders to these academic types, she didn't want to interrupt them. She looked around again.

The other person she wanted to speak to was Iona. She wasn't in the main hall, but she wouldn't be far away. She had barely left the guild building since Pringle had gone. If she did go out to her temple at all then she made sure that she did it when no one else was about to see her. She was usually to be found in either the kitchen or the Guildmaster's private chambers which were technically hers now by virtue of being his wife, even though he wasn't currently around. Mori had been forced to revise her opinion of Iona of lately. She could not honestly say that she liked her, but she had now come to see that she had some uses. She was also the only person who was likely to have an idea about Pringle's present location and that was what Mori needed more than anything else. She couldn't put her finger on why, but she had a deep-seated feeling that they needed him back.

Mori found Iona in the kitchen chopping turnips and flinging them into a large pot. She didn't need to ask Iona why she had taken to helping with these tasks, Mori knew full well that these mindless repetitive activities were a very effective distraction. As Mori entered the kitchen, Iona looked up and half-smiled at her. Mori wasn't about to beat about the bush.

"Iona," she said in a quiet, solemn voice, "Where's Pringle? We need him." Iona looked at her and paused for a moment, her face wandered through a gamut of emotions and Mori could tell she was holding back tears. Mori didn't wait for Iona to try and express her answer, it was plain from her facial expressions that she didn't have an answer to Mori's question. "It's okay," she said, in the same steady tone, understanding but not sympathetic. "But we do need to find him, if you have any idea where he might be?" Iona simply nodded and returned rapidly to the turnips. Aware that she had just caused Iona a certain amount of distress, Mori didn't hang about. She left her to her mountain of turnips without delay.

Elor stood up and stretched out the ache in his back. He had been curled over the manuscript for so long he couldn't remember what it felt like to stand or indeed walk. At last he had finished it and it was almost to his satisfaction. He could not be completely sure that it would work, a fact that he had tried desperately to conceal from Mori and Daisy. He was unsure how successful he had been at this either. Looking out of the clerestory windows he could see that it was daylight again. Well that was fine, it would give them a few hours to get things organised before this evening. He put his quill down and wondered off to collect together a few people.

Til-Dar scowled. The Adventurers Guild were up to something. They always were. The word on the street was that they had been burning the candle at both ends and in the middle as well. Activity on that scale meant a plan and he wouldn't be surprised if that bloody Trickster priest wasn't in some way behind this. The arrogance of the man was astonishing. Something had to be done. He'd seen that interfering dark elf running about in the Temple District a number of times over the last couple of days too looking pre-occupied and self-important. It could not wait. They would need to strike today. They had more than enough strength of arms to take on the Adventurers Guild and win. He went into the temple, the day light was hurting his eyes.

The greenskins were bored. Everybody else was praying. Apparently, something was going down this afternoon because all the pinkies and pointies were flapping about like a load of geese in a farm yard and nobody was telling them anything. This lack of information usually meant something important was happening. They were quite used to this and had found many and various ways of entertaining themselves whilst they were being kept out of the loop. Clench, the tiny little goblin, had started making interesting sucking and popping noises using her nose, mouth and fingers and two of the orcs were beating out a rhythm on their legs and feet to accompany her.

Usually, GerVal would have found this amusing but today he was too involved in thought. It was an unfortunate assumption that people tended to make. They assumed that if it was green, or grey, it didn't think, it wasn't even entitled to a gender apparently. It was a very stupid assumption because in fact greenskins thought a great deal. They just rarely thought about the same things as the other seemingly more civilised species or in the same way. For example: goblins hate water, which is why they don't wash but they do go on boats because boats stop you having to go in the water. Simple, indisputable logic that left most other races open-mouthed, wondering why goblins didn't just stick to dry land.

GerVal was not a goblin, he was an orc and a very large one at that. As such, he usually thought about what he was going to kill next and how and sometimes he extended these thoughts to include what he was going to drink an awful lot of when he'd done that. Right now however, he was thinking about something else entirely. It occurred to him that he was guarding a very, very old and important suit of armour that in about three hours was going to contain a feeble-looking religious nit-wit with a slightly weak chin. Once they'd dressed him up like a tin-covered numpty, the god-bothering types were going to ponce about doing something that looked like the Bard's Guild had tried to concoct a new form of folk dancing. Then, in theory, and GerVal had noted that Elor had repeatedly failed to say that it would definitely work, this would make the chinless nit-wit the champion of the Younger Gods. What GerVal was struggling with was this: once they'd done all of this and the nit-wit in the armour had been imbued with whatever it was he was going to be imbued with, what happened then? He wanted to know but not enough to bother the wizards in their flurry. He just continued to mull it over. No doubt someone would explain in due course, or not. It didn't really matter. Until then, he would just do what he was told, mainly because it was no bother to him and he'd just made the piece of ground he was sitting on warm and comfortable. Reaching out lazily, he cuffed Clench around the back of the head and hissed "Shut up," at her. Then, he burped loudly, stuck his finger into his ear and furtled about.

GerVal was asleep, and snoring like sludge descending a down-spout, when Daisy appeared three hours later looking pale and tense. The orc Danz and Clench the Goblin were wide awake and still on guard the others having sloped off to an alehouse the moment that GerVal had nodded off. They were balancing various different things on their sleeping leader in an effort to cover him in bits and pieces without waking him up. It was probably a good thing he hadn't fallen asleep with his mouth open Daisy thought as she watched Clench trying to stick a snail on his dagger hilt. Heaven only knew where she had found the snail indoors but Daisy had decided it was best not to inquire.

Daisy never knew how to start talking to the greenskins. She wasn't particularly good with people in the first place and from what she understood greenskins needed special handling - she wasn't entirely sure why, it was just the impression she had been given. She cleared her throat and Danz looked up.

"Alrigh'" he said languidly. "Wha's up?" Daisy shifted her

weight from foot to foot, she did really know how to phrase her request, so she went for straight forward.

"We need the stuff, if you could bring it over that would be great."

Danz nodded to her, winked and said "Right you are boss." Daisy mumbled

"Thanks" uncomfortably and left as quickly as possible, unsure whether the use of the word boss was facetious or not. When the greenskins arrived in the main hall laden down with the items they found Elor, sweat beading on his brow, surrounded by a gang of distracted, sombre-looking religious types.

"Excellent," said Elor as he saw the three greenskins arrive. "If you could bring the items this way."

GerVal, who still had one or two snails crawling up him and a salt spoon hanging out of his hair, was intrigued to note that Elor's voice was quavering and as he approached he could see that the whole wizard was vibrating. Jarell the chinless seemed to be the only person in the room who wasn't palpably nervous. GerVal thought that this was probably a pretty good indication that the silly sod had no notion what was actually going on because being a greenskin he was naturally suspicious of people who made claims about ridiculous things like destiny and divine provenance and turned down offers of liquor. The items were dumped unceremoniously in front of the serenely smiling idiot, and the greenskins stepped to one side. They stood together leaning on the wall and looking on with the same air of mild fascination used by people with standing room tickets for the latest Bards Guild farce.

Elor coughed affectedly and the last of the mumbling stopped. "We're ready to begin," he said trying to steady his tremulous voice, and with a wave of a hand he indicated that the gathered clerics should form a circle. He looked over at the greenskins opened his mouth to ask them to leave, and then thought better of it. He just nodded curtly at them and GerVal touched his imaginary cap in acknowledgement, dislodging the spoon."Are we doing it here?" demanded a sweaty faced priest in a grey and red robe, that was probably the representative of the Celestial Flame.

"Yes," said Elor tartly, not enamoured of the priest's critical tone. "This is as good a place as any and the writings specify the need for neutral territory," he added with a sniff and the grey-clad cleric pursed his lips unable to argue in spite of the fact he clearly wanted to. "So," said Elor, his voice taking on a much deeper timbre as he forced confidence into it.

"Welcome and gather. We come together in this ritual to show the unity and strength of all the Younger Gods who work in harmony and balance…"

As he spoke his words filled the hall completely amplified by their gravity. All the gathered priests were completely consumed, hanging on his every word. He welcomed each God and their representative by name, and as he did so the magical power in the room built and blossomed until it was possible for even the uninitiated such as GerVal to feel it tingling on their skin. GerVal was amused to see the Iceni Whitefire representing Amroth and some of the other less important followers, glowering openly at Iona who was representing Kesoth. Elor continued to expound on the need for unity among the Younger Gods and their followers. He spoke extensively about the meaning of the ritual and then, when GerVal thought he was going to have to start plucking the hairs in his ears to keep himself awake, Elor changed tack. In turn starting with the red-faced Celestial Flame priest who was to present the armour, he called on the representatives to dress Jarell. The champion stood in the centre of the circle and continued to smile beatifically throughout. Stepping forward one at a time the priests added the scabbard, sword, dagger, shield, cloak, scroll case and helm to his costume. It was just as the Aesthetics representative, who possibly the strangest smelling man that GerVal had ever encountered, stepped up to Jarell to hang the amulet around his neck that Elor realised he had made a mistake. The Chaos Brother was standing beside him, a curiously angelic smile on his face and his eyes fixed firmly on Jarell

He was apparently completely unaware that there was no item for him to add to the champion. Elor's pulse quickened and he felt sweat soaking unpleasantly into the back of his robes. The Aesthetics chappie, as Elor had come to think of him, was performing a complex and incongruously low bow, signalling that he was about to return to his place in the circle. Elor looked about in panic. No one seemed to be wearing a belt. Every member of the ritual party had, as instructed, arrived clad in a free flowing ceremonial robe of some kind. Fortunately for Elor, or possibly unfortunately depending on how you viewed the situation, none of the ritual participants noticed his obvious distress as they were far too wrapped up in the significance and spirituality of moment. On the other hand, the three greenskins who were off to one side watching with expressions of confused amusement, were all well aware of it. GerVal sidled around the edge of the circle to Elor and out of the corner of his mouth, in a gesture that was probably an attempt at subtlety, hissed,

"What's up Guv?" Elor looked askance at the orc, the last person he had expected to be of use right now.

"What's up?" repeated GerVal through his teeth again, this time louder and more urgently in case Elor hadn't heard him the first time because of his subtlety. Elor cast his eyes down the orc and saw exactly what he needed. Judging by the number of buckles on his frontage, the orc was wearing at least three belts. Elor's eyes lit up.

"Belt," he grunted to GerVal, trying not to disturb the final words of the Aesthetics chappie, who was thankfully making a seven course banquet out of taking his leave from the Champion. "Give me your belt."

Greenskins have more sense than to say things like 'why?' to wizards. GerVal just took one of his belts off. There was an incongruous clattering sound as one of GerVal's knife loops hit the floor and the orc held the strip of boiled leather out in front of him. It still had a snail wending its way merrily up it, completely unconcerned by what was going on around it. With trepidation and a look that suggested he thought it might be contagious, Elor took the belt from GerVal and passed it directly on to the Chaos Brother, who had just become aware that it was his turn to approach the champion. The Brother took the belt happily and without any indication that he was in anyway perturbed by the presence of the snail moved forward to address the champion.

The moment he had fastened the belt up over the Armour of the Celestines the grimy metal buckle became brighter and Elor breathed out. The assumption had been correct. In a strange kind of way, Elor would reflect later, the method of obtaining the buckle and even the snail, had been perfect really.

The Chaos buckle was the last item in the jigsaw of the Champion's Armour and as the Brother finished his blessings and returned to his position in the circle, the ritual moved on to the second stage. Elor turned back to his scroll and began to read the segue. GerVal collected his knife and stepped back to the side wondering if he could get Elor to cough up for a new belt after all this was over. It was in these moments as Elor's transitioning speech came to a close, that several things happened and didn't happen at the same time.

The room darkened as the light coming through the clerestory windows was obscured by thick black clouds and the floor shook. Several of the ritualists fell over screaming in pain and clutching their sides, blood flooding between their fingers. The hall door burst open and just as it did the glass of the windows imploded, showering everyone with fine shards that clung in hair and gashed skin. A harsh wind whipped into the hall, thick with some kind of powdery dust. Iona let out a shriek and ran towards the door. The clouds of dust started to form into humanoid figures. The green-skins picked up their weapons. Iona leapt bodily at Pringle who was standing in the doorway, so that she was wrapped entirely around his skinny frame causing him to stagger back against the wall. A hideous high pitched jangling sound filled the room and Elor tutted.

The wizard had not moved throughout the tumult of the last few seconds, concentrating solely on Jarell, who was now apparently in full regalia. Elor had been expecting some kind of magical change or shift at this point but from his readings of the magical signatures, it had happened. He was too busy assessing this to be fully cognisant of what else was occurring around him. Pringle regained his breath, shoved Iona to one side and blurted out the message he had come here to convey.

"The Fae are coming," he panted grabbing Elor's robe by the

sleeve. "We need to move, now." Elor looked at Pringle with a curled lip, he was tempted to stamp his foot and spit his irritation that the ritual didn't seem to be working in any case, but he didn't. The room had been plunged into chaos. As he looked at the wheezing cleric, a dozen shimmering figures with greyish skin, spindly claw-like fingers and black fangs had formed out of the dust. Their dark, wicked eyes were fixed on the ritualists. Elor could not argue. Even if the ritual did need to be re-scripted, there was no question that they needed to leave this room as soon as possible. The creatures that had burst in through the windows were already prowling around the fallen ritualists, slimy black tongues licking their thin lips greedily at the sight of their mortal prey. The three greenskins, who were just as pleased as the Fae to have something to injure had set about three of the nearest. The Fae had responded to this attack by hissing and spitting corrosive saliva at the greenskins, who just cackled and carried on, ignoring the smoking patches on their armour and battering them with as many weapons as they could hold. Teign and Whitefire were defending the weeping sea god priestess and the body of the Chaos Brother.

It took Elor a mere five seconds to take all this in and process it enough to make a decision. He reached for his staff, which he had propped against the wall behind him. He raised it above his head, bellowed a complex incantation in his best wizarding voice and slammed the end of the staff down on the floor. Immediately, a vortex of white and blue light started to form around the bottom of the staff, slowly flickering and expanding outwards.

"Come on," yelled Pringle, horrified by the lethargic response of the ritualists. He leapt over the prone form of the Aesthetics chappie, grabbed Jarell by the shoulders and started pushing him towards the slowly expanding portal. Iona, who had picked herself up from her ignominious disposal, raced back into the circle and scooped up the Enigmas priestess who was shaking and weeping in an ever expanding pool of her own blood. Iona did her best to heal her as she carried her towards the portal, but she wasn't the most powerful of clerics. Suddenly aware of what was going on, the others were starting to take action, although some of them were struggling against the Fae creatures. Mori and Daisy were trying to wrestle the Aesthetics chappie from the grip of one of them. Mori had sunk her ankh-hilted dagger deep into its back and was grimly removing her blade for a second blow. Daisy had hold of the limp form of the priest and was pouring healing magic almost continually into him as she struggled. Mori struck again and sent a bolt of lethal magic crackling down her dagger into the creature's back. It let out an ear-piercing screech and whipped around, relinquishing its grip on the limp figure in its arms as it did so. Daisy snatched the priest, staggering back under the weight and Mori darted out of its reach. Then, dragging the still delirious man between them, they raced towards the portal.

"Run," bellowed Teign, shoving the tearful sea god priestess towards the swirling pool of light as he and Whitefire started backing towards it. They were the ritualists left in the hall apart from Elor. The greenskins were showing no signs of trying to leave.

"Come on," bawled Pringle through the portal at them. "Let's go!" Danz to turn around, gleeful winked at Pringle and said,

"Nah, it's okay mate, we'll sort this." This lapse in attention cost him his advantage and it was all he could say before ten foetid black claws were sunk deep into his chest. He let out an anguished yelp and turned back to the fight. Pringle didn't pause. He took the orc at his word and nodded curtly to Elor, his Guild-master's authority restored. Elor stepped through the portal himself and with a flick of his staff drew it closed behind him.

A sorry sight met Pringle's gaze. They were in the relative safety of a small glade in the woods outside the City walls. He counted up and found that there were fourteen gathered including himself, one for each God, Elor who was, for want of a better term, the master of ceremonies and Jarell, the supposed Champion. Mori and Daisy, themselves not entirely unscathed, had taken firm control of healing and welfare and were working their way steadily through the injured and panicking. Whitefire and Teign, still hyped from the fight were stalking the edge of the glade either attending to matters of security or, if one was feeling less charitable, walking off their adrenaline. Iona was sitting on the floor, cradling the Enigmas priestess who was pale and worryingly still in her arms. Iona was stroking her hair and humming gently under her breath, having discharged all the healing magic she was capable of before she had reached the portal. Elor was comforting the Sea God priestess who seemed to be uninjured but somewhat hysterical, wailing about wanting to return to temple. Jarell the champion clad in the regalia of ages, stood stupidly to one side of the group with a slightly dazed expression on his face and his hand on the hilt of the Sword of Death like a militia officer unsure if he ought to intervene in a bar brawl.

Pringle shook his head and sighed. Jarell may not be the true-blue-hero type, but then this was Aberddu and not Albion and in Aberddu you made the best of what you had. If Jarell was an All-Gods follower and a willing sacrifice then Jarell was the right choice. They had to finish the ritual. Overcome by melancholy for a moment, he looked across at Iona again as she gently brushing her hair out of her eyes. She would make a wonderful mother, he thought. After all this, he hoped he would find out. He desperately wanted to go to her and embrace her and tell her it would all be all right but he couldn't. First of all, he had to make sure this would not be a lie. Turning the other way, he went to Elor and in a low voice said,

"So, what next?"

Elor opened his mouth to complain about the ritual not working when he looked down at Pringle's hand.

"Er," he said stupidly, pointing at the glowing ring on Pringle's hand. The ring, that had begun to buzz and shimmer several days previously was now flickering with red and yellow pulses"Yeah," said Pringle, as though that were an explanation. "It brought me back here." Elor's mouth opened and closed again, his eyes suddenly lit up as though the florin had finally dropped.

"Take it off," he said urgently, "and give it to Jarell Quickly." Pringle didn't argue. Although he didn't entirely understand what Elor was on about he followed the instructions. He slipped the ring over his knuckle, and grabbed Jarell's ungloved hand. The champion stood there impassively and watched with only mild interest as Pringle manhandled him in this way. Once he had wedged the ring firmly on Jarell's little finger, the only digit onto which it would fit, he leapt back and looked the champion up and down unsure what he was expecting to see.

Initially nothing happened, Jarell just stood staring at his latest acquisition. Then, very gradually, as though clouds were slowly parting around him, he began to shimmer and glow until a halo of soft white light surrounded him. Elor scanned the magical traces and breathed a sigh of relief. This was the change he'd expected, later there would be time to puzzle over why it had taken Pringle's ring to bring it about now he just needed to finish the ritual. The nimbus of light around Jarell had attracted the attention of the ritualists, who stopped whimpering and bandaging each other and turned to stare.

"Come on," shouted Pringle with a theatrical gesture reminiscence of a circus ringmaster. "We have a ritual to finish." Almost as one, the ritualists flooded back into a circle and Elor reached into the pocket where he had safely stowed the script of the ritual. As they resumed, the woods became hushed, the air was thick with magic. The breeze calmed and the clouds froze in position. As each representative added their scripted contribution to the proceedings, tension rose. Still serene and glowing Jarell stood in the middle of the circle and looked on with what appeared to be only gentle curiosity. The chanting grew louder, the nimbus grew brighter and Jarell was obscured from view. If anything had moved in the clearing none of the ritualists would have noticed, they were far too absorbed in what they were doing.

The cadence escalated and peaked. There was a blinding blue-white flash and they were all thrown to the floor.

Some time later...

Daisy lifted the baby carefully and cradled it the way she had been taught in the orphanage. Judging by its size it was a newborn but it was far more alert than she would have expected for an infant so young. It also seemed remarkably placid given that it had been left lying naked on the forest floor. With her free hand, she dug about in her bag. There was usually some cloth knocking about for emergencies. It wasn't the most salubrious of swaddlings but it was better than nothing she thought as she folded the stained muslin around child. She noticed as she covered the child – a girl – that she was warm, clean and apparently not hungry. Tenderly, she stroked the soft blonde down on the baby's head and cooed gently. Mori, far less naive than her friend, was looking fractiously around the clearing. She didn't like it. For one thing, the last memory she had was of daylight and there being a dozen people there. Now it was dark, nearly midnight she sensed, and the clearing was empty apart from the two of them and this child. Newborn babies don't fall from the sky, and they certainly don't grow out of the forest floor spontaneously, that meant someone had put the child down there. It wasn't cold, hungry or agitated, that meant that it hadn't been there for very long. Squinting, she peered into every dark corner, her elven eyes searching out the shadows of movement. She knew there was no point in hoping that Daisy would know what had happened, she was too preoccupied with the baby. Far more used to young children than Mori from her time as a nurse in the temple orphanage. The child seemed to be smiling serenely back at her.

For a moment Mori almost thought the baby was humouring Daisy, then she snapped back to her wits. Whatever was going on was not good. If this baby was a trap it should have sprung by now, and if this baby was not a trap then what in blazes was it? She shivered, the cold damp air of the summer night was soaking through her ritual robes. Whatever they were going to do, they needed to get back to the city and safety as fast as possible. People who leave babies lying about don't deserve an explanation when those babies are collected by well-meaning priestesses.

"Come on," she whispered urgently to Daisy, drawing her knife without thinking, "let's get back to the City." She put her free hand on the baby's head and suddenly the world changed.

The ground shook, and both priestesses fell to their knees. Daisy flailed to maintain her hold on the baby and found nothing but muslin in her arms. Mori righted herself quickly casting about, her dagger at the ready, but she did not get back to her feet. There was a warm wind and a glow in the sky and suddenly a young girl was standing in front of them. She was maybe six or seven, fair-skinned and red- haired, she had a smattering of freckles across her nose and a serene, knowing smile. She was wearing a plain green slip dress and no shoes and she glowed. Both women bowed their heads. It is not difficult, if you are faithful, to know when you are in the presence of the divine. The girl reached out both hands and gently lifted their chins so that they were looking at her. Then, in a voice like the song of a thousand larks, she said,

"I am Aurora, the Goddess you have prayed for. I am born tonight as a mortal, and you will look after me. I must live and grow on this plain before I can ascend to divinity. If I am to be the Cycle, I must first know the Cycle." Then, she kissed them both on the forehead. Later, they realised that neither of them had any idea who she had kissed first as they were both under the impression it was them. Then, as suddenly as she had appeared, she was gone and the baby was back in Daisy's arms. The sky was dark again. The women looked at each other, hearts overwhelmed with elation and terror. Without another word, they both began to run.

AFTER THE RITUAL

Iona sat in the warm bath water trying not to wince as it stung every cut and scratch on her skin. Soap first, and then luxury beyond belief, oils and a warm drying cloth. It was even clean bath water, well it had been when she stepped into it. Now, flakes of mud and leaf-mulch floated on the surface. She yawned and reached for the ball of soap. She was still fighting to get her head around the scenes she had witnessed earlier that day. She had asked Pringle if he wanted to go and pray, but he had just smiled at her and said he could pray later. The way he had said it made her blush, she still felt slightly ashamed of herself for the way she turned into a simpering wench when Pringle showed her kindness or smiled at her with those miraculous eyes. Instead of the temple or the Adventurers Guild, places you would expect to find a cleric or a Guildmaster after such an important event, he had brought her to the Black Wolfe Tavern, the poshest establishment Iona had set foot in since leaving Ambassadorial service.

They had a quiet dinner and he booked them a room for the night. He had not said that he was leaving in the morning and that he might not come back but Iona knew. She was pushing that to the back of her mind now, along with what she had witnessed in the clearing. There would be time for analysis and grief later and if there wasn't then she didn't want to waste what remained on glum reflection. Once all the grubby patches had gone and the aches had soaked away, Iona stood up and reached for the small clay flask. The rose perfumed oil smelt exotic and alluring. It took only a few drops to cover her whole body. She couldn't remember the last time she had actually used bath oils, and even then she had never felt as special as she did now.

"The moon's up I see," announced Pringle as he walked in just as Iona bent over to replace the flask on the floor.

"Cheeky," she said, straightening up and turning around. Pringle was standing in the door way holding a large drying cloth. Clearly, he had just bathed himself and was wearing a long cloth robe, his large bare feet poking out of the bottom of it. She shivered as a cool breeze tickled her damp skin. Seeing the barely perceptible shudder, Pringle stepped forward and draped the drying cloth around her. It was warm and soft on her skin, it must have been hanging by a fire. Iona let Pringle wrap her and scoop her up in his arms. She lay there blissfully as he kissed her forehead and carried her over to the bed. Gently he placed her on the expensive cotton sheets and a wistful smile crossed her lips as she remembered her wedding night. The linen on Pringle's guild bed was scratchy and unwashed but it had felt just as good.

Pringle bent forward and blew out the candle and Iona heard his robe fall to the floor. As he slid across the sheet beside her, Iona felt herself tense in anticipation.

"Iona," he whispered, his breath hot on her cheek, "there's something I should tell you. There's a chance that... " At this point Iona interrupted him.

"I already know," she whispered, "but that's tomorrow." Then, before he could say anything else, she kissed him.

JUST BEFORE MIDNIGHT

Aberddu City East Gate

The two priestesses paused panting in a hazel coppice. Nothing seemed to be following them but Mori was still not satisfied. They were almost within sight of the city gates, but both of them were breathing hard. The baby was still wide awake but placidly looking about. Whilst they recovered their breath, Daisy rigged up a sling for it with the fabric of her tabard. They could hear the noise of the gate traffic through the quiet of the forest night. Voices, involved in what could generously be termed 'a spirited exchange' but was more akin to an argument, carried through the air. The priestesses, aware that they were extremely vulnerable held fast where they stood and listened. "I said dismount and state you're business," bellowed the gate Sergeant again. Krieg just looked at him, his white eyes glaring wildly out of the black, his nostrils flared.

"Open the gate," came the reply. The voice was familiar to the priestesses, and on hearing it they looked at each other and couldn't help but smile. "This is important."

Greery was tired and cold. He had done three double shifts already this week because of a run of particularly virulent pig-blisters that had probably come in with those stinking pilgrims. Even the kid was down with them and Greery had almost felt sorry for him when he had called around. However, today was market day and he was exhausted. He had spent the better part of the day counting geese, sheep and goats, he'd had to make his own tea and worst of all they were out of lardy bread because Coombes was also down with the pigging blisters. Consequentially, he was even less in the mood than usual for people swaggering up to his gate on very large horses and making demands. "Oh is it really?" he said in his snottiest sergeanting voice, the one that clearly indicated that after that, the person on the receiving end would be lucky to get a kick in the *you-know* never mind about anything else.

"Yes," said the mounted tartar levelly, somehow his word carried across the night cutting through all other noise but Greery was too involved in his sarcasm to notice.

"Let me guess," he said sardonically, "you're here to see Krieg Clan Dragon of the Aberddu Adventurers Guild?"

"No," said the tartar with the same calm resonance, dismounting his horse and striding deliberately towards Greery. The Sergeant, not a small man himself, had not been able to appreciate the full physical stature of the tartar until he had seen him standing on the road. Exactly where tartar stopped and fur armour started was difficult to discern, but it made for an impressive bulk. Greery found himself standing opened-mouth, his hand still on his sword hilt, as the tartar approached. Krieg reached out a sinewy hand, grabbed the front of Greery's oil-skin and lifted him clear off the ground. Then, without so much as drawing a deep breath slammed him into the gate and in a very soft, reasonable voice that seemed to carry just as well, said,

"No, I'm not here to see Krieg Clan Dragon. I *am* Krieg Clan Dragon, now let me in."

If Greery could remember the events between being pinned to the gate by Krieg and the cup of tea that Baker pushed into his hand a quarter of an hour later he never let on, but he must have been involved somehow because it was indisputably his signature in the log book beside the entry and Baker hadn't opened the gate all on his own. This was happening more often than he liked. He sat in the door way of the sentry box contemplating his future.

Perhaps he could get himself transferred to the Docklands patrols. Word had it that the sea captains paid well in barter for the occasional blind eye and the hookers were cheap and obliging. When he saw two priestesses waddling up the road out of the darkness he sighed deeply and sent Baker to deal with them.

Greery had had it, any more of this and he was going to hand his notice in. Perhaps the Docklands wasn't far enough - perhaps he ought to try the Albion navy or something a bit more interesting. If life was going to be hard work then at least a change of scenery and time away from his wife might make up for it. Being the gate Seargent was not an interesting job but it had, until recently at least, been a quiet life with good pay. He had been working diligently on a comfortable middle- aged paunch, made mostly of strong tea and lardy bread, designed to keep him warm on long damp winter night duties. That had long since vanished, it took time he no longer had to drink enough tea and scoff enough lardy to have some to spare. And then of course there was the war. If you could really call it a war at all. All those lice-ridden, scabrous pilgrims that had come in over the years to take up space in the Temple District and the poor quarter, all the religious nuts, all the hangers-on – **all of them**. They had all decided to leave town at once. Through the East Gate. He had had to resort to double entering in the ledger, because he was fast running out of space.

THE PLAINS OF BLOOD - BATTLEFIELD OF THE GOD WAR

Timier dodged the claws of another horrific beast and dived into a hollow behind the stump of a blasted willow tree. Fighting for breath, he wiped his bloodied knife on his surcoat. With sadness, he realised he could no longer pick out the blazon of the Law Army. He had been getting progressively more and more grubby and now his whole front was stained a nasty reddy-brown colour. It was becoming more and more difficult to tell who was on which side at a glance. Timier felt that there might be some kind of philosophy in that but his brain was too exhausted to fathom it through.

For a moment he closed his eyes trying to block out the battle, but it didn't work. Those creatures were still there whenever he closed his eyes, burnt on to his retina. The dark gaping maws, the rotting facial features wreathed in flames and the overwhelming taste that came to his tongue every time he remembered them. He couldn't remember when he had last slept. It did not matter, it was impossible to tell night from day any more. A world with sunshine, laughter and feather beds seemed unconscionable right now. He opened his eyes again, he was still half sitting, half lying in a stinking hole and would probably never see Aberddu again. He heaved himself to his feet, and crouching behind the stump so that he could see the whole field, he tried to work out where he was.

A few days ago, if he'd been separated from his unit like this he would have received an extensive dressing down from his Captain for breaking ranks and flouting protocol. Now, when he turned up at the camp, if he made it back there alive, he would be greeted with open-armed relief by the deputy who had taken command when the Captain had bought it. So few of them remained that even the Paladins were losing faith. They never said as much because they didn't need to; it was written in their eyes. It was then that he realised hot tears were sliding down his cheeks.

Timier had run a long way into enemy territory. He hadn't really known just how far until now. Between his position and the Light Alliance lines were a sea of Dark Alliance and their malevolent creatures. Handmaidens, Angels of Kesoth and dozens of other monsters were swarming over the ground in front of him, picking off the few remaining survivors and feasting on the carrion. It was a sickening sight. His heart sank with grief as he was transported back to the Galivara Wastes to the last battle he had seen like this. Not like this really, not anywhere near as brutal or bloody but just as frightening in its way. He could still hear the words of Josef de Clariar. "A holy war is a thing of glory, Timier. It is the ultimate and final test of faith. You will know as you walk from the field what your heart believes." He felt cold every time he remembered those arrogant words and saw again his final sight of Josef de Clariar - his wide lifeless eyes staring in terror at the sky, blood drying on his flesh and tabard. He had been right in a way. After seeing that, Timier had never aspired to be a Knight of Justice again. He knew in his heart that he loved Law but he would never, ever believe that his faith was superior to anyone else's, whether he agreed with them or not.

Timier was just weighing up his options when he felt the midnight power rush coursing through him restoring his limited magic. Even with that he doubted he'd make it two hundred feet across the battlefield, never mind the half a mile needed to reach the Light Alliance lines. He sat down again and put his head in his hands. There were two choices really, in all of this, and they weren't really choices at all because they both culminated with the same sticky ending. He could either make a brave run for it and get cut down as he ran or he could stay here and wait for an unimaginable horror to happen to him. He knew he should make the heroic dash for it, but really with weary limbs, a pounding head and burning blisters on his feet he just wanted to sit here and wait for the inevitable.

He curled into a ball, perhaps if he lay very still he would pass for a piece of the landscape and be ignored. He was just wondering how ludicrous an idea this was when there was a thunderous crack and the world was momentarily bleached white by a flash of blue-white lightning. For a moment Timier thought he had been partially deafened by the noise because the sounds of the battlefield had dropped to almost nothing. He could hear the clamour and clash of steel on steel but the guttural roars and groans, the menacing hisses, the jarring melodic singing of the Handmaidens, they had all gone. Cautiously, Timier lifted himself up and peered around the blasted stump. All the monsters had vanished.

And it broke like a tide. Suddenly, the God War ended. Although it would be some time before all sides could be convinced to stop fighting and all divine creatures left the mortal world. For those that witnessed this incredible event it was as though someone had flicked a switch, turning off the surety of war and bringing in the hideous tumult that followed. For some, the rebuilding had to start, for others there was still another threat to face.

Just after midnight

Aberddu Adventurers Guild

The clang of the warning bell startled Clench awake, causing her to flail wildly and topple out of her hammock. Walloping Danz on the way down, she landed heavily on Dremmel's massive stomach, knees first. The gigantic troll grunted and swatted at the tiny creature as though she was an oversized bug. Knocked out of his dream by the falling goblin, Danz sat up sharply and almost immediately tipped sideways, landing with a thud across Dremmel's legs.

GerVal woke in the middle of a scrum of green and grey arms and legs grabbing at trousers, weapons, boots and other people's body parts, accompanied by the sound of the emergency bell. With a look of deep-rooted resignation, he reached for his giant spiky mace and heaved himself out of the pile of hide he'd been sleeping in. This was the second warning bell in as many weeks, and GerVal was wondering if they were going to have to contemplate new employment options as this adventuring lark was turning out to be harder work than it looked.

"Let's go," he grunted, and at once the collection of half-dressed greenskins trooped out into the hallway, dragging whichever weapons they had been able to lay their hands on. Down in the main hall, they joined the crowds of yawning adventurers who had gathered at the sound of the bell. They were in varying states of undress, some of them had clearly been in bed since the curfew bells, whilst others were still fully clothed and red-faced from drink.

Most of them were muttering under their breath about how the bell was only for emergencies and how this was a bloody liberty, ringing it twice in two weeks when it barely rang once a month normally. The sour-faced night porter was flinging logs from the recently filled wood basket on to the embers of the guttering fire whilst a bloodshot and scrawny stable boy in a thread bare night shirt and holey woollen socks pumped the bellows for all he was worth. Clench, who was about the same height as most people's elbows, pushed her way to the front of the clustered adventurers, curious to see what had pulled her from the warm comfort of sleep. It was bound to be over-hysterical pinkies, most likely yet another snivelling woman or a panicking wizard. The other common use of the bell was the Warriors Guild indulging in what could charitably be called a bout of late night inter-guild high-spirits, but that wouldn't have had the night porter stoking the fire. Also, the Warriors Guild was shut.

In her recollection, she had never before seen about a hundred stone of tartars with blood and fire in their eyes. Even a goblin can be stirred by the sight of a towering tartar in full furs and war paint, and the five that stood before Clench were quite an impressive collection. She recognised the leader. He bore a striking resemblance to a former guild member who Clench seemed to remember hung around with those uptight priestesses and was mostly drunk. To give him his due she had thought, if she hung around with the those two she would also be mostly drunk. Having said that, Clench was convinced that the tartar she was thinking of had been somewhat smaller than this gargantuan figure.

It wasn't long before GerVal had shoved some of the smaller, younger adventurers to the side and joined Clench at the front of the rabble. Unlike the goblin he was not awestruck by the spectacle, he simply wanted to know what these tartars thought was so important. He held out hopes that it might be something worth hearing as tartars were less prone to histrionics than most pinkskins but so far it was difficult to tell. The tartar in charge, whose name he thought might have been Krieg, was howling with laughter much to the confusion of this clansmen. Beside him, a scrawny-looking warrior in stained combinations was looking at him with puzzlement unable to work out what he had said that was so funny.

Eventually, Krieg choked out the words,

"Really? Dakarn Pringle, the well-known Trickster-bothering, amnesiac piss-artist is the Guildmaster?"

"Yes," muttered the warrior still confused.

"Fair enough," conceded Krieg, trying to catch his breath and looking about him. "Well, I guess beggars can't be choosers. Where's Elor?"

"Mr Nybass is probably in the Mages Guild," ventured another young lad in a knee-length doublet and bare legs. He spoke tentatively, clearly anxious that the vast tartar didn't laugh at this information with such gusto as he had at the news about Pringle being Guildmaster.

"Mr Nybass is it now?" chuckled Krieg kindly, "Okay, what's your name boy?"

"Derek," mumbled the lad in the doublet. "Peterson," he added when Krieg seemed to be waiting for more.

"Can you go and fetch him for me?" asked Krieg in a tone that suggested this more of a command than a question and Derek nodded. "Put some trousers on first though," added Krieg with a straight face but a glint in his eye as he saw Derek trying to work out if he ought to go right away.

GerVal was conflicted. He had heard the name Krieg Clan Dragon bandied about before, although from what he had heard he had gleaned an impression of an irresponsible, inebriated oaf. In GerVal's eyes, this was not necessarily a damning description, many of his best friends were irresponsible, inebriated oafs, however what he had not expected was the man in front of him. There was no doubt in GerVal's mind that this was a man whose time had come. He had not woken them all in the night to invite them to a dock-side piss-up. This was going to be worth waking for. GerVal sat down on the floor by the edge of the fire place and made himself comfortable. If the other adventurers wanted to stand up and wait for the wizard and gods knew who else to show up then that was their look out.

Daisy and Mori scurried across the near pitch-black square towards the Adventurers Guild. The kitchen door was usually open after curfew. They were used to the empty darkness of the largely deserted District but even so they were both gazing about them urgently, eyes finding their way into every corner, every shadow. Mori didn't expect to sleep tonight, she just wanted to get back to the safety of the Guild Hall and sit in the quiet kitchen with a cup of mead. Then, in the morning they would try and find Elor and see what he had to say about their latest arrival. As she passed the grand frontage of the Merchants Guild she picked up her pace, for some reason she found the towering columns disconcerting in the dark. Daisy, who was already moving quickly to keep up with Mori's larger strides was forced to break into a jog. They were drawing level with the Mages Guild when Mori heard something that caused her to pull up short and fling out an arm to stop Daisy. It was the sound of movement from the side passage and in her keyed up state, Mori wasn't taking any chances. She pulled Daisy into a patch of shadow by the wall and indicated that her friend should keep quiet.

They were only there for a moment, when the source of the noise became more apparent.

"Hold this for a moment," barked a familiar voice from the shadow and the pale flicker of a candle lantern cast a puddle out of the end of the passage.

"Do you need a hand Mr Nybass," said the beleaguered lantern holder who sounded as though he was beginning to regret being useful.

"No thank you," snapped Elor tersely, "Just hold the lantern steady." There was no reply.

Mori looked at Daisy, they had both heard it. Mr Nybass. Unless there were two of them, that was Elor. The question they were both dying to ask was what in the name of all that was holy was he doing in the side passage of the Mages Guild after midnight? They didn't have to wait long to find out. It became evident almost immediately exactly why Elor was so clearly disgruntled. He emerged from the passage way and stood in the grubby half-light of the lantern tapping his foot.

"Come on," he grumbled, "Let's go if we're going." The voice of his companion was just about audible, saying something placatory as it closed a door with a thud. Then a young man with a tousled shock of dark brown hair and a weary expression appeared next to Elor. The lantern light made it possible to see that Elor was standing in the Guild Square wearing his long flannel night shirt, a night cap, a knitted bed-jacket, a shawl and a pair of thin leather slippers. "What was so damned important that you needed to drag me from my bed then Derek?" Elor continued in an irate whisper.

"Umm," began Derek, clearly stumped. "I don't actually know," he admitted after an uncomfortable pause. "I didn't stop to ask. Krieg was just so adamant that you should be fetched that I came right away."

"Krieg?" croaked Elor, his uppity tone completely gone. "Krieg Clan Dragon?"

Derek nodded cautiously. He wasn't keen on a repeat of what

he had already started thinking of as 'The Dakarn Pringle' incident. "The great big tartar," he added to underline his point. "I think his name is Krieg anyway." Elor nodded and said in a choked, tremulous whisper. "Yes, that's him." Then recovering his senses slightly, he suddenly stood bolt upright, stamped his foot and yelled,

"Damn-it I thought we'd have longer." Then, without pausing to explain or wait for Derek, he stalked off across the Guild Square as fast as a wizard in pyjamas could go. Mori and Daisy exchanged looks again. If anybody knew what to do about their current situation it would be Elor. Without another word, they broke their cover and scurried after him. Derek, who had been too busy concentrating on fetching Elor to realise who else was there, started back with surprise and then watched in confusion as the two priestesses chased after the wizard. Derek sighed. This was definitely more interesting than life on the pig farm but sometimes, just sometimes, he wished the adventurers were as easy to deal with as the pigs. By the time Derek had found his way back to the guild building, he was starting to wish he had gone to a tavern instead. He could certainly use a large mug of something, and he didn't particularly want to go back into the Guild Hall. He had the feeling things were only going to get worse. Perhaps, if he was very quiet, he might be able to slip into the kitchen without attracting too much attention.

As he opened the door, Derek realised this was unlikely. Krieg, Mori, Daisy and Elor were still in the antechamber, embracing each other enthusiastically. The small room echoed with the excited greetings of people who were overwhelmingly pleased to see each other. Derek tried to slide past unnoticed, but before he made it as far as the hall door he felt a spade-like hand clap him on the shoulder. He turned to see Krieg smiling back at him. The tartar then winked at him and mouthed "thanks mate," before letting him go. Derek smiled bashfully at his feet and shuffled his way back into the main room.

When they had finished greeting each other, Mori grabbed Krieg by the elbow and whispered to him urgently,

"There's something we need to tell you." Then without giving him much choice, she dragged him through the heaving guild hall and into the pantry. Daisy and Elor followed cautiously. When they finally managed to pick their way through the press of bodies, they found Krieg sitting in one of the chairs by the range, his eyes wide and his mouth open as Mori recounted the events that had taken place after the ritual. The moment Elor grasped what she was saying, he sank onto a stool beside Krieg his eyes fixed on the priestess. He made Mori repeat the salient points twice before Krieg cut across him and said,

"So where'd you put it?"

Mori was about to say put what? when Daisy cut in, speaking for the first time.

"She's in the Life Temple," she said. Elor opened his mouth to object but Daisy quickly added, "she's in the orphanage. Only Sr. Imelti knows that she's not just an ordinary baby." Krieg nodded slowly,

"Is she okay?" he said quietly, clearly struggling to trust this unknown nun.

"No," said Mori before Daisy could respond, "She's a miserable old bat, but she knows how many beans make five, so don't worry."

"Okay," said Krieg. It was clear from his facial expression he was searching his brain for more things that may need to be handled. Looking at him now, Daisy thought how far removed he was from the happy-go-lucky drunk she used to know. "She'll be safe enough there. There's something else we need to do and we need to do it now."

ABERDDU CITY TEMPLE DISTRICT

With most of the Brotherhood of the Lady's Justice away on the plains of blood, the temple had been left in the hands of the Sisters of the Chalice and the Morning Brethren. The Morning Brethren were a joyful collective who believed it was their duty to procreate as much as physically possible in order to spread the gift of Life. They were generally agreed to be great fun, but not the people you want to defend your temple. It was only a matter of time before someone realised this weakness and exploited it.

Til-Dar felt a rush of divine power crackle through him and he bellowed the command to attack, The Hunter's Army - half enthralled mortals, half terrible, dark Fae - swarmed forward and overran the Life Temple in minutes. The brief screams of the gate guard soothed his bruised ego. Since the Adventurers Guild had slipped through his fingers earlier he had felt disjointed and his rage had slowly escalated. The guild no longer seemed like a satisfactory target. His eyes had turned to the temples, the home of those interfering priestesses. Someone had seen them both go into the Life Temple earlier, perhaps they hadn't left.

Sr. Imelti had been on her midnight rounds when she heard the first signs of attack. She had darted back to the Sisters' dormitory and woken the sleeping women before the temple alarm bell had rung. She didn't pause to explain, she just barked out orders to wake the children and evacuate. She then thrust her ring of cast iron keys into Sr. Leonora's hand, tore off her wimple letting her silver braid fall down her back and snatched a baby from a crib by the door. Before Leonora had time raise an objection, Sr. Imelti had gone through the step-door.

She ducked down the alley that ran behind the Life Temple and slipped between the buildings into a higgledy-piggledy little courtyard. She raced up a narrow stairway and popped out in a grubby passage at one end of the Brightling Bridge. She was now a matter of yards from the Guild District. Behind her, she could hear the sound of the escalating attack on the temple. She didn't pause to look back, she just kept running with the baby clutched to her chest. When she had handed this child over, she could worry about everything else, hopefully without explaining to Leonora.

Even though she was aware that adventurers kept different hours from temple-dwelling nuns, Sr. Imelti was still surprised to see that the building was brightly lit at this hour. She could hear the noise coming from the hall before she had even opened the main gate. As she rang the warning bell, she was not amused to hear the mixture of raucous laughter and uncouth language filtering through the gap under the door. As she waited on the step, she pursed her lips and offered her prayers to the Lady for the redemption of these sinners.

Five minutes later, she had completely changed her mind about the Adventurers. She had walked into a room that she had unconsciously labelled as a den of debauchery and within moments of her saying the words 'temple under attack' the whole atmosphere had changed. It was like watching a very eccentric but well-oiled siege-engine rolling up to a battle line. A massive tartar who had introduced himself as Krieg Clan Dragon was now barking orders at groups of warriors, wizards and other outdoorsy types. Sr. Imelti just stood to one side and watched, the baby still clutched in her arms. She was still staring in fascination when Daisy took the baby from her and thanked her profusely. Then accompanied by her dark-elven friend, a slender tartar woman and a wizard in a nightshirt, bed-jacket and cap, Daisy had disappeared through a portal.

Standing in the Temple Square beside a breathy Death cleric who was wittering on about healing supplies, Sr. Imelti's whole world view changed irrevocably. The Life Temple was still standing but crawling with vicious hissing dark-lipped creatures. She didn't care that the temple had fallen, she could see from the rage in their eyes that they had not found their target. The Sisters had evacuated and everyone was safe. She had expected to be relieved that they had escaped but distressed about the temple. Instead, her relief was absolute. For the first time in all her years, she saw the temple building as nothing but a pile of stones.

What surprised her even more than this was how she felt about the woman beside her. It seemed that in the time she had been in the Adventurers Guild the Fae-children had over-run the Life Temple and in their dissatisfaction at finding the building empty had taken their wrath to the Death Temple. The Death Temple had not been left so unguarded. The Fae had met quite a sizeable resistance. Unfortunately, this had not worked in the Death Temple's favour. The temple was now burning, the main tower had been blasted to pieces and death followers of all stripes were fleeing the falling masonry and flames.

The woman beside Sr. Imelti stood elegantly weeping at the scene. In spite of herself, Sr. Imelti actually found herself reaching out and embracing her. Less than an hour ago she would have had nothing but vitriolic words to say about this woman and now here she was comforting her. From where the pair stood, in the shadow of the Chaos Temple, Tollie and Sylas watched the scene before them. Chaos seemed somehow an appropriate temple for this night. The denizens of the district, those that had chosen to remain behind, were not ready for this battle. The war was supposed to be miles away. The whole place swarmed with the children of Krynok inflicting their terrible will on the followers of the younger gods. Habited and wimpled nuns scurried this way and that, white with terror, their vestments splattered with blood. Elders and sages leaning heavily on staffs hobbled as fast as they could in the direction of safety, whichever they thought that happened to be; there was very little consensus. Upright scholars laden with scrolls and tomes argued urgently on the steps of the Law Temple. The Death Temple burned, drowning the tableaux with a sickly orange glow. And in amongst all of this, there were people, ordinary people. The sick, the destitute and misplaced who had turned to these temples for safety and salvation. All hope of that now gone, they were crowding in the square, panic rising, filling the air with terrified cries.

A fork of blue lightning flashed for a moment turning the world monochrome and a thunderclap cut through the cacophony. Heads turned to the Docklands road. Elder Dmitri was an impressive sight, even without his massive cloak. Tollie had never found out how exactly Sylas had got hold of the large sheep-skin garment, there hadn't been time. If there was a 'later' then he was going to ask him then. For now, he would just stay here and marvel at the Elder's impressive flare for the dramatic.

Tollie would have bet all the money in his pockets and in the stoneware jar that Sylas didn't know he kept behind the bar in the Rotting Dog, that this was the moment that Elder Dmitri had been preparing for. And what preparations. Few had questioned the decision of Dmitri not to take his temple to war on the Plains of Blood. Thinking it over, Tollie had to admit that it did make a certain amount of sense - let the others fight it out, stay in the city and reap the rewards of not deserting the people in their hour of need - then side with the victors when they returned. Of course Tollie had no way of know if that was actually Elder Dmitri's intention, but being the cynic he was it made sense to him. There was another flash of lightening, and Tollie was able to see the full extent of what approached. An army, Tollie hazarded at one hundred to two hundred strong armed with shields and pikes, wearing the Sea God livery marched towards the Temple Square. At the head of this army was Dmitri himself, driving a chariot pulled drawn by a team of a dozen oxen. The beasts', their harnesses and the chariot itself crackled blue with magic. Someone had found him a smaller, blue cape which billowed behind him in the night breeze.

Tollie and Sylas were fixated, both aware that they were witnessing one of those pivotal moments in history and something the Bards Guild would never truly manage to replicate. Apparently Til-Dar and his Fae army had felt exactly the same thing, because with frightening unity they all turned to look at the approaching forces and started moving towards them. Tollie was rather worried by the look on Elder Dmitri's face, because in the half-light of the Death Temple flames he appeared to be smiling.

The enormity of what followed took some time to digest, but eventually Tollie and Sylas, and all those who survived that night to think on it further, realised exactly what they had seen. Elder Dmitri opened his mouth and let out a shrill, spine-chilling cry and the Fae Army stopped dead in its path. Then, continuing to issue the same hideous other-worldly noise, he reached out his arms in front of him. Streams of pale blue light shot from his palms and wove their way through the crowds. They found Til-Dar surrounded by a dozen dark winged creatures, and wrapped themselves around him. He struggled but to no avail, as the tentacles of light tightened and grew, squeezing him tight. Once they had a strangle hold on his neck, they lifted him up and when he was about twenty feet above ground Dmitri made a sharp gesture with his hands and Til-Dar's eyes bulged. The sound of his neck snapping reverberated around the Temple Square. His voice echoing through the bedlam, the priest began to speak.

"It will take more than this to overthrow the faithful of the Younger Gods. Return to your own world Children of Krynok, before we who champion the Younger Gods are forced to destroy you."

On hearing these words, Tollie and Sylas exchanged significant looks. Had they just heard that correctly? Neither of them dare to speculate. They were still looking at each other a moment or so later, when Elder Dmitri's plan started to unravel. There was a sudden shift of power, and the Fae Army over-rode the thrall that Dmitri had placed on them. One or two dropped down to Til-Dar's body, but the vast majority of the creatures swarmed forwards. When Tollie looked up again, Elder Dmitri was no longer visible. Instead, the chariot, oxen and the front row of the Sea God Army had all disappeared beneath a wave of dark Fae. The pike-men flailed and stabbed wildly, but it was clear that they had not been trained to face actual combat with the unwieldy weapons they were carrying. Had Elder Dmitri really thought he could just march into the Temple Square and shout the Fae down? Apparently so. Tollie was unable to look away. Carnage was a word that sprang to mind. Beside him, he could feel Sylas tensing and shaking, he too apparently couldn't drag his eyes from the horror in front of him. It was a few moments after he first heard the sickening noise filtering through the cacophony that Tollie realised he was listening to the sound of thousands of fangs on flesh and bones.

When asked how long the next few events took to occur, no one who witnessed it could give an accurate answer. Stunned as they had been, no one had moved when the Fae had first swarmed, but then the spell had suddenly broken and people had rushed forward from all quarters. Law clerics with shields and swords side by side with ragged, dagger wielding Kesothians and Chaos followers of nearly every conceivable stripe. Grave-diggers from the Death Temple, wielding shovels like axes and Sisters of the Chalice armed with little more than sticks. Tollie was almost inspired to join this united force but a cough from Sylas brought him back to his senses. The pair stayed in the safety of their shadow and looked on as mixed clerics from every conceivable background charged into the Fae Army to defend the Sea God followers. It was possible to see from where they stood the vast amounts of magic that were being poured into both healing and defending the fallen, the green flashes of the Life priests mixing with the crackling purple of the Kesothians and the Amrothian red and gold in an awe-inspiring light show.

It was too late for Dmitri, as the dark creatures moved away from him Tollie could see that very little remained of the seven-foot zealot but the blue cape and a pair of boots, with ankles sticking out of them. The oxen on his chariot team had been unharnessed, and those that had not been devoured had bolted and were trampling fallen fighters under-hoof in their blind panic.

The fight lasted a matter of mere minutes before the next in a long string of extraordinary events occurred. A column of pure white light erupted from the middle of the square, dispersing as it moved outwards into all the shades of the rainbow. The wave of light knocked the breath from every creature in the square, including Tollie and Sylas, and many of them fell to the ground. There was a moment of absolute silence and all eyes turned to look at the figure that had just appeared. Tollie recognised the cloak of the Sea God before he took in anything else, but as he looked he realised it was all familiar: the helm, the shield and sword, the scabbard and the dagger, even the belt buckle. Without realising what he was doing, he dropped to his knees. Beside him Sylas had done the same, and he could see they were not alone. All around the square, stunned onlookers had dropped to their knees and some of, presumably the more faithful, had bowed their heads or flattened themselves prostrate to the ground.

The Champion of the Younger Gods, because this was certainly no longer the bemused and non-committal man that Tollie had met in the Guild, must have been about eight or maybe nine feet tall. With commanding presence and without drawing his sword, he strode forward and the Fae cowered and cringed away from him as he approached the body of Til-Dar. He reached down to the broken heap and lifted it up. Far from the brutal acts of mutilation Tollie was forced to admit he would have stooped to in this position, the Champion handed it tenderly over to a woman a few feet away who was obviously a Child of the Hunter. The look of puzzlement and then terror on her face was so pronounced that Tollie could see it from nearly two hundred yards away. The clearly mortal woman then turned on her heels and fled from the Champion's sight. She was not alone, dozens of the Krynok followers followed her, their thrall broken. With the mortals gone, the Fae Army were not so many, but they were far more vicious. With the same disconcerting unity that they had attacked the Sea God followers, they turned and started to move towards the Champion. At this point, he drew his sword and Tollie chuckled. He had never actually heard a sword make a metallic ringing sound as it was drawn from its scabbard before, but the sword of Death shone as it was pulled from the Scabbard of Life, and as he wielded it the champion stepped forward and for a moment the Fae paused. Only for a moment.

Meanwhile, in Tartaria...

Indya froze. She looked up at the stars and then back at the bones. The whorls of smoke from her dying fire were barely visible in the indigo night. Pricking up her ears like a hare hearing a hound, she scoured the skyline. Something was coming, she could feel it. Something extraordinary and unexpected. There was a crackle of light beneath the Indaba tree and for a moment her breath stopped. She thought the tree was burning, but it wasn't. Four figures had appeared in the shadows and now every tiny hair on her was tingling. There was some divine presence with them and she sensed danger, or at least desperation. She snatched up her staff and in her clattering gait hurried to the tree. Her worldly eyes were weak with age, but her spirit eyes were sharp. The four figures she had seen outlined were nothing of note really, although two of the souls were shimmering. However, among the them was the thing she had sensed; a tiny ball of the purest white light Indya had ever seen in all her years gazing into the spirit world. As she approached the group, one of the figures broke away and moved towards her.

"Indya," called a voice that she recognised. "Indya quick," shouted Tian "We need you."

Just after dawn

Aberddu City - back in the Adventurers Guild

Elor and the priestesses were in the kitchen when Krieg and the others finally returned to the Adventurers Guild. Daisy was standing at the range pensively stirring a large bubbling pan and Mori was organising cups of wine. Elor, still in his night-shirt, bed jacket and slippers was sitting at the table with his head in his hands. Krieg still had both his swords drawn when he barged his way in through the pantry, his nostrils flaring and his eyes wide with adrenaline. The other three did not react to the blood and filthy sprayed across his face and clothes, they just quietly acknowledged his presence as he slumped down on to the settle by the fire and let his swords go with a clang. He sighed. The light of excitement that had been there when he arrived had faded in his eyes. His brow was lined with worry, the gravity of the tasks at hand seemed to be drawing a web on his face. Mori pushed a cup of wine into his outstretched hand and squeezed his shoulder companionably.

The sounds of adventurers returning are never as joyful as those they make when they depart. The clatter of people removing their armour and weapons belts and the staccato snaps of exhausted conversation filtered through from the main hall. For a moment no one in the kitchen spoke. Mori poured herself a cup of wine and sat down next to Krieg. She didn't want to ask about the state of the Temple District and found that the longer she wondered the less she cared of what had become of the bricks and mortar. She knew that there wasn't much time to pick over the nitty-gritty of what had happened tonight, it was imperative that the guild were not allowed to disperse or become distracted from the original mission at hand. She looked at Krieg, his eyes were red and watering with exhaustion as the adrenaline waned. Mori reached into her pouch and pulled out a tiny wooden pot. Cautiously, she opened it , not daring to breathe in too deeply. The tiny dried leaves in the pot were still as pungent as the day she had last closed the lid. The sharp, astringent aroma wafted up into her face, with great care she took a minuscule pinch of the herbs and before Krieg could comprehend what she was doing enough to object, she dropped them into his cup. Too late to stop himself from taking a drink, he realised what his friend had done. The herbs hit his tongue and he felt the whole inside of his mouth start to dance and burn, he spat the wine out spraying it all over the side of Daisy's habit but it was too late. The tiny little leaves were clinging to his tongue and already beginning to work their tricks.

Barely five minutes later, Krieg was up out of his chair, bouncing from foot to foot.

"Where's Tian?" he asked, his eyes flicking around him and his lips quivering. "Where's she gone? Where?"

"She's in Tartaria," sniggered Daisy, with ill-concealed amusement. She always found it funny when Mori gave Krieg what she thought of as the 'jittering leaf'. "She stayed with Indya, she said she'd catch us up." At this point, Daisy lost all pretence at decorum and returned cackling to her stew pan. Mori took charge. Firmly grabbing Krieg by the hips, she turned him so that he face the door back into the Guild Hall and shoved him forwards gently.

"Go on," she said unapologetically, "You've got a guild to rally. I'd go now before any of them disappear." Krieg nodded, and with an expression that suggested he was having to concentrate quite hard in order to walk forwards without bouncing off the walls headed back into the Guild room. Mori picked up her tray of wine cups and followed him. With three purposeful strides, he crossed the room and leapt onto a bench. Eyes turned from grubby weapons and partly-repaired armour and as he cleared his throat everyone else fell silent. Daisy, who had appeared in the door carrying her large pain of stew could barely believe her eyes. In all her years in the Guild she had never, ever, witnessed a silence like this. There must have been nearly fifty people in the room, all told, and not a single one was inattentive.

Krieg talked for nearly half an hour and the Guild sat spellbound like children at the feet of the story-teller. Daisy and Mori served the stew and wine, and collected in the cups and bowls with little disturbance. Elor, who had transplanted himself to a rocking chair by the fireplace when Daisy had brought the dinner through, was taking extensive notes with a shaking quill. When Krieg finally fell silent no one moved. There were no questions, arguments or passive aggressive comments. No one even made a joke. They were all very carefully running over various details in their heads. When after nearly thirty seconds still none of them had stirred he cleared his throat and said,

"We're leaving at dawn tomorrow, you have twenty four hours," and with that the spell was broken.

Twenty four hours later at the East Gate ...

Greery lit his pipe and puffed extensively. He had started preferring the dawn shift. Sure it meant keeping anti-social hours, but it was better than the evening shift, fewer tartars. He yawned. It was going to be a glorious day when the sun had finally burned off the thick river mist that had rolled up from the Ddu. The kid had gone quiet, presumably nothing much was happening, but still he ought to join him on the parapet and show some kind of willing. At this time in the morning most of the traffic was for the Market Districts and didn't trouble the East Gate. Greery yawned again as he climbed the ladder and dragged himself up on to the platform. He rubbed his eyes with a slab-like hand and was about to say something jovial but unimportant to the kid when he looked down into what ought to have been deserted city streets. He really couldn't believe it. Marching up the road toward the gate, four a breast, armed to the teeth and brazen as you please were a group of what appeared to be nearly sixty tartars, led by none other than Krieg flaming Clan Dragon himself. Greery was so cross he forgot to breathe out and nearly choked on his pipe-smoke.

The party and its assorted hangers-on halted five feet from the gate, and at this point an on-looker who was not Greery would have observed that whilst a significant number of them were tartars, the large majority were not, but to Greery that really didn't matter. All that did matter was that these furry bastards wanted to go through his gate, and at least this time they were heading in the right direction. He shouted to the kid to open up, did a cursory head count and entered 'five dozen out' in the ledger. As the gate swung closed, he knocked his pipe out on the parapet rail and grunted "Good riddance."

Later that Morning

Aberddu City State - on the border with the Middle Kingdoms

Krieg rolled his eyes, it was going to be a bloody long way to Tartaria is Daisy had started whining already. She was standing petulantly beside him, her arms folded across her chest

They were both looking at a large Tartarian Bay.

"I thought you could ride a horse?" retorted Krieg, still slightly trembling with the after-effects of the jittering leaf. "You rode that horse in Hasselt."

"That wasn't a horse," snapped Daisy, and before Krieg could retaliate with a comment like "well it wasn't a cow," she qualified her statement. "That was a fat little pack-pony. This is a sixteen hand Tartarian Charger. That's not the same thing." Krieg let out a chuckle not unreminiscent of the one Daisy had let slip the morning before.

"Fine," he snorted, not bothering to cover his amusement with Daisy's indignation. "There are alternatives." It was a cruel comment he realised when he saw the look of hopeful relief on Daisy's face, but there was nothing else he could do. "Well," he said, "You could always ride with me, I'll be taking point most of the way but I'm sure you won't mind the speed, or," he paused dramatically and watched Daisy's eyes narrow, "Tartaria's in that direction," he pointed towards a mountain range in front of them, "I'd get going now, it's going to be a very long walk." Sullenly, and without saying anything, Daisy stomped over to the horse and started to fasten her pack onto its saddle strap.

Although she was standing close by her two friends, Mori wasn't listening. She was lost in a very peculiar thought. Even though the group was now seventy five strong, with the addition of the tartars who had been husbanding the horses, there was still one person she was missing - as loathed as she was to admit this. Krieg's point, which she had to admit had would have been valid twelve months ago, was that Pringle had had as much time as everyone else to show up at the Guild. He had even had the privilege of two, count them two, messengers neither of whom had been able to locate him or Iona. He was simply one man, they could not wait for him to show up. Mori had closed her eyes and sighed at this, she didn't agree with Krieg but after the tumult of the last forty eight hours didn't have the words to disagree. Now, standing in the sunshine on the borderlands, looking at the sleek pure-bred in front of her she was kicking herself.

The exercise of seating sixty or so people, many of whom were inexperienced riders, on to horses took quite some time. Once helped into the saddle, most of the adventurers who had barely ridden before were able to steady themselves and make a decent fist of walking and trotting. However, there were some notable exceptions. Mauna Evanga, the limp Death cleric who was still recovering from the 'extreme trauma' of watching her temple burn had shrilly insisted on riding side-saddle. The horsemen shrugged and pointed out that they only had the saddles that were on the horses. Sniffily, she consented to ride astride and spent the following twenty minutes squealing and falling off. In the end, a tight-lipped tartar woman with half a dozen feathered braids pulled her up into her own saddle and hissed that she had better sit still if she knew what was good for her.

The problem of the greenskins was not so easily solved. The first issue was purely dimensional. Tartars, although they vary in size the same way as other humans, are pretty much all of the same build. Therefore, Tartarian warhorses are bred to fit that size. This makes them difficult mounts for dwarves, whose legs are naturally short. It makes them near impossible for goblins.

There's no such thing as an average goblin, but there are a few universal facts - they are all smelly for one, regardless of whether they wash, and for another they are all fairly tiny. The most usual mount for a Goblin is a mountain goat, and it has been said that Goblins are able to harness the innate goatness to great effect. When faced with a Tartarian Charger, Clench's first response was to shriek with laughter and ask how many people would be riding it.

At the other end of the green skin spectrum are Trolls.

Predominantly, these are creatures that are six times the volume of a goblin, with about one third the brains. Often, their foreheads keep the rain of their feet - or they would do if their feet weren't so big. Dremmel, who was large and stupid even by troll standards, took one look at his allotted horse and snorted. Apparently the horse had had the same thought because it also snorted and bolted, with one of the horsemen still hanging on to the bridle. Eventually it was resolved. Clench scrounged enough rope to tie herself onto Danz's mount like a large squirming parcel by passing the rope through his belt, wrapping it several times around her waist and fastening it on the saddle pack- hooks. GerVal, who was a particularly large orc, Dremmel and the other trolls agreed to travel on foot.

Krieg gathered them all together once they were safely mounted and reminded them once again that they would be riding across the Middle Kingdoms and into Tartaria, entering the Dragon lands via a hostile mountain pass. At that point, he indicated to a clutch of about a dozen very young tartars who were grouped together around a large, muscular youth in heavy furs. They had rode with the guild from Aberddu but until now, no one had really questioned who they were.

"This is Syrne," said Krieg, and the youth nodded a curt acknowledgement of his introduction. "And the rest of Clan Stallion." Some of the young tartars smiled slightly, a few others nodded but the rest just returned the stares of the adventurers with sullen silence. "They will be riding point," said Krieg with a tone and look that dared anyone to argue with him. "They know this ground well, they know the threat we are dealing with better than any of you," As he said this, his eyes swept across the faces of the waiting adventurers, inviting a challenge. "If you get in front of them, then you're on your own." The greenskins were nodding attentively, well used to following orders but Krieg was worried by the arrogance he was seeing on some of the other faces. They'll learn, he thought as he turned his horse and shouted for Stallion to move out.

Meanwhile, back in Aberddu...

Pringle and Iona strolled contentedly through the city, heading towards the Guild by a meandering, unhurried path. They had been enjoying the morning sun, the air by the bay was fresh and sweet, as though a storm had broken a few hours before and it had just finished raining. Hand in hand they made their way through the Trade District. It was oddly quiet for this time of day. There was some activity, but it was muted and stilted as though people were doing only the bare minimum. Boarded up booths and empty shops were a common enough sight these days - the war had dragged so many traders and merchants away. Iona sighed, hopefully that all be over soon. The champion had ascended, that should bring the war to an end.

She wasn't naive enough to think that this was the last tragedy that would devastate the city, but she did hope there would be some time to breathe and heal before anything else happened. As she thought this, she squeezed Pringle's hand. He smiled, lifted her hand and gently kissed it and looked at her again in a way that softened her soul. Even in this, his most blissful smile, there was a hint of melancholic resignation in his eyes that this too would someday pass. She turned to look at him, and then standing on tiptoe stretched up to kiss him.

Slowly, the Guildmaster and his wife wandered through the back alley markets towards Little Nippon. Light-hearted and wrapped up in each other, they laughed and chattered. They stopped at a Kchonese trader and with the last coins in his pocket, Pringle bought Iona a jade and a silver ring to replace the one they had borrowed from the Trickster Temple. It was a cheap carving of an ouroboros that had probably never been as far as Alendria, never mind Kchon but Iona didn't care. It meant far more to her than any of the fine jewels she had been showered with by the men who had traded for her affections. Carefully, he slipped the borrowed ring off her finger and pushed the new one on in its place, then he took her hand in both of his and lifted her palm to his lips.

That was it. That was their perfect moment, standing in a

grubby side-street in the Trade District. Years later, Iona returned to that street but the trader had gone, she looked down at her empty finger and knew that it was just as well. Even if she could have replaced the ring, she would never again be able to capture that moment.

It was nearly lunch time by the time they reached the point where the Trade District begins to bleed into the Guild District. This part of the city was far more business-like and far less entertaining. The clientèle in this part were not open to exotic merchandise, slick patter or charming smiles they were here seeking services. Not that the Guilds had fared any better than the temples or the markets in this time of war. They made straight for the Adventurers Guild. Iona was not surprised to see the building empty. Had she been here the night after the ritual, she too would probably have drunk a significant amount of cider. No doubt all those that weren't in the temples were in bed, nursing their heads. Pringle pushed open the gate and bounded playfully up the steps pulling Iona with him.

Then moment he opened the door, they both knew something was wrong. They had expected a quiet guildhouse, full of slumbering, hungover adventurers, but this wasn't that. The guildhouse was deserted. The fire place was cold, and the main hall was dark in spite of the sunlight and the air was stale. They looked at each other and in unison drew their weapons. A sudden clatter from the direction of the pantry caught their attention and they both wheeled round to see what might be coming their way. The clatter was followed by another more resonant thump and a string of rather ripe expletives that seemed strangely incongruous in a clipped Paravelian accent. The Pringles looked at each other, both of them recognising the voice and Iona mouthed the word

"Elor?" to her husband, who creased his forehead in puzzlement and nodded. They both stood stock still and waited. They weren't there for long, because in less than a minute Elor appeared in the main hall carrying a bowl of pease-pudding and holding a shawl around his shoulders. There was an obvious stain on the hem of his nightshirt that was presumably the remains of whatever had caused all the swearing. He appeared completely oblivious to the newly-weds as he ambled across the guild hall and in fact was almost standing on Iona's foot when he finally looked up, let out a quivering screech and flung his bowl at her.

While Iona scraped pease-pudding from her hair and Elor tried to steady his heart-rate, Pringle took in the wizard. It was clear from the state of the man that he had been in some form of work-related frenzy, as he had not shaved or brushed his hair for what Pringle hazarded to be twenty four to forty eight hours. He was dressed in a grubby nightshirt and sturdy adventuring boots, and under one arm he had tucked a thin leather tome and a notebook.

When Elor had finally recovered himself, he looked the pair up and down and instead of making any kind of pleasantry said,

"Why aren't you in Tartaria?" Taken aback by this abrupt question Pringle retorted,

"Why are you still in your night shirt?" whilst Iona, still partially covered in pease-pudding only managed

"What?" as a response.

The three of them went back into the kitchen, and as Elor helped himself to another portion of pease-pudding he explained what Pringle and Iona had missed. Iona, who had started washing her face at the stand-pipe stopped dead when Elor said the word Salamander, and Pringle sunk down into one of the arm chairs. At length, Elor went through the plan and as the rest of the guild had done when Krieg explained, Iona and Pringle listened in awed silence. When he had finished talking, Pringle got up and helped himself to a large measure from the brandy bottle and Iona, who had now wiped her face with a drying cloth said,

"I've got a couple of questions."

"Fire away," said Elor, with a little more pomposity than was sensible for a man in grubby bed wear.

"Actually, it's three," said Iona with a dry smile, "Why are you still in your night shirt, why aren't you in Tartaria and how come you're wearing boots?" Elor looked somewhat taken aback, he had clearly been expecting something either more arcane or logistical in nature.

"Oh, er," he started, "Well, because I can't ride a horse, I needed to go to the library and because I don't like reading in leather breeches," and then, on seeing Iona's look of total bemusement, added, "but not necessarily in that order." Iona merely nodded in response, as much as she respected Elor she sometimes found it better not to ask questions. "Anyway," he said clearing his throat and picking up his things, "my pease-pudding is now stone cold and I still have several chapters to finish before tomorrow. Do excuse me."

It was several minutes before Pringle spoke, and when he did he only needed to say one word. In the silence, Iona had walked over to where he now sat at the table, stood behind him and rested her hands on his shoulders. After a minute or so, he reached up at took hold of one of them. She did not want to see his face as he processed the information, she knew what his pained expression must look like and she didn't want to see the sadness in those eyes. When at last he drew in a heavy breath and turned to look at her, she could see he had been crying. Only a few tears, but they were still poised on his cheeks. He opened his mouth, and his lips trembled, in a hoarse whisper he said,

"Iona," and she shook her head.

"I know she replied softly,"I know." Then she kissed his damp cheeks, forced her lips to smile - although she could not persuade her eyes - and whispered, "Go."

TARTARIA - STONESNAKE-DRAGON BORDERLANDS

Twilight

Marta knew the others were laughing at her, she could hear them. She didn't care, their arrogance only served to reinforce her opinion. So they had seen nothing, not a single sign that the Dragon were ready to move against them. That told them only one thing for definite - the Dragon weren't stupid enough to leave their army somewhere Salamander's scouts would see them. She refused to believe the legend that the others seemed to buy into - that Salamander was so feared that no one would dare stand against it. She knew better. The Dragon may not be able to bring down the whole of the Salamander Army, but they would certainly be able to do some serious damage, and possibly disrupt the magic. Unlike the others, she did not underestimate the passion of the Dragon. They would sooner die than become Salamander.

The General himself believed her. It was he who had insisted the others accompany her on this scouting mission even though they obviously thought it a waste of time. She was not looking forward to reporting back that they had been unable to find any signs of... well that was just it, they hadn't found any signs of just about anything. Not even the flaming dragon guardians that normally marked out the borders had been in evidence. They had ridden clean onto Dragon land without any resistance whatsoever.

The more she thought over it, the more it troubled her. She slowed her horse to a walk and let the others get far enough ahead of her that she couldn't hear their sniping remarks. Unlike the others that had come over to Salamander, Marta had not turned her coat in the pursuit of power or influence. She had also not sought out Salamander, in a very roundabout way he had sought out her. She had realised long ago the naivety of thinking that working for Salamander was somehow helping her protect the Boar. She had been flattered when one of the commanders had approached her after she had attended the first negotiations, offering her a deal. She had been foolish enough to believe his flattery, that she was somehow caught his eye as a talented war-leader. She had meant her words when she had told the chieftain that they should fight till their last breath, but when they returned to camp they found a scene of utter devastation. Marta had panicked and done the only thing she could think of to save the clan. She knew that the chieftain was dead now, but she had no idea if he had ever found out exactly where she had gone and why.

It was only when she had crossed over and spent some time talking to the others that she discovered that she had not been singled out at all. The same offer had been made to every single deputy that had come to a negotiation and most of them had never made it back to their clan - some of them had even helped overthrow their own chieftains. Marta was horrified. When she had heard them say that she had felt the blood drain from her face as she imagined the sad eyes of the old man that she had abandoned and it made her pangs of shame worse. At least she had held out against the implanted gem that the others had taken so willingly.

Marta thought of the old man again as she dropped her horse to a walk and halted him under a tree. She was so angry she could feel hot tears prickling on her lashes. She had made an enormous mistake and she couldn't think how to undo it. Gulping back her fury and shame she jumped down from the saddle. This horse was the only living creature left whom she loved, and who possibly loved her, she didn't want him to see her in her moment of shame. She walked around the base of the tree, and felt the ground warming beneath her feet. Scuffing at the ground she found what she had been looking for - the remains of a small fire not long extinguished. This place wasn't deserted after all. She let out a small yelp of triumph before she realised that she was now standing alone in hostile territory. Pulling her tomahawks from her belt, her started to scour the skyline for movement her lonely despair completely forgotten.

Meanwhile back in Aberddu...

Weepy goodbyes were not in Iona's nature and she had been both gratified and a tiny bit wounded to see the look of relief in Pringle's eyes when she took her leave with a simple kiss. She had left him with Elor in the Adventurers Guild. She understood completely why he didn't want her to go to Tartaria with him – having someone you care about more than the others changes the dynamics of the group. Had Iona been a different kind of woman, she would have been stayed in Aberddu and been flattered by this. Had Iona been a different kind of woman, Pringle would not have loved her. As she walked away from the Guild building her mind was buzzing. She was not going to go to Tartaria *with him*. She had not given him the opportunity to express his opinion on the matter of her going to Tartaria without him. He may be her husband but he was not her keeper, and there was no way she was going to miss this. She would just have to find someone else to go to Tartaria with - and fast. She had a few people in mind, surely some of them would be gullible enough.

Nearing Midnight

The Middle Kingdoms - Stonesnake borderlands (the other side)

Entering Tartaria in the dark was a bad idea during peace time. Entering the hostile Stonesnake Territory, with known enemy troops in tow was nigh on suicide. Krieg had instructed the Stallion to take them as far as the borderlands and find a secluded spot to wait out the night. They had followed his command to the letter, and the whole group was now carefully ensconced in a small hollow about half a mile from the edge of the thick pine forests that were the border of the Stonesnake lands.

At very least they could rest the horses. He doubted many of the adventurers would sleep, although the greenskins were already snoring in a large fidgeting heap. Krieg wished dearly that he could go back to that kind of carefree simplicity, but that road did not go both ways. He looked about for old friends. Mori and Daisy were at prayer, and not to be disturbed. He could not blame them, in these times it must be a comfort to have an anchor like faith. The Dragon was not something that you prayed to, but on some level at that moment he wished it was. The only other face he really wanted to see right now was Pringle - but that had proved beyond the ingenuity of his messengers. Listlessly, he dropped into a crouch and rested himself against a tree.

Jamar was restless, riding always left him out of sorts. He was not a natural horseman, and the combination of the fresh air and the concentration required to keep the beast under control left him agitated and mentally and physically exhausted. From this ill-feeling, he had grown a lingering annoyance with the Stallion, who seemed to find his lack of skill in the saddle highly amusing. In fact, he was sure he could still hear them chuckling about it now. He scowled, bit into his bread and chewed irritably. After all he had seen and all he had done these children dared laugh at him. His mouth was dry, painfully he gulped down the chunk of bread and flung the crust into the undergrowth.

Between the low muttering of the Stallion and the snoring greenskins he doubted he would sleep and lying on the cold floor wasn't exactly restful. He got up and stretched his back out. There was only one thing he could do, he would have to walk this mood off. They were half a mile from the borderlands - if you could be a specific distance from an area known as borderlands - that should give him enough space to stretch his legs and clear his head without straying onto enemy territory.

For a priest, even on devoted to Kesoth the dark God of betrayal, Jamar moved extremely deftly. As he passed the huddled groups of adventurers and tartars, he attracted no attention whatsoever. His boots made no sound on the forest floor and he disturbed nothing. As he walked down a side-track, he fancied he was one of the stealthier movers present, if not the stealthiest. Tartars may be strong, fast and resilient but they were not subtle. They were loud and arrogant and obvious, that was their flaw. He was like the shadows, feinting and never quite solid. So he couldn't sit a horse, but he could certainly do things that those children, and he thought the word children with venom, could not. His hands tucked under his arm pits for warm he strode up a slope, aiming for the brow of the hill. Open country, almost

- no tartars hiding here, although he would have been able to conceal himself. Never mind he thought, disturbed at how vehemently this bitter little voice was hanging on, there would be opportunities to show them what he knew. He would stop on the brow of the hill and sit for

a while, until his boiling rage had quietened. Pushing himself up the last, steepest bit of the slope he put his foot on a rock jutting out from the ridge. Then he felt a hot sharp pain in the small of his back and a heavy leather gauntlet clamped over his face.

TARTARIA - SALAMANDER TERRITORY

Formerly Clan Ghostbear lands

Marta was red in the face as she pulled up her horse just within sight of the camp. She and her prisoner had covered quite a lot of miles at speed and she could feel her horse's pulse thumping in his neck from the exercise and she wondered if some of it was also because he was picking up her anxiety.

"Get down," she hissed to the woman behind her, "you'll have to walk from here." Obligingly, Tian hopped down and held out her wrists so that Marta could shackle and collar her.

The two women entered the Camp at a sedate pace, Tian trotting obediently behind Marta's horse. Even at this hour, the camp did not sleep. A soft pinky-red glow spilled out around the smiths and armourers as the atonal chorus of their hammering filled the air. Carts of supplies rolled back and forth, messengers rushed and darted through gaps and everywhere people were talking. It was not the idle chat of those with time to pass, it was deep discussion of important matters. Marta nodded politely to several people as she paraded her prisoner down the main roads of the camp. Tian was very distinctly Dragon, and she attracted quite a significant amount of attention as they went in the form of jeering and catcalling. She kept her eyes down and concentrated on her footing.

As they approached the command tent, Marta could clearly hear the General's voice echoing through the hubbub. He was obviously displeased by something. He never quite shouted, but he had a certain voluble tone that let you know he was not happy. Right now it was directed at Janx.

"Let me get this correct," he said with dangerous precision in his voice, "as far as you know Marta was with you when you left the Dragon border, but when you got back she wasn't." There followed a reply with Marta could not make out and the General continued with, "and nobody knows where she went or when?" The escalating incredulity in his voice forced Marta to smile, she could see the others now pretending that they didn't want to grovel in the face of Salamander's tightly-restrained, icy wrath. Everything suddenly went quiet, and as she dismounted and tethered her horse outside the tent, she couldn't tell if the general had stopped talking or had switched to a menacing whisper. When Marta entered the tent the General was facing away from the door, his hands clasped behind his back. The others were all together on the other side of the fire, varying looks of shame and anger on their faces. Apparently, she had disturbed the air as she entered because the General turned around, his nostrils flaring, his face cast in shadow by the flames of the fire. She was glad she could not really see his expression as he set his eyes on her, although the moment he saw Tian the atmosphere in the tent changed palpably.

"Marta," he said coolly, "who's this?" He nodded to Tian. He didn't show any signs of pleasure, but he showed no signs of displeasure either and that would do right now thought Marta as she shoved her captive forward.

"This is Tian Clan Dragon, General" she said in a small but solid voice. "and I think she might be useful."

ABERDDU CITY - FIRST LIGHT

As they passed the end of the Bryony Bridge, Iona felt her heart sink. She couldn't quite see the Guild Square from here, but she knew if she stepped about a hundred yards in the right direction she would. She knew that in all probability Pringle and Elor had already left, they were also supposed to be departing with the morning six-hour, but that didn't help. She looked away. This was exactly what Pringle had meant, this was a distraction of the sort that might just get you killed. She shook her head and looked ahead. They would be at the transport circle in less than an hour and on the Tartarian border by midday. Where they went from there wasn't her business, she wasn't in charge she would just following orders.

Something told Pringle that all the effort he had put into assembling his kit was wasted. As he pulled the straps on his sleeping mat tight he had a strange feeling that he was not going to need it. He would have said, had he been more romantic or dramatic, that the last few hours had been hell without Iona but truth be told he'd been too busy to think about it. It was only in the last minutes that he had enough spare thinking space to really be aware of what was happening.

Elor was repacking his scroll case for the ninth or tenth time. he had finally changed into adventuring breaches, a white doublet and a smart black frock coat - which he styled "his outdoor clothes". Pringle, who in spite of his position in the temple and allegedly in Albion Society, still thought of himself as a street-scum adventurer, smiled when he had said that. The idea of indoor clothes was something Pringle couldn't quite postulate. As Elor screwed the lid back onto his scroll case, he looked up at Pringle and said,

"Right, let's be off. It's going to take me a while to triangulate on to them when we get there."

Pringle shouldered his pack and nodded politely, unsure what Elor had said. The wizard slung his satchel across his back, checked his belt buckle and picked up his staff. Then, without saying another word he put one hand on Pringle's shoulder and slammed hard on the Guild room floor with the staff. A white-blue swirling portal opened and the fresh snap of Tartarian morning air wafted into the Guild.

"After you," he said, and Pringle stepped through.

STONESNAKE BORDERLANDS

Krieg must have slept because he didn't remember the night turning to grey, but it had been a fitful and unsatisfying rest. Judging by the faces around him, he was not alone. The Stallion, who had youth on their side, were bright eyed and the greenskins, who did not suffer with the same kind of anxieties as everyone else, seemed in good spirits. Apart from that, faces were ashen and eyes fixed on the tree line. The tartars were readying the horses and it wasn't exactly the moment for jollity. Expedience was the order of the morning and in very little time, everyone was ready to leave. Sullenly, the adventurers divided into two parties and group leaders started counting heads.

Krieg understood the need for prayer. He really did. He was just less understanding of the priestesses timing. They would at least keep it quick he supposed. That was the trouble with selecting the elite guild members for your part of the mission. It was rare that adventurers made old bones without some kind of faith or at very least the understanding of one. When Daisy and Mori had announced that they wished to pray before they set off, Ferrin and Whitefire had asked to join them and not to be outdone Teign, Knight of the Brotherhood of Justice, had dropped to his knees then and there. This had the tartars that were accompanying the group high and dry and looking at Krieg with pleading expressions. He simply shrugged. He wasn't about to upset the best weapons he had by telling them that they couldn't spare a few minutes for prayer. As he waited, he couldn't help noticing that the other party was also still here.

"Are you all here?" Erin demanded of GerVal, the de facto greenskin leader. She never felt the need to treat any of the greenskins with civility. GerVal who was well aware that he was both smarter and more awake than Erin was giving him credit for looked her straight in the eye and said,

"As far as I know, I ain't got any missin' bits." Erin scowled. "You know damn well I meant you as in your people," she said your people with such poorly veiled contempt that GerVal narrowed his eyes but let it go. "Yeah," he said in a tone that let Erin know he was unimpressed, "We'z all here. None of us wondered away in da night."

"Fine," she grumbled as she turned away to recount her party. Erin was sulking because she had been what she considered to be 'lumbered'. Not only had she been assigned all the greenskins and Clan Stallion, she had been given Mauna Evanga who was about as much use on an adventure as her jewellery would be if it came without her, and Gul the odious shaman with the semi-sentient beard. All the respectable adventurers - Teign, Whitefire, the two priestesses, Lord de Andro, were going with Krieg to his destiny. They were the sort that one expects to take on a mission of that significance, none of them were new, none of them were scruffy or insubordinate and none of them were green. Erin looked over her group bitterly, she really had just been assigned what was left. And now she was one short

"Who's missing?" she snapped a little louder than she intended, as though one of the adventurers was deliberately hiding in the bushes trying to avoid latrine duty. They all looked around each other, and nobody seemed to know. Then, one of the newer recruiters, whose name she had hazarded as 'Derin,' said,

"Where's Jamar?"

"Jamar?" she said, fighting to recall a face that when with the name. "Dark hair, olive skin, dark eyes, about a foot taller than me, Kesothian I think," reeled off the warrior, who come to think of it was not called Derin at all, perhaps his name was Derek. As he spoke, she did bring the image of the man to the front of her mind. Shifty type, she thought, when she had been Guildmistress she had never sent him anywhere that she hoped they may be invited back, particularly not if she thought there would be anything for him to steal. She just about remembered him being with them as they left Aberddu. She had been riding behind him until it became apparent that he was a liability on horseback. She couldn't see him in the clearing, and she knew that he had not been assigned to Krieg's party. Where had he got to?

"His pack's down there," piped up on of the younger Stallion, who's name she hadn't even bothered to guess at. "And his sword." One of the other Stallion immediately dropped into a squat, and began to examine the ground with his nose about an inch from the mud. Then scuttling on all fours, he began to make his way out of the clearing and along a side path. Syrne turned to Erin and said,

"Give us a moment, we've got his tracks," and chased after the boy with his sword drawn and two or three of the others in tow. His curiosity piqued, Krieg wandered over as the Stallion departed. "What's wrong?" he said bluntly to Erin, this was no time for pretending he was a diplomat.

"We've lost Jamar," she said in the same business-like manner. "What?" snapped Krieg. Erin just shrugged. The conclusion of the Stallion trackers was that his tracks had mysteriously stopped on top of a ridge about three quarters of a mile away, just inside Stonesnake territory. Judging by the surrounding area, there had been another tracker there with enough skill to conceal traces because as the Clan Stallion tracker so eloquently put it,

"Nowhere's that tidy, everywhere has bloody squirrels."

Krieg looked at Erin, and Erin looked back. Strictly speaking this was not an Adventurers Guild commission, therefore everyone here was a private citizen who just happened to be a member of the illustrious guild. However, it was difficult to argue that that meant usual guild protocols should be abandoned. Death was sometimes unavoidable every adventurer accepted that, however being left behind was not. It was a well-known fact that if you returned from a job with fewer adventurers than you had departed with there were going to be some very difficult questions and on more than one occasion, Guild members had been charged and fined with 'not performing reasonable actions to ensure the safe return of all party members'. However, they were in extremely hostile territory with less than twenty four hours to get to their final target before all hell broke loose across Tartaria and then the rest of the World and no clues as to where Jamar had gone. Krieg closed his eyes and exhaled loudly. From the sounds of it Jamar had been snatched, but it also sounded like he had wondered off alone in the dark, less than a mile from enemy territory. Krieg shook his head and sighed.

"Go without him," he said softly, "if you find out where he is, try and get him back but your mission is more important than one man." Erin nodded. She quite agreed, she didn't want to hang about Tartaria with a bunch of kids and greenies, looking for the kind of twit that thinks orders don't apply to them. "Right," she said with a less-than-amused tone, "leave him. Let's go."

CAMP SALAMANDER, FORMERLY GHOSTBEAR LANDS

Janx let out another unintelligible bellow, and his battalion moved out. Between midnight and dawn they had managed to muster nearly two thousand troops who were now ready and waiting for further orders on the open fields outside the camp gate. Marta was at the head of a small select unit of skirmishers. Tian rode beside her on her own mount, with her hands and feet shackled carefully so that she could not flee. Salamander let his mouth smile as Marta let out a cry and they departed.

The General had been very well pleased with the prisoner and the information she had eventually divulged relating to the sorry state and current location of the Dragon army. It was the opportunity he had been hoping for. With the Dragon army taken care of he would be able to complete the ritual without interruption. It seemed he had credited them with more intelligence than they deserved. They had no notion that soon all their efforts would be too late. In twenty four hours there would be nothing they could do to stop him, and then even the mighty Dragon would have to succumb. He watched as the last three battalions moved out and disappeared into the horizon. Then, without changing a single muscle of his facial expression, he turned his horse and rode back into the camp.

And then, as the noonday sun broke the back of the day, all eyes were focused on one destination.

Silently the adventurers lined the edge of the gorge, looking down at the plunge pool of a massive water fall. From the cliff edge they could see up and down stream for nearly two miles. Right now the whole length of the river was relatively placid, but a few minutes ago that had not been the case.

The greenskins were sodden. They had waded into the river about half a mile from the drop with the intention of damming the main flow. They had, by means of little other than a lot of rope and sheer brute force, felled half a dozen trees and were heaving them into the water. It turned out it was just as well that Erin had insisted they rope themselves together in spite of their objections because no sooner had they positioned two trunks substantially narrowing the stream, than the river itself started fighting back.

As ludicrous as it sounded, that was the only way to describe what happened. Suddenly, plumes of water fountained up out of main flow, covering them all. Rip currents and vortices appeared with no warning and stated to pull the smaller ones under, Clench was totally submerged and had she not been tied to the others would have plummeted over the falls. As it was, she was badly bruised and shaken but still with them. It had taken the rest of the party and all the horses to pull them free of the raging torrent. Danz and Tomp had lost consciousness by the time they were heaved to shore but were suitably revived by means of some kind of revolting liquor that was tipped up their noses.

It took less than thirty seconds for the tree trunks to be dislodged by the force of the water and swept over the falls. They met the plunge pool at the bottom with a cacophonous crash. Then as quickly as it had started the tumult ended. Most of the greenskins were all for trying again but GerVal concurred with Erin when she had said there was no reason to assume that it wouldn't do the same thing again, and this time one of them might not make it out. Now they were sitting on horseback, steaming gently in the noonday heat gazing up and down the length of the river. They needed a new plan. However, given that this was the cleanest most of the greenskins had been in several years, it was making it tricky to think.

After two or three minutes of complete silence, Gul slipped carefully out of his saddle and wandered towards the undergrowth. Erin was about to shout at him to come back where she could see him, when Severin held out a hand for her to stay quiet. The shaman waded into the brambles until he was knee-deep, reached out an arm and without seeming to make any other movements or sounds, stood and waited. Not ten seconds later, a small starling swooped out of a tree and landed on his arm, followed by another and another. After about twenty seconds, a dozen or so starlings had perched on Gul, covering his head, arms and shoulders almost completely. The adventurers watched in open-mouthed awe as he let out a soft, modulating note that replicated exactly a starling call, and as one the whole flock took off. The starling cloud rose up out of the trees and dispersed and Gul returned to his horse. The party members fixed him with a whole range of expressions from quizzical irritation to plain bemusement in hope of an explanation. These inquiring looks were completely lost on Gul, a man so embroiled by his wild magic that there had been some conjecture that he was only half in the material plan. The other half of him was floating about in the spirit world somewhere. The greenskins tended to assume it was largely due to the quantity of hallucinogenic berries he ate but other people kept insisting it was part of his magic. He simply leant across to Severin and in a hoarse whisper said.

"You're an Evoker aren't you?"

Incredulously the ageing elf nodded. Over the centuries, he had seen fit to learn many skills, and as it happened elemental magic was something he had taken to with ease. Why in the world this was important was a total mystery to him.

"Excellent," said Gul smiling broadly. At this point Erin lost patience, "Look here," she hissed viciously, "I'm in charge you need to tell me what exactly is going on, do you hear?" Gul froze, and turned to face her with an expression of cold determination that actually frightened her.

"It's quite simple," he said in a clear, sharp voice, obviously unhappy at being spoken to like that by Erin. "The enemy control water and they control fire, if we wish to defeat them or even engage them successfully we need to use the powers of earth and air. Is that exact enough for you?"

The look of angry disdain in Gul's eyes as he spat the last words into Erin's face was so unexpected it caused her to reel backwards. She didn't dare respond other than to nod. Gul carried on, and for the first time Erin and the other adventurers were aware that he was more than just a grubby backwoodsman. His power didn't usually manifest itself and when you were watching him eat raw fish or read the portents in a bowl of cawl it was difficult to believe that somewhere beneath it all was a powerful arch-mage. Just then, they had all seen it and were glad that most of the time it remained hidden.

"I can manipulate the earth, but," he said, speaking in the same patronisingly slow tone that people tended to use when they addressed him, "unlike an elemental mage, I cannot manipulate the air. Severin is an elemental mage, and therefore he can."

"Okay," croaked Erin flushing deep red. To her credit she knew she had deserved this treatment and willingly capitulated. "What did you have in mind?"

"Well," said Gul, softened slightly by Erin's submission, "first of all we need to get down there." He pointed to the bank of the river, about a mile downstream. "That's within throwing distance of the ritual site. Once we're down there, I'll explain."

Gul's plan was simplicity itself. Erin had to admit it was stroke of genius, and the thing she liked most about it was that basically all she, and the majority of the others had to do, was hide. They had abandoned the horses at the top of the ravine, with three of the Stallion. The rest of the Stallion disappeared into the undergrowth on either side of the river before anyone else had a chance to see where they went. The greenskins headed for a large patch of soft leaf mulch, and began to burrow with their bare hands like a family of ungainly giant moles. That left just four adventurers, apart from Severin and Gul, who were both going to have to risk being slightly exposed.

Brazka and Derek had a quick scout around and came back with news that there was a largish drainage ditch not far from the main path just downstream. Erin nodded and Mauna Evanga let out a feeble yelp which earned her a searing look from the former Guildmistress. Erin was still smarting from the dressing down she had received from Gul and wasn't about to take any nonsense from this drippy priestess. Mauna shrugged her acquiescence and they left Gul and Severin to secure themselves in the trees on either side of the river.

The still of the day was broken fifteen seconds later by an affronted shriek, that was very rapidly stifled.

"Shut up you stupid girl," hissed Erin into Mauna's ear, she had one hand clamped hard across the priestess' mouth and her ponytail firmly gripped in the other. "It's only water." "It's green," whimpered Mauna, her kohl-rimmed eyes wide with self-pity. "and there's probably things living in it." At this Erin rolled her eyes, how this woman had ended up in the Adventurers Guild was anyone's guess, probably took a wrong turn on the way to the useless fops and dilettantes guild she thought cruelly. Surely Mauna had toughened up in the years she had been adventuring. Well, if she hadn't it was too late now, this was something of a kill or cure situation. Moving her face so that they were basically nose to nose, Erin explained in a low voice.

"Yes, you're right. It's green and there are almost certainly nasty things living in it but it's quite simple, either you get into that ditch with the rest of us or you can sit on that log over there." Erin removed her hand from Mauna's mouth just long enough to point to a log about ten yards away. "and wait quietly for General Salamander to show up and kill you. The choice is entirely yours. I don't really care one way or the other, but I'm getting into this ditch. Okay?" Mauna's eyes were now so big that they looked like they might just pop out and roll away and her colour had drained so she was even paler than usual. Erin held her gaze for a few seconds longer and then with deep scorn, let go of her and turned away. Mauna hesitated for a moment as though there was actually a choice to be made, then with a long languid look at the log, she hitched up the shirts of her robe and stepped one foot at a time into the stagnant water.

DRAGON

Krieg looked nervously over to one of the Dragon scouts, who raised his eyebrows and inclined his head almost imperceptibly to the left. He didn't want to admit that he didn't know where he was going in front of the adventurers, and this scout seemed to understand that. He had been hoping to have Tian back, but obviously something had come up. It was a strange feeling to be so embroiled in this event and yet so out of control. Krieg didn't like it. His memories of adventuring had been of laughter and excitement. Riding in silence through Tartaria surrounded by po-faced clerics was alien and troubling. This wasn't exciting, this was stomach-churningly frightening. He was almost certainly riding to his death, and probably the death of many of his friends and all because he had the hubris to refuse his fate when he was young. He should never have left the clan, he should never have gone to Aberddu and the Guild. Then, he would be here with Tartars, maybe even his brother. He let out a deep sigh. He doubted that even his brother would have been in better spirits right now, but at least he would not have dragged these out-landers here to meet an end in the defence of Tartaria. Why had he even thought it was their fight? He gulped and sighed again, desperately wishing someone would speak to take his mind off it but aware that this was unlikely.

All of a sudden, there was a disorientating flash that caused two of the lead horses to rear and bolt. Krieg, and several of the other warriors, had weapons drawn before they had even established the nature of the threat. The rising tension was suddenly broken as someone sneezed and then began to hiccough. Standing in the middle of the path, about twenty yards ahead of them were two men. Both were long haired and dressed in leather adventuring breeches, but there the similarities ended. One was diminutive and distinguished, he wore a smart jacket over a white doublet and was carrying a satchel and staff. His companion, who clearly had the hiccoughs, was wearing a threadbare red shirt and cracked leather jerkin. He had a comprehensively stocked adventuring pack on his back and a very large hammer resting carelessly on his shoulder.

"Ah," said the smaller man, in a manner of fact tone, "there you are." Krieg and the other adventurers lowered their weapons, although the Dragon did not.

"Elor," said Krieg smiling. He had almost forgotten that the mage had promised to join them in Tartaria. Then he turned to the other man and with an even broader grin said, "Pringle, you're late and you look like crap, you been out in the Docks entertaining the hookers again?" "Close," replied Pringle acidly between hiccoughs, "I was with my wife." His hand was clutched to his rib-cage as he continued to spasm quietly. Then he added, "What are you doing with my guild?" The tense silence between Pringle and Krieg expanded to cover nearly everyone for a moment, and then Pringle let out another hiccough and it was shattered. Elor looked over to Mori and said, as though he were explaining to a class,

"It's the pressure change that causes the hiccoughing you know, it messes with one's diaphragm something awful." Pringle and Krieg were still locked in a gaze, neither one prepared to back down. Pringle let another spasm contort his face into a picture of discomfort, and then repeated,

"Well? What are you doing with my Guild?" Krieg looked him dead in the eyes and said calmly, "I'm taking them to kill Salamander, why?" At this retort, Pringle's face broke into an almost semi-circular grin. "Okay then," he said, "let's get on with it."

For a wizard, Elor was a surprisingly competent horseman. It was at times like this, as he levered himself deftly onto the back of Mori's saddle, that it was obvious that he had not always been the desk-bound wizard they were familiar with. Pringle climbed on behind Daisy and the group moved off again without any further delay.

"Alright shorty?" he whispered into her ear as he balanced his hammer carefully between them. Daisy didn't respond, she just smiled. Everything was going to be fine, Pringle had arrived.

After an hour or so, they arrived in a wide clearing, and the scouts indicated that they should stop and dismount.

"The rest of the journey must be on foot," said one of them pointing at a path that headed out the other side of the clearing and up towards the bottom of a rocky outcrop. "Only two or three of us can go, the rest must stay here with the horses." Krieg nodded. Looking around the gathered adventurers, at his closest friends, he didn't know how to choose. Obviously he would have to take one of the Dragon scouts with him, which meant he could select only one adventurer to walk the rest of the way with him. His eyes fell on Mori and Daisy, how could he pick one over the other? He knew very well he couldn't. They would both have to stay. If he was leaving them, then he would have to leave Pringle too. Ferrin, Teign and Whitefire were all good men but he didn't know them. That left him Elor. He looked at the wizard whose face, like his own, was prematurely worn by the cares of the world and thought he could make a much worse choice.

Before they departed, Krieg let the priests bless them once more and Daisy hand over a substantial amount of the potion bottles she was carrying. Then, she flung her arms around the large tartar and he could feel her trembling with suppressed sobs.

"You're not going to die," she blurted out. It wasn't a question, it was a statement, made with total conviction. "I promise," she continued, "I'm not going to let you die, unless I'm dead." Krieg squeezed her hard and then pushed her away.

"Thank you," he said smiling. Mori appeared beside him and squeezed his arm.

"Good luck, and bless you," she said with a gentle half-smile that meant as much to Krieg as Daisy's dramatic embrace. He nodded and with a deep breath turned and, accompanied by Elor and the Dragon scout, headed towards the path up to the outcrop.

Indya banked up the fire with moss to make the steam thicker. If they didn't arrive soon then it would be too late. She told herself to not worry, they would arrive, the portents did not lie. She shook her head. It was getting harder and harder to stay in this world. She closed her eyes. The cave was stiflingly hot and the steam was making her groggy. She opened the wooden chest and pulled out the tiny clay pot. She had mixed the herbs already - in fact she had mixed them nearly a year ago before she even knew what they were for. She scattered them into the fire and the steam changed colour slightly, glowing faintly green for a moment. The vapours filled the cave and Indya inhaled deeply. Wormwood and cuckold grass, a familiar astringent scent that sent her head reeling. Eyebright and rose-hips danced sweetly on her tongue. Mugwort made her eyes water and dandelion root made her tingle. She lowered herself to the floor with great care, and lay herself flat on the furs she had put out. If one was going to walk in the spirit-world, it was probably a good idea to make sure that one's material body was safe and comfortable. She inhaled again deeply, taking in more of the psychedelic vapours.

And then she could smell the enticing scent of sun-warmed rain on grass, and she could feel the dampness on her ankles, and she was walking on a very green steppe. The sun was high and white hot, the sky was perfectly clear, even though it must have rained not that long ago. She inhaled again, enjoying the smell and the feel of the warm air on her cheeks. The steppe stretched out for miles around her, flat and featureless and she was completely alone on it. She ran and whirled about in the grass as though her body were young again. Her limbs moved freely without aching or creaking, she held her face up to the sun. After a few minutes, she realised that she was wasting precious time and began to look around more seriously. Indya had seen the Dragon many times before, she had been spirit-walking since she was a girl and she had first seen the totem himself when she was just 19. Now, he was like an old friend. She smiled as he approached, but she had to admit she was concerned with what she saw.

It was difficult to describe the nature of a clan totem. They were the essence of Clan, the soul of the clan - a living entity separate from its component pieces. They were not divine, nor were they demonic, Fae or undead, but they were other-worldly. The best the scholars had been able to like them to was Wyld Guardians, but even then they didn't channel magic like that. They were an embodiment of what it meant to be Tartar and Clan. They told the clans what they were. Dragon was strong, and fierce and fearless. It appeared differently to each shaman, preferring some to others. As Clan Shaman, Indya had had a close relationship with her totem for a long time. She saw it as a giant scaled drake when it was still, but when it walked it was a very tall man with long limed hair and a bare, woad-patterned chest. Even as she had grown older, he had not changed, and neither had her spirit form. In her heart, she felt as though Dragon were the closest thing she had ever had to a romance. In the dark of the night, she even dreamed of the man she saw when she spirit-walked but that was another story.

What worried Indya was how suddenly Dragon seemed to be aged and frail. When they had last met he was as young and vital has he had always been, now although he was not bent with age, he was moving with the slow deliberate stride of an older man, his eyes dulled by care and his brow lined. Indya tried to hide her worries and held out both hands to greet him. They both grasped each other's left arm with both hands and Indya was troubled to see a look of relief in Dragon's eyes.

FALL

Elor was leaning heavily on his staff with about twenty feet of path still to tackle. He was breathing hard and wishing he spent less time hunched up in the library. The two tartars had not waited for him, this was the fourth or fifth time he had stopped and he had worn out this courtesy after the first two. He could see Krieg standing on a ledge outside a cave-mouth, stripping off his layers of fur armour and weaponry. The Dragon scout was helping him, making a neat pile of his things. As Elor looked more closely, he could seem shimmering whorls of steam coming from the small black aperture in the rock face. Some kind of herbal concoction to aid the journey to the spirit world. Elor's knowledge of Tartarian spirit walking was not extensive, but it had grown manifold in the last few days. The exact recipe that was used was not of particular interest, but he was very interested to learn more about the power exchange that was about to take place. He heaved himself the last twenty feet and slumped onto a low rock panting. Krieg was now clad in nothing more than his leather breeches, and the scout was daubing his bare chest with spirals and dashes of woad. Elor was interested to note that Krieg had even removed his boots, his bare feet were leaving sweaty prints on the rock.

Once the scout had finished the woad adornment, Krieg dropped to his knees, and began to crawl into the cave without another word. Elor watched with fascination as Krieg disappeared into the darkness. He could see the Dragon scout eyeing him suspiciously but he ignored this. As he understood it, the role that they had in this was largely ceremonial. Spirit-walks attract attention and anything that attracts attention attracts trouble. Spirit walkers traditionally have guardians in the material plain, who protect their bodies as there is no magic or healing that can retrieve a soul trapped in the spirit world if it has no body to return to. This is usually only an issue when Spirit-walking takes place on a large scale and in the open, it was not unusual for all the Clan Shamans to go together. Fifty or sixty of them at a time, all openly lying prone in a sweat-lodge or yurt needed considerable guarding from unscrupulous attack. Guardians had become part of the tradition and so even when the walkers were lying well concealed in a remote cave, they must still be guarded. There was only so long Elor could remain interested as he stood outside the silent and slowly steaming cave mouth. He sniffed the air, but he didn't have enough knowledge of herbalism to identify the component smells. He felt his head swim as the vapours hit his tongue and took several steps into the fresh air. Wandering to the edge of the outcrop he tried to pick out the adventurers in the clearing below but the trees were in the way. Restlessly, he ambled back towards the cave-mouth avoiding the fumes. The scout, who had taken up a position about five yards from the cave mouth and had not moved since, was giving Elor a look of disapproval as he scampered about like a vaguely curious child. Apparently this was not done. Elor was about to make himself even less popular by asking the scout if this was all that was going to happen, when the mouth of the cave started to glow. Dimly at first, but gradually strengthening, rays of light started to spread out across the ledge. There was still no sound coming from the cave, other than the faint crackle of the fire. Elor went to inspect it more closely, suddenly unconcerned by the heady smoke, but the scout held out a hand barring his way. With a stern look, the scout communicated that Elor would do well to take up a position perhaps just out of the scout's arms reach and stay there until Krieg and the shaman re-emerged. It was at this point that stillness was broken by a piercing shriek from below. Elor's first reaction was to run towards the cry, but the scout shot out a hand again and grabbed his arm.

"No," he said in a low voice, speaking for the first time since they had reached the ledge. "Whatever happens, we stay here. Let them deal with it."

It had been a very welcome break from time in the saddle. Daisy had so relieved to finally put her feet on the ground and stretch out her aching back. She, Mori and Pringle had installed themselves under a tree and were making the best of a pack of adventuring rations and a small bottle of cider. Whitefire had taken the opportunity for some yogic meditation, at least that's what they assumed he was doing. Teign and Ferrin stood swaying from foot to foot, weapons drawn gazing in opposite directions both unable to relax. The three clerics were laughing quietly at their expense when suddenly everything changed.

Out of the tree line shot a single flaming arrow, it went straight past Teign's ear and landed in the dry grass beside Whitefire which caught immediately. The flames spread into a robust little fire. Before any of them could act, tartars started appearing out of the fire and another flaming arrow hit the ground fifteen feet from the last. Then another and another, so that they made a square.

Four fires sent a continuous stream of tartars at them from all sides and in moments they were surrounded. Teign and Ferrin who had had the wherewithal not to put their weapons down ploughed into the onslaught but they were outnumbered. The three clerics flung aside their picnic and leapt to action but it was a little too late. The tartars split second advantage meant that their numbers became overwhelming extremely quickly. The fighters were falling faster than Daisy could pump healing into them, Mori and Pringle flung holy fire as fast as they could but it didn't seem to be doing its usual damage to the tartars. Whitefire was managing to hold off four or five at once, but mainly it seemed to Daisy, because they were toying with him like a groups of cats with a shrew. Teign fell on the other side of the clearing and Daisy, praying through her teeth, sprinted across to where he lay, casting magic on him before she had even reached his side. One of the tartars took a swing at her, and she felt the blade hit her back. She tumbled forward, and her face contacted with the warm pool of blood on Teign's chest. She heard a distant snort of amusement before she passed out. Mori saw Daisy fall and shot a glance around behind her to see if Pringle had noticed but he wasn't where she thought he had been. She didn't stop to look for him, if he'd run off that would be his hard luck later when he came back and they were all dead. She just concentrated on trying to get to Daisy, so that there would at least be a little time longer when they weren't. Only when she had made it to Daisy's side did she see exactly what Pringle was up to. He had emptied the contents of the cider flagon onto one of the fires, which was now gently steaming and he was stamping his way across the second, trying desperately to extinguish the flames that hopped easily across the tinder-dry grass. It looked for all the world like he was performing some kind of bizarre folk dance to mark the coming of the sun.

Mori looked a moment too long, she didn't see the tartar raising his sword, the first she knew of his presence was the sharp pain in her shoulder blade, then she keeled forward onto the warm body of her friend. Pringle looked up, he saw Mori lying motionless, Daisy's legs sticking out from beneath her, and the top of Teign's helmet beneath that. That meant he was the only healer left, but what was the use of running across the clearing to meet the same fate as Mori and Dee? Someone else could pour a healing potion down their throats, he was needed for something else.

RISE

If there had been anyone left to witness what happened next, then in all probability Pringle would never have done it. This was part of a deal he had made in the dark hours when he had thought the Trickster was dead. He had prayed and prayed and prayed until his knees were raw and his back was numb and in the darkness he had heard a voice, and that voice had taught him to hope. He had become more than a priest that night, he had offered himself up to the Trickster. The Old Man, hiding on the material plane, weary and earth-bound, could not return to the heavens without the faith of his followers. Such was Pringle's faith, and his lineage, that he could supply a substantial amount of that power to the Old Man. The deal was struck: when Pringle chose to sacrifice his mortal body the Trickster would get his soul but in return the Trickster must grant one, last request. Save these souls was a last request worthy of any high priest and as Pringle made it, his lips began to tremble and his eyes began to sparkle. A kaleidoscopic light poured out of him, or was it into him, it was difficult to tell. The irises of his eyes turned from piercing blue to purple, then green, yellow, orange. As they spun and flashed his body rose off the ground and he hung for a moment spread-eagled in the air as the light poured. The tartars, who were not easily distracted from their quarry, paused in their annihilation and looked around. Then, at once Pringle exploded or was it imploded. The clearing filled with a flash of multi-coloured light and the enemy tartars crumpled where they stood, the remaining fires went out and then, with a faint chuckle echoing through the trees, Pringle was gone.

Do this properly he had said, and when you get back to Aberddu there will be something waiting for you. Show us what you're made of he had said, and when you return I'll explain further. If that wasn't an incitement to come back then not much was.

Tollie had been surprised to see Janus Montgomery alive because he could have sworn that he had seen him on the bone-carts on One-way Walk. When he thought of that day on Gallows Hill he still shivered, but he had the sense not to say that or mention it to Montgomery at all. He had just listened to what he had to say, nodded a lot and rounded up a couple of old faces. Why exactly Janus Montgomery wanted them to go to Tartaria was anyone's guess, and really wasn't that important. What was important was that they got themselves to Tartaria to witness what was happening, see which way was the wind was blowing and see what fortune they could make on the way. That last part went without saying really. Tollie had contemplated going along with the guild, but on balance this was probably a safer option.

The land was flattening as they reached the Tartarian border, their directions only took them so far, which is the problem when you are given directions by someone who'd overheard them in a pub. Apparently they had to find their way on to the Ghostbear lands and look for the river. Which bit of the river was anyone's guess. Iona had somehow acquired a map, but that hadn't been much help. It was several years old and the cartographer had been of eastern origin which meant that it was proportioned differently from most western maps and didn't have the same orientating information. What it did show them was that the bit that they thought was the Ghostbear lands, after a lot of argumentative conjecture about which was up, did in fact contain a very large river that had half a dozen tributaries. When questions about which branch of the river they were aiming for Montgomery simply shrugged his shoulders. Resourcefulness was one of the things that he expected from his employees, so Tollie, Sylas and Iona slouched off to think it through. Unfortunately, go to Tartaria and keep climbing trees and other high things until they could see something big happening was the best they had managed to come up with in the limited timescale they had. They'd been bloody lucky to get the passage through the transport circle as it was, never mind anything more complicated in terms of magical aid.

As they tramped across the borderlands, Sylas kept scratching. Having tried hard not to appear too conspicuous, they had dressed themselves in furs and leathers similar to those traditionally worn by tartars, and whilst there was no way they would have passed a close-up inspection they would at least not appear to be outlanders from a distance. The problem with this was that unlike tartars, Tollie, Sylas and Iona had soft western skin unused to the feel of animal hide on sweat. It was quite unpleasant and the way that Sylas wriggled and writhed it made him look as though he had some kind of very active infestation. Tollie sighed. At least he wasn't whining. When they got to the river he was going to suggest Sylas take a dip.

When Elor saw the bright, multi-coloured flash he finally snapped. He didn't care whose tradition it was, he wasn't standing around outside a steaming cave whilst his friends were facing something that could produce that much light. He couldn't even work out what kind of magic it was to start with, but then after a second or two it dawned on him and he let out an anguished yelp as he over-powered the bemused tartar who had been holding him by the shoulders to stop him leaving. In a flash, he vanished from where he stood and reappeared a hundred yards down the path. From there, he simply picked up his feet and ran, hampered slightly by his staff.

He could see the horror that awaited him from about two hundred feet away. The light seemed to have exploded most of the enemy tartars. The clearing had become a charnel house, flesh and bone shards strewn across the pine needles, blood from tartars and adventurers mixed together drenching every available inch of ground. Elor paused for a moment and took in the horrifying scene. He could see the bodies of most of the adventurers lying among the carrion, worryingly still. The ground was charred in several places and the smell was repulsive. Over-riding his initial instinct to step back and analyse, he flung his staff to one side and hurried through the viscera towards Mori and Daisy. If he could bring them round then they would be able to fix everything else he told himself as he tried not to notice what was sticking to his boots.

Erin found it very easy to ignore the fact that Mauna was crying. When you're mostly submerged in stagnant ditch water a few tears only serve to make the experience more theatrical, because frankly you can't get any wetter and at least the silly girl was weeping silently. She had to admit she was praying, probably as hard as the soppy cleric next to her, that the tartars turned up sometime soon. The smell was starting to get to her, something had crawled into the top of her boot and it felt like it was starting to nest. She tried not to think about it, and then found herself staring at that bloody toad again. It had been eye-balling her with suspicious inquiry for god knows how long, and she was starting to think that it might not be just a lowly toad at all. It could be a shaman's familiar acting as a second set of eyes or even worse a very patient wizard. It was this sort of paranoia that kept adventurers alive and Erin was seriously considering the merits of trying to off the toad when she heard horse hooves approaching behind her. Instantly all thoughts of batrachian treachery and murder vanished. She plunged Mauna, spluttering, below the water line and taking a deep breath herself followed. From his perch, Severin had an unparalleled view of the whole scene. The river here was a placid shining expanse, a far cry from the turbulent plunge pool a mile and a half upstream. The water was just too deep to see the river bed, but clear enough that it was perfectly possible to see the plentiful supply of river weeds. It would have been beautiful had it not been for what approached.

A dozen or so tartars were trotting up the path on horseback. It was definitely better than a horde of hundreds, but he had to wonder about the strength of these twelve. It had struck him the first time around, all those centuries ago, how much larger Salamander's tartars were than those from other clans and it wasn't as though the others were small. The two riders at the front were gargantuan. Even from this distance he estimated that they were both easily in excess of seven feet tall, riding sleek chestnuts that must have been at least twenty two hands high. The riders had the wild, staring glaze of hemlock and wicked magic, their eyes darting about for approaching threats. Severin held his breath as they passed the ditch that contained the adventurers. Mercifully, neither of them looked down.

Behind them rode three much smaller figures. It was difficult to tell what gender they were but it was clear from their general appearance that they were shamans, and powerful ones at that. Their hair was solid with lime, and liberally adorned with feathers, bones, shards of gemstones and all sorts of other trinkets. The skin on their faces and bare arms was stained and scratched with sacred markings and each of them rode with one hand on the reins and the other holding a long, ornate staff. The staff of a tartar shaman was as personal as a fingerprint. They cut the wood themselves and adorned it over the years, building power as they did so. It wasn't unheard of for a shaman to die after the destruction of their staff, although this was not overly common – tartars tend to be made of sterner stuff, and dead shamans can't avenge their staffs. Unlike the front riders, they were not looking around, their eyes were entirely focused in the other world.

Behind this vanguard rode two figures of phenomenal potency. A tall, proud man stripped to the waist, his clearly defined muscles rippled against his shining, tanned skin. His torso was covered in symbolic tattoos and the stains of war paint. He had jet black hair and a face used to authority; dark piercing eyes scanned every inch of the undergrowth and Severin found himself nervous of his magical concealment ability for the first time in nearly a century. The man had a single marking on his cheek - a salamander. Beside him was a much smaller woman with paler skin, her untamed red hair flying in the breeze. She had the same dark piercing eyes and authoritarian bearing and she rode with nonchalant confidence, as though she were enjoying herself. They must be Salamander and Flamehair, or very good decoys thought Severin. Suddenly over-run with suspicion, he tried to identify the magical signatures echoing from them and found himself winded by the sheer ferocity of them.

In the slow thoughts of his hind-brain, he realised that that had been the moment when his life had become a clear dichotomy. On one hand the power he witnessed was quite literally breath-taking, on the other hand in more practical terms it is far easier to burst a full water skin than a half-empty one - and so it went with magical power. Severin dared to smile. All they needed to do was poke it gently and it would pop. Poking it gently was something they could probably just about manage.

Behind the pair came another three shamans and two body guards - one of whom had the infamous red banner of Salamander trailing from a pole strapped to his saddle and the other one had a large cloth-wrapped parcel draped over his saddle – about the size of a body.

By the time the last riders were in sight, the front riders were almost within range. Severin took a deep breath and found himself praying for the first time in nearly a decade. Gul's plan had seemed such a great idea in explanation, but now they were about to execute it Severin realised it was basically suicide. The seconds dragged by until the front hoof of the first horse landed on the marker line and then time tumbled out of control. What happened next took less than thirty seconds in total but in memory seemed far longer.

The basic premise was simple - get as many of them to ride their horses into the river as possible. To this end, Clan Stallion had concealed themselves in the ground-cover that spread up the steep bank on the far side of the river. Severin had to admit they had done an impressive job. He had watched them hide and he still had no idea where any of them were. It wasn't until the first arrow flew out of the foliage that he had any inkling at all. The first the riders knew about it was the sound of it hitting one of the shaman's horses. The animal reared, but the rider was not unseated. She simply lay flat on the horse and whispered to him as she removed the arrow gently. Although the horse was easily healed, the arrow had performed its function, all eyes were now scanning the far riverbank. Well, nearly all eyes. It seemed a lone archer was not enough of a threat to attract the attention of either the General or his sister. Flamehair seemed completely uninterested by the whole thing, even when the first arrow was followed by a shower of more than a dozen moments later. Salamander was now scanning the nearside bank suspiciously. Severin held his breath, aware that this was stupid. If Salamander could see through his magical concealment then he was a dead elf, regardless of whether he exhaled or not. The General's gaze fell on him and lingered momentarily. Severin felt his pulse rate quicken, but then suddenly the sound of the commotion behind him pulled Salamander's gaze away.

Whilst he had been scouring the ravine most of the riders had taken their horses into the water, staring up the bank trying to locate the bowmen. Another shower of almost silent arrows had fallen. Some of them grazed the tartars, but most missed entirely embedding themselves in the ground and the roots of trees. Flamehair snorted with derision as one skidded to a halt in front of her mount.

"Pathetic," she hissed under her breath. She hoped that the resistance was not tartar, she liked to think that even the renegades would be more effective than this. She wasn't really looking at the river when the noises started. The horses had already disturbed the glassy stillness of the water, but now it seemed that it had ideas of its own. The river started to bubble and chop, and several of the riders let out startled yells. They tried to manoeuvre their horses back on to the bank, only to find that they were unable to move at all. The river weeds that had been lying languidly in the stream were now coiling up around the horses' legs, winding tighter and tighter. The horses were starting to panic and even though they were unable to move their legs, they jolted and tried to buck. Several of the riders jumped down to calm them and found themselves also trapped by the plants. Having witnessed the fate of their comrades, three of the riders still on the bank leapt out of the saddle and ran straight into the water, only to find that the weeds then grabbed on to them too. One of the warriors was so unbalanced by the sudden halt to his motion that he actually toppled forward and plunged under the water. In his tree, it was all Severin could do not to let slip a chuckle that would have exposed his position in an instant. The whole thing couldn't have been more perfect if it had been orchestrated by the Bards Guild as a piece of theatrical business. Between the riders stranded atop panicking horses, those who'd gallantly tried to calm their steeds and the ill-considered rescue attempt there were now nine out of ten of the guards in the river. Only one of the rear-guard warriors – the one with the large cloth bundle - remained on the bank with Salamander and Flamehair. He seemed completely at a loss as to the best course of action, which Severin felt was fair enough. Flamehair's face had switched from an expression of arrogant nonchalance to one of blind fury. Only Salamander seemed to be fully in control and ready to respond. Letting out a ferocious howl, he flung a ball of flames at the under-brush about ten feet from the bass of Severin's tree. The dry leaves and grass caught immediately, and the fire began to spread rapidly. Within moments, it was licking the bottom of Severin's tree. He couldn't risk jumping down,there was only one thing for it. Taking a deep breath, he dropped his concealment spell and shot a forcefield around the trunk of the tree, so that it formed an invisible, impenetrable disc ten feet wide, about twenty foot below him. That would keep the flames at bay and provide him with a sturdy if uncomfortable safety net. Then, he recast his concealment spell praying to any gods who would listen that Salamander hadn't spotted him in that moment's exposure. He was on borrowed time unless someone put the flames out anyway because once they reached the force-field it would be blisteringly obvious that someone had cast magic, and he knew the General already suspected there was something in the trees. With no idea how he was eventually going to get out of this situation, Severin was faced with little choice but to do what he had originally climbed up the tree to do, even though he was well aware that it was very likely to make his situation a whole lot worse. Half closing his eyes, he held his hands in front of him, palms up and concentrated. As a cloud elf, he had a natural affinity for the air and as an Evoker - a wizard of elemental magic - he had been trained to fine tune this affinity until he could perform acts of caeliomancy that would leave others breathless, in this case quite literally.

FLAME

A faint breeze rustled the leaves in the trees, gently fanning the flames below. It did not gust as you would expect a natural wind to, it maintained a constant speed and intensity. The warrior that had remained on the bank looked across. His face was contorted into a grimace of discomforted confusion, he put a hand up to his throat. Severin could see the tell-tale red whorls starting to appear on his neck. He opened his mouth wide but no sound came out, his face was paling as the oxygenated blood flowed away. His chest started to heave which was in fact the worse thing he could have done. It simply expelled the air from his lungs faster allowing Severin to pull it away even quicker. Severin watched the tartar with sinister fascination as he became limp, his eyes rolled back and he collapsed forward onto the horse. Concentrating hard, Severin moved his hands down fractionally. The air kept flowing, fuelling the fire below. In moments, the unconscious rider's horse had dropped to its knees, and then very gently fell sideways tipping the rider onto the ground, where he sprawled across the grass. Flamehair reeled around at the sound of the horse collapsing and span back almost immediately. She glared up at the trees above the fire. Severin froze, the bolt of magic she shot in his direction passed so close to the top of his head that he wasn't sure she couldn't see him. Undeterred as her magic failed to find a target, she took aim again and this time, the lightning connected with Severin's chest. He actually felt his heart stop beating for a few seconds, then he let out a strangled shriek and toppled sideways from his perch. Flamehair snorted indifferently as Severin fell towards the fire, and then exhaled irritably as he halted about five feet above the flames. Severin hit the forcefield with a jolt that knocked the air out of his lungs. He had forgotten he had even cast it, and now he couldn't remember how long it would last. In his panic, he snatched at breath, taking in a substantial amount of smoke causing him to choke. His head spinning, he poured some more magic into the force-field just in case it was weakening then he flopped backwards.

The objective was simply to hold the tartars up for long enough that the others had a chance of arriving before the ritual was over - hence the attack of the ferocious pond weed and the air sucking stunt. The greenskins had reluctantly agreed to hide in a very big hole and leave things to the two mages and Clan Stallion because there wasn't supposed to be a fight, so they weren't 'chickening out' or missing anything. That had all been fine and dandy until the crazy tartar general set fire to the undergrowth and his bitch of a sister knocked Severin out of his tree. With most adventurers there would have been several minutes of uncomfortable indecision before they threw the plan out of the window in favour of an ill-conceived escape attempt. The greenskins didn't bother wasting the time with discomfort or indecision, they just leapt out of their hiding place straight onto the road.

Their new plan, if you can even call it that, was in no way sophisticated. It mainly involved making a lot of noise and throwing things until they were within weapons reach of any tartars. Neither Salamander nor Flamehair seemed remotely shocked by the sudden appearance of about half a dozen orcs, trolls and goblins charging headlong at them waving maces and swords and had they been other than they were the greenskins may have been concerned by this lack of reaction.

It took the General barely seconds to respond with a wave of his hand, as he sent magical pulses charging through the atmosphere causing two or three of them to drop their weapons. GerVal let out an irate grunt as he dropped his spiky mace onto his boots but it didn't stop the charge, the greenskins were ready for this eventuality and armed to the hilt.

Seeing that he had failed to stall the charge, mere moments before it reached his sister, Salamander shot another bolt of magic, this time with visible flames, hitting one of the trolls - Tomp - square in the chest and knocking him flat. Trolls hate fire - to be fair to them they hate anything that causes them pain because it takes a lot of effort to cause a troll pain, but they particularly hate fire because in the words of a well-known scrap of trollish wisdom: fire hurts more. Tomp's reaction to the flames was to yelp, then roll over and over in the dirt in an effort to put them out. Unfortunately, given he was burning on unfamiliar ground, he misjudged his stopping point and rolled sideways into the river. As he said later, whilst it was true that he had spent most of the rest of the ensuing fight bound up in water weeds, at least he wasn't on fire any more and being a fairly smart troll he would take embarrassment over burns any day.

Flamehair also reacted, although far less swiftly than her brother. She made a single, imperious hand gesture, and the brambles on the road-side began to grow at an alarming speed. If you're going to go charging into places without much of plan, as the greenskins tended to, then you either developed lightning-fast reflexes or you didn't charge in anywhere, with or without a plan, ever again. Most of the greenskins simply outpaced the plant-life, only tiny goblin Clench did not have a long enough stride to avoid being caught in the bramble trap. Danz paused to try and wrestle her free. Flamehair's face creased with irritation and she waved her hand again. Danz was just leaning into the thorns, trying to pull Clench out, when they suddenly started moving again towards his feet. With a nimbleness of step that defied his bulk and his gangly legs, he performed several acrobatic moves that took him nearly fifteen feet away in a matter of seconds, landing him within inches of Flamehair herself. Beaming widely, his mottled teeth on show, he smirked,

"Ha. Missed. Nice norks by the way love." Then he winked and ran out of reach as she tried to snatch at his furs. Flamehair let out a frustrated yell and with another flick of her wrist sent a bolt of yellow energy straight at his back. It connected with his lower portions but it only made him stagger forward, he didn't so much as lose his footing. She was about to strike again when Dremmel popped up right in front of her, shouted

"Boo," and bounced a stone off her forehead. As he did this, Danz caught up with GerVal. A brief amused look passed between the two enormous, sinewy orcs, one of whom was surreptitiously patting a smouldering patch on his left buttock, and they both grinned. Moving at the same time, they dropped their right shoulders, put their heads down and charged straight at Salamander. For all his powers and legend Salamander was at the very base of everything still a tartar, and whilst it had been a long time since anyone had charged at him like this he did recognise a full body tackle when he saw one coming. When Danz and GerVal hit him he was braced and ready. They had originally planned to tackle him to the floor and roll him into the river, but they hadn't calculated the fact that he might be able to withstand their combined force. Not sure what else to do, the green skins simply clung on to the General and refused point blank to be shaken off. This left them struggling in an incongruous scrum that looked like some kind of offbeat three-man polka. From the ditch several yards away, the rest of the adventurers could do nothing but listen, drip and sulk as they heard the plan going tragically but predictably awry.

When Krieg emerged from the Cave he could almost feel the power of the Dragon crackling from his skin. In his normal state, he would have been shocked at how frail Indya appeared right now, leaning heavily on her staff, the blood drained from her face so that she was almost grey. The daylight had taken on a new crisp edge, he felt more alive than ever before, and taller. He looked around for his other companions, and was surprised to see only his tartar guard remaining.

"Where's Elor?" he said, a little shocked that his voice hadn't changed at all.

"Something happened," said the tartar gravely, "I couldn't stop him." When Krieg gazed down into the clearing, he could see exactly why. He didn't pause, he just sprinted down the mountainside.

By the time he was standing in the clearing, he didn't need to ask what had happened, or what it had cost - he already knew. Teign and Ferrin were kneeling beside Whitefire's lifeless body, tears silently falling down their blood-splattered faces, eyes closed, hands outstretched and faces upturned in prayer. Elor was standing beside a scorched tree, at his feet sat Mori, her face flat and her eyes staring into the distance as Daisy sobbed into her lap and Mori distractedly rubbed her back. He looked about for Pringle momentarily before he realised why Daisy was crying. For a fleeting moment he wanted to sit down next to her and join in but then the force flowing through him took over and he realised that unless he made a move to lead, this would be as close to the ritual as they were going to get.

Krieg did not try to inspire them with speeches he simply indicated it was time to move on without a word. It was a silent party that picked themselves up and made their way along the mountain pass to the vast flat grassland. From there, Elor would be able to portal them to within a mile or so of the river. Then it was just a question of hoping they were in time to stop anyone else from dying. Tears were streaming down Daisy's face as she walked but she didn't speak because she knew that there was nothing she could say that would be in any way productive. Krieg knew that when they got to the river they would be snatched from the morosity that was currently gripping them, or if they weren't they would die.

ON THE OTHER SIDE OF TARTARIA...

Marta had to admit that the Salamander army was a heart-stopping sight. She had ridden out with the Boar war bands many times, but they would have had to mobilise the whole clan in its heyday to have any hope of having anything like these numbers. As they approached the far-eastern reaches of the Dragon lands, she could finally see what they had been searching for. Just as promised, there was a small clutch of Dragon army, maybe two hundred or so, idling on the dried-out river bed. They did not seem to have noticed that they were slowly being outnumbered by the might of the Salamander. Marta snorted with amusement and looked over at Tian who returned her look with a cold stare.

The commanders led their battalions along the edge of the ravine, and still the Dragon didn't seem to react. Marta could see the triumph in Janx's eyes. So much for the great might of the Dragon army, this would be like shooting fish in a barrel. Neither he nor any of the other commanders had paused to consider the situation, they just saw what they had been told to expect - a worn-out battalion, with no pride, no spirit left. To Marta it would have smelt of a trap, but she knew the others wouldn't think like that. It was this arrogance that had scared her more than anything else she had seen. The General himself was not complacent, but those who surrounded him believed that he could not fail, and that their strength was superior to anything.

By the time she had arrived at the edge of the canyon with her unit, everyone else was in place. A cautious leader, a merciful or wise leader perhaps, would have sent a single battalion to deal with the two hundred. Janx was neither merciful or wise. He was going to flood the gorge with troops, they were all going to go at once on his signal, riding head-first down the steep rocky slopes. Gilfdan trotted over to Marta, nodded an acknowledgement at her that presumably translated as 'well done,' and then came to a halt beside Tian. He leaned into her, his sour breath on her ear and cheek.

"Enjoy this, won't you?" he hissed, running a salacious hand down Tian's thigh. Marta saw Tian's shackled hands ball into tight little fists, and she turned her head and spat full into Gilfdan's face. Gilfdan leered, apparently he'd expected that kind of retaliation, and looked sickeningly gratified as he wiped his face with his hand.

"Watch, quisling, as we destroy your people, and I'll find you later," his voice got softer and crueller as he spoke, "and we'll celebrate together." Tian turn her head away, she would have spat in his face again but he seemed to have enjoyed it. As she felt Gilfdan move out of her space and ride back to his own troops she smiled. A quisling was she? That was good coming from him. She smiled to herself, she would have been enjoying the irony of this situation right now, had she known what irony was. She certainly was going to enjoy watching this and she would celebrate later, but not with him.

Squinting into the sun, she could just pick out what she knew was on the far side of the chasm. She had to commend the soldiers below, waiting so calmly as the bait in this massive trap. They knew full well that the Salamander were coming for them, and no doubt were aware of their presence. Tian was not sure she could have resisted glancing up, but then that was why she was a shaman and not a warrior.

Marta could feel her heart beating, meting out the seconds until what may well be the last charge she ever made. She realised in these long seconds, that seemed to take almost days to pass, that she was more afraid of her horse dying than she was of dying herself. Should she survive this attack, she could guarantee it would not be for long, but that was not her horse's fault. Would he forgive her? She was trying to make amends but she had no idea if he would know that or appreciate it once she was gone. She lay down so that her cheek touched his coarse black mane and she ran a soothing hand down his neck. She could feel his steady heartbeat through her cheek and knew then that it was only her that was worried. A single, cold tear fell onto the mane. There would have been more, but the air was filled with a trill echoing war-cry and the sound of two thousand horses thundering. Marta sat up and made to join the charge but something stopped her - Tian had hold of her arm. She didn't say anything she just shook her head and indicated with a glance that Marta should hang back. It was a matter of seconds before she found out why. The thunderous charge descended at speed, pulled down to the river by gravity as much as anything, and then with in ten or twenty yards of the ravine floor something happened. Horses in the front rank started to stagger and fall, throwing their riders as they tumbled. The air was filled with a cacophony of yells and distressed braying. The second rank unable to halt their descent trampled the fallen horses and riders underfoot, falling themselves and adding to the pandemonium. The third and fourth ranks saw what had happened, but were also unable to react in time, and they to became part of the chaos until most of the Salamander army were caught up in the calamity that had befallen them at the bottom of the slope. They didn't notice the slowly growing size of the Dragon army, as more troops appeared seemingly from nowhere. Relatively few of the Salamander had made it past the concealed pit-traps on the lower slopes, and found themselves face to face with an enemy that was not what they had expected. Far from the dispirited rabble that they had been led to believe they would find, the warriors were healthy, well-armed and baying for blood. Marta looked at Tian and the two women exchanged a gleeful half-smile.

Back at the river...

It was inevitable really, thought Erin as she moved carefully into a crouch. The guild's plans tended to range from 'a bit of a farce' to 'unmitigated cock up', Erin had no idea why she had thought that this one would be any better. It was no good hiding in a ditch when you were supposed to be saving the world and it sounded like it was all going to hell. She heaved herself to standing trying to ignore the slimy leaf mulch as it slipped into her boots, and grabbed the top of Mauna's arm, pulling her up as well. Brazka and Derek stood up too, so that they formed a bedraggled, dripping line. They attracted no attention, as they were significantly out of the way, but they could see quite clearly that things were not going well. The greenskin plan seemed to have involved one very simple strategy: run at the tartars and shove them into the river. This was having varying degrees of success. At least two trolls were in the water themselves and bound by the snaking water weeds, and GerVal, Danz and Salamander seemed to be locked in a teetering stalemate that was going to end with one of them in the water, it was just a little unclear which one. Somehow, one of the mounted tartars in the river had leapt from her saddle to the river bank and was scrambling upwards presumably trying to locate Gul. There was forest fire spreading happily into a raging inferno, surrounding the still unconscious Severin on his magical platform and only the tiny goblin Clench seemed to have noticed. She was scampering back and forth from a small rivulet, using her helmet as a bucket, flinging pitiful amounts of water on the flames. Erin let out a snort of melancholic amusement, realising that if she paused to consider the tragedy of the sight she might not be able to go on, the situation was already incalculable. There was no obvious course of action, in fact it was looking suspiciously like they had only two choices: stand here dripping and watch everyone else die or run screaming into the melee and join them. It was one of those choices that isn't a choice at all. Some people are simply incapable of standing back whilst others are in distress, at which point everyone else looks like a selfish spineless bastard if they choose option two. Brazka started running and the rest of them, ditch water flying off them, followed. Erin drew her sword as she ran with no worldly idea what she expected to do with it when she finally reached the fight.

SALAMANDER: ENDGAME

The final battle of the Summer of Fire was not the epic affair that legend suggested. The whole thing took barely quarter of an hour all told, once the second party of adventurers arrived. This was such a disappointment to one particular bard that he invented a ferocious storm, siege-engines and a whole extra army. So well-crafted was his tale that no one questioned exactly how this cast of thousands fitted on the banks of the river until much later. His story is far longer and probably more entertaining than this one, but not a faithful account of events in any way.

It would have been glorious to think that the battle that finally brought it all to an end lasted longer but had this been so then there was a significant chance that it would not have ended at all. As Krieg, Mori, Daisy, Elor and the others set foot on the path down to the river they were greeted by a scene of horrific destruction. Flames were sweeping up the side of the valley, crackling through the undergrowth, licking the edge of the road, scorching the earth and heating the stones. The ground was blackened and steaming, fire-drakes dancing amongst the sparks and embers, taunting several shapes that Daisy assumed were adventurers. She could make out the tiny goblin Clench, who was lashed motionless to a smouldering tree stump, but the human-sized lumps were indistinguishable. She felt bile rise in her throat, even if they managed to defeat Salamander, it looked as though they would be too late to save them. It surprised her as she thought this that no tears came to her eyes.

In the river and on the road, were soaking wet tartar guards who had managed to crawl free of the weed trap. One or two of the greenskins were still bravely tussling with the tartar guards, but from this distance it was more than obvious that they were simply objects of amusement like valiant shrews facing up to a farm cat. Across the river a couple of the Salamander tartars who had managed to jump from their saddles and were now scrambling up the bank in search of Gul, who was further up, clambering on all fours and barely five feet ahead of them. Several of the Stallion were hanging lifeless from trees and stumps. Had this not been enough, it was quite clear to see that they had arrived in the very nick of time.

Not far away, the ritual had begun. Flamehair, Salamander and six shamans were standing in the river just downstream, the water around their ankles bubbling and swirling. The pulse of the drum echoed down the valley like a heartbeat, a low chant weaving through it. Two of the shamans held a limp figure between them, it seemed to be wearing a surcoat that Daisy recognised but she hoped that she was wrong.

Krieg and the Dragon tartars broke into a sprint, and the adventurers followed suit. Salamander did not pause in his ritual to acknowledge the approaching force. Later, Elor pinpointed this moment as the General's fatal mistake. It was a miscalculation based on one poor assumption: not all groups of adventurers are of equal power. Behind the angry Dragon were not a clutch of two-a-penny mercenaries, instead there were two powerful priestesses, two paladins and an arch-mage wizard all of whom were beside themselves with fear and grief. The first group may have been no match for his guard but now his guard had more than met their match.

Krieg and the Dragon arrived first, ploughing straight into the ritual guards. The Dragon tartars were smaller but faster than the massive Salamander guards, and in seconds the fight dissolved into a deadlock of flying fur and axes. When the rest of the adventurers arrived on the bank they were able to run straight past the squall towards the ritual. Teign and Ferrin made straight for Salamander himself, Elor for Flamehair. Mori and Daisy homed straight in on the fallen adventurers in hopeless desperation that they may be able to save a life.

As Daisy raced on to the charred earth, she could feel her feet blistering through her boots but this did not stop her. She dropped to her knees beside the motionless body of Mauna Evanga, ignoring the heat as it baked her leather breeches. A single touch gave her hope as she sensed a pulse, and she reached out to lay on hands in blessing. She did not see the drakes as they eyed her, attracted by her movement. She was not aware that they were circling her, drawing in on their new living, prey. She was simply concentrating on saving a life. Mori, more worldly-wise than the idealistic dwarf leapt to her defence swinging her sword wildly to keep the flaming reptiles at bay. One dark elf, however powerful, is no match for a pack of blood-thirsty fire-drakes. The blade of her sword crackled with magical energy as she swung it boldly. Slowly, they surrounded her – the new target of the hunt.

When Mauna opened her eyes and looked up into soft blue eyes she almost shrieked with irritation. She had never gazed on the face of Hecate, but she knew in her heart that she was not a grimy dwarf with a creased forehead and a chalice in her hand. That was a healer - which meant she was still alive and on that gods-forsaken battlefield. Daisy gave her only a moment to recover herself before she reached down and hauled her to standing by the shoulders.

"Help," hissed the dwarf, pushing her towards the forms of two other adventurers. This was not a plea it was a command and although she could feel her feet burning she did not dare disobey the dwarf's fury.

The tartar guard that was fighting Danz looked and saw Elor approaching at speed with his staff above his head. In an instant, he weighed up the threats and put Danz down with a single boot that broke two ribs and sent him flying into the river. He then turned his attention to Elor. Tartar magic is naturalistic and land-based, a shaman's staff being a symbol of his or her bond with the land as well as a weapon. They are unused to the more arcane practices of book-learnt wizards, who consider staff to be theatrical props that add to the drama of a good spell rather than an actual necessity. The tartar lunged forward, and with both swords broke Elor's staff. The wizard's response was not what the tartar had been expecting, instead of reacting as though he had been injured he let out a scream of annoyance, flung the shattered wood to the floor and sent a pulse of magic flying from each hand towards his attacker.

This knocked the tartar off his stride, causing him to stagger and giving Elor time to draw his sword. When his blade hit the recovering tartar it was crackling with flames. At last in familiar territory, the guard was able to fight back. For a few seconds at least he was dominating again until with a barely perceptible motion, the wizard shattered his off-hand sword. Elor summoned every ounce of courage and strength, aware that he could not leave this to the warriors alone. Unless they eliminated the ritual guard, they would not be able to disturb the ritual and if they didn't disturb the ritual Salamander would become nigh on impossible to kill and this would all be for nothing. He could feel sharp pains darting down his sides through what he thought of as his reading muscles - normally used only for hefting giant tomes from library shelves.

Had Ferrin and Teign had a moment to pause they would have been impressed with Elor's tenacity and skill with a sword. However, they were themselves faced with several ritual guards who were not bemused by their opponents. Warriors the world over recognise each other as being of the same stripe, knocking out any possible element of surprise. Fighting styles may differ, but ego and the will to triumph do not. Once again, a fight was at stalemate.

Danz recovered himself and scrambled out of the river. The guard he had been fighting seemed to be losing shamefully to a wizard with a flaming sword. He looked around for his comrades. Something had to give, and he was damned if it would be the adventurers. Clearly what they needed was more greenskins.

Sadly, he recognised there was nothing to be done for Dremmel as he floated face down in the river but less than five feet away, Tomp was lying limply in a rivulet gurgling. If he could get the troll standing they might have half a chance of dragging GerVal out of the shrub that had him pinned down within feet of the spreading flames. Three greenskins was a veritable army in this situation thought Danz feverishly, as he plunged his hand into his pouch, rummaging among the shattered bottles and pots for anything that might still contain a potion. When he found nothing he inhaled sharply and plunged his hand back into the debris. Trolls are hardly folk and a guts-full of glass shards was better than death. He snatched out a handful without really looking, flung a bandage to one side and skidded to Tomp's side on his knees. With a grunt and heave, he rolled his friend onto his back and pushed the sticky shards into his open mouth. Nothing happened. Danz reached down and scooped up a handful of river water and poured this into Tomp's mouth as well, so that it washed some of the viscous mixture down the troll's throat. Tomp opened his eyes, went to speak and immediately vomited the broken glass onto Danz's leather-covered knees. Danz had never been so pleased to be covered in blood, sick and broken glass in his life.

"Ouch," wheezed Tomp struggling to his feet with a half smile and the pair of them headed towards GerVal without another word. Between them, Daisy and Mauna had revived Derek and Brazka who had immediately dashed away to aid Mori. Mauna was now cradling the charred remains of something Daisy could not identify. She did not have the patience to put up with the piteous wailing, she knew that at the moment her efforts had produced no positive effects. All she had succeeded in doing was healing enough people to save Mori, who was only in trouble because she had chosen to protect Daisy whilst she healed.

"Come on," she snarled at Mauna and dragged her away again. They could count the cost later if they made it that far and the drippy Hecate priestess could wail as much as she wanted then.

Whilst neither innovative nor elegant, it cannot be denied that three large, armed and irate greenskins are often the most efficient solution to a problem. In this case the problem was that

Elor had started to lose his advantage against the tartar he was fighting. Somehow he had found himself on the defensive and it was testament to his eclectic talents that he had yet to sustain a major injury. GerVal didn't even break his stride. He had just spent the better part of half an hour tied down and humiliated by these bastard tartars and he was not going to stand for any more. He lifted his axe above his head and with one swift, unblocked blow sank the blade three quarters of the way into the tartar's muscular neck. To the tartar's credit, he did not yell or falter, he simply swung up with both his swords to where Elor had been, only to find that as he toppled forwards with the axe embedded in his flesh, that the wizard had vanished. GerVal didn't pause, as the tartar hit the floor the orc's boot was on his back giving leverage so that he could pull his blade free. With a second, unnecessary swing he brought it down again, this time severing the tartar's spine cleanly. Arterial spray hit him full in the face and moments later the body exploded flinging out hot bone and viscera. GerVal let out a deep, guttural roar, blood and sweat running into his mouth. Blinded by fury and his head spinning, he felt better.

At this moment, Mauna and Daisy managed to free Clench the goblin who, with similarly wounded greenskin pride, scuttled towards the battle without so much as a look back. The Dragon and the Salamander were still hacking into each other, fur and frenzied hatchets flying. Mori, along with Brazka and Derek, was taking on another clutch of drakes that seemed to have materialised out of the flames. Skirmishes the length of the bank occupied the rest of the adventurers and the ritual guards, leaving a small but obvious path straight to the ritual. From this distance, Daisy could see that the limp figure was definitely Jamar. The front of his tunic had been torn and his head was lolling forward. She could see a deep gash in his chest into which a gem had been pushed.

Daisy admitted later that she hadn't really thought her actions through, and she really wasn't comfortable with the idea that she had done anything heroic – in spite of what others might claim. She had just seen a fellow adventurer in distress and a clear path towards him and run into it. It had never even occurred to her to draw a weapon, she just ran straight for the river and launched herself onto him. The force of a whole lightly-armoured dwarf hitting Jamar full in the chest caused the shamans who were holding him to lose grip and he fell backwards into the river. Daisy went with him and they landed with a loud splash.

The noise of them hitting the water, and the subsequent sounds of the shamans following them brought Krieg's attention to the river. Stepping out of the reach of the guard he was fighting, he saw the submerged dwarf kicking and scrabbling to get purchase on the slimy river bed. She was trying to pull herself out of reach of an angry shaman, who was wading through the river towards her with a knife raised. In spite of this chaos, and the fact that the shaman beating the drum had stopped, neither Salamander nor Flamehair had been phased at all and the ritual was still under way.

Krieg's mind was racing, he carried the power of the Dragon with him, but he had expected to feel different. He had expected the totem to take control of his thoughts and guide him every step of the way but it was not like that at all. He was still just a man, uncertain and unconvinced by his supposed power. The fate of Tartaria weighed heavily on his shoulders and all he could think about was what would happen when he inevitably failed. He had paused a little too long, he was disturbed by sound of his name. Elor bellowed it again.

"Krieg," he yelled urgently, diving out of the reach of a raging tartar, "Krieg, look!" He refocused his gaze on the river. When he had first looked, he could clearly see the adventurers and tartar in the tumultuous current, but during the seconds he had been locked in his melancholic reverie the ritual had progressed and the water around the ritualists was starting to form vicious foaming eddies. The figures in the river were pulled under and started to wash down stream. It may well have been the sight of Daisy, helplessly flailing that spurred Krieg on to finish the task. Even if he couldn't defend Tartaria from this evil, he could at least save a friend from drowning.

Elor was at his side as he charged - the wizard apparently

unarmed, Krieg holding nothing but a knife. There was no formal plan, no discussion of tactics, instinct took over. Elor wasn't even conscious of what spell he was casting until it had begun to discharge. It was breathtakingly simple, when he analysed it later, and brilliant. The tartars would have considered every possible physical threat carefully, and there was no doubt that they would have warded themselves against just about every kind of possible offensive magic and damage, therefore it would have taken a great deal of power to break down the protections, more than a single wizard would normally possess. However, the spell that Elor found himself casting wasn't usually considered to be offensive or dangerous - unless you took into account that the victim was standing in a river. Flamehair saw Elor approaching and smirked scornfully, she was not worried about the wispy magic she saw flying towards her. It contacted with her temple and she felt no pain, then the world blurred, her eyes rolled up into her head and she sank down into the swirling pool fast asleep.

Krieg was not so fortunate as he approached Salamander. The General was not as complacent as his sister, he had been waiting for this attack. Nothing that had attacked so far had been a match for him, but he knew Tartaria too well to believe he'd be able to take this power back unopposed. Power was to be fought for, and the harder the fight the more valuable the power. He also recognised the power that this approaching tartar carried with him, it was raw ancestral magic similar to his own but almost certainly not as potent. Clan Dragon had been resistant to his attempts to unify Tartaria but surely he would have felt the Dragon totem rising. He had to admire the courage of his attacker, to run at him with nothing more than a knife. The ritual could continue after this hiatus, once he had revived his sister and dispatched this brave fool. One sword was enough, he reached into his back scabbard. Whatever his doubts may have been, Krieg was still a born war- leader. He saw Salamander reach up to his sword hilt and he knew instantly what would happen when the General drew his katana. It was a rookie trick really. The feint that Krieg pulled off was simplicity itself but simple things should never be overlooked. He sprinted the last few yards towards Salamander head on, and the General began his swing to connect cleanly with Krieg's shoulder. At the very last second, just as the blade should have connected with his flesh, Krieg dropped to his knees and skidded forward inside Salamander's reach. With a single powerful thrust he drove the knife deep into Salamander's gut.

A blinding flash of blue-white light and a sharp crack filled the river- valley. With the same slow inevitability as a pan boiling over on a fire, a pin-point of orange light started to expand from the centre of the light column, roughly where the knife had connected with the General's flesh. After the crack, it seemed all sound had been sucked away, even the water made no noise. Those that survived the blast remember the slowly expanding light, that filled them with an overwhelming sense of foreboding that pushed up from their very souls forcing them out of the way. Those that did not survive must have been transfixed by it. Daisy had just reached Jamar and was about to heal him when the explosion happened and his gemstone detonated, along with those of all the other Salamander tartars still standing, and she was thrown backwards into the rapid flow so that she was carried away downstream. As Mori pulled a tearful Daisy out of the river later, she pointed out that it was probably the force of Jamar's blast that had saved her life.

Iona had a feeling something was wrong. Indicating to Tollie and Sylas that they should stop where they were, she shinned up one of the massive spruce trees in front of her to get a better view. These trees were easier to climb than some of the more spindly species in the Elven Forest, the rougher bark provided more natural footholds. Soon she was nearly fifty yards up and gazing down into a burning river valley. She could barely make out the figures below that were fighting below, she didn't try to guess which one was Pringle. As she watched, the battle suddenly turned into something else. A column of blinding light shot high into the air and a slow, orange blast wave started to spread out from it. The wave boiled the river water into ferocious clouds of steam, incinerating everything in its path as it began to climb the sides of the ravine. The figures on the riverbank were scattering in panic, some caught by the blast. Transfixed for a moment, Iona realised that the wave was going to spill over the edge of the ravine. She would never get down the tree in time, she could warn the others but she was trapped.

"Run," she bellowed to them, and they did not question her, the fear in her face louder than her words. Tollie and Sylas, aware that they were working for the Other Guild and not the Adventurers, took to their heels and were gone before either of them had time to look and see what was coming their way. Blood pounding in her ears, Iona had a split second to make her choice. She couldn't escape, she might make it to the ground before the wave reached the bottom of the tree, but she would not be able to outpace it. If this was the end, then she would be the master of her own fate. There would be one, final, act of rebellion, one last rush of adrenaline. She pulled herself to standing on the branch. Then, with her face upturned to the sky, she sucked in one very deep breath and sprung into the air.

She fell for less than ten seconds before her plummet was halted. The sky flickered with red and yellow and she looked up into the face of an angel. Pringle's face, much bigger than it had been as a mortal, looked down on her with gentle, sad eyes. He did not need to explain, she knew what had happened. She looked up at him, dazed and winded as Pringle flew directly upwards, just missing the edge of the blast wave. She didn't look as the tree she had just jumped from crumbled to ash, she was too busy looking into her husband's kaleidoscope eyes.

"Pringle, I love you," she uttered "I love you too," he said, but she did not hear him because she had already passed out.

Marta could hear Iri's voice calling her a coward for hiding, and Malik defending her as a pragmatist. In truth it was a bit of both. The battle below was beyond anything that Marta had seen before in terms of passionate hatred. A turn-coat has comrades of a fashion, whilst they may not trust her they expect her to trust them. That was not the case for a turncoat twice-over like Marta. She had no allies on the battlefield, she had sold out her clan and now she had sold out the Salamander. Her biggest fear was that Janx or Gilfdan would come looking for her having worked out the trap was her idea, partially at least. She had cut Tian loose as soon as the battle was under way, and after a moment's pause, she had galloped away to join the Dragon army. She hoped that Tian was still alive because it would be nice to have a friend.

Marta felt rather than heard the explosion. By the time the wave hit her, it had become nothing more than a searing wind that rushed over her, knocking her to the ground and sucking the moisture from her lungs. She fought for breath momentarily and then with a big gasp cold air poured back into her lungs and she rolled over choking. The noise of battle had been instantly silenced by the wave, and Marta looked down onto the battlefield expected to see a horrific frozen scene as soldiers and horses tried to re-orientate themselves. What she did see, she never would have imagined. The wave was still pushing across the veldt chasing several dozen souls who were desperately trying to outrun it. As it hit the Salamander tartars their gems detonated causing them to explode, drenching the ground with blood and bone shards. Many of them let out anguished yelps that were cut abruptly short. The Dragon were so stunned and repulsed by the sight, that they could not react - they simply let the wave flatten them.

Lying in the grass, watching the handful of ungemmed Salamander tartars bearing the brunt of the Dragon's angry retreat, Marta had no idea what to do next. She didn't dare ride down on to the plain, her red stripe was too obviously Salamander. She had no clan to return to, and no idea if Tian was still alive.

And back at the Aberddu East Gate

Greery was furious. If he had to sit through one more smug lecture from an uptight Law cleric about the importance of gate security during times of martial law he was going to lose it and tell them exactly where they could stick his well-greased smooth-running, triple cog ratchet mechanism. He stumped around the gatehouse banging the kettle against whatever he could get it to contact with. He'd like to see one of those self-satisfied be-robed bastards this far through what had started as a ninety hour shift and looked as though it might get even longer.

The trouble with the kind of young lads who get assigned to the gate patrol is that they all fancy themselves as soldiers but don't have the aptitude for regular militia patrol. They are sent to the gate, where all they have to do is light the brazier, brew the tea and wind the crank until they can be trusted to do something more complicated - like ask someone for papers. However, in times of war armies are not so picky and more than half the shift had joined up and consequentially been killed. They'd been forced to beg the old guard out of retirement, which was all very well but most of them couldn't wield the wood axe or climb the steps to reach the crank, and whilst they could be trusted to ask for papers they couldn't necessarily see to read them. They did at least know how to brew tea and slice lardy, when they hadn't dozed off.

"Gate security, my hairy arse!" thought Greery to himself as he slammed the kettle down on the fire and hauled himself back up to the parapet. The city was leaking like a sieve, and a damaged one at that. If he was any judge every scabrous, lice-infested god-botherer that was left in the city had flooded out in the last few days. The traffic out of the East Gate had never been so heavy, and whilst he hadn't had time to find out what was going on at the other gates, he could only assume it was as bad. Rumour had it that the Temple District, Docklands and most of the poor quarters - basically the entire north side of the river- had been reduced to rubble and that was enough to make people leave even without the continued threat of violence. In light of that, it made him wonder exactly who they were trying to keep out and what else they could possibly do to the city. He was just winding himself up for another internal rant when he looked down the road. Gods-dammit if it wasn't those priestesses again, waddling like mother ducks at the head of a gaggle of dishevelled-looking adventurer-types.

Greery liked to think of himself as an every-man, or at least he would have done if he'd known what one of those was. He was very proud of the fact that he had no idea how 'the other half' lived. The 'other half' in Aberddu, a city free state without its own nobility, included priests, wizards and those guild members who made enough money to have a room just for the bath and an indoor privy - which included the adventurers. The only dealings he usually had with them was as they sidled through his gate on the way to some ill-gotten gain or other, and he fervently hoped every time he shut the gate behind them that he wouldn't have to open it to allow them back in. But open it he did, with alarming frequency, to let the smug, self-satisfied bastards back into the city. As he wound the crank for the horse-gate this time, he looked down on them and his ire turned to pity. He had to admit that he felt quite sorry for them as they loped up the road in silence, caked in mud and dried blood and looking sour and weary. It wasn't often you saw them return home so sullen. Dirty and blood splattered pretty much normal, exhausted and limping as well - but silent was disconcerting. More worrying was the solemn compliance that greeted him as he asked for names and papers. He had never known so many adventurers pass through the gate without a single self-important, snide or uncooperative remark. He almost wanted to ask what was wrong.

EPILOGUE - THE DAYS THAT FOLLOWED

Mori came to find Daisy. She had eaten, bathed, rested and prayed alone, it was time to approach the future. Daisy was lying fully clothed on her bed in the guildhouse, having removed only her boots and her weapons belt since they had arrived back twenty-four hours ago. She stared blankly at Mori, who had knocked on the door and opened it without waiting for a response. Daisy had cried herself out on the journey back, and Mori knew that she had been lying there sullenly for hours dwelling on the fact that they had lost so many including Pringle and Krieg, particularly Krieg. She knew Daisy had promised him she would keep him alive. Having no bodies to bury had made the grief harder, those who had fallen had been disintegrated by the blast wave.

Mori understood why Krieg had not told them what was likely to happen when he finally killed Salamander. The raw power of the Dragon was forced through him, shredding his body and producing the column of light. Daisy had been inconsolable when Mori had first dragged her from the river, but slowly she had become quieter and quieter. She hadn't spoken for nearly thirty-six hours now, it was time she stepped forward. Mori moved to her bedside and offered her friend a hand up.

"We need to go, we have a child to take care of," she said simply and Daisy sat up. With glum determination she took

Mori's hand and pulled herself to standing. "You're having a bath, then we're going to find Elor, he's going to take us to Tartaria."

Iona woke up crying in the Guildmaster's bed in the bright light of early morning three days after Salamander had died, with no memory of the intervening time. She dragged herself to a sitting position, propped up on a pillow and let the tears fall down her cheeks. She looked over at the empty space in the bed beside her, the rumpled sheets, the dented pillow that still smelt of him. She reached out her hand, she knew it was madness to be surprised that they were cool to the touch. Her hand came to rest on something rougher than the bed clothes and she picked up a piece of parchment. It was in his handwriting.

Iona – I have 10,000 Guilders, it's in the guild vault. Use it well, use it wisely and remember me. I love you.
D x

Iona was so stunned by what she read that she stopped crying. Surely this wasn't her husband's idea of one last laugh? Whatever he might have been, he was not essentially a cruel man. Stiffly, she stood and hobbled to the window. She pulled back the ratty drape at the window and looked out. It was a sight that no amount of explanation could have prepared her for. The Guildmaster's bedroom had a glorious view over the majestic city, taking in other Guild Buildings and some of the larger temples as well as the mottled patch roofs of the shanty town that filled every available gap between these grander structures. At night it was almost magical with the lanterns glowing. Or it had been.

Iona stood for some time trying to taken in what she was looking at. Apart from the Mage's Library opposite, and the Scribes and Cartographers Guild, there wasn't a single undamaged building in the Guild Square and beyond that things were far worse. She realised with horror that she could now see almost as far as the Docklands, because where there had been temples there was now rubble. Only the Life statues were still standing, the four towering marble sculptures towering over the destruction with sadness in their eyes. She back-tracked. The Temple District may have been destroyed, but she had no worry that it would be raised up again, more glorious than ever. However, the debris of the poor quarter was beyond words. It was only possible to tell it had been destroyed because it was all strangely level, and one closer inspection crawling with people. They were scuttling over the piles of stones and timber like ants trying to scrape what little dignity they had left off the street. Iona reread the note and knew what she had to do.

The crater left by the blast, nearly a mile and a half in diameter, was a near-perfect circle. The shock wave that had swept across the land had eventually curved upwards forming a dome that flickered and flashed - trapping drakes and flame-spirits inside it. Slowly, the river had started to fill the crater with water. The dome dissipated releasing the creatures and the lake formed. The land repaired itself. The man stood on the cliff and looked down at it. As though remembering a dream, he knew he had somehow caused this destruction but he could find no jubilation or remorse in his heart. He blinked in the sun.

The passage of time meant little to him, he had no idea how long he stood and looked, only that day became night and night grew darker. Then in the slow break of the dawn, as the night faded to blue-grey, a hand touched his bare shoulder and whispered a name in his ear. When he turned, an old woman and two young tartars were standing there. They seemed familiar to him. The youths looked serious but Indya looked at Krieg and smiled. He smiled back, he could not remember who this woman was but he knew she was powerful and important. She laid her hand on his shoulder and in a soft whisper said,

"Welcome back Krieg. You are no longer just Dragon, you are Tartaria."

Dear reader,

We hope you enjoyed reading *Summer of Fire*. Please take a moment to leave a review, even if it's a short one. Your opinion is important to us.

Discover more books by L.G. Surgeson at https://www.nextchapter.pub/authors/lg-surgeson

Want to know when one of our books is free or discounted? Join the newsletter at http://eepurl.com/bqqB3H

Best regards,
L.G. Surgeson and the Next Chapter Team

AUTHOR'S NOTE

Pronunciation Guide

Aberddu – *pronounced 'Aber-thee' – is Welsh and translates as 'Mouth of the Black River'*
Kesoth – *pronounced 'kee-soth'*

Explanations

Indaba – *this is a Zulu word meaning 'business or matter'. It is the word given to an important discussion and would take place under a tree for shade. (It also used widely within the Scout Association for the same purpose). Colloquially, it has also come to mean a great fuss. I've pinched it for the Tartarians and stretched its meaning somewhat. Other than that, the Tartarians bear very little resemblance to the Zulu... except perhaps that you wouldn't want to start a war with either.*
Iceni – *in this world, the Iceni were a tribe of ancient Britons. Under the leadership of their queen Boudica, they lead the violent opposition to the Roman invasion of Britain. In the world of the Black River, the Iceni are a race of divine creatures created by the Goddess Amroth. They are the embodiment of honour and duty,*

and according to legend are unable to act against the tenets of Amroth without potentially fatal consequences.

Missing apostrophes - *no doubt the lack of apostrophes in the names of Aberddu's city guilds will have driven some of you barmy. This is a deliberate choice by the council of guilds. The proposal was put forward by the Merchants Guild - on the grounds that extra punctuation makes signage more expensive - and seconded by the Weavers & Dyers - because punctuation can cause terrible arguments, and the Warriors - because they thought it looked silly. The proposal was put to the vote, and passed eight votes to five, with a number of abstentions. The representative of Scribes and Cartographers Guild was forced to go for a lie down in a darkened room.*

Acknowledgements

First of all, the usual thanks to Mum, Michelle, Louise, Meg and various other women who have been pushing me when it comes to writing. It took a long time for me to believe you weren't just being nice and that actually I may have written something worth reading. I'm glad you didn't give in. A special mention is due to Ruth (Mori Sil'erbanis) – my 'punctuator in chief', whose editing comments kept me giggling through the long process of proofing - and the best friend a terrified Life cleric could want.

I'd also like to thank my epic team of 'crowdproofers' who helped me by reading sections and highlighting errors – as promised here is your credit:

Delwyn Gee , Gavin Duck, Anne Esslemont, Susie Freeman, Lily French, Deedee Davies, Helen Williams, Jonny Jones, Imogen Jones, Jane Gimber, Lynda Crunkhorn, Rebecca Taylor, John & Debbie Jackson, Emily Baker, Sian Pearce, Paul Arnold, Sarah Moore, Rose Hogan, Victoria Henry, Jen Brammal, Pete Hughes, Sarah Stephenson, fellow Next Chapter author LE Fitzpatrick and, of course, the incomparable Ruth Burns (aka Mori Sil'erbanis). Thanks also to the #Awethors – my wonderful 'virtual' writing buddies, who see each other through the highs and lows of being writers.

As well as the people in my life who have helped me as a writer, there is another group of people I need to thank even more: a group of live action role-players based in Aberystwyth called 'Aberddu Adventures'. For 12 years, I was a prolific game coordinator for this group, and a large amount of the setting, stories and characters in the Black River Chronicles have been the result of that. They are the reason why all of the books in the chronicles are dedicated to characters in the stories.

In recognition of this, I would particularly like to acknowledge: *Ian Shires (Godfather of Aberddu), Pip & Dan Walker, Will Robinson (aka Dakarn Pringle), Karl Hatton (aka Krieg Clan Dragon), David Gibbins, Rob Gardener, John Blower, Matt Palmer (aka Elor Nybass), Phil Bettinson, Hannah Johnson, Pete Hughes (aka William Freemonte) and Ian Hatch (aka Derek Peterson)* all of whom poured passion, time and creativity into our little world, worked with me and inspired me as game coordinators and creators. Also, Cerys Robinson who christened our city 'Aberddu'. However, my biggest heartfelt *'diolch yn fawr'* goes to our players over the many years, who bought into our crazy vision and built Aberddu brick by brick around us. Without you guys the city, the state and the whole continent – not to mention about a dozen other planes of existence – would be empty and lifeless.

About the Author

LG Surgeson is a writer and teacher from Mid Wales, UK. She lives in a cottage full of fairy doors by a river in the middle of nowhere with her long-suffering partner Michelle and their four cats: Ocean, Terminal Curiosity, Pickles & Puddin'. She prefers it to the real world because it smells better and you can see the sky. Her other hobbies include quilting, gardening, sleeping and wearing a dent in the sofa. She writes in the time she saves by ignoring the housework. The cats like to help. They aren't good at it.

LG was born in South Africa in 1980 and emigrated to the

UK with her folks when she was just four years old – hence she's no idea what it's like to be actually warm. She grew up in Dorset on the South Coast of England, and having decided that this was neither rural nor cold enough she packed herself off to university in Aberystwyth in 1998.

She successfully qualified in a fancy pants mathematics masters in 2003 that can basically be boiled down to why jelly wobbles and custard gets thicker when you stir it. The following year gained her teaching certificate. Since then, she's been gainfully employed in a range of educational settings trying to convince teenagers that maths, or at least maths teachers, aren't all evil – well not very evil any way.

As a writer, LG started at a young age. Her first masterpiece was a book about a naughty black and white cat that she penned at the tender age of seven or eight. It was lovingly illustrated by her mother. After that she was hooked and has had books on the go ever since. It took her until 2011 to work up the courage to unleash her work on an unsuspecting world. The Freetown Bridge was released as an e-book and was met with a warm reception.

Since then, LG has released 4 more books in her Black River Chronicles, a fantasy series following the exploits of a bunch of misfit adventurers who frequently find themselves being forced to 'Do The Right Thing' when all they wanted was to make a small fortune.

The series, and LG herself, owe an unending debt of gratitude to the Aberddu Adventures Live Action Role-play system in Aberystwyth, which she played in and ran for twelve years and on whose game world the series is based.

As well as fantasy novels, LG also writes fiction novels based on various life experiences – predominantly those she has had in her during her career working with young people with emotional, social and mental health difficulties that lead to extreme and challenging behaviour. (This is often more amusing or heart-warming than it sounds). She hopes these books will touch the souls of their readers in the same way that the experiences have touched her.

She hopes to release some of these in the near future, but currently they aren't yet perfect enough to leave her laptop.

As if all this wasn't enough for the unsuspecting readers, LG also writes the occasional article and blog posts on subjects about mental health, the education system and anything else that makes her hot under the collar. She has two blogs for this: Scaling the Chalkface - educational ranting for the terminally exhausted and Good Mental Hygiene, a blog about her own and other people's experience with mental health issues focussing on coping mechanisms and positivity. As well as appearing on her own blog, LG's articles on mental health have appeared in various internet journals.

LG is very excited to be working with Next Chapter so that she can spread her own personal madness further afield. She hopes they realise what they've let themselves in for.

Follow the Black River: Find out where it leads

Thanks for joining us. If you enjoyed this book, why not try the next in the series and find out what happened in **'The Winter That Follows'**.

CPSIA information can be obtained
at www.ICGtesting.com
Printed in the USA
BVHW082051030521
606340BV00005B/1278

9 781034 826309